THE DEVIL'S BREATH

Also by David A. Waples

Non-fiction
Approaching Infinity: A Practical Workbook to Help Us Achieve Our Goals in Life
The Natural Gas Industry in Appalachia: A History from the First Discovery to the Maturity of the Industry

Novels
White Widow
Piano Dreams

THE DEVIL'S BREATH

A Novel

David A. Waples

Author of The Natural Gas Industry in Appalachia

iUniverse, Inc.

New York Lincoln Shanghai

The Devil's Breath
A Novel

iUniverse books may be ordered through booksellers or by contacting:

iUniverse
2021 Pine Lake Road, Suite 100
Lincoln, NE 68512
www.iuniverse.com
1-800-Authors (1-800-288-4677)

This is a work of fiction. All of the characters, names, incidents, organizations, and dialogue as well as any locations that are identified in this novel are either the products of the author's imagination or are used fictitiously.

ISBN-13: 978-0-595-42924-0 (pbk)
ISBN-13: 978-0-595-87263-3 (ebk)
ISBN-10: 0-595-42924-6 (pbk)
ISBN-10: 0-595-87263-8 (ebk)

Printed in the United States of America

To the memory of my father

PART I

▼

DISCOVERY

C H A P T E R   1

▼

Northeastern Ohio, April, 1865

One more kick and Zeke Snodgrass could be filthy rich. *Or,* he thought, *I might as well be dead.* Worse than poor or dead was the prospect of finding his ultimate pursuit was only a dry hole. There had to be more to life than this farm of dry, cracked earth and chicken shit. Rich was something he could envision. Maybe as wealthy as Vanderbilt, on whose railroads he once toiled. *Rich as a sultan.* Yesterday, a no-name from northeastern Ohio—tomorrow, Snodgrass may be synonymous with Rothschild.

"What will you do with the money?" asked Gabriel, Zeke's brother.

Zeke pretended not to hear. He swiped at the river of perspiration on his brow with his dusty biceps, leaving a streak of glistening mud on his forehead. The spring day's strangling heat was as unwelcome as a visit from an annoying relative. But for a farmer, the sweat and grime adhered to Zeke's aging body like a second skin.

"I'd like a big-ol' brass bathtub," Gabriel answered himself.

Zeke never thought about it that specifically. What would he buy? A topcoat. A mansion. Servants. Fine food. Dancing girls. A new carriage with healthy horses. A ship to navigate the Great Lakes. A verdant estate of fertile land. Cigars to smoke in a plush office in downtown Cleveland. Who knows? Maybe he'd even take a wife. Zeke was not sure what the crowned heads of Europe spent their riches on, but he would find out. The fantasies erupted like a sudden geyser, but first things first.

"Keep pulling on that rope," Zeke said.

Gabriel Snodgrass pinched a wrangling rope taut with one cattle-rancher's glove hand and gripped the crude wooden apparatus with the other. Zeke slipped his narrow-footed boot into a stirrup-shaped loop of rope dangling a foot above the ground. It reminded him of a hangman's noose. But instead of his neck in the gallows, the oval ring of rope held one foot in a prosperous future. The other end of the fraying hemp cord was tied to a ten-foot-long hickory sapling suspended over his head, parallel to the ground. The pole rested on a vertical Y-shaped log from an old locust tree, its butt end buried two feet into the ground like a fence post. It towered upward like an Indian totem pole. The log acted as a fulcrum for the rudimentary mechanism—a man-powered springpole-drilling device used to sink saltwater wells. But saltwater was not Zeke's quest. He sought the black blood of the earth—liquid cash that transformed the lowly into the mighty.

Zeke kicked down in the stirrup with all of his 150 pounds of bones and muscle. His weight on the rope bent the flexible sapling downward. A metal chain tied to the springpole was fed through a five-inch-wide hole, tunneling sixty-seven feet below the surface. An iron spike, filed sharp and fire-forged by hand, was attached to the base of the chain. It lifted by the fulcrum pressure of his weight bending the springpole, and as he took his weight off of the stirrup, the hickory pole whipped upwards, and the heavy, pointed tool barreled down deep in the hole, chipping at the limestone rock far below.

Zeke and his younger brother worked the drill for two weeks on their pitiable farm, boring through dirt, shale, and now, the hard part, solid rock that he hoped held below it a porous limestone formation that contained oil like water soaked in a sponge. Zeke heard that the simple drilling derrick rig was based on a design once used by Chinamen to drill for saltwater more than two millenniums before, and it was a model that he didn't see the need to improve upon. The structure bore little resemblance to the newfangled oil rigs supported by wooden cross braces and girders used by most serious petroleum explorers that sprouted over the Pennsylvania countryside during the oil rush that began six years before, just prior to the War Between the States. Those structures called derricks earned their name from a seventeenth-century English hangman, whose gallows resembled the tower-like configurations now used to find oil beneath land previously worth pennies an acre. It was first-come-first-serve and soon the Pennsylvania woodlands were littered with the triangular edifices. But Zeke possessed neither the know-how nor the money for that. The only similarity between the Snodgrass device and a derrick was his crude setup had a noose.

The four-year-long war that separated the union was nearly over, or so the newspapers said. Sherman burned Atlanta, Grant had Lee on the run in Richmond, and just about everyone was sick of the carnage. Zeke hoped it was true. The two brothers were lucky enough to be too long-in-the-tooth to be called to serve in the Union Army, but survival was a fierce battle even for civilians during the conflict. Fortune, however, could turn. The discovery of rock oil ninety miles east in western Pennsylvania back in 'fifty-nine made the region crazy with "oil on the brain," now the lyric of a popular ditty pounded out on pianos in local saloons. It seemed that everyone was looking for the oleaginous black substance that could be refined into a new product—kerosene—for lighting. Whale oil, used to illuminate most lanterns in Zeke's lifetime, was no longer affordable as the once plentiful sea leviathans were getting harder to find. The Snodgrass brothers, who once worked as stevedores on the docks of Cleveland and then struggled for years to make a decent living by farming on the flat, supposedly fertile fields south of the Lake Erie shoreline, were running out of time to wait for their ship to come in. A decade before, Zeke heard of the 'forty-niners in California striking it rich by panning for gold nuggets. But the West Coast seemed as far away as China to go to find a fortune. If there was *black* gold underneath the surface of the foothills of the Alleghenies in Pennsylvania, he surmised, it might also lay hidden underneath his own feet a few miles west. New oil discoveries were rampant in the southeastern part of Ohio. If Zeke didn't drill for it where he was, eventually someone else would. So, with the help of a "proven" forked divining rod rented from a salt-well driller he met in an Ashtabula tavern, Zeke searched for a suitable location on their farm to drill their well. Not more than 200 feet from their back door, the Y-shaped hickory prognosticator Zeke gripped horizontally in his hands bent portentously downward like a hunting dog's snout on the scent. At that point, he drew a cross in the barren earth with the heel of his boot. X marked the spot.

Zeke adjusted his well-worn, shin-high leather boot in the low-hanging noose. The rough rope's friction against his ankle left tan vertical abrasion lines up the sides of his boot from his arches to his shins. He breathed heavily and his muscles ached. He hoped his endurance would hold on as long as his determination. He built his upper-body strength unloading crates from Great Lakes shipping vessels, and toned his lower body from steadying a mule-driven plow through the arid, rocky land the previous owner of his farm hoodwinked him into buying. He could not show any sign of weariness. Zeke was the dean of the Snodgrass clan, an incredibly fit sixty-seven-years-old, strong as the day was long. His sinewy figure belied his advanced age. No one who met him guessed he was a day past fifty. Though the snow-white hair of the long-time bachelor was rapidly becoming sparse, his handsome, tanned, ashen-bearded face and sparkling ice-blue eyes still caught the eye of every lonely widow in northeastern Ohio. And he was proud of that. He sopped up the gusher of afternoon sweat once again from his only age lines—deep crevice worry wrinkles that meandered across his forehead like two thin canals.

"I'm losing hope in this," Gabriel said, heaving. His younger brother's lungs wheezed like the leaking bellows of a church organ. He was shorter, stockier, and not as comely as his brother. Zeke also felt Gabriel lacked his patience, strength, and fortitude. This was his brother's fifty-ninth birthday. *That's probably depressing him*, Zeke thought.

"Liven up little brother," Zeke said. "You need something left for your old age."

Zeke literally bet the farm on this venture, and it must pay off. Last year's corn crop disappointed because of an extended dry spell. His dairy cattle were not lactating like they should. And the debt payments on his twenty-acre plot were falling into delinquency. But Zeke had faith. Zeke told his brother there was nothing to worry about. But Gabriel wasn't the only cynic doubting the prospects that the springpole water-drilling rig would lead them from rags to riches. Zeke's disagreeable mule also looked on skeptically from a distance, ears twitching to shake off biting spring flies. It brayed as if to say, "Give it up."

"Oh ye of little faith," Zeke said, his marble-sized eyes reflecting avuncular disappointment. The hoary man jumped up on the rope stirrup once again with the jolt of a mule's stubborn kick.

Blow-by-blow, inch-by-inch, the hopeful drillers tunneled down through the ground finding little but almost impenetrable rock that dulled their drilling bit. Recent progress amounted to only about a foot of ground excavated per day.

"Hurry up with that new drill bit," Zeke hollered to the only other human witness to their drudgery, Gabriel's slow-witted son, Jake.

Jake sat nearby, forging another curved iron spear-like tool over a small fire, a replacement for the dull spike below that was worn after hours of pounding solid stone like endlessly knocking on a door when no one was home. Jake, a disheveled, longhaired man dressed in threadbare overalls, was born thirty years before after an arduous delivery that took the life of his mother. The inebriated attending doctor, who stumbled in during the hard labor too late to be of much help, told Gabriel he didn't think the child would survive the trauma. Something about the lack of oxygen in the birth canal. But Zeke heard through an assisting midwife that the damage to Jake's brain might have occurred when the doctor tried to pull the infant's head with iron forceps that resembled tongs a stableman used when shoeing a horse. The babe emerged an overripe plump twelve pounds, but his wide girth tortured his petite five-foot-one mother during the ordeal, ripping her reproductive parts inside causing her to bleed to death. Yet, Zeke knew his brother loved his matricidal son, dullard or not, and kept him constantly by his side like a fawning dog. Zeke did not resent the simple oaf of a nephew who possessed the mind of a five-year-old, but he worried that the ignorant helper would only get hurt. Drilling for saltwater, or anything else for that matter, Zeke learned, could be dangerous business if not approached cautiously. Occasionally, those seeking the brine, which could be boiled down for salt to preserve food, sometimes found dangerous carberetted-hydrogen gas—"natural gas" some called it. The invisible, inflammable vapor blew violently out of the ground and, if accidentally ignited, could explode with disastrous results. Oil, Zeke understood, could be bailed out of the ground safely with a bucket, poured into a whiskey barrel, and sold for a decent profit to Mr. Rockefeller's new kerosene refinery in Cleveland. Those unlucky enough to find the transparent hazardous gas instead of oil not only didn't make any money, but also sometimes paid the price with their lives.

"Uncle Zeke," Jake said, "da bit's just 'bout done." The muscle-bound, but dense boy-man lifted the huge, spiked drilling tool, still glowing lava-red from the blacksmith's cauldron about twenty feet from the well. Jake knew his appointed task, but had no idea what was the purpose of drilling such a small hole no bigger than the entrance to a ground hog's lair deep below the ground. But what the youth lacked in brains, he made up in brawn. Zeke often left the tedious job of bailing the well, scooping out broken rock, mud, and earth from the drill hole with a small wooden bucket, to the strapping younger Snodgrass. Jake didn't seem to mind. And when not bailing, he occupied most of the time stoking his fire with dry kindling of ash wood, hay, and a catalyst fuel of dried cow chips. Though the smell revolted Zeke, he was pleasantly surprised that the idiot maintained the blaze by the crap from the scrawny cattle. They weren't good for much else. He only wished his dumb nephew built the fire a little farther away from the well.

Zeke didn't notice anything out of the ordinary at first when the drilling bit deep in the borehole seemed to vibrate a bit. His muscles were already trembling from the backbreaking work pounding through stone with the heavy tool. However, after the next jab into the ground, Gabriel leaned over the hole's opening at just the wrong time. A geyser of water squirted out of the borehole like the piss stream of a giant stallion and soaked his younger brother with a greenish, greasy liquid. Then, suddenly, the vertical stream stopped as quickly as it started.

Gabriel coughed, fell backward, and landed on his rear spraying a puff of dust around him. He came up groaning and spitting, a viscous substance dripping from his bearded face.

"What?" Zeke asked, ready to jump on the stirrup once more. "Oil?" Pangs of excitement ran up and down his spine like racing spiders.

"It's dang awful," Gabriel said. "It's salt—the most god-awful salt I ever tasted."

"Blazes," Zeke cursed as vulgar as the God-fearing man ever did. He smelled it now. A sour, foul stench, like the worst mule fart he ever inhaled. He jumped on the rope's stirrup, raising, and then dropping the drill bit in the bottom of the hole once again.

This time the ground rumbled like an approaching stampede. The sound of clanging metal emanated from deep inside the hole, and then a whistle and hiss screeched louder than anything he heard before. It sounded like one of the Pennsylvania Railroad's steam locomotives roaring down the track with the brothers in its path. Before Zeke took another step backward, a plume of water and vapor blew out of the well hole like a shotgun blast, followed by the thirty-pound drilling bit attached to a metal cable, fired out of the opening like a cannonball out of a Union Army's artillery battery. The force of the high-pressure vapor bent the springpole log backwards, snapped it in two, and hurled it directly in the path of Jake, who stood and stared at the spectacle transfixed, hands still gripping the red hot tip of the drilling tool at the end of metal tongs that looked like the forceps that probably squeezed his mushy newborn skull. The pole crashed down onto the dumbfounded man's head, pummeling him to the ground and finishing the job begun by the drunken physician. Then came the piercing smell—an odor so pungent it seemed to burn like acid in Zeke's nostrils and drill into his brains.

"Sulfur!" Zeke gasped. No one heard him. The violent howl of escaping gas out of the borehole was as deafening as a passing twister. The two brothers crawled away from the blowout, which threw water, dust, and the pungent exhale of a dragon's hideous breath fifty feet into the air. The iron drill bit, a moment ago deep inside the ground, now suspended magically, whirling twenty-five feet high in the air, dancing in the middle of the tornado of the blowout like the showgirls at the Cleveland saloon where Zeke used to burn his stevedore paycheck. Zeke's obstinate mule, grazing disinterested several rods away moments ago, leapt into a gallop he never saw the likes of before.

Zeke heard stories of greenish to black crude bubbling up the borehole, pushed to the surface by the imperceptible natural gas held in the same rock formation deep below the earth. He also heard of brine propelled out of a drilling hole with a fury, pushed by the earth's belch of the mysterious vapor. He thought he was prepared for either occurrence. But the degree of this violence was inconceivable. The ferocity of the foul blowing wind stunned him, and the fetid stink of sulfur seared his lungs. Gabriel crawled to his motionless, if not dead, son, whose dense skull was smashed by the six-inch-wide log like an over-ripe pumpkin trampled by a horse's hoof. Zeke's lungs now hurt so severely, he couldn't even call his brother's name, and if he could, his voice would not be heard over the catastrophic roar of the well. This was a disaster. It could not get any worse.

But it did.

The burning embers from Jake's cow-shit-fueled smote scattered in countless directions when the springpole snapped backwards. Gabriel appeared not to recognize the danger, but Zeke's eyes registered the fear of Hell.

"No!" Zeke croaked, crawling backward, crab-like, staring at the plume of white-ish propellant spitting out of the well hole. He knew that open flame and the hellish fog that shot from the ground did not mix. As Gabriel crawled toward the lifeless body of his son, Zeke knew there was little his brother could do for the boy. In fact, there was little they could do for themselves.

It happened in a flash. The flammable spit from the hole reached a smoldering ember. A giant whumph! And then an explosion so powerful, Zeke thought he put his head in a cannon's barrel. The force of the blast blew Gabriel's stocky body off the ground and into the air, ripping off most of his clothes and flinging him like errant cannonshot. By the time Gabriel returned to earth thirty-feet away, every remaining piece of cloth and hair on his body was in flames. His head struck one of the many large stones that clogged their planting field, and his life most likely ended as abruptly as that of his son. Though Zeke was farther away from the point of ignition, he wasn't as lucky as his brother. The optimistic oil pioneer was greeted by a blasting kiss of Satan's fire that blew him backwards, rolling him along the ground like a tortuous dragging behind by a wild mustang. His clothes also spontaneously ignited, and his flesh burned in painful waves.

Zeke was conscious, but passage of time did not register with him. He thought it perhaps was the end of the world as Preacher Heath always threatened from his pulpit anytime he suffered to attend the weekly service at the Baptist church in Ashtabula. Fire and brimstone. He was blinded, his olfactory sense singed, and the only thing he could hear was a loud ringing. After some time, he could no longer feel the pain of his burns or the scorching heat from his hopeful well that now was a fifty-foot torch in the ground.

The initial whistle of the well blowout and subsequent boom of an explosion naturally attracted the Snodgrass neighbors. The first to arrive was John Davis, a broad-shouldered blacksmith known as "Little John," who grew string beans and corn on a nearby farm. He was perplexed as he passed the Snodgrass mule galloping in the opposite direction. He didn't notice anyone sprawled on the ground, but instead gawked at the horrific flare that grew right out of the earth like a giant undulating cornstalk, casting an eerie, orange glow that could be seen for miles on the backdrop of the late afternoon's darkening bruise-colored eastern sky. The rancid reek of sulfur and roasting flesh pervaded the air. Davis thought the Snodgrass brothers were two old God-fearing farmers digging a senseless hole in the ground like two blind moles. Now it appeared they opened a door straight into Hell.

Davis heard a weak, but agonizing groan for help over the thunderous flames howling from the depths of the earth. He bent down over a fallen body, barely a shred of clothing covering torched red skin. The few clumps of white hair remained on the old man's head, but his eyebrows, mustache, and scraggly beard were gone. Davis didn't recognize him at first. His crumpled body looked more like a two-legged, stillborn foal than a human being. As Davis bent down to get a closer look, he recoiled from both the man's hideous appearance and the miasma of burnt skin.

"Zeke?" Davis said. He reached down to hold Zeke's head up, but then pulled away when the stricken man's sticky flesh peeled off on his fingers like the skin of an eel. "Oh lordy, Zeke!"

The old man struggled to somehow speak through his painful fog. There was nothing Davis could do. The other two bodies on the ground were motionless and were likely dead. It was too late for Gabriel. It was too late for Jake. But Zeke wanted to speak. The old farmer held up a weak finger that looked like a warning.

"Dev—" Zeke groaned through his scorched throat.

"What happened?" Davis asked. "What happened Zeke?"

"Dev—il's ... Br—, br—,"

"What?"

"D-devil's ... b-b-breath ..." Zeke gasped. The stricken man's throat relaxed and his body fell limp.

Davis glared at the conflagration roaring from the ground and the steeple of fire reaching upwards. He prayed that Zeke's soul would be lifted in the current of the hellish flames soaring toward the heavens.

This crazy old man, Davis thought. His greatest dream transformed into a hideous nightmare. He uncorked a devilish genie out of the bottle. Instead of granting ready wishes, the phantom arrived to destroy.

CHAPTER 2

▼

Six months later, Fall 1865

By the size of the crowd, you would think President Andrew Johnson himself was going to visit and kiss all the babies. Who would have thought that an afternoon at a desolate farm near Ashtabula, Ohio, would be the hottest ticket in Cleveland? Daniel O'Day, a promising petroleum business executive, read about the incident in the Cleveland newspapers, saw a daguerreotype illustrating the marvel, and knew he must investigate. O'Day even talked his employer into the laborious trip from Cleveland, and that was not easy since his superior was as parsimonious with his time as his money and not fond of rough rides on carriages. But it was a fact-finding mission of a business opportunity. O'Day audaciously hinted that this natural wonder may be a mother lode discovery that could rival, or even eclipse, the discovery of petroleum. It could make poor men wealthy. And rich men kings.

The Snodgrass clan finally hit pay dirt. Unfortunately, Zeke, Gabriel, and Jake would not see the bounty of their discovery. The reward fell into the lap of the only surviving Snodgrass, a cousin with the given name of Quincy, but who insisted others call him by his middle name, Abraham, to identify with the recently assassinated president of the United States. It adorned the former circus barker with a regal air of respectability. But the financial benefit of the Snodgrass unearthing did not come from the output of their fiery well, but from the admission price to a regional tourist attraction. "Someone should benefit from the tragedy," cousin Quincy was quoted in the newspapers. The Snodgrasses sacrificed their lives for the spectacle that everyone in northeastern Ohio now wanted to see with their own eyes.

"Satan's Belch" is what the whitewashed sign read at the dirt road entrance to the Snodgrass farm. How that name was adopted no one was sure. But to see the spectacular burning plume close up, you first paid ten cents to Quincy, a.k.a. Abraham, Snodgrass. And most people forked it over. From miles around, families gathered picnic lunches and traveled to the rural farm in their mule-drawn wagons or horse-led buggies to see the latest wonder of the world, a giant torch that roared out of the bowels of the earth like the bellow of Lucifer himself. By now, the orange tips of the blaze stretched upward only forty-feet, as the pressure of the natural gas-fed flame dwindled. Some speculated that the well would soon peter out. So Abraham Snodgrass was raking in some cash while the going was still good. The Snodgrass cousin was rumored to be a drunk, a freeloader, and an all-around scoundrel. But thanks to the last will and testament of Zeke Snodgrass, no one could prove otherwise that he did not legitimately hold title to the previously worthless land that now was home to a curious cash register.

At first, neighboring farmers wanted the surviving Snodgrass to extinguish the huge flame. The roar of the blaze echoed for miles on a still night, and the hellfire lit up the horizon, making their livestock uneasy. The dairy cows wouldn't lactate and chickens were reluctant to lay eggs while the devilish torch roared like a pack of restless wolves howling in unison. But Abraham said that was nonsense, and vehemently refused once he found out that nearly everyone in nearby Cleveland would travel miles just to peer through a window to Hades. Besides, Abraham couldn't put out the conflagration even if he wanted to. In fact, no one could get closer than twenty feet to the natural inferno without getting scorched.

It was Sunday and the crowd was thick as a swarm of yellow jackets at a picnic. A threatening overcast indigo sky in the distant horizon was perfect contrast to the ghostly orange-yellow flame. The bitter stench of sulfur faded some over time, making observation at close range tolerable. Children played in the Snodgrass's rocky field, tossing stones at one another, while their parents snuggled on picnic blankets pretending they were courting once again, stuffing cheese and sausages into each other's mouths like insouciant French nobility. Brazen teenage boys attempted to roast the sausages on the ends of ten-foot-long saplings in the giant campfire, but usually could not stand the intense heat for long. Abraham spent time embellishing the tale of his cousins' fatal discovery of the burning well and how they paid with their lives as they battled to control the fiendish, vaporous vomit from Beelzebub's own belly.

Rolling up a rutted, dusty path, Daniel O'Day maneuvered an elaborate mahogany buggy pulled by two majestic black Cleveland bay horses. His round face was accented by a bushy moustache and wiry black hair splashed with plenty of tonic. O'Day was dressed in a common black suit, and topped his presentation with an English bowler hat. His robust sun-reddened cheeks saw the outdoors much more than the pale-complexioned passenger who rode in the buggy with him. O'Day's boss was an ashen-faced, stern-looking, steely-eyed man with *à la Souvaroff* brown muttonchops sideburns growing into a well-trimmed moustache, leaving a determined jutting chin clean-shaven. He wore a silken Iverness—a dapper greatcoat with a large cape that shielded his expensive suit from the road dust. On top of his head rested a black silk chimney-pot hat, made popular by the recently deceased President Lincoln. Both men sat primly on the padded leather seat of the luxurious buggy, like they were watching an opera. O'Day pulled back the reins of the muscular, well-groomed horses, which looked as if they belonged in a fancy European circus. The two approached the newly installed gate into the farm, festooned with a rope. A reconstruction of a crude springpole-drilling rig stood inside the roped-off area.

"This is it," O'Day said, subdued, though with a latent bubble of child-like excitement in his voice.

The taller man looked impassively at the distant flame shooting out of the earth, lifting his head and silky stovetop hat, his protruding chin pointing to the scene like a dagger.

"Carburetted-hydrogen gas," O'Day continued, dusting trail dirt off his well-tailored waistcoat.

"No oil?" his stoic companion asked, raising one eyebrow not as a query, but in contempt.

"No sir. But look at that fire! Can you imagine how that could light up the streets in Cleveland at night?"

"It smells."

"Yes sir, that's sulfur. This well apparently hit some *sour* gas. But there are reports of dozens of other similar sweet wells that have hit powerful pressures of largely odorless gas. There are some towns in the central part of the state already trying to pipe the vapor to light their streets—at the cost of pennies. Imagine what the town-gaslight leaders would do if we could get this product to the city at a fraction of their cost. Their dirty coal-gaslight operations would crumble at the competition."

The taller man still looked unimpressed, his gaunt, bearded face as animated as a dead man. He was a cautious accountant and produce merchant by trade, and O'Day knew he did not favor risky or quixotic investments. He was usually frugal with words as with funds, so he was difficult for O'Day to read.

"This gas is invisible," O'Day's employer said. "How can you capture this genie once it is out of its bottle?"

"I think it can be done through long wooden, or maybe, cast-iron water pipes," said O'Day. "Some have piped it through rifle barrels. But gaslight is just the beginning. This natural fuel provides a hotter flame for manufacturing uses than coal or wood. And others claim it can even be used to heat a home. Most important, it doesn't need to be *refined.*"

O'Day knew he said the wrong word.

The pallid-faced man shot a sudden, piercing glance. "Mr. O'Day," he said, "refining is our business."

O'Day bowed his head. His normally taciturn employer continued in the tone of a Sunday sermon. "Capturing this product from the earth looks like a job for God. I feel we would be much better off sticking to the knitting by pursuing the transportation of Pennsylvania rock oil for kerosene. Oil can be contained and is well behaved in a barrel, and we can control its transport by railroad. Besides, our competition to the coal gaslight men is kerosene. This *natural gas* element seems like folly." He paused, but added, "But ..."

O'Day's eyes peered upward like a brash servant.

"If you can find a way to safely move this ghostly fuel from the middle of nowhere to the cities and convince people to bring this incendiary apparition into their homes or factories, then keep me informed. Until then, our bread is better buttered by petroleum. We can see it, feel it, smell it, taste it, and, most important, get paid for it."

"Yes, sir."

"Howdy!" a shrill voice broke the lecture. Abraham Snodgrass stood at the roped-off entrance to the farm, spinning a straw hat in his stubby pink fingers, an unctuous grin on his pasty face. This man was no farmer. O'Day knew a con man from the city when he saw one.

"Welcome to Satan's Belch, the eighth wonder of the world," Snodgrass proclaimed in his carnival-barker's voice. It must serve him well to get attention over the bellow of the nearby flare. O'Day and his companion on the well-cared-for carriage must look like big-city investors. They were not dressed for a Sunday afternoon pleasure ride. O'Day knew Snodgrass smelled money. A lot of money.

O'Day's employer looked at Snodgrass contemptuously, and then reached inside his cape for his gold pocket timepiece, attached to his vest by a fancy Albert chain. He was always "on the clocker" O'Day knew, obsessed with time as if every second was costing him a fortune.

"You fine gentlemen chose a wonderful day to look at the burning well," Snodgrass continued. "*Satan's Belch* my cousin called it—his dying words. See how it burns against the distant storm clouds in the east. I usually charge ten cents a head, another five for a buggy, but you distinguished individuals look like you are here for serious business. You both can enter for only fifteen cents total."

"Fifteen cents?" O'Day's boss finally conveyed emotion in his voice. "For using our eyes?"

"Well, as I said, I would charge others two bits for two and a buggy. The money goes to the children of Zeke and Gabriel Snodgrass," he said, grasping his hat against his portly chest as in dutiful respect. O'Day read that there were no surviving children of the two brothers. This man was not just an opportunist, but also a bald-faced liar.

"They gave their lives for this discovery," said Snodgrass.

"Then it appears they were well paid for their foolishness," the stern man responded. "Let's go Mr. O'Day."

O'Day shrugged, tapped dust off the round, curved brim of his derby before returning it to his head, and then tugged the leather reins.

"Yes, Mr. Rockefeller," he responded.

The horses turned, and the elaborate buggy rolled away leaving Abraham Snodgrass in a cloud of dust.

The ingenious wheels in O'Day's head spun. *I'll tame this invisible tiger,* he thought. *And I'll convince Mr. John D. Rockefeller that this miracle of invisible fire might someday surpass his blessed dirty crude.*

PART II

▼

CRISIS

CHAPTER 3

▼

Fall, 1979—Tel Aviv, Israel

Akmed Abram clawed at his heavy cotton jacket, flailing with his hands as if the garment was on fire, but there was no way to tear it off. He heard the stories of both pain and rapture, but what he really needed now was more strength to rip this cloak off from his sweaty skin. *You need more courage,* he told himself. He hoped his death would not lead to suffering, his own or anyone else's. He was suddenly less concerned with the next world than with the world he would leave behind, miserable as it was. He heard a clock ticking. An alarm rang. But he was alone. Far from his target. *I need more faith.* He needed to get to the crowd. No, not yet. He cannot die here. This cannot end in vain. *I need more time.*

A blinding flash. No pain, only separation. He floated into the air as easily as a canvass sail lifted by an updraft sea gust. He tried to focus his cloudy vision. He saw blood and bones cascading from his chest like a breaking dam. And on the top of his torso, there was nothing.

He could now see himself on the ground from a great height. But not all of himself. Only his decapitated head rolling on the ground, eyes open as wide as plates but lifeless. Mouth ajar but no sound coming out. What his friends said was true. The telltale sign of a suicide attack was the severed head of the bomber as the explosives easily separated the entire skull from its delicate perch upon the spine. His body continued to rocket upward and his detached head screeched its silent scream from below.

Akmed woke in a panic. He wiped a rivulet of salty sweat dripping down his prominent angular nose. It was a typical arid, blistering day fueled by heated Mediterranean breezes in the Israeli seaside capital of Tel Aviv, but the perspiration oozing out of Akmed's pores came not from the radiance of the sun, but from the stress in his gut. The stiff western wind off the sea did nothing to cool him. He fell asleep in an alleyway waiting for the chosen moment. He never slept well at night. The dreams. No, nightmares. And when stress consumed him during the day, he escaped reality by dropping into dreamland at a moment's notice as if hit in the head by a rock. He could walk in his sleep for an hour. The somnambulist Akmed puzzled his parents and everyone who knew him. Akmed, the sleeper, they called him. But the terrors behind his closed eyes roused him in short order.

Akmed adjusted the bulky vest under his knee-length dusty cloak one more time. It was not comfortable. And it weighed a ton. But he would not wear it long. As soon as the lunchtime crowd of one of the posh marketplaces in downtown Tel Aviv was fully involved in commercial activity, he would shed this heavy skin like a snake. The young Palestinian wore a jacket filled with steel ball bearings, small scraps of jagged metal, and sufficient explosive material that would blast with the force of several sticks of TNT, sending shards of death in every direction.

Akmed was only seventeen-years-old and he was about to die. Or rather, as he believed, begin to live. At last, a solution to his nightmares. The dreams of dread would soon end. And so his puny life would now have purpose for God. *What is life?* he thought. Akmed grew up in abject poverty in an Egyptian-administered refugee camp near the shores of the Mediterranean in Gaza. An Israeli soldier gunned down his father in 1967 during Israel's invasion of the Gaza Strip and West Bank during the Six-Day War when Akmed was only five-years-old. Controlled by the Israeli army along with 1 million other Palestinians, he was weaned on resentment of the occupation. His mother was run over by a bulldozer seven years later, as she protested their family's displacement in favor of one of Menachem Begin's Jewish settlements on the Gaza Strip after the Arab-Israeli War in 1973—what the Zionists called the "Yom Kippur War." Their stone villa, dilapidated as it was, and small olive orchard in sight of the blue seawaters were destroyed. He himself, at the tender age of fifteen, was flogged with leather whips by whom he believed were Israeli agents attempting to silence protesting Palestinians. Now, six years after his mother's death, he had no home, he had no parents, and he had no country. All he owned was scars on his back and faith that his death would lead to freedom for Palestine as well as a one-way ticket to Paradise for himself.

The deadly vest wrapped around his torso was not his idea, though. He was more accustomed to tossing rocks at Israeli tanks and dodging the reprisals of non-lethal plastic bullets. The deadly garment was suggested by an officer of Fatah, the Palestine National Liberation Movement, one of the oldest and most

influential resistance groups that made up *Munazzamat at-Tahrir Filastiniyah*—
the Palestinian Liberation Organization, better known as the PLO. This Fatah
officer, known to Akmed only as Omar, guided the orphan teen since the death
of his mother. The carriers of the *sacred explosions* were volunteers, but Akmed
noticed they were lured by the Army of God with the flair of a savvy street vendor. Bombers were almost always boys like him—in their late teens, often without nuclear families, on the run from authorities, and angry. Some of the recruits
were mentally slow and were even more effortlessly swayed to blow themselves up
and take as many Israelis as possible along with them. For this they could pay the
Jews back for the exodus of the Palestinian people from their natural homeland.
The volunteers were immediate heroes among their people. And Paradise was
paved with endless happiness. And the chosen few arrived early.

Akmed, however, was no dunce. He liked school, when he attended. He had a
flair for math and science, his teachers said. And Akmed once had vivid day-
dreams of fantasy instead of the devilish nightmares that plagued his thoughts
once his eyes closed. Growing up in sight of the docks at Gaza's chief port, he
dreamed of becoming an oceanographer, lured by the siren call of the cobalt-blue
waters of the Mediterranean. He wanted to sail, fish, and feel the salt breeze on
his copper-toned face, and perhaps even explore the liquid world below like the
wily Frenchman he saw on television, Jacques Cousteau, on the research vessel
named *Calypso*. But that was when he did not think of all the agonies. His father
was killed because he stood before at an Israeli tank, unarmed. His mother's
bones were crushed by the greed of the Jews taking their land, claiming the occupied territories as "God's gift" to the Israelis and their reactionaries' desire to rein-
habit all the ancient land of *Eretz Yisrael*. But he and many others of his
countrymen vowed the Jews would not succeed. Akmed was raised a proper man
of God, dedicated to the five pillars of Islam including: repeating the creed that
Allah is the one God and Muhammad is his Prophet, regularly studying the
Qur'an, and repeating the *Salat;* kneeling in prayer on his mat toward Mecca five
times a day; practicing the *zakat*, the giving of alms; adhering to the month of
Siyam and fasting during *Ramadan*; and hopefully participating in the *hajj* to
Mecca to visit the sacred sites. But there was no time for that final pillar in his
short life. He would substitute a sixth pillar of Islam's colonnade—self-sacrifice
for God. There was only one light at the end of the tunnel of his dark depression
that lasted throughout his teenage years. And that was revenge and death. His
adventure with the *Calypso* would have to wait for the next life.

He drank bitter date wine and toasted his superiors at Fatah just an hour ago.
A week before, he even received a blessing from Yasser Arafat himself. *A servant of*

Palestine who dies for the sake of their nation will not die in vain, the gallant hero of the Palestinian people proclaimed. Akmed's younger sisters still lived in Gaza. His handlers within the freedom organization pledged that they would be taken care of financially for the rest of their lives because of Akmed's heroics. They would be honored greatly and attract important husbands who sought to marry into a celebrated family.

Now the talk was over. It was time to act. The lunchtime crowd was milling about through the open-air restaurants built by rich Jews with their American money. He despised the young women and men, strolling together hand in hand knowing they someday would inherit the riches of their parents. The Jews and their acolytes were totally clueless of what it was like to be a Palestinian teenager. There was no future for young men like him. Little did the Jews know their future ended here as well.

Akmed was tall for seventeen, though he only had 150 pounds of flesh on his six-foot-two frame. He stood head and shoulders above his compatriots and did not blend into a crowd easily. So he would have to act quickly or would surely be noticed by soldiers that regularly patrolled the commercial thoroughfare as regularly as taxis moving through the Israeli capital. He quickly stepped into the narrow marketplace street from an alley between two shops that had no windows on the side. He slipped into the stream of walking traffic of Israelis moving along the boutique-lined street. He immediately walked unnoticed into a crowd of teenagers off from school for a spring vacation. The teens flocked to the posh shops to spend their parent's money. Akmed stared at a kinky-haired Israeli teen—probably his age—wearing a silken yarmulke on the crown of his head, smiling as he took the hand of a shapely woman with hair the color of fire. A red-haired Israeli? Maybe she was a European. Maybe even an *American*, Akmed thought. Her reddish hair contrasted with her bronze-tanned skin, probably earned by afternoons lounging on an exclusive Tel Aviv beach in the Mediterranean sun. He found it humorous once when a Palestinian teacher told him that Caucasian Americans went to great lengths to darken their epidermis, while they condemned and oppressed their fellow Americans with red, brown, and black skin. There were riots in the American cities over such things. America was the land of violence, greed, and godlessness, and satanic partners to the Jews.

Akmed listened to the conversation of the two smitten youths in front of him. *Yes, they are speaking English!* Akmed understood, and somewhat spoke heavily accented English himself. His teachers insisted he learn the wicked tongue of the West so he could be a leader someday for Palestine and stand up directly to the imperialists from across the Atlantic. He learned English in a Palestinian school—despite their indigence, Palestinians were among the most highly educated people in the Arab world—and his language skills were supplemented by watching American television shows on a black-and-white set at a seaside Gaza restaurant where he catered to fisherman. It was fascinating. Every American television show was full of killing and violence, Akmed noted. Everyone carried a gun. Cowboys they called them. The jingoist American heroes slaughtered the red-skinned native population of their continent with their superior weapons and then stole their lands. Then, they enslaved the Africans like an imported commodity. Perhaps they now help the Jews kill or potentially enslave the Palestinians for sport.

But the proud people of Palestine resisted. The "pulse of the street" revolt began with strikes, boycotts, tax resistance, and rock throwing. But easily suppressed by the Jewish military might backed by the United States, the passive protests were proven to be insufficient. Now it was Akmed's turn to do his part. He would die, but so would many Israelis. And an American standing right in front of him! Wouldn't that be great? Not only was he to kill the vermin of Israel, but also take the life of an ignorant rodent from America that propped up the Israeli occupation of Palestine. Wouldn't that be a message television could broadcast across the globe? Recently, Akmed learned the Persian Islamists in Iran stood up to the Americans, revolting against the American-puppet Shah, seizing their embassy, and taking American hostages. The mighty America was powerless to stop it. This is part of a worldwide revolt against the evil western culture, many in Fatah said. America, the Iranians claimed, was the "Great Satan" behind the Zionist pigs at every turn and must be confronted. Fatah would show it was also not afraid to take on the power of America.

The crowd of teens slowed near the entrance of a trendy restaurant that opened only a month before. The eatery was a favorite of on-leave Israeli soldiers as well, *taking a respite from their brutality in Gaza and the West Bank*, Akmed thought. This was originally the target of the plans of Akmed's handlers. Kill as many soldiers as possible, but remember, the civilians in the area were not innocents, but merely collateral damage. It was standing room only and a half-hour wait greeted those who wanted to make a social statement and eat where the in-people dined. The restaurant played hedonistic American disco-music and served disgusting western-style food. This was the perfect opportunity. How could he get so fortunate? Chances are he could take out dozens of Israeli soldiers crowded around the entrance, along with the arrogant grinning Jew and his American slut girlfriend.

As Akmed reached his sweaty palm inside his coat, his eyes met those of an Israeli military policeman, standing guard at the busy restaurant's entrance. Nothing in Akmed's coal-black, narrow eyes communicated fear or worry, but that is not what the policeman noticed. It was a hot day, and Akmed was wearing a heavy cloak. He stood out in the crowd like a poorly disguised wolf among sheep. Akmed wanted to make it inside to maximize the damage, but he could not wait any longer. His hand grasped a handle inside his coat. The vest bomb he was carrying was modified from a parachute backpack. To detonate the explosive, all he needed to do was pull the ripcord. Instead of a parachute popping out to safely bring him down to earth from the sky, the device would blow the steel ball bearings and serrated metal pieces through the bodies of everyone around him, and send his soul rocketing from earth to heaven.

The policeman was now more than suspicious. He was on the move. Akmed was found out. He gritted his teeth, closed his eyes, and in his penultimate act, screamed *"Allah Akbar"* (God is great). He yanked the handle with the fury of revenge for the deaths of his parents and thousands of his countrymen.

Nothing happened.

As the Tel Aviv military cop pushed himself through the crowd of anxious teenagers, Akmed looked down at the parachute ripcord handle gripped in his white-knuckled fingers. The cord ripped out of its holster, but there was no detonation, no explosion. Whoever designed this parachute bomb was a fool. And now Akmed failed in his mission. He was not in Paradise. He would be captured by the Jews, and worse, suffer the unlivable embarrassment of surviving when he was supposed to die for his people and Allah. The policeman edged closer, shouting. Akmed was pushed from behind by more impatient teens trying to elbow their way into the popular restaurant's queue, unaware of the commotion in front. He could not be taken into custody. He must flee. Since his height made him obvious, he ducked into the crowd, but he had to shed his worthless killer jacket. He must create a distraction. He ripped off his cloak and threw the heavy jacket over the head of the teenage redhead who stood obliviously in front of him.

"A bomb! A bomb!" Akmed shouted in both Arabic and English.

The girl screamed and cowered, the weighty jacket full of hundreds of steel balls and metal scraps landing on her shoulders. She fell to her knees. Panicked, she looked directly in Akmed's cold, dark, assassin's eyes. Her Israeli companion reached to grab Akmed's sweaty shirt. The young Palestinian barreled backwards just as the policeman fought his way through the pulsating crowd of teenagers that were pushing their way from the scuffle in the center.

"A bomb!" several teenagers cried.

"Get back!" the policeman shouted, and the crowd moved away from the young woman who fell to the ground, covered by the tan jacket that must have felt as heavy as a metal awning.

"Do not move!" the policeman ordered the hysterically crying woman.

When Akmed arrived at the safe house several blocks away, he wished he was dead—even if the pursuing Israeli policeman shot him in the back. Who could stand this shame? The jacket did not explode. But it wasn't his fault, was it? He practiced right in front of his handlers. But would they believe him? Would they believe the Israeli media if the police admitted the bomb was a dud? Or would they conclude that Akmed was a coward who abandoned his ethereal mission? He wanted to die now, more than ever.

The look on the faces of his PLO handlers was as if they saw a ghost. Those who were sent to do Allah's work to save Palestine did not return in the flesh. If bodies were returned to families they were often in several pieces. Usually the head came in a separate sack. Akmed was in one piece. And his head was firmly attached. They must be shocked to see him whole without his jacket. Akmed fell to his knees and tried to explain, but did not expect mercy.

"I deserve death," he said. *Better to die at the hands of your brothers than your godless enemy.*

But Akmed would not die. The ever-efficient Israeli radio and television stations were all over the story within a half hour, interviewing the policeman who spotted the suspected terrorist.

"The terrorist's detonator failed," the policeman told the cameras and microphones. "However, there was enough explosive on him to kill many, many people. But thank the God of Abraham, it did not go off."

Akmed's handlers frowned disapprovingly, though not at Akmed. He was only the missile housing. They seemed to be more disturbed that they lost the payload.

"Akmed, listen to me," said a frosty-bearded man wearing a black-and-white kaffiyah headscarf. He was a senior officer in the PLO Akmed knew as Omar. There were few old people in the freedom-fighting organization, Akmed knew. Most were killed in the struggle before they sprouted gray hairs.

"Yes," Akmed whimpered, his head between his legs.

"Were you followed?"

"No, I don't believe so."

"Were you seen by this policeman?"

"Yes," he said. *Please spare me this shame*, he thought.

"He can identify you?"

"Probably."

The officer frowned, stroked his bushy, salt-and-pepper beard thoughtfully, and mumbled something to another companion.

"Akmed, listen to me," he said.

"Yes."

"You must leave Palestine. You will be found. We will have another mission for you someday. There is no need to feel shame. This is Allah's will."

"I don't understand," Akmed sobbed.

"If you stay here, you will eventually be caught. But we have ways to get you out of Israel. Through the West Bank, then to Jordan, and from there, perhaps to England. We have plenty of friends there who can take care of you. You will be safe. You may be more use to our nation there."

"I don't understand," Akmed cried again, tears streaking down his face.

"You will, young soldier. Some day you will."

CHAPTER 4

▼

December 1979, London, England

He called himself "Cowboy," and he looked the part. A broad tan Stetson on his head, leather western boots with intricate designs riding up to his calves, and a leather string pull tie that resembled Roy Rogers' attire. His speech echoed the folksy vernacular of a protagonist in a Zane Grey dime western. However, his muscular, svelte build had all the college girls at his table swooning over him. And he enjoyed it. He lifted a large glass mug of dark English ale to his lips and polished it off, leaving a thick web of foam lacing on the inside of the glass and on his upper lip. Warm beer was something he was not used to, but he became acclimated without much effort.

The bar of the King's Rook Hotel was full—it was New Year's Eve in London, and every pub was packed. A rare three-inch snowfall deposited on London's streets during the evening caused traffic tie-ups and fender benders as the natives went about their planned celebrations. Loud voices were common throughout the crowded room, but were especially raucous at Cowboy's table, where a group of American college students on holiday laughed uproariously. Though the hotel pub contained people from many different nations and persuasions, Cowboy's manner and accoutrements stood out, as he would put it, like teats on a snake.

"I'm just one wild and crazy guy!" Cowboy roared, doing his best impression of the comedian Steve Martin, who was all the rage back in the states. "And I would like to touch your big American breasts!"

The young college-age girls with him, most sophisticated, giggled as if he made up the lines himself. They were on a University of Oklahoma-sponsored theater tour for three weeks and he was just a tag-a-long with his drama-major girlfriend, who was upstairs in her hotel room in bed with an intestinal virus. Bruce "Cowboy" Rhodan was a petroleum geology major at U of O. He had washed out of the U.S. Naval Academy and didn't miss it. Unfortunately, except for lively sex, he knew he and his thespian girlfriend mixed like oil and water. She was a prissy drama queen and she hated his desire to puff on large cigars. Her companions probably found him ribald and uncouth as well, and probably not all that bright. That was okay with him. He was entertaining, especially after a few brews. And by the attention he commanded, he knew he was handsome as hell, rugged and tough, but in a baby-faced sort of way. A cross between Steve McQueen and that new heartthrob of the silver-screen's newest blockbuster, one of girls said, though she could not remember the name of the movie star.

"You know, that cute guy who plays Han Solo in *Star Wars*," said a petite blonde biology major. He stared at her button nose, prominent cleft in her chin, and *kind* mouth—the kind Cowboy wanted to stick his tongue into.

"Harrison Ford," Cowboy answered. "Get that all the time. Want to see my light saber?"

A nearby jukebox shifted from a syrupy Elton John instrumental that Cowboy thought sounded like a cheap windup music box to an earsplitting punk-rock anthem, with a burning wall of guitars and acrimonious shouted lyrics. Cowboy winced.

"Is that what these limeys call music?" he said. "I don't suppose they have any Waylon Jennings in that thing?"

"So your girlfriend Cindy says you are a son of an oil billionaire or some-thing—like J. R. Ewing on *Dallas*?" said a sassy brunette—*eyes as black as the inside of a well bore*, Cowboy thought.

"No, I'm not, but my son will be," he said. "All I need to do is find the lucky mother."

"Oh, you don't think she is here do you," the girl said, laughing at his bra-vado. She was a business major. *A boardroom mind with a bedroom smile.*

"No," Cowboy said. "Not the mother of my future child. The *mother lode.* The Big Kahuna. The Great Gusher. The Gargantuan Gasser. The hole to hell that will make me so rich that, well, I can afford a lot of sons to a lot of mothers."

Cowboy did not deny that his ego was a long as the Oklahoma panhandle. But he knew there was something in his eyes that led everyone to believe that he would do exactly as he claimed. He certainly exaggerated his influence and poten-tial in the oil and gas business to his girlfriend, who obviously relayed his bullshit to her companions. His immediate family wasn't even in the business. But his uncle did work on an offshore rig. And he yearned to get back to the oil and gas platforms in the Gulf of Mexico where he spent his summers. But the only drill-ing Cowboy was currently engaged in was with his girlfriend. Until she started puking—and claimed her monthly "friend" arrived. So tonight, saying good-bye to the 1970s, Cowboy was out on the range trying to rope another cow. And he had his eyes on either the elfin blonde with the Kirk Douglas chin or the brown-haired beauty with midnight eyes like big drops of black gold.

"We are on the verge of something big off the coast of Louisiana," he said with a wink of his blue eyes. He lifted his empty mug of ale. "And with the price of oil and gas shooting up, when we hit it, compared with me, J. R.'s going to look like he lives in a trailer park. I tell ya, when we hit the gusher in the ol' U.S. of A., that Ayatollah is going to shit in his turban."

He needed a refill. The warm beer went down like a soft drink. He knew his natural unquenchable desire to engage in bullshit artistry was only surpassed by his thirst for alcohol, taste for cigars, and propensity for finding trouble.

A severed head in his hand, Akmed Abram held his victim's long, pinkish-blond hair that was turning more crimson by the moment. It was the decapitated head of the American girl who accompanied the Jew. Heavy and pendulous, it felt like a bag full of figs. It was true—her head did come clean off when the jacket blew up. Just like a cannonball. His friends were right. And here was his trophy. A woman's head, vacant eyes staring, mouth agape in a soundless scream. He dropped the skull and it bounced hard, as if on a wooden floor. And from her head, warm fluid, frothy and bubbling, suffused over him, drenching his hands, arms, and hair.

A firm hand nudged Akmed's shoulder.

"About time to call it a night, mate?" the bartender asked, drying off one beer mug with a towel with one hand, and uprighting a now empty mug of ale in front of Akmed. He had fallen asleep right on the barstool, face in his arms. The clunk of the bodiless head in his dream was the heavy glass mug toppling to the bar top and the flowing blood was room temperature sudsy ale soaking the sleeves of his overcoat and the side of his head that lay on the counter after he slumped forward.

Akmed the sleeper. This time, his tendency to fall into sudden slumber was aided by ale. Until a month ago, Akmed never drank alcohol with the exception of the ceremonial wine that was a precursor to blowing his body parts all over a Tel Aviv marketplace. His Islamic tradition forbade wallowing in drink. But his nightmares and insomnia! He was terrified by day and sleepless at night. But he was not indefatigable. He met a companion he hoped would bring him solace and rest—alcohol. He was no longer in the ancient land of Palestine; he was in decadent downtown London, just three blocks from Trafalgar Square and not that far from the Queen's Palace with its silly Beefeaters, the black-booted, red-jacketed guards that stood stoically in their cylindrical, fuzzy bearskin hats. He was told to blend into the rest of the Arab population of London—there were more and more all the time. It would not be difficult—there were thousands of believers there. Do what the Londoners do. So that is what he did. He just turned eighteen and had a passport to prove it. He could consume alcohol legally, and despite the bitter hoppy froth on top of the draught, after a couple of warm ales made him woozy, he developed an affinity for the beverage.

"Pardon?" Akmed replied to the bartender. Soggy pound notes and wet pence coins covered the area in front of him. He was not done imbibing. He had a little money left. Then maybe he could sleep without the night terrors. The barkeep tightened a smile, shook his head in regret, and moved on to another customer.

Akmed frequented this hotel bar since it was a short walk from where he was living. Escorted to Jordan through PLO operatives, he boarded a plane to London, complete with a legitimate passport that even permitted him to keep his own name. He was a homeless teenage orphan, a Palestinian refugee hosted by sympathizers in London. Akmed lived with an elderly British couple, Charles and Elizabeth Walpole. Charles was a former diplomat in the Foreign Service based in Palestine during World War II, and Elizabeth was a British Army nurse who met him near the conclusion of the conflict. When the state of Israel was proclaimed in 1948 by the United Nations, the armies of Syria, Egypt, Lebanon, Transjordan, and Iraq attacked the next day. Caught in the middle of the conflict and soured by years of war, the Walpoles fled back to England. They married, worked nondescript lives back in the United Kingdom, and now enjoyed retirement in a three-bedroom flat, intoxicated a good portion of the time. Still, they had a life purpose. They had many friends among the Palestinians, and despised the UN-created state of Israel, though they were not anti-Semitic. They were Christians, but they simply resented the treatment of the Palestinian people after the 1948, 1967, and 1973 wars. So in response, they contributed thousands of their retirement dollars to the Palestinian refugee cause, and held their small flat as a temporary safe haven for refugees or PLO operatives fleeing the Holy Land. They did not inquire why the refugees left. Scotland Yard was well aware of the Walpole's support of Palestinian efforts—Charles, in fact, was a public leader of the Londoners for Free Palestine Association—but the old folks broke no laws, and every Palestinian who stayed with them carried a legitimate visa and had every right to reside in Britain. The British authorities were consumed with identifying Irish Republican Army terrorists, not Palestinian freedom fighters.

"One more," Akmed said to the bartender, holding up a long index finger. Silently, the barkeep reluctantly complied.

Akmed did not work, but instead leached off of his English hosts. There wasn't much work around, anyhow. England was on the brink of depression it seemed. Inflation, unemployment, and interest rates were at record levels. The English socialist-democratic state appeared as if it were on the edge of collapse. Jobless, he spent his days wandering through London, visiting historic sites. He toured the British Museum and Charles Dickens' birthplace, window-shopped the affluent and famous western department store Harrods, and gawked at prostitutes and spiked-haired youths with safety pins through their noses loitering around Piccadilly Circus. He even sat in on a debate in Parliament, waiting in line for three hours to listen from the gallery high above where the Members of Parliament (MOPs) and British prime minister screamed at one another. He noticed that the tourists were searched, which made him nervous. But the British police were not suspicious of Arab teenagers, but instead were ever on the lookout for IRA bombs. The day Akmed attended the Parliament debate, a brown-haired, throaty-voiced woman vociferously berated the gray-haired MOP for his party's role in creating inflation, unemployment, the energy crisis, and every pestilence known to mankind. *How could they let a woman talk that way to a man?* he wondered. This was so strange. And he later learned that this bombastic, insolent woman was the country's new Prime Minister. The West was full of puzzling mysteries.

The hotel bar bustled with New Year's revelry. A group of teenage Americans were causing commotion in one corner of the pub. They talked in weird, facetious Eastern-European accents and said abstruse things he did not understand and broke into hysterics. A jukebox boomed a wall of irritating sound, horrendous western music by sick young Brits in a "musical" group. They sang something called "Anarchy in the UK." To Akmed, it sounded like the braying of donkeys undergoing castration, though the disrespectful devil-filled youths might be right about the state of affairs in Britain. Over the bar a television set was on, with the sound turned low. A BBC news program was airing a story about the continuing hostage situation at the American Embassy in Tehran. News film footage of the blindfolded Americans with their hands tied behind their backs was shown repeatedly. On Akmed's left at the bar sat an unattractive, tall red-headed woman slurping gin, leaving a sloppy imprint of red lipstick on her glass. Next to her, a British teenager with spiked flame-red hair and pierced body parts who looked too young to consume alcohol, smoked an unfiltered cigarette. On his right, stood one of the gauche American tourists, a young man wearing, *what else*, Akmed thought, one of those "cowboy" hats. Akmed was told that the American cowboy was a thing of the past—only seen on television—but there he was, a pink-cheeked young American, with a huge hat that you could cook a meal in, leather boots, and a wide silver belt buckle in the shape of some kind of pot on his blue-jean pants. All that was missing was the holster, six-shooter, chaps, and little sharp spurs on his heels to stab horses in their flanks. Akmed was puzzled. And Americans, he had heard, ridiculed people in traditional Arab dress!

The Palestinian looked at the silly American in his ten-gallon hat and then the rooster-haired British teen dressed in leather, chains, and a huge metal object the shape of a fishhook jutting out of his earlobe. *What is he? Oh yes, a punk rocker*, Akmed learned when he asked his hosts who the queer-looking men were lurking in the underground train stations waiting to buy narcotics. They were worthless vagabonds who listened to satanic music and consumed mind-altering substances—parasites on this polluted society. *Yobos*, the Walpoles called them, misguided thuggish young males. Akmed felt like he was in the alien cantina portrayed in that American science-fiction film he saw the week before in a London movie house—*Star Wars*, it was titled. Interestingly, all the English-speaking heroes did in that motion picture was kill people, just like the cowboys exterminated the denizens of America. The United States was full of killers. Killing for no purpose. There was no invasion, no unwanted occupation, and no revolution. Instead, killing there seemed to be some kind of national sport. Even Akmed's English hosts hated the Americans.

"They are an impudent people who think they own everything," Charles Walpole told his Palestinian guest.

The Londoner punk-rocker's eyes glazed over most likely from his consumption of a plethora of illegal pharmaceuticals and excessive doses of porter. The half-burned cigarette, an inch of ash protruding from the end, dangled from his swollen lips as he ran his tattooed hand over the breasts of the ugly redhead. *The British Crown ran its iron hand over the tender breast of Palestine for many years. Disgusting.* Meanwhile, in a loud abhorrent voice, the arrogant American demanded several draughts for his stupid friends. Now the Americans picked up where the British left off, helping the Jews exterminate his people. They all deserved to die. But Akmed was told to do nothing and wait. Omar would contact him when he needed him. Did he have to wait before he could defend Palestine and deliver retribution to these swine? Akmed swallowed his refilled tepid brew and grimaced.

"Oooo you think you're lookin' at?" the drugged and drunken punk rocker said with a thick Cockney accent, his glassy eyes wandering like snooker balls after a break.

Akmed was involved with his own ale, and didn't realize the teenage waste product was speaking to him. The young Palestinian was going to violate his Muslim upbringing again—he was "pissed," as his hosts called becoming intoxicated, in hopes of drowning his horrid dreams.

"'ey!" the safety-pin pierced punk in the leather jacket said, pushing Akmed's left shoulder, spilling a good portion of his drink on the bar surface. "I'm talkin' to you A-rab!"

Akmed turned and glared at the English youth. The drunk's multi-spiked hair bobbed like the blood-red comb of a barnyard cock.

"What you want?" Akmed said, in his best attempt at the native tongue. Akmed's eyes were bloodshot and black circles hung below them like dark crescent moons. He was sleep-deprived, intoxicated, and he was still a neophyte with English. He could understand it spoken with an American accent, thanks to television. But he could barely understand a word from this drunken English fool.

"What the bloody 'ell are you doin' here—you some kind of Sheik?"

The foul stench coming from his belligerent mouth must be his breath, Akmed surmised. He hadn't smelled anything like it except from the mouth of a donkey.

"I am Palestinian," Akmed said proudly.

"A bloody terrorist?" the youth responded, breaking into a pathetic intoxicated laugh displayed to his unlucky lady of the evening, who giggled, and then gasped for air with a smoker's wheeze. She exposed her decaying yellow-green, tobacco-stained teeth.

Spittle dripped from the teen's swollen lip. "Workin' with the Irish bombers are yeh? Some kind of tag-team terrorists? Are you goin' to blow your bloody self to 'ell at the stroke of midnight?" The ridiculing laughter continued, followed by a tobacco tar-induced cough. "Fuckin' 'appy New Year! Kaboom!"

Akmed gripped his pocket. In it, he kept a switchblade knife he stole from his host's writing desk. After all this time, he felt he may have to finally kill someone.

CHAPTER 5

▼

"Hey friend," a third voice interrupted the confrontation between Akmed and the Londoner. It wasn't the barkeep—he was retreating to a phone to contact the hotel security. It was the baby-faced American in the cowboy hat two sizes too big for his head. He stepped forward and tugged on his pan-shaped belt buckle, which every American would recognize as the silhouette of the state of Oklahoma. "Is there a problem here?"

"What the 'ell do you want, cowboy?" the punk rocker replied, again sliding into a mocking laugh for his harlot audience of one. "Fuckin' American, you can go to bloody 'ell too."

"We're celebrating New Year's Eve and we don't want any trouble," the young American replied. Akmed scanned him from hat to boot. The American had the same clueless puppy-dog look as the tanned redhead in the Tel Aviv marketplace—devoid of the problems of the real world, living in their false paradise. The American's locks of curly, dirty-blond hair puffed out of the back of the huge hat. His cheeks were rose-red from too much drink. Akmed quaffed from his refilled mug and drops of ale foam stuck to the shaved tips of his thick moustache.

"Go back to the Alamo, cowboy," the punk rocker said, pointing at the television. "Those Iranians 'ave you by the balls, they do. They're going to gut 'em and feed 'em to their camels."

The drunkard continued his phony belly cackle better than the best Shakespearean actor in Stratford-upon-Avon.

"Why don't you mosey on over there, sit down, and drink your drink?" the calm voice of the youth from across the sea said, tipping his hat back a bit on the top of his forehead.

"Fuck off, Hoss," the punk rocker said and swung a right hook at the face of the American. He dodged the blow, though his huge Stetson flew off his skull, exposing thinning hair the color of the sand on a Gaza beach. Instead of striking the American, the drunk's hand glanced the chin of Akmed instead, knocking him into the bar. Before the inebriated English youth regained his balance from his wild swing, the American left jabbed the skinny attacker in the stomach. When the Brit doubled over in pain, a roundhouse right undercut caught the nose of the verbally abusive man and he flung backward into the lap of the repulsive hooker, toppling her off her bar stool. They both crashed to the floor with all the grace of two bags of sheep manure off the back of a pull cart. Without his hat, Akmed noticed that the young American's blond hair was sparse on the top, like one in his middle-years, though the fair-haired hirsute curls in the back of his head hung nearly to his shoulders, like a woman. The American picked up his western hat with a sweep of his arm, dusted it off, and placed it back on his head—*just like in the cowboy movies*, Akmed thought.

When the American turned, he saw the barkeep talking with two hotel security officers who had rushed to the scene.

"Shit!" the American said.

The security men promptly ejected both of them out onto the snowy curb. The American's big-mouthed college friends swore at the security guards, calling them "redcoat fascists." *Shocking talk from women*, Akmed thought. The semi-conscious punk rocker was still on the floor, dazed. The Bobbies would be called to haul him away and into a London drunk tank where on this evening, he would have plenty of company.

"Well I guess I ruined New Year's Eve for both of us," the American said to Akmed. "Howdy, my name is Bruce Rhodan." He offered his hand.

Akmed did not reply, nor did he move a muscle.

"Rhodan—you know like the flying monster in the *Godzilla* movies?" he replied.

Still, no answer.

"Well, people call me Cowboy—even Sid Vicious in there did and I hadn't the opportunity to properly introduce myself."

Akmed tilted his head and stared at the American curiously, like a biologist observing an unidentified species. "Cowboy" offered his hand again, in traditional western fashion. "Your name?"

"Akmed," he finally answered, still trying to figure this American out. He still did not shake Cowboy's hand. This was the ugly American his British hosts talked about.

"Well, howdy Akmed," Cowboy said. "Where the hell can we get a drink around here without getting involved in a brawl? The locals don't seem to like me much around here."

More silence followed. Then Akmed said cautiously, "I have drink at my flat."

"Well, where do you live?" Cowboy answered. "I want to celebrate the New Year—the new decade! I wouldn't mind gettin' rip roarin' drunk and piss on the window of the Old Curiosity Shop. These damn limeys aren't the most gracious of hosts."

Akmed pointed down the street and walked. What was he doing? Who was this aggressive fool? He was fascinated. He had to learn more about these Americans. *Know your enemy*, his handlers had told him. They stepped into a slush-covered zebra crossing, a section of road featuring several diagonally painted white lines designating a purportedly safe passage for pedestrians across a dangerous London thoroughfare. A 1950s-era black taxi nearly ran the American over. Akmed reached and seized his arm, pulling him backwards from a certain hit and run. Neither spoke. They were both drunk. They dodged more cabs and erratically driven lorries, who might have pub-frequenting truck drivers behind their wheels. Before they reached Akmed's adopted apartment in a neighborhood of middle-class rowhouses, Akmed heard the entire life story of "Cowboy" and his assessment of his trip to England.

"I had that streaky fatty bacon they serve at the hotel," Cowboy said. "Disgusting how they can ruin a pig in these parts. I'd rather eat jerky. And the coffee—puke! The beer is okay though. But those breakfast rolls? What do they call them—scones? It tastes like a lump of cardboard with plaster-of-Paris on top. Fine hotel, hooey! What a tourist-trap!"

The American talked faster than an angry woman arguing over prices of withered fruit at a Palestinian bazaar. The only thing Akmed understood was that "Cowboy" was from an American province called "Oklahoma," and was visiting London for the first time. He did not appear to like it much.

"I'm here with my girlfriend—she wasn't in the bar, she doesn't drink much. She's here on a theatre tour—I'm along for the ride. She's here to see Shakespeare, George Bernard Shaw—y'know, that fag light-in-the-loafer-shit. I'm here to check out the London brew. Man, that piss-warm dark ale will mess you up if you're not careful. I'm used to smooth southern whiskey—some homemade by my uncle. Frankly, I'd rather be in the hotel room with my honey showin' her the long little doggie, if y'know what I mean, but she claims she's ridin' the cotton pony. Y'know? Flyin' the red flag?"

Akmed did not have the foggiest notion of what the American was talking about. He did not recognize any of these words or expressions from the movies and television shows he had seen. He knew that, according to the English, "fags" were cigarettes. He did not know why Cowboy was comparing some man named "Shaw" to a tobacco smoke. But he wanted to understand what made this American tick. He led Cowboy into an unpretentious flat that smelled of mothballs and cabbage. Akmed's English hosts were out on the town, boozing it up for the holiday. Akmed pulled out a bottle of scotch, another one of his new western alcoholic favorites. The two filled their glasses and knocked back a shot. Cowboy tipped his hat backward and wiped his brow with his forearm. His hairline was indeed receding on top, unusual for such a young man. But his gray-blue eyes appeared full of mirth—exaggerated by the pints consumed earlier in the evening—with little seriousness to his character. He was gregarious and appeared not afraid to generate conversation with anyone at anytime about anything. He acted as if he expected everyone to like him. And perhaps if they didn't, the loquacious American would not notice. But the boyish young man had the confidence of an elderly tribe leader, Akmed observed, and based upon his actions in the hotel bar, he was no coward. A short time before, another shot of liquid courage may have urged Akmed to kill this American just for his abhorrence of the West. Now, he was captivated, as if he was observing a rare zoo animal that deserved live study rather than post-mortem dissection.

"Tell about … America," Akmed said slowly. He was hoping he could understand the Cowboy for he spoke so rapidly.

"America is the greatest goddamn country in the world," Cowboy said, pouring another drink. "Well, Oklahoma is anyway."

"Tell about Ok-la-homa." Akmed offered a plate of shortbread cookies. "Biscuit? From woman who lives here."

Cowboy perused the snack with no appetite.

"No offense, but they look like she baked them during the blitzkrieg," Cowboy said. He declined with a wave of his hand.

"*Oklahoma!*" Akmed's guest sang, "*where the wind comes sweepin' down the plain!*" breaking into hearty laughter like the intoxicated Englishman did.

Cowboy stopped laughing. Akmed was not familiar with the tune.

"No, Oklahoma is real nice, Akmed," Cowboy said. "Blue skies, clean air, beautiful land that stretches as far as the eye can see, corn stalks as high as Wilt Chamberlain. You should come to America sometime."

"America," Akmed pondered. "So much woilence."

"Excuse me?"

"Woilence," Akmed said. "I watch American television—killings all the time. America is full of woilence."

After the third time, the American understood.

"Oh, you mean *violence*? No way, José. America is the land of opportunity, of freedom, of business."

"Business?" Akmed said. Of course, Americans thought of nothing other than money that they used for their business of violence. "What business you do?"

"My family owns a gun shop."

Cowboy waited a beat and then laughed again. Realizing the irony, Akmed actually smiled.

"Actually, I'm a senior at the University of Oklahoma, majoring in petroleum engineering and geology. I have an uncle in the oil drilling business in Texas— big oil and gas is waiting to be found offshore in the Gulf of Mexico. Those damn towel-heads need to know there's more than one way to skin a cat."

Akmed didn't react. He was generally puzzled. Was this an insult? Cowboy's rosy cheeks seemed to turn white.

"Sorry," Cowboy said. "My girlfriend says I always put my boot in my mouth. I didn't mean anything against the people in your neck of the woods."

Yes, you did, Akmed thought. But the fast-talking American was backpedaling.

"We're in a bit of an energy crisis and economic trouble down home, and we're gettin' the drilling shaft if y'know what I mean," the American said. "We need to be a little more self-sufficient."

"Woilence, energy shortage, economic trouble," Akmed said. "America does not sound like such a good place."

"No, Akmed, you got it all wrong. America is great. Sure, we got our problems as much as anywhere else. One of the problems is our peanut-growing president, but I think we are going to get rid of him. Hate to say it of a southerner, but he's not the best thing for business. But that's the thing, Akmed, we can change our government policy without putting a bullet in the back of someone's head. America is about freedom, not violence. Again, no offense friend, but you folks in the Middle East seem to doing a good job at the violence thing yourselves."

"Free-dom," Akmed pondered, mulling over both syllables in his creaky English. He rehearsed his thoughts many times in English to his British hosts. "My country wants freedom."

The Palestinian looked away. Thousands of his countrymen in Israeli prisons charged with what? Being Palestinian? Teachers, political leaders, religious men deported. There is now talk of the massive expulsion of Palestinians from their own land. Land stolen, houses and vineyards destroyed, curfews and travel bans keep people from their jobs, unfair taxes, and they had no voice.

Akmed returned his attention to Cowboy. "Did not rebels in America kill the English because of … how you say … tax without presentation?"

"Yeah," Cowboy said, "taxation without *representation*. I guess we did." He cleared his throat. "Enough politics," Cowboy said. "I'm here for the broads and the booze." He filled both shot glasses with Scotch and they drank again.

"What do you do here in London?" Cowboy asked, seemingly eager to change the subject.

"I not a job," Akmed replied without emotion. "But I look. Bad economy in this country."

"Ever think of the oil and gas business?"

"No," Akmed replied. "We no have energy business in Palestine."

"Well what do you like to do?"

Akmed looked at the ceiling, puzzled why the American was so curious. "I want to work on ship," the unemployed Palestinian said. "I like ocean."

"Well, hell, then you might like the oil and gas business. Drilling is picking up in the North Sea—it's the *dash for gas*, man. The Brits have some great prospects underwater. They're hiring lots of non-English workers. Damn nobles think they're too good for the work. You could earn a good buck on a drilling platform and see all the sea you want. My uncle knows some of the Brits involved in the projects. Met them at an international conference on offshore drilling. The drilling business is kind of a tight fraternity, if y'know what I mean. They travel the world sinking holes in the ground for a buck. My uncle's been in Singapore, Saudi Arabia, Norway, you name it. He might be able to put in a good word for ya."

Akmed remained silent and knocked back another shot of Scotch. His hosts would be annoyed when they arrived home to find he and his unexpected American guest drained the entire bottle and were partying in their flat. The alcoholic English couple already showed irritation to Akmed's freeloading, though to his face they claimed the contrary. This cajoling American was most likely disingenuous, but remained an enigma. Working on an oilrig? On the ocean? He thought that this American may not be so worthless after all. But he hated all Westerners. This greedy American rube was so abominable. On the other hand, he said interesting things. Akmed rubbed his pocket. The knife was still there. He must choose. If it would solve any of Akmed's problems, or if he received instructions from Omar, he would not hesitate to kill this drunken American fool in the blink of an eye. Omar said to wait. Wait and do what? Perhaps he should pursue what he dreamed about and still serve his native people. As the American would say, there was more than one way to skin a cat. When Omar called on him, he would be ready.

PART III

▼

AGENDAS

CHAPTER 6

$$\blacktriangledown$$

Modern day, Norfolk, Virginia

The cranking whine of the helicopter rotors roared like an approaching subway train. The foam-padded helmet on Danielle O'Day's head did little to insulate the thunderous sound repeating *chop, chop, chop.* The vibration of the entire aircraft shook her like a rag doll in a clothes dryer. She was not a fan of heights. That made her woozy. But her acrophobia was not what disturbed her now. She was terrified of the water only a few feet below her. A dozen years before, Danielle refused to jump in her high-school pool for swimming lessons, resulting in a failure of physical education for the term. She was teased relentlessly, but only she knew why she would not dip her toe in the water. When she was four years of age, her toddler cousin crawled unsupervised into a child's swimming pool and drowned. She discovered the lifeless body of the two-year-old boy, skin as blue as the bottom of the plastic pool. Like being bitten by a dog as a child, Danielle's aquaphobia manifested over time, and she would not tread near the smallest body of water, fearing it somehow was alive and ready to snatch her from below with its stealthy aqueous jaws.

She screamed in terror when a classmate prankster pushed her in the deep end of the high-school pool, supposedly to help defeat her fear. Instead, she floundered about in the water, swallowing what seemed like a gallon of chlorine before her fireplug-shaped gym teacher, a 245-pound lesbian—or so the high school girls rumored—jumped in fully clothed to drag her out. Danielle was sickened as the teacher known as Manly Martha lugged her along to the pool's side in proper lifeguard form, with the back of Danielle's head wedged in the cleavage of the big woman's chubby bosom. Her classmates said it was a sexual thrill for the PE teacher who often stood at the entrance to the women's shower clutching towels and gawking while the pubescent girls washed themselves. Danielle's girlfriends kidded her about getting mouth-to-mouth after the rescue from the wet and blubbery instructor, though it never really happened.

Slender and lithe as a marathoner, Danielle was not unfit; she only preferred to exercise with feet on firm ground. In fact, she lettered in track in her late high-school years. But the gym grade in her sophomore year didn't really matter. She carried straight As in every other subject and scored a near perfect 1580 on her SATs. That resulted in a generous scholarship to Boston College. Later, after devouring her undergraduate education in three years like a hungry lioness, she graduated with honors from Princeton Law School. She thought of life as a trial lawyer, but eventually backed away. Her deceivingly slight frame and fragile, almost squeaky, voice did not command courtroom presence. A few chauvinistic classmates warned her that she would be better off back at the firm up to her ass in research than masquerading in a man's job arguing before a judge and jury. She was not intimidated, but decided to pursue corporate, rather than trial law anyway. She was more comfortable behind a desk cranking out industry position papers than playing Ms. Perry Mason.

At her father's urging—though she rarely listened to him—she agreed to apply for an open attorney position at American Energy, a multi-billion dollar asset energy company that served millions of natural gas and electricity customers on the East Coast. Her father was a union foreman at the utility, a welder by trade, though her lineage could be traced to the firm's predecessor companies operating since the inception of the fossil-fuel industry. A great, great uncle, Daniel O'Day—her namesake—was a major figure in John D. Rockefeller's Standard Oil empire when the energy plutocrat seized control of the nascent American oil industry. In fact, O'Day was the American pioneer of natural gas pipelines in the late nineteenth century, solving the enigma of how to transport an invisible and dangerous product—natural gas—up from holes in the ground in sparsely populated Appalachian woodlands to cities dozens to hundreds of miles distant. There were O'Days in the energy business ever since, including her father, who worked for one of American Energy's natural gas utilities in a small city in northwestern Pennsylvania. After only three years on the job, her lawyer-dominated executive brethren promoted Danielle to vice-president. Women in the previously white male-oriented business were on the fast track, though she was as capable as anyone else with her experience. She pushed a lot of paper, made a lot of money, and was doing what she was put on earth to do, practice law, albeit from behind an office desk rather than before a jury box.

But how did she get here in the back of a chopper about to be dunked into chilly water? It was tenth-grade gym class all over again. She was strapped in the back seat of the lightweight flight cabin as it swayed from side to side, preparing to dive into the drink. Warning buzzers droned in her ears. Red lights blinked on the chopper's control panel. It was going down, the intercom said in her helmet. She would be underwater and imprisoned by her safety belt. *I will probably drown, here and now,* she thought.

The helicopter jerked violently once again, and plummeted into the water. Danielle screamed. Immediately, the chopper's bubble tipped to its side and filled the cockpit with frigid water. Danielle wore a life jacket, but the cold liquid paralyzed her. *I am going to die.* When the helicopter's cabin submerged, she would drown in her safety harness. The pilot in front of her could not save her—he was as lifeless as any car-crash-test dummy.

Pull the ripcord, pull the ripcord, her logical lawyer mind shouted in her head. *That will disengage the safety harness and I can escape!* She always listened to her logical brain, not her irrational heart. The emotional side of her was anesthetized, after enduring an upbringing under an overbearing father and then a disastrous brief marriage to a man ten years her senior. She let that arrogant son-of-a-bitch break her heart, and was swept into analysis. She vowed never to be controlled by girlish feelings again. She would be in control. But now her latent fears seized her rational mind from behind.

She was as upside down as a drowning bat, the bubble cockpit engulfed, water encapsulating her in a liquid prison. *Is this how I will die?* she asked herself. *A stupid, incompetent woman in a man's world? Will I let them kill me?* She would not.

Danielle grasped the ripcord on the side of the seat and yanked it with all the power of an Arnold Swartzenegger Terminator robot. The body-pump classes at the fitness center were good for something. Immediately she was free of the harness and she floated on the inside of the water-filled cabin like a disengaged fetus in the womb. Still disoriented—she was upside down—she reached for the cabin-door opening and pulled herself free. She couldn't swim, that much she knew. But she was wearing a lifejacket. Her instructors told her not to fight the water or thrash about, but let the vest do the work of bringing her to the surface. *Hold my breath, hold my breath, and I will survive …*

As her head broke the water's surface, she thrust open her mouth for a breath too soon and swallowed a huge gulp of water. It tasted like an old fear. It was saturated with chlorine. She gagged and coughed, spat and choked. A huge hand grabbed her life-jacket collar from behind, and pulled her upward. In a moment she was on the side of a huge indoor pool, still coughing and spitting out water.

"For a moment there I wasn't sure you were going to come up," an avuncular male voice said. It was that of Jerome Jefferson, the Norfolk, Virginia, flight school safety-training instructor, who had led the survival classes on helicopter water landings. He was a slight man with a college-professor gray beard and affable royal-blue eyes. The federal government mandated the classes for those American Energy company employees who would need to travel by helicopter over water surfaces.

Danielle shivered as a couple of assistants helped her remove the lifejacket, and then threw a huge beach towel over her shoulders.

"It's s-so c-cold," Danielle stuttered to no one in particular.

"Pretty realistic, isn't it," Jefferson said, helping Danielle to her feet. "Chopper rotors loud as a rock concert. Ice-cold water. This is nothing. The Atlantic Ocean is a lot colder. Been there. Done that. But we wanted to provide a little chill to show that you weren't in your bathtub. But the good news is, you pass."

The mock U-1 Huey helicopter cabin was lifted from the water by a large wench over the pool for the next test passenger, who must prove he or she could escape from the pod without assistance before receiving fly papers. Its mannequin pilot stared its blank don't worry, be happy mien at her. Danielle almost wished she failed, just like high-school gym class. She yearned to be safe and warm behind her oak attorney's desk covered in white papers and bulky law books, munching on a bag of M&Ms. Getting dumped in a crash-training school's pool, or heaven forbid, splashing into the rough waters of the Atlantic Ocean, was not her first choice of leisure activity. But that is what American Energy wanted her to do. And the risk management attorneys at her firm did everything by the book, following government safety rules and regulations to the letter. Consenting to government edicts was good financial business. The only thing more expensive than following the sometimes-redundant government regs was getting caught violating them. A sign in the energy company's legal floor read, "Remember Enron."

"You have a one-in-a-hundred chance of hitting the water in the ride from land to an offshore platform," Jefferson instructed the class of the crash trainees, stroking his gray beard like a cat. *One in a hundred!* Danielle figured he would say one in ten thousand or something. This is not what corporate law was all about. Her job hazards included long hours, sore eyes, and endless Chinese take-out—not combat duty.

American Energy was noted for vigorously cross-training its senior management, and Danielle evolved into a "bungey" boss. Her frequent appointments to head various departments gave her a taste of the various facets of the industry. But before she even knew the names of the employees in several departments during her ephemeral reign as general manager, she was recalled and whisked off to a new assignment. Her latest venture was to head the company's public affairs department. Public relations was not her forte. She was an introvert by nature, but was not about to turn down another potential promotion and pay raise from the company brass. Her first major assignment as the company's PR head was a critical one—to inspect the firm's experimental biofuels-gathering operation off the coast of North Carolina in advance of a visit by the president of the United States. The assignment came from the head of the corporation no less. But there were no mid-town Manhattan taxis to an offshore platform.

"If you want to run with the big dogs, you have to get off the porch and lift your leg high," American Energy's CEO said to her, who incidentally, was a woman.

Danielle remembered her analyst's advice: *Feel the fear and do it anyway.* She had plunged into the cold water. She survived. Her ambition surpassed her trepidation. She felt the fear and did it anyway. But this was only a pool.

CHAPTER 7

▼

American Energy Headquarters, New York City

"Are you going to put the petroleum industry out of business just like Rockefeller's kerosene snuffed out the whale-oil trade?" asked Jake Chavez, energy reporter for the *Wall Street Journal.*

Alexandria Raven, the CEO of American Energy, chuckled, revealing a string of perfect teeth. On entering her fifties, she was both physically attractive and matronly at the same time. Generous platinum-blond hair surrounded a distinctive face that could display a range of emotion. Depending on whether she smiled or frowned, she could look like a blissful Marilyn Monroe or a humorless Margaret Thatcher with a dye job.

"Well, let's say than instead of saving the whales, we're here to help save the planet," said Raven, sporting a car-salesman grin.

Chavez was a black-bearded man with an academic visage, and when he chuckled, his eyes squinted into slits on his face the size of dashes from a Sharpie. He wrote the comment down, laughing contemptuously all the way, and then put the end of his pen to his mouth. "I doubt Mr. Rockefeller had the ecological concerns of the pell-mell extermination of sperm whales on his mind when he squeezed out his competition in the oil industry in the nineteenth century to become one of the richest men on earth," he said.

"That was then," Raven said, "and this is now."

Raven was cautious with the financial press. Though the *Journal* editors were philosophically sympathetic with business, the reporters were as untrustworthy as any bottom-feeding journalist from the major television networks. The interview took place in Raven's spartan Manhattan office. Chavez admitted to her that it was downright homey. Instead of oil paintings of past corporate presidents and golf trophies stacked on walnut credenzas and end tables, the cream-pastel-shaded credenza of the chairman, president, and CEO of the sprawling energy company was adorned with fresh flowers and numerous pictures of her several grandchildren. Conspicuously absent were photographs that adorned the office of her predecessor hobnobbing with smiling influential politicians and professional golfers at exclusive country clubs. In fact, the head honcho of one of America's fastest-growing energy companies played the game rarely. It wasted too much time and reflected the old-boy network of years past. Frankly, she hated the sport. It took far too much time that she did not have. *What did Winston Churchill say about the silly game?* she thought. *Striking a very small ball into a very small hole with implements ill-designed for the purpose.*

If she had the time, she would redecorate. Something on *Martha Stewart Living* recently caught her eye. She had the bucks. Soon, her company's net worth might make Bill Gates and Microsoft look a seven-year-old with a lemonade stand. For now, rudimentary function took precedence over panache.

The financial reporter continued. "You've headed American Energy for the past five years, and already doubled the company's asset base. You've engineered the firm's geometric growth as a producer, transporter, and distributor of natural gas from wellhead to burner tip. Any natural gas consumed in the eastern United States probably flows through a storage well, pipeline, or meter of an American Energy subsidiary. Some would say you are bent on taking over the entire industry."

Raven perched on the edge of her chair like a jaguar stalking prey, preparing to launch her attack with a sprinter's speed. She did everything fast and those who stood in the way were torn apart. When she started her career as a manager of the company's phone bank she proved her mettle by being the only supervisor who did not abhor firing people. After a new company policy required call operators to reduce their time on the phone with customers by 50 percent, one operator achieved the goal by hanging up on every other caller before saying a word. On average, she met the target. Raven immediately terminated the woman, a single mother raising three young children, ignoring her tears and apology. Since that time, her orders were carried out without question.

"Natural gas and electric takeovers were posh in the 1990s," she answered, now backing down and primping a potted plant on her credenza. "But everything came to a halt after the Enron fiasco brought national attention to shenanigans in the energy-trading industry. We are much more cautious now, and conduct due diligence."

"Yes," the reporter countered, "but since corporate misdoing fell from the headlines, your consolidation of one of the nation's largest industries resumed.

Critics in Congress say federal regulators turned their heads and rubber-stamped your recent massive acquisitions."

"Well, the industry has changed," she said.

It surely had, she thought. American Energy was once a sleepy utility company that served mostly remote areas of the Appalachian states. As contiguous natural gas distributors no longer had long-term supplies of fuel, shortages and escalating costs of gas strangled their markets. Energy-intensive industries such as steel, glass, automaking, and chemical plants could not afford the high costs and either shut down or severely cut back their consumption, resulting in massive layoffs. Natural gas-fired electric utility stations that had replaced mothballed nuclear plants and discontinued high-pollution coal-burning facilities hiked electric rates to pay for the fuel that generated the power. Many residential and small commercial utility customers could no longer afford their escalating electric and gas utility bills, and delinquencies were hemorrhaging the cash flow of small utilities. American Energy stepped in.

"Something had to stabilize the industry," Raven said.

The bearded reporter grinned. "And American Energy's deep pockets came to the rescue."

"The regulators agreed that we provided strong capital support for the crumbling distribution infrastructure. As a result, we now have 15 million customers dispersed across nineteen states. Growth is good."

"Growing like bamboo—dormant for years and then shooting up several feet in one day," said the reporter.

"That's an apt metaphor—I like it."

"What about *your* long-term gas supply? You are not on the LNG bandwagon."

Raven pondered her response. American Energy refused to sink its capital in the latest rage in the natural gas industry—liquefied natural gas, or LNG for short. She nearly caused a mutiny among the company's board of directors, which favored investment in the foreign import of natural gas as the only cure for the nation's shortage. Raven resisted intense pressure from the sinecure board members, irate shareholders, eminent industry experts, and many government leaders who felt LNG from islands in the Caribbean, West Africa, and the Middle East was the savior of the United States' energy supply. American Energy's rival on the East Coast, National Gas and Electric Corporation, invested in a new $30 billion government-backed LNG plant that bought the product in long-term contracts from foreign countries for U.S. domestic consumption. Previously uneconomical, LNG was now competitive with the shrinking North American supply of gas, whose price was escalating as fast as its supply was shrinking. But the idea of the globalization of natural gas supply was anathema to Raven. She refused to be wooed into a partnership with National Gas and Electric, which was looking for co-investors. She vowed to buy her competitor's assets for a song if the LNG strategy blew up in its face.

"American Energy would prefer to stay *American* energy," Raven said.

The recent Islamic revolution in the Middle East and resulting turmoil in LNG exporting countries such as Algeria and Qatar, along with civil-war-torn Nigeria and labor strikes in socialist Venezuela, accentuated the prophetic wisdom of her decision. And there was always the threat of terrorism, once thought endemic to the Middle East. For example, 900-foot LNG tankers received U.S. Navy escorts to bring the fuel to America's coasts. Though LNG would not explode in its liquid state and did not lend itself to rapid combustion, if spilled it could burn. LNG's worst U.S. disaster occurred in 1944, when nearly 130 Cleveland residents were killed when a substandard tank ruptured and the vaporizing LNG caught fire. Alexander Raven learned the lessons of industrial accidents such as the Exxon Valdez in Alaska, Union Carbide in Bhopal, India, and, of course, how could anyone over forty forget Three Mile Island in Harrisburg, Pennsylvania?

Instead of investing in foreign gas supplies, American Energy's seemingly rapine acquisition strategy absorbed as many regional pipeline systems and domestic natural gas reserves as it could. The company's girth spread faster than a teenager's waistline with a steady diet of quarter-pound hamburgers, super-sized trans-fat fries, and bovine growth-hormone-enhanced milk shakes. In addition to natural gas, the company's latest trend was the purchase of electric power plants, most generating the juice through new combined-cycle turbines fueled by natural gas, or older coal-burning facilities converted to gas. Coal not only produced pollutants, but also tons of global-warming gases that the environmental movement targeted for extinction. Though natural gas produced half the CO_2 than coal, Congress recently tightened restrictions on carbon dioxide emissions with an onerous $200 a ton carbon tax and that was hampering even the more environmentally friendly natural gas-generating facilities. American Energy responded by implementing the technology to reinject global-warming carbon dioxide produced by the plants back into the ground rather than release it in the air, a process known as *carbon sequestration*. Ample government research dollars flowed in for the experiments. The process appeared simple: remove several hundred pounds of carbon dioxide from the air a day from the firm's natural gas burning electric plants by pumping it under the earth via wind-powered machines.

Though it was expensive and, according to some scientists, of dubious benefit to the environment, it made most regulators and some environmentalists happy.

"This biogas demonstration project American Energy is involved in off the coast of North Carolina—generating natural gas from *seaweed*?" Chavez said, scratching his beard as if it would release some mysterious journalist-truth-serum dandruff. "Come on, Ms. Raven, the United States possesses only 3 percent of the world's supply of natural gas. Federal law prohibits offshore drilling. Where are you going to get your future long-term supply if not from foreign sources?"

Raven leaned back in her office chair as if the issue dawned on her for the first time. She said, "I guess we will have to get lucky."

CHAPTER 8

▼

American Energy Chesapeake Electric Generating Station, Central Maryland

The homemade white placards looked as if they were slapped together with kindergarten finger-paint the morning of the protest. *Stop the Lie—We Won't Fry! Greenhouse Gasses Kill. Remember New Orleans.* Despite the crude designs, professional artists produced them weeks before. All were paid for by the environmental activist group called "Americans Need Greenhouse Effect Rage," known by the acronym ANGER. The signs splashed across television screens in bright primary colors adorned with pithy slogans. The placards protested the opening of a retooled coal-fired electric power plant in central Maryland that would now burn natural gas.

Save the World, Someone Else May Want to Use It, proclaimed another placard. A troubadour in a Lands End polo shirt cradling an acoustic guitar followed that sign singing the George Harrison song of the same name.

"We must help awaken the American people of the real danger of the assault on the earth—not global terrorists, but global warming," espoused ANGER president Herbert Winkle to his members in a news release. The activist group's leader was affectionately known in the press as "Hurricane Herbie" for his Cassandra portents of the increased number of intense hurricanes and tropical storms that he maintained were the calling cards of catastrophic climate change.

Herbert Winkle felt Islamic terrorists weren't the real enemy of civilization. Carbon was. Carbon linked with hydrogen was the heroin the modern world was not only addicted to, but also the drug with which it was poisoning itself. There was so much coal in the world—so much that the atmospheres of cities like London and Pittsburgh became inhospitable environments for humans in the nineteenth century. Then, the twentieth-century energy junkie switched to the next black drug, petroleum. It was more efficient than coal, but still the creator of smog that poisoned people in Los Angeles, Mexico City, and Peking. And what took millions of years to cook below the surface of the earth, humans wastefully consumed in a century and a half. Now, natural gas, the most efficient of the fossil-fuel gang, was the friendly narcotic power of choice. With the spilling of carbon dioxide in the air when fossil fuels burned, the heating blanket of the earth was turning up so high the human race was cooking itself to death.

The environmental advocate neatly arranged the ready-made protest signs for those volunteers who agreed to picket the morning of a news conference christening the refurbished power plant. The electric generator's reincarnation was generally a welcome event on the East Coast, after it was shut down two years before because of noncompliance with various clean-air-emission standards. The federal government's recent acceptance of the revamped United Nations Air Quality protocol—dubbed Kyoto II—required a 20 percent reduction of greenhouse gases, known as GHGs, from automobiles, industry, and especially, power-plant emissions in ten years. Though the former owners of this coal-burning facility thought the plant would be mothballed and eventually rot away to a rusting, industrial skeleton eyesore in the Maryland countryside, the white horses of American Energy Corporation came to the rescue, vowing to meet or exceed the EPA regulations and provide much needed electric power to the Washington, DC, corridor. Though American Energy did meet the federal government guidelines for reduction in sulfur dioxide, nitrous oxide, and the more innocuous carbon dioxide, as far as Winkle and the radical ANGER group were concerned, any fossil fuel burning was another nail in the crucifix of Mother Earth. Winkle felt too much CO_2, the harmless, odorless gas expelled by human lungs and absorbed by trees, was not only melting the ice caps and drowning polar bears, but also would eventually convert the lush bread basket of the United States into the uninhabitable surface of Venus.

"Hey, hey, American Energy, how many degrees did we warm today?" chanted the well-choreographed protesters, pronouncing "Energy" *Ener-jay,* so the ditty echoed the mantra of the 'sixties Vietnam-era protest ditty: "Hey, hey, LBJ, how many kids did you kill today?" The collection of protesters marched in step in fanfare as if they were a corps of proud majorettes, bobbing their sturdy cardboard placards like celebratory flags.

Unlike many environmental protests that featured mostly radical college students and their antisocial bearded professors dressed in pre-torn, stone-washed blue jeans and bandannas, the ANGER flock was a diversified group of soccer-moms with toddlers in tow, casually dressed grandmothers, and clean-cut middle-aged men of various creeds and colors. In order to appear in an ANGER protest, you first registered with the group's headquarters, received approval on your planned dress, and agreed to carry a designated protest banner. No home-made signs were permitted because they did not show up clear enough on televi-sion. ANGER did not advance its cause by attracting a motley mob of malcontents and nihilists who would be dismissed by common-sense Americans. Winkle envisioned a protest that would look good on the tube—full of passion and outrage, but as respectable as the girl next door.

ANGER boasted a nationwide following of 100,000 paying members, earning the influential clout of the Sierra Club or Greenpeace in the U.S. Congress. Win-kle, a no-name environmental attorney who won several critical lawsuits against natural gas utilities, launched it into national prominence.

"Though many natural gas utilities brag about their squeaky-clean environ-mental image, many have an Achilles Heel as they have inherited the sins of their fathers," read Winkle's written testimony submitted to a congressional subcom-mittee. "In nearly every major urban center across the eastern United States, there are toxic dump sites once created by manufactured gaslight companies dating back to the nineteenth century when the only gas most people used was produced by a gasification process that roasted coal or oil. Unfortunately, the byproduct of the romantic glow of gaslights that once lit the streets of New York City, Phila-delphia, and Boston in the 1800s was benzene, cyanide, and a plethora of other deadly contaminants that would not make the carcinogen list of the Environmen-tal Protection Agency for another century. At the time there were no objections in dumping the lethal chemicals into rivers or covered pits that would someday be the sites of homes and schools."

Although the bowler-hatted chieftains who ordered the dangerous chemicals dumped and buried—usually in low-income urban neighborhoods full of immi-grants or African-Americans—were food for worms, the companies that eventu-ally purchased the assets of the Gilded-Age firms now were the proud owners of the contaminated land. Fresh out of a small law school in Dayton, Ohio, the young environmental attorney launched his self-proclaimed jihad against the util-ities when he filed a lawsuit after one West Virginia firm sold a former unidenti-fied coal-gas chemical dump to a local school district. Five years after the construction of an elementary school on the site, children digging on a play-ground unearthed blue soil that turned out to be saturated with cyanide deriva-tives. Though no detrimental health effects could be proven, the entire school was abandoned, and the subsequent legal action bankrupted the local utility com-pany, whose managers claimed they had no idea the dump existed.

The original case attracted national attention, and it propelled the small-town attorney who spearheaded the action into superstar status. Herbert Winkle, however, did not resemble a Hollywood star. The bony and balding legal activist, who was habitually clad in a dated and rumpled charcoal suit, resembled a nerdy kid who would be the easy target of any schoolyard bully. Thick TV-screen eyeglasses magnified Winkle's already bulbous brown eyes. His left pupil was cross-eyed, always wandering like an errant planet out of its orbit, confusing anyone who made close eye contact with him. Those engaged in conversation with Winkle would not know which eye to center their attention. In addition, he walked with a slight hobble for his left leg was one-inch longer than the right. In addition to his scrawny, feeble frame and strabismus stare, Winkle was afflicted with a profound stutter, especially when excited in front of a crowd or television cameras. Though markedly improved since childhood, his stammer would often delay the beginning and end of his statements by several seconds. Despite his physical and oral challenges, he was a brilliant attorney with an IQ of 140. The distractions of his meandering gaze, shuddering speech, and crooked gait were overshadowed by the eloquence of his legal arguments. His lawsuit against the utility firm in the contaminated elementary-school case resulted in a $20 million verdict for the school district and a $20,000 settlement for every one of the rugrat's parents in the schoolyard. Only some of the verdict was paid out when the local utility filed for Chapter Seven. Seeing a value, American Energy scooped up the small gas firm's assets and immediately unleashed its corps of lawyers get a stay on further payouts to the so-called "victims" of the buried chemicals. The new owners had deep enough pockets to deal with the legal challenges.

As a result of American Energy's utility takeovers, the short, frumpy, stuttering lawyer now declared American Energy "Corporate Enemy Number One" and the largest threat to the public's health. Winkle declared, "Though the ivory-tower executives claim they had nothing to do with the pollution from the past, they are collecting millions of dollars in bonuses and stock options while children in poverty-stricken city neighborhoods are making dioxin mud pies with deadly chemicals dumped by their predecessors."

American Energy, on the other hand, publicly committed to clean up any old manufactured-gas sites they currently owned, though coal gas was a thing of the past, something to be reminisced about while reading a Charles Dickens' novel. Still the ghosts of manufactured-gas past haunted the legal offices of natural gas corporations who could not shake responsibility for the toxic dumps, even though the firms' contemporaries may have had nothing to do with them.

Winkle transformed his toxic-site celebrity into wider recognition for environmental issues with his latest cause célèbre, global warming. With effective media relations, Winkle became a household name across the country. His stutter and wandering left eye became affectionate trademark mannerisms endeared by his supporters. According to the polls, an overwhelming percentage of Americans who were aware of the dragon-slaying environmental advocate had a favorable opinion of him. With Hurricane Herbie "keeping an eye" on the utility polluters, many slept more sound at night.

As the orderly protestors strode past the front gate of the spruced-up Maryland power plant, Winkle administered an impromptu news conference with national television cameras whirring in front of him.

"The c-c-cost of this power plant reopening is one our environment cannot af-f-ford," Winkle blurted as best as he could through the fog of his speech impediment. "American Energy must shut this plant d-d-down."

A press release alleged that companies like American Energy were responsible for devastating, and possibly irreversible, climate-change effects including melting Arctic ice sheets, rising sea levels, the spread of insect-borne diseases around the world, violent hurricanes, global-wide droughts, and crop failures. When asked what the plant shutdown would cost the economy in American job losses and lack of electricity on the grid, Winkle unrolled a chart of too-complicated-for-television figures, stammering his way through a lecture of how solar, geothermal, and wind power could replace the greenhouse-gas-producing fossil-fuel power plants on the East Coast. *The reporters were dolts*, Winkle thought, *and would follow him like sheep as long as he was David flinging stones at Goliath.* Reporters hovered around like rubbernecks at a car accident.

"What about this effort by American Energy to plant new forests on their lands to help absorb carbon dioxide, a process known as *carbon sinks*?" asked a balding, male wire-service reporter.

"C-C-Carbon sinks?" Winkle quipped, "Y-You would have to plant a forest the size of Nebraska to offset one of American Energy's power p-p-plants."

An emaciated local female television reporter who did not appear to be far out of high school queried, "What about that bio-gas project American Energy is making waves about in the ocean—generating methane from sea kelp?"

Winkle knew that PR song and dance—even the president of the United States was humming the tune.

"P-P-Public relations p-p-poppycock."

His stutter faded a bit as he delivered a well-rehearsed short lecture on global warming. Greenhouse gases such as CO_2, produced by the burning of fossil fuels, formed an atmospheric layer that held the sun's heat near the Earth like smudge pots in a fruit-farmer's field during a Florida freeze, heating the planet and potentially leading to cataclysmic weather effects. Winkle pointed out that Quelccaya, the world largest tropical glacier south of the equator in Peru, was melting. The 7.5-mile-long mountain glacier towering 18,600 feet above sea level was losing about 100 feet a year, forty times what it was in the 1970s. An ancient ice shelf the size of 11,000 football fields recently broke off in the Canadian Arctic. Also, U.S. climate researchers found a long-frozen specimen of Distichia muscoides, a 5,177-year-old moss-like plant, when the ice melted. Greenland, most of which was usually covered with snow and ice, was now actually becoming green. In Europe and Asia in the depths of the previous winter, ski resorts were making fake snow in the melting Alps, butterflies were plentiful in Denmark, and daisies were blooming in Moscow.

"The t-t-ten hottest years have occurred since 1990," Winkle warned. "Glaciers are the canary in the coal mine when it comes to global w-w-warming."

Though Winkle knew his protest would have little material effect on this plant's operation, and only a marginal impact on public opinion, his presence continued the sow the seed of suspicion that nothing utility companies did was in the public interest. Rather, they were callous institutions led by gluttonous executives who put profit and self-interest over public safety and the future of the planet. No, he would not shut down American Energy's new electric-generating plant. But he would remain a burr on its PR butt. Though the electricity to be produced there was sorely needed, it would be expensive power, four times the national average, because of another upswing in the price of natural gas. Therefore, as far as Winkle was concerned, the general public would not be sympathetic to American Energy and their new plant. It was only a cash cow to milk consumers' bank accounts, while filling the air with more carbon dioxide that would crank up the earth's thermostat and convert Buffalo into Miami Beach, and Miami Beach into Dante's Inferno. Sooner or later, Joe Lunchbucket would raise enough hell to his local Congressman to take over the robber-baron utilities, enforce mandatory conservation, and produce only clean energy at affordable prices for everyone. *Now that would be a perfect world*, Winkle thought, not a stutter in his mind.

CHAPTER 9

▼

Erie, Pennsylvania

The gasoline station sign read in bold, black letters: $8.40. A couple of years ago that price per gallon was a shock. But now, gasoline was sold by the half-gallon. The price was actually $16.80 a gallon.

Just like the '70s, Dan O'Day thought, when pumps did not have three digits to display the price when the cost rocketed beyond ninety-nine cents. When gas surpassed ten bucks a gallon, the digital displays didn't have room for a fifth numeral. So selling by the half-gallon repackaged the same old product in a smaller wrapper. O'Day squinted through the dirt-streaked windshield of his Ford F350 in the November morning sunshine—a rarity for this rust-belt north coast town—and could just make out the price for unleaded regular. The most expensive gas in town. But why the line? He knew why. The small independent service station was one of the few in the city with any gasoline left at all.

O'Day's patience was wearing as thin as the slices of chipped-chopped ham his wife stuffed in his sandwich for lunch. His truck burned more fuel idling than most passenger cars did driving down the highway at sixty-five miles-per-hour. One bumper sticker on the rear of his pickup read, "LIKE YOUR JOB BENE-FITS? THANK A UNION." Another displayed a pair of hands strangling an Arab sheik with text that read, "HAVE YOU HUGGED AN ARAB TODAY?" O'Day looked in his rearview mirror. The line of cars extended four blocks to city hall.

"C'mon, goddamn it!" O'Day groaned. He leaned on his horn causing an echo of responses from the queue of motionless automobiles that resembled multi-colored segments of a disgruntled caterpillar. The drivers did not lay on their horns in a furious roar of anger. It was more like a whiney bleating of sheep that realized that the circumstances had them by the shorthairs, and they would remain in line and be sheered at the appropriate time.

O'Day dug under his square index fingernail removing some oily grime, a consequence of cleaning out dirty gas relief valves. Though callused and showing signs of arthritis, his hands were his profession. His first love was welding. He melded steel pipelines together in roadside trenches for thirty years. The pipelines were often full of gas on both ends, separated from his acetylene torch by leather bags blown up to fill the insides of the line to block the flow of the flammable vapor while he worked. This was probably how welders received the appellation "spark idiots," he would tell his coworkers, who stepped back from the ditch when he fired up. But he had not picked up a welding torch for a couple of years.

O'Day was a foreman in American Energy's customer service department and the union president for the local chapter of the International Gas Workers (IGW) union. His current duties were annoying, ugly tasks at times, but he was lucky to be still doing it. It was better than running from dogs while reading meters, and until recently, most of the customers were pleasant enough. Though he was supposed to refer all home appliance maintenance work to the customer's own plumber or heating contractor, he would gladly conduct minor repairs as a courtesy, which usually garnered him an under-the-table ten-spot tip. One buddy of his regularly got laid on the job by a lonely customer who repeatedly called in a gas leak, but O'Day was too smart to get tied up with that stuff. He was a burly man with an ample mop of graying-brown hair rarely combed. A growing paunch that his wife told him was "as cuddly as a teddy bear" distorted his once linebacker-sized frame. He dressed in scuffed steel-toed black work boots and indistinct gray-green pants and shirt that hid splotches of grease, dirt, and other contaminants he picked up during the workday. He liked his former job at American Energy better, before the company contracted out the welding work to non-union outfits. That, he thought, was not only anti-labor, it was downright dangerous. He likened his adroit welding skills to the ability of a deft surgeon. But instead of splicing veins, he joined sections of metal pipeline, the vascular system of the natural gas industry. He mended large major steel arteries and smaller-diameter distribution capillaries that ran through the cities and towns that carried the fuel of life to customer appliances. The work did not belong to rookies. He pined for the days when he worked with his union brethren in the trenches, repairing pipeline like the best of cardiologists operating on the Goliath gas system.

"Welding is like a heart bypass," he told his coworkers at a long-ago Christmas party, when his company spent money on such frivolous things.

"More like removing a tumor on an asshole," one wisecracking friend retorted.

He took the insult with a grain of salt. His buddy owed him a life for he once dragged him out of a ditch full of leaking gas that forced out all of the oxygen out of the hole, causing him to lose consciousness. O'Day barely made it out alive himself. His friend's way of saying thank you was by calling him a dexterous proctologist.

Today, most of the low- and medium-pressure gas pipeline system was linked by plastic tubes, fused together with the help of a sophisticated computer, leaving little work for the seat-of-the-pants welder. Only major high-pressure lines were still constructed out of metal, and contractors, not the utility workers, installed those. As a result, O'Day was transferred to customer service. But a job was a job—nice work if you could get it. And he invested thirty-five years at the utility company, slowing building a workingman's pension. Though close to retirement, he would be one of the union's negotiators with American Energy for the next contract. He would give those suits what for. He had nothing to lose—he was *outta' here*. The corporate sons-of-bitches wanted to break the union that had represented the gas laborers for three-quarters of a century. Management would find they had a fight on their hands.

But what did the future hold for his industry anyway? The western world's shortage of petroleum crippled numerous industries in the United States, causing layoffs that contributed to a 17 percent unemployment rate. World chaos was the cause of it all, centered in the Middle East of course. *Fucking ragheads*, O'Day cursed under his breath. A Wahhabi cleric coup usurped the Saudi Arabian kingdom thirteen months before. Rich petroleum and natural gas countries including Kuwait, Oman, Qatar, Abu Dabi, and even some African countries such as Nigeria, were in the midst of bloody revolutions. The most recent victim was the old French colony Algeria, toppled in a purist Islamic coup. Bucking the rest of the generally sane OPEC ministers, the Islamic radicals in several nations cut off most of the North American and European oil supply, joining Iran, Iraq, and a few other Middle-East fig republics in the largest oil and natural gas embargo ever implemented on the western world.

This came as a shock to most erudite Western politicians, but no surprise to O'Day. *Dumb ass politicians got us into it.* The United States increased its dependence on foreign oil four-fold since the oil embargo of the 1970s. The muscle-bound U.S.A. spread its legs wider and wider, giving the biggest weakling on the sandy beach in the Arab world opportunity to bring the American Charles Atlas economy to its knees with a swift kick in the cohonnes.

We asked for it. And we got it.

O'Day remembered the dark winter mornings in 1974 when a caravan of automobiles waited for the corner gas station to open to buy their five-dollar limit during that decade's first oil crisis. Even-license-plate numbers on even days and odd numbers the following day were permitted their meager portion like malnourished concentration camp prisoners. Rationing. How glad he was in 1974 that he was too poor to buy a car.

But that was then, and this was now. O'Day owned three antique cars besides his truck: a '38 coal-black Dodge that looked like something Al Capone would fire a Tommy gun out the window of; a '59 fire-engine-red Plymouth Fury with a push-button automatic transmission; and a '66 cobalt Mustang convertible. Each sat silent in his garage, symbols of America's love affair with gaudy, gas-guzzling personal transportation. How little things changed over the years. Not only did the United States face another oil crisis as a net importer of the fuel, the predicament extended to other energies as well. Ironically, though the U.S. sat on one-fourth of the world's coal supply, the environmental lobby prevented the nation from using it. Most of his company's electric plants were now fueled by natural gas, and because of shortages, brownouts were common.

Shouts interrupted O'Day's ruminations. He rubbernecked out of his window like a mutant turtle sticking its head out of the side of its hard shell. A scuffle and a fistfight erupted as the cars in front of him inched forward toward the gas station. Drivers behind their SUVs and small trucks threw their hands in the air and jerked their heads backward to see if they could get out of the fruitless procession. "Baa! Baa!" the sheep-sounding car horns echoed among the flock of vehicles.

O'Day knew what was going on. Some joker jumped the queue and a near riot raged on before the pumps. Up ahead, a burly, bearded Caucasian man with a bright red beard wearing a hunter-orange wool coat was duking it out with a slim, bald, African-American man clad in a gray pin-stripe business suit. The police might return to the filling pumps for the second time that morning. The supply of gas was depleted, and those closest to the pumps did not take the news with a high degree of mirth. O'Day was tempted to get out and referee. Few would challenge his broad-shouldered, six-foot-four frame. His steely-glare hazel eyes, square jaw, and flat nose gave him the essence of a jarhead drill sergeant or a retired boxer. But he was getting too old for settling bar fights. He barely had the energy to take on his sometimes-contentious wife.

"This sucks, huh?"

O'Day looked up and a teenager who abandoned his sun-yellow Camaro in front of his truck was standing at his driver's side window. The brown-haired teen, bearded the best he could grow it at his tender age to cover his blemishes, apparently wanted to commiserate to pass the time. O'Day wondered how the youth got the scratch to buy the sports car. *Must be a rich college kid.*

"Can you believe this?" the teen said again, gesturing toward the fight ahead.

O'Day grunted an affirmation.

"Yeah," the kid said, "America is an oil junkie looking for a fix."

O'Day didn't answer.

"And that's not all," he said, as if he were opening up a textbook to opine. "We're importing vast quantities of liquefied natural gas from the Middle East and South America to generate our electricity. Do you know we can't flick on the light switch, turn up the heat, or crank the key to our cars without big oil execs and the Arabs sucking money out of us?"

Yeah, O'Day thought, *faster than you probably do out of your Daddy's wallet.*

"Damn oil, gas, and utility companies are all in it together," the teen said. "One big fucking cabal."

Here it comes. This bozo doesn't know I work for the gas company. O'Day was used to it. Instead of kicking the family dog when frustrated, American Energy's customers now vented their frustrations on the closest victim—the utility employee. Just the day before, O'Day's service truck was pummeled with eggs and the air let out of the tires—not by bored, prankster teenagers, but by furious middle-aged customers who suffered sticker shock by their utility bill. As a union man, O'Day did not have much sympathy with the white-collar types in the ivory towers who pulled the strings at American Energy. However, he knew the blame for the energy crisis could be shared by many, including this idiot joy-riding in his yellow Camaro.

The teen continued his harangue. "That boob in the White House is afraid of the wrath of energy company PACs."

O'Day remained mute. *How about hotheaded, loudmouth consumer activists and the Luddite environmentalists who are always protesting against drilling for oil and gas here, there, and everywhere because it threatened the nesting place for some microscopic sea creature? How many times must the country go through this mess before it learns its lesson?*

"How many times do we have to go through this before we learn our lesson?" the teen uncannily repeated O'Day's thought. "I read in the 1970s—"

"Fuck it," O'Day said. He wrenched the wheel of his seven-year-old monster truck to the left and bucked out of the slaughtering row. The teen darted out of the way at the last moment. *Who was to blame? The Arabs? The politicians? The corporate tycoons who seemed to profit from every crisis?* But that would include his only child, his attorney daughter whose stock seemed to be rising in a company he never seemed to get ahead in. *Someone will have to pay for this*, he thought. O'Day headed home, his gas-guzzling pickup sputtering on fumes.

CHAPTER 10

▼

New York City

"To finance the acquisitions, we are going to pawn off some of our previous shining stars," Alexandria Raven lectured American Energy's mostly titular board of directors. She stood at the head of the twenty-foot oblong mahogany table in the boardroom of the firm's Rockefeller Center headquarters, more than assure of herself. "Thousands of oil wells in the United States and Canada, our foreign power investments, and numerous other assets are now on the block."

"Including the kitchen sinks?" asked one cynical board member who ran a chain of pharmacies. Ernest Moore was an impeccably dressed chrome-haired man with distinctive Grecian statuesque features, including a wide nose, thick gray eyebrows, and full, ripe lips. Raven's CEO predecessor appointed him to the board, and she could not wait to get rid of him.

Raven smiled though she found nothing humorous.

"In fact, it includes the kitchen sinks," she answered, clicking her peach-painted fingernails on the glass-covered conference table. Despite the feminine manicure, her hands were strong and callused from pulling many a weed from her spacious garden. Now, she was going to yank the weeds in American Energy so the real crop could grow. "Several executive gold-plated basins that looked like they came out of one of Saddam Hussein's Iraqi palaces will be soon sold at auction."

After Raven glared at the inquisitive director, Moore fell back in his chair, nostrils flaring. *Cost cutting should be familiar to him*, she thought. Moore's corporation over-expanded in the 1990s and now was forced to shut down dozens of drug stores that were hemorrhaging cash like a severed femora artery. However, the pompous drug company CEO most likely never let the cutbacks reach his executive floor. She was speaking a foreign language to him—she had always been thrifty. *I must bump him off the board before he gets indicted for SEC violations in his own firm*, she thought.

"We will consolidate corporate staffs and reduce the workforce 20 percent," she continued without fanfare. Raven knew she would receive little flack on that issue. Raven and the board were far away from where the hatchet met the wood. The financial headquarters of the firm was located at the base of Broadway, near the site where John D. Rockefeller directed his Standard Oil empire more than a century before.

American Energy's investments in several electric-generating plants in Europe and some third-world countries had already been liquidated to other more risk-tolerating investors. The corporate giant's latest divestiture was a phased severance of its minor stake in the Palestinian state-owned "Yasser Arafat Offshore Gas Project," off the coast of the Gaza Strip in the Mediterranean Sea. Constantly changing laws, perplexing and arbitrary draconian regulations, and rocky political regimes caused Raven to abandon the foreign investments that became posh the previous decade. Of special concern were terrorist attacks by Islamic fundamentalists in Pakistan and Muslim-dominated former Soviet republics. America, and therefore American Energy, was a terrorist bull's-eye, and the savvy businesswoman wanted nothing to do with foreign dalliances. Raven told the board when she assumed the CEO job early in 2001 they would eschew business in unstable Islamic countries.

"Pakistan, Uzbekistan, Afghanistan—we're not investing American Energy dollars in any country with a fucking *stan* in it," Raven said with uncharacteristic vulgarity, added for unquestionable emphasis. Her decision was prophetic as the terrorist attacks later that year on American soil and subsequent threats to American investments by militant Islamists around the globe made such bets a hazardous, if not deadly, gamble.

Raven stood before a wide-screen monitor in the boardroom that displayed a projected map of the eastern United States, one hand on her hip and the other gripping a laser pointer. She was fifty-years-old, but her platinum-blond hair, magnetic hazel eyes, and curvaceous hips filling out her conservative pantsuit always kept the eyes of the mostly male board of directors focused on her. She opened the meeting by unveiling pictures of her newborn grandchild, but once the meat of the meeting ensued, she sounded more like an annoyed Hillary Rodham Clinton than a doting new grandmother. She transformed into a commander, hands behind her back, marching back and forth in the front of the room in a leisurely goosestep. She fired the laser light pen on several circles on the map that represented facilities owned by American Energy and finally rested the red dot on the firm's electric plant in Maryland.

"This new plant is up and running despite the public protests," Raven said robotically.

"Tree-hugging Socialists!" cursed Nick Cavone, American Energy's vice president of Electric Generation and the board's most recent appointee.

"Calm down now, Nick," Raven said.

She knew Cavone, a thirty-year veteran of the electric business, was furious that the ribbon-cutting dog-and-pony-show scheduled at the company's revamped electric-generating station was cancelled because of the protest by the environmental group ANGER. Cavone was a hothead, but a Raven loyalist. He sported a gray crew cut, its top as even as a serving platter, and resembled Nixon-aide H. R. Halderman with olive-tinted skin. Told he had the most "level head" in the company by an associate, he was flattered until he realized it was a joke about his haircut. He was volatile, but he got things done. Unlike Cavone, however, Raven maintained her equanimity under the greatest pressure.

"Don't those card-carrying commie weenies know that this plant is generating power as clean as possible so they can plug in their electric clown cars at night?" the exasperated utility VP protested to his boss.

"Hybrids don't need to be plugged in Cavone—they charge themselves," said Moore, the drug-store tycoon, attempting to reassert his dignity with sarcasm.

"Whatever," Cavone said.

"Apparently," Raven interrupted to brief the rest of the directors, "the local congressman and both Maryland's U.S. Senators had little desire to run the gauntlet of well-orchestrated environmentalists in front of television cameras. Therefore, we cancelled the whole event. Bad publicity would get played up in the media more than whatever goodwill could be attained by our photo opportunity, especially when the heavyweights refused to be caught dead pictured in our corner."

"But we had a nice spread," Cavone whimpered.

"Forget it," the matriarchal head of American Energy said. "One day they will have egg on their faces. They are counting on long-term high energy prices to rally the public. Only a prolonged energy crisis will add fuel to their fire. When all of this is over, their protests will fizzle."

"What the hell am I going to do with all that damn cheese?" Cavone said.

"Send it to a homeless shelter." Raven knew Cavone was probably more upset the catered lunch and hor d'oerves that was uneaten by the press would have to be absorbed in his budget.

Drug-exec Moore piped up again. "Don't you feel that the nation is becoming more dependent on natural gas, even though it's in short supply?"

"Yes," said Raven.

"Do you agree that the use of natural gas to generate electricity is expected to jump 40 percent in the next twenty years?"

"Sounds about right."

"Are you not aware that the experts on Wall Street warn against the *In Gas We Trust* energy policy with growing dependence on imported liquefied natural gas?"

"Of course."

With each question, Moore's voice rose in crescendo and became more antagonistic.

"In addition," he continued, "won't increased natural gas use hike carbon dioxide output?"

"Possibly."

"What about the price shocks of higher-cost natural gas—do you believe your customers can afford the product?"

Raven clicked her colorful fingernails on the glass-top table once again like drumsticks. "It has entered my mind."

Moore stood and addressed the board as if it was a jury. "So there are massive shortages of natural gas, the cost is going through the roof even with imports from unfriendly countries, the government is slapping new environmental regulations on the industry, Wall Street is dumping our stock, and there you are fiddling while Rome burns."

Raven stood stolid. After a long, uncomfortable pause, she said, "The pessimists will soon be debunked. American Energy's plan to reinject carbon dioxide far under the earth will not only meet, but also exceed new government edicts. The energy crisis will eventually subside with our new supplies coming from within the United States."

Moore shook his head in disbelief and appeared to rest his case.

Part of his cynicism was understood. Raven could not elaborate on her optimistic view of natural gas supply. It was a matter of national security that buffoons like Moore would leak to the press. Everyone involved was on a need-to-know basis. The board members knew only that American Energy operated a demonstration project to generate natural gas from sea kelp off the East Coast.

"And our plan is to create so much additional supply," she said, "the price will plummet, pleasing consumers. Our company makes the lion's share of its profit by transporting clean-burning natural gas no matter what the product's cost, and also, by generating electricity from it. The cheaper the base cost of the fuel, the more energy we will move, and thus, increase our profit."

"All from a bunch of seaweed a hundred miles offshore," Moore said sarcastically. "Bullshit!"

Cavone, suddenly the fawning corporate cheerleader, suggested, "Natural gas might become so inexpensive it might be too cheap to meter."

Moore sneered at him. "Someone once said that before about nuclear energy, and later ate their radioactive words." He pointed a finger at Raven, who returned the assault with a glare of daggers. "This plan is foolhardy. Seaweed gas! This is absurd; I must resign from this board."

The other board members stared at Moore as if he just farted loudly in church. The pharmacy tycoon stormed out of the room.

"A pity," Raven said to the remaining group. "We did not get Mr. Moore's input in the proposed elimination of our employee prescription-drug plan."

After nervous laughter, she went on as if nothing happened. American Energy's fortune would not go sour like the dashed dreams of the atomic power industry. It was foolproof. America would feast on clean, affordable energy with no waste, pollutants, or greenhouse gasses and the domestic supply would be delivered through the pipelines of American Energy. And there would be no cataclysmic accidents.

There will be no more Three Mile Islands, she thought.

CHAPTER 11

▼

The White House, Washington, D.C.

"The only nation in the world that bans oil and gas drilling off its coasts is the United States of America," said the president of the United States. "Don't you find that odd?"

The elderly woman sitting opposite the nation's leader puckered her lips like she just sucked a slice of lemon. "America contains only a fraction of the world's population, but consumes a quarter of the world's energy, wasting more and polluting more than any nation on earth," countered Olga Stevick, president of the Silver Union, the most powerful public lobby since Ralph Nadar's Citizens' Action.

"That, unfortunately, is true," President Nathaniel Patrick "Nate" Freeman admitted. "But the fact remains—our economy runs on energy, and without it, we will have trouble keeping our head above water. Conservation is good. I support new CAFE standards, but it will take the automakers years to comply and some time before it has an impact on the country's oil consumption." He spoke with unbridled confidence, a resonant voice projecting from his chiseled face and football-player-sized frame. *But we can't conserve our way out of a crisis*, the president thought. And, his energy experts told him, increasing the gasoline mileage of cars—like lower oil prices—only encouraged *more* energy consumption because it enabled people to drive more.

"What are we senior citizens supposed to do in the meantime?" Stevick asked.

"I am working with Congress on the alternative-fuel provision in the energy bill."

"Better late than never," Stevick huffed. "Detroit and the oil companies have been in bed together for years. It is time for a divorce."

The president winced.

Stevick swiped at her stringy gray hair, as she was as unkempt as her caricature drawn by the leading newspapers' editorial cartoonists. No matter how hard the satirical artists tried, they could not seem to exaggerate her witchy appearance. Stevick wrinkled her nose and her bifocal glasses bobbed up and down. She held her trademark yellow legal pad in her lap with her age-spotted hands. Long, unpolished, and chipped fingernails gripped the rumpled tablet like the talons of a falcon. Despite her grizzled mien that resembled that of a bag lady, the president knew she was as sassy and spry as a cougar.

The eighty-one-year-old woman has more balls than a Navy Seal, he thought. And the Commander in Chief knew plenty of them in his years as a Midshipman. Olga Stevick rose from a humble grandmother of eight to one of the most powerful women in America without individual wealth, celebrity fame, corporate power, or PAC contributions. It started five years before, when the ever-increasing electric and gas rates of American Energy Corporation in Ohio caused her to attend a public hearing on a rate-hike request before the state's public utility commission. Speaking as a widow on Social Security, she decried the higher costs while utility executives raked in millions in salary and stock options. She said the high cost of energy didn't force her to choose between feeding herself and feeding her dog. She said sarcastically that she "already ate the dog" to howls of delight by a hoary lynch mob of senior citizens attending the hearing. The television reporters attending the session found Olga a natural before the cameras and before long, the once craven old crow metamorphosed into a ferocious consumer advocate hawk excoriating the utility industry and those lawmakers who supported it. She garnered thousands of names on petitions of protest and launched the Silver Union, a full-fledged 501(C)(3) nonprofit organization dedicated to the proposition that all utilities are created evil. Thanks to the Internet and satellite TV, the hollow face, haggard hair, and gravelly voice of the crag became nationally renown. Her take-no-prisoners style vented against the nation's energy firms was admired coast to coast. Soon, oil and gas producers, major automakers, and energy-producing state congressmen allegedly in the pockets of the oil industry were also in her sights. *Olga's Army,* as the Silver Union was nicknamed, soon attracted a gusher of funding via the Internet, and logged in millions of members of all political persuasions. Three years later, *Time* magazine named her "Person of the Year," calling here the "little old lady that could."

The president owned a delicate problem. He invited Stevick to the White House for public-relations purposes. Spurning her would be an insult to millions of potential voters. And elected with only 35 percent of the popular vote as an independent in a three-way presidential race two years before, the president's political capital was more borrowed at usurious interest rates than earned. Stevick not only criticized the energy producers for the higher costs of their product, but also at the same time, aligned forces with environmental interests condemning energy industry captains for polluting the nation's water and atmosphere. The cabal of populist interest groups opposed additional drilling off the coasts of the Atlantic and Pacific seaboards, as well as in Alaskan and Rocky Mountain wilderness regions. They vigorously opposed federal loan guarantees, accelerated tax depreciation, and tax credits for companies to build a natural gas pipeline from Alaska to the lower-forty-eight. Instead, the radical consumer and environmental groups espoused conservation, wind power, and other burgeoning renewables, all subsidized by windfall profit taxes on the fossil-fuel industry. Currently, renewable energies provided only 6 percent of the nation's energy supply. Most important, the president knew, Stevick and her cohorts favored a return to price regulation, if not actual government takeover, of the oil and natural gas companies, or at least the breakup of the monolithic energy firms that dominated the industry. The aged activist had her own public affairs Internet podcast sponsored by member contributions, including the "green" millionaires who suddenly found Jesus after exercising enough unbridled capitalism to acquire a fortune. The recent energy embargoes against the United States took a little wind out of her sails, the president thought, as many commonsense Americans demanded that the country become more energy self-sufficient. That is, keep gasoline, heating oil, and natural gas affordable while they continued to drive huge SUVs and open their windows in the winter in case it became too warm inside with their thermostats set at eighty degrees. *Am I being too cynical?* he wondered.

"We hope you support the country's new effort to produce natural gas in an environmentally safe manner," President Freeman said. He relaxed behind the Oval Office desk. A jaunty salt-and-pepper-haired man in his late-forties, the former Navy Communications officer was noted not only for his rugged good looks, but also his persuasive abilities. He hoped he could charm cagey social-activist grandmothers as well as he did starry-eyed soccer moms.

"You mean American Energy's public relations stunt," Stevick sneered. She perched on the end of her chair in the famous ovoid White House room as if she sat on a dirty bus stop bench.

This old coot is a tough nut, the president concluded.

"Stunt or not," President Freeman said, "it is a step to help alleviate our country's energy crisis, and," the president paused and emphasized, "increasing the supply, along with the nation's conservation plan, will reduce prices in the long run."

"I don't have a long run if I freeze to death this winter," Stevick said, peering over her spectacles like a wary schoolmarm. *You can't fool an old fool,* she seemed to say with her pewter-gray eyes. "Cutting down American Energy's obscene profits collected from the wallets and purses of defenseless senior citizens, already struggling with medical costs—"

"Mr. President?" a voice interrupted from the open Oval Office door.

The president looked up, and Stevick sighed, irritated at the disturbance. It was the president's chief of staff, a portly, balding man of sixty-five with bushy gray sideburns and remnants of kinky hair on the back of his head the color of lead. *He looked like John Quincy Adams,* the first lady once glibly remarked. The interruption came just as planned by the president.

"The UN Secretary-General is on the line," the chief of staff said. "This is about Nigeria."

"I'm sorry," President Freeman said to Stevick. "I have to take this call. But I will look over your most remarkable suggestions."

Freeman knew she thought the interruption too convenient. *There is a snake in the woodpile,* her cold stare said to him. Stevick pursed her wrinkled lips and her mouth reminded the president of a picture of an infected rectum he once saw in a medical text.

In her arthritic hands, she held the "Ten Commandments for Safe, Reliable, and Affordable Energy" as drafted and approved by the Silver Union board of directors. Twenty minutes later, President Freeman guessed, the consumer hawk would verbally rip him apart like a captured rodent before the TV cameras when she shuffled off the White House doorstep.

"Of course, Mr. President," Summerville said with dripping sarcasm, as if she were Cinderella's stepmother suggesting that she could go to the ball after all. She then thrust the typed sheet of paper with her manifesto into Freeman's chest and hobbled toward the door.

"The Oval Office will always be open," the president said as he returned to his desk.

Stevick stopped, and then peered at the leader of the free world.

"Mr. President," she said. Freeman's eyes rose.

"I would hope you would have a little more respect for your elders. I am not impressed or intimidated by you, the mighty energy companies, or their acolytes in Congress. I am eighty-one-years-old. I have raised eight children and endured an abusive marriage with an alcoholic husband. I have not just fallen off the back of a turnip wagon. Please don't patronize me. I'm too old to take crap from anyone."

"Yes, mamm," was all the president of the United States could think to say.

CHAPTER 12

▼

Maureen O'Day's husband glowered over his gravy-covered meatloaf. She did not like a brooding husband at the dinner table, especially when her world-famous meatloaf was served. He could be difficult at times, and she was willing to live with his ranting and cursing while watching sports teams on television in the den. But not in her kitchen.

"It would be a little more firm if you remembered the breadcrumbs on the way home, Dan," she said.

"Well, if I didn't have to push my truck two blocks, I would have stopped and picked some up," Dan O'Day said. "I can't get a goddamn gallon of gas in this town."

A lock of Maureen's chocolate-brown hair, streaked with line of white, fell in front of her high forehead. Maureen felt she was going bald. Her hairline was receding faster than her husband's and it was driving her crazy. So she teased her hair toward the front in large loops to camouflage the embarrassment. Dan said she was imagining the whole deal. Despite in full-fledged middle age, her husband claimed his green-eyed Irish bride was just as beautiful as a "morn' in spring." Maureen knew that was bullshit.

"Why can't you bring the service van home?" she said. "You're on night call aren't you?"

"Yeah, I'm on call all right. But the brilliant folks at the gas company have a new policy because of the *energy crisis*. If there is a gas leak in the middle of the night, I have to find my own way to the shop, and then pick up the van. The three-piece-suit big shots think that little folks like me will drive around town using up the company's precious fuel on personal business. So if someone's house is in danger of blowing up, or if their expensive gas is blowing out of a line somewhere, they'll have to wait that much longer before I get there. That's real economy."

Maureen waved a wooden spoon in a circle. Her prominent crow's feet danced like barn spiders at a hoedown when she laughed or frowned. "That doesn't make any sense. I thought those vans are *natural*-gas vehicles anyway."

"They are, but the powers that be are as stingy as ever. You figure they would brag about the NGVs, especially with the gasoline shortage and all. Natural gas may be expensive, but at least they have some. They've screwed around with that technology since the 'seventies and still can't get it off the ground. Ever since the fuckin' lawyers took control—"

The conversation between Maureen and her husband was broken by the entrance of a slim woman with rusty-colored hair that flowed liberally over her shoulders. It was their twenty-eight-year-old lawyer daughter and father's namesake, Danielle. She inherited her mother's movie-starlet high cheekbones and emerald eyes as well as her father's Marine Corps drill sergeant square chin and petulant personality.

"Still bitchin' in the kitchen about the gas company, I see," the long-legged woman said. She was dressed in tight faded blue jeans, one of her father's Cleveland Browns' football sweatshirts, and sheep-wool-lined slippers.

"I was just sayin' Dannie," her father said. "Ever since American Energy gobbled up every independent gas firm on the east coast, we make decisions from some fiftieth-floor executive dining room in Rockefeller Center, not locally where the rubber meets the road."

Dannie. Maureen knew her daughter hated the masculine pet name her father called her since she was a six-year-old playing T-ball. They had a son who died in infancy named Daniel. A few years later came Danielle, his next son who happened to be a daughter. The sparks flew between the two since childhood. Thank goodness the *mother* was there to referee.

"Dan, you keep blaming every problem at work on the executive *suits*, and us *fucking* attorneys," Danielle said, sipping coffee from a delicate china cup. "The reason we are in this energy mess is because of the government—not because of our company. We are doing everything we can to—"

"Eliminate your old man's job, I know." He brought his plastic convenient-store coffee mug up to his face.

"Now, now you two," Maureen said, introducing several slices of cinnamon toast like diplomatic envoys into the feud. Her husband slugged the final drippings of coffee down his throat, and then signaled with the empty mug to his wife that he wanted more. She dutifully retrieved the pot, and he reached for the newspaper sprawled out on the kitchen table.

"Where else does the blame lie?" the elder O'Day asked. "The suits never worked in a ditch. They never laid an inch of pipeline, fixed a leak in a snowstorm, got bit by a dog in an attempt read a meter, or forced to personally shut off an indigent grandmother in the ghetto for nonpayment of a bill. All they do is collect stock options and go to Club Med."

"You're full of it," Danielle said.

"Now, my own offspring is one of them," he bemoaned.

Danielle bit into the cinnamon toast and she ate silently. Maureen moved between the warring family members and tried to apply a balm.

"Tell us about your big trip," Maureen asked her daughter.

"Well, I don't know much," Danielle said. "Just that it involves a press event with the president and the new source of gas from ocean kelp."

"Ah yes, Madame President," her father said.

"The president *of the United States*," Danielle corrected.

"But Raven will be there too," the father said from underneath his newspaper. "Going offshore to announce more layoffs."

"Don't swallow that union bullshit," Danielle answered.

He dropped the paper. "This union bullshit got your butt through your fancy-ass college. I've worked my tail off to earn a living while these Johnny-come-lately baby-boomer lawyers cash in on the investment your family helped put in the ground a century ago."

"Oh Jesus, not this again. Mom!"

Maureen offered more toast to her husband to try to nip the argument in the bud. But it was too late. Her husband was in diatribe mode.

"Your great-great-great uncle got that goddamn cheapskate Rockefeller to pay pipeline men a decent wage in the late nineteenth century," he began, "back when the ordinary guy worked seven days a week in the jungle for slave's wages earning riches for those greedy Gilded-Age sons-of-bitches. The pipeliners loved Danny O'Day, even though he was one of John D.'s lieutenants. They used to say, "If you stuck one pipeliner with a needle—"

"Yeah, yeah, they all bled!" his daughter finished the phrase.

The O'Day's green-eyed daughter laughed derisively, stared at the ceiling, and then took another sip of coffee like it was poison. Both mother and daughter heard this tirade too many times before.

"I've got to pack," the young O'Day said, only to Maureen. The mother of the family stood on the sidelines, feckless, like a coach watching her team get trounced on the field. Danielle rose from the table. Even with the cloak of the baggy sweatshirt and jeans, she couldn't disguise her feminine curves that taunted every male lawyer in the American Energy legal department. But as far as Maureen knew, Danielle wasn't interested in any of them. She was an overachiever. As a child she had to hit the ball farther than the boys—her father insisted. She could not be a sissy-girl. Now, as an attorney, she felt she had to out-man the men as well, as if every O'Day, male or female, had to sport testicles.

"Don't walk away from me," Maureen's husband said, knowing his parental influence was feeble, if not nonexistent.

Maureen whispered harshly, "She is almost thirty years old. You cannot control her life."

"Listen here young ma—"

He didn't have time to retract his emotional outburst. *Young man! Damn him,* Maureen thought. He would tease their daughter when she would be reluctant to do boyish things in her youth—taunting her by calling her "girlie" as if that were an insult to a nine-year-old female. Danielle now called her own father Dan, not Dad. Maureen wanted to step in and slap her husband in the face, but it was too late. Besides, her daughter did not need help defending herself.

"I'm your daughter, Dan!" Danielle bolted back into the kitchen and pointed at her chest. "See, Dan, these are teats. Little boys don't grow teats. They grow dicks. Only little girls get teats—even those you wanted to grow dicks." She stormed out of the room.

Her father sat open-mouthed, realizing there was no way to backpedal down this road.

"Daniel Sean O'Day!" Maureen exploded. Now, her mercurial Irish temper boiled over. There was hell to pay when she used his middle name. She was usually quiet around her husband, content to prepare the meals, clean the house, and promote domestic tranquility through food, drink, and innocuous conversation. But when her sometimes-oafish husband threatened to split the rock on which she built her life—her small family—he would have to answer for it.

"Go right to her and apologize!" she scolded. "You should be ashamed, don't you know?"

"I didn't mean—I just misspoke," her husband said, shaking his head, defeated.

"Get your own goddamn coffee," she said, removing her apron and tossing it in the sink. She flew out of the room following her only child, a daughter—a beautiful, sagacious lawyer—who was named after her father and that insufferable great-great-great uncle.

In the doorway of the bedroom where her little girl spent many a lonely night playing with the dolls her father didn't want to see, Maureen silently watched her throw items in a suitcase. She wondered if family life would have been different if her first born had not died moments after birth. There was nothing to be done—a genetic defect. His name would have been Daniel Sean O'Day, Jr. The unspeakable pensiveness that swamps a mother after the death of a child took its toll on Maureen and her marriage. He husband fared no better. Maureen lost a piece of herself, more important than an arm or an eye. Her husband lost an heir, and he seemed to mope for months like a childless king of a crumbling empire. Their solution was another child, another chance. After a troubling pregnancy, diabetes, and bed rest, the next slid out of the womb healthy, but female. Maureen was warned not become pregnant again and underwent a hysterectomy. And so the baby became Danielle Sarah O'Day.

Danielle stuffed her clothes into a black leather Gucci suitcase, part of a set that cost her $2,000. She was obviously angry, but there were no tears in her eyes. She inserted a rectangular object about the size of a large walkie-talkie into the bottom of a bag and laughed. It was a GPS satellite phone, a global-positioning device her father gave her for her birthday.

"Your father thought you would appreciate the James Bond gadget since you always have the latest picture-phones, Ipods, and whatnot," Maureen said from the doorway.

"Why does he do this again and again mother?"

"He's only frustrated about his job."

"He's frustrated I don't have a penis."

Maureen knew she was right. He did always treat her like a boy. He didn't buy her tea sets and rag dolls as a child. He bought her racecars and footballs. He took her hunting for deer, turkey, and ducks, lecturing about different types of firearms as if she were a member of a militia. But she endured. And when she was a full-grown woman with a law degree, her father did not bless her marriage to that well-to-do, twice-divorced Wall Street broker.

"He only wants her ass to parade around at New York Café Society parties," her husband sneered. On that point, Maureen agreed. Thank God Danielle dumped him after six months.

Maureen hugged her daughter from behind.

"Your father didn't mean that, don't you know?" her mother said. "His job is getting difficult—this economy, the irate customers, and no gasoline. You know how your daddy loves his cars."

"Apparently much more than me."

"No, no." Tears streamed down Maureen's cheeks.

"I curse the day I decided to work for his damn company," her daughter said. "I thought he'd be proud. But I'm a lawyer, not some union slug, shame on me. It's like I left a Georgia plantation in 1861 to join the *Union* army."

"That's not true and you know it."

"I shouldn't have come here, Mom. I should have stayed in New York. I have to leave in two days anyhow for that offshore project."

Maureen lifted the satellite phone from her daughter's suitcase.

"Your father says this phone will work where cellphones can't," Maureen told her. The electronic device stood about six-inches tall, two-and-a-half-inches wide, and two-inches thick. It weighed a little over a pound and had a continuous talk time of nine hours and twenty-four hours on standby. "Now look at this contraption. What in the world will they think of next! Your father says all the drillers out at sea use it—he wants you to use it on your trip. Do you remember what his instructions were?"

"Yes, mother. What I remember most is that it costs about $1.50 a minute; he was complaining about that so I wouldn't waste money."

Maureen smiled. What her husband didn't tell Danielle was the device itself cost $1,000, his entire raise for the last two years.

"Your father said with this you will always know where you are and how to get home," Maureen said. "And through some Internet website, he can find you anywhere on earth."

"Is that a threat?"

Maureen hugged her daughter again, squeezing her almost too tightly.

"You'll never know how proud your father really is that you are a lawyer—an executive no less—in the company where he has worked for thirty-five years."

"That's right Mom," Danielle said. "I'll never know."

As Danielle left, the father of the family never left the kitchen, and he never refilled his coffee mug either. When Maureen returned, her mulish husband cracked open a beer and hummed to himself the traditional Irish ballad.

Oh, Danny boy, the pipes, the pipes are calling.

He hummed that tune for months after the death of their infant boy. He took a swig from the can and wiped his mouth with his forearm.

Oh, Danny boy, oh Danny boy, I love you so.

One-hour later, Danielle O'Day was in a cab headed to the small hometown airport. The brief visit to her birthplace didn't work out. No matter what she did, she felt she would never get the acceptance of her father, let alone his love. Did she even want it? He was old school, pigheaded, and an ungrateful bore. The hell with him. In two days she would be aboard an American Energy helicopter flying over the Atlantic to land on an experimental offshore natural gas collection platform to inspect the facilities in preparation for a visit by the president of the United States and an elaborate media entourage. The thought scared the hell out of her. Why did she want to do this? To jump-start her precipitant career and impress the president of the company who had taken her under her wing? To spite her Neanderthal father? What a wasted effort that would be. Her father wanted a boy, but was awarded a girl. Her mother cried when she walked out the front door of the unpretentious ranch-style home in suburban Erie, Pennsylvania. She felt the wetness of her mother's tears thirty feet away as the taxi pulled out of the driveway. And her own eyes became moist when she discovered her purse was stuffed with homemade chocolate chip cookies—the tollhouse recipe, her favorite.

As the small plane soared off the short runway, an ominous thought darkened her mind. A feeling that she might never return home again.

CHAPTER 13

▼

After Olga Stevick stumbled out the Oval Office, Thaddeus Mann, the president's chief-of-staff, reclined in the same chair that Stevick vacated. The pungent, unwashed stale-closet body odor of Stevick stung his olfactory senses.

"Phew!" Mann said, wrinkling his nose. "She's gone, but her aura remains."

"I tried not to breathe much," President Freeman responded. "But it will fade. If only solving the energy crisis was that easy."

"Well, unfortunately, the oil and gas shortage, as well as that old bag, is not going away."

Mann was an experienced politico whom the president counted on for frank advice, especially when it sawed across his own grain. A Mississippi native, Mann joined the Navy at eighteen and flew rescue choppers in Vietnam, receiving a bronze star and two purple hearts after rescuing three stranded Marines under fire in a Viet Cong ambush. After returning stateside, he won an open seat in Congress and served six terms in the House and one in the Senate, becoming a champion of military spending, especially for the Navy. After his political career, he joined the lobbying ranks of a defense contractor for a few years. He was in comfortable retirement when the newly elected president of the United States rang his phone and asked for one last mission. Mann had supporters and detractors on both sides of the aisle, but he was a man of his word and respected by both parties. The president was a former Navy communications officer, public relations executive, and presidential spokesman. Freeman was not a politician by trade. He needed coaching in the legislative arena, and Mann fit the bill. The president wanted to be a political gambler, but Mann was the one who really knew how to play the game. As Kenny Rogers sang, he knew when to hold 'em and when to fold 'em.

"Thanks for your positive thinking," the president said. He nicknamed his aide "Eeyore," after the saturnine donkey from the Hundred Acre Wood.

"The politics of realism," his wizened aide ruminated, stroking his nineteenth-century-style sideburns. "Another major glass plant announced it will shut down in six weeks. The company is blaming the high cost of natural gas. About 3,000 will be laid off in western Pennsylvania. It is the last major glassmaking facility in the nation. With current energy prices, they can't compete globally."

"Right behind the steel and chemical industries that depend on cheap energy. Last one out turn out the light."

"Without new natural gas supplies in the pipeline pronto—we'll have the light turned out for us."

"How is the project going, by the way?"

"That's the silver lining," said Mann. "Nothing but positive reports from *Project Hades.*"

The president sank in his chair. "*Hades* … couldn't they come up with a more inspirational name than that?"

"Well, it is the deepest exploration below sea level. Sometimes we have to make a deal with the devil. They are waiting for your presidential order to proceed."

The president rose and sauntered across the royal-blue carpet of the Oval Office. *How many great and dreadful decisions have been made in this very spot,* he thought. Now Nathaniel Freeman had to make another one that might not only determine the success or failure of his presidency, but also the fate of the nation.

"What's the status on the platform visit?" President Freeman asked.

"It should be a great one, Mr. President. We will travel from Norfolk to inspect a Navy destroyer—one I saved from the scrap yard I might add—and then tour the nearby liquefied natural gas plant there. Then we will helicopter to the offshore platform, along with a slew of press and industry leaders. From what I understand, American Energy has put together a dog-and-pony show that should wow them. We'll fly right over one of the company's electric-generating wind farms off the Outer Banks. And they say you can even see the underwater kelp farms from the air, the green stalks of the plants waving in the currents below like palm branches at the gates of Jerusalem."

"Sometimes, your similes are stretched a bit too thin," the president said.

"It's what political campaigns are all about," Mann said, a chuckle shaking his steel-wool-pad sideburns up and down.

"Imagine, getting natural gas from seaweed," said the president.

"That's a proven fact, Mr. President. Our concern is, will the press be satisfied with that? Convincing them that a bunch of green sea spinach is going to solve the country's energy problems may look as comforting as Jimmy Carter on television wearing a cardigan sweater next to a wood fireplace."

The president remembered the image. He was in the Naval Academy when President Carter declared his "moral equivalent of war" on the energy crisis in the 1970s. Carter's symbolic conservation gesture of the sweater and fireplace did nothing to solve the energy crisis, and instead made him appear weak. *Didn't that mild-mannered peanut farmer know that most wood fireplaces consumed more energy than they produced?* Carter found his political rear end bounced out in the next election not just because the Iranian militants held hostages in the U.S. Embassy in Tehran, but rather because you couldn't get a tank of gasoline in Brooklyn to jaunt up to the Adirondacks for a weekend holiday. It was déjà vu all over again as Yogi Berra would say. The same fate awaited him at the end of his first term unless things turned around fast. More important, the economy of the United States was about to go down the tubes because of crippling energy shortages and rocketing price increases. The press was already making Carter-Freeman comparisons. In one political editorial cartoon, the child-like Freeman stops at President Carter's brother Billy's gas station to fill up a gas can with the "moral equivalent" of gasoline with alternative-fuel peanut oil to power his presidential moped.

The president knew that only more domestic energy would save the country from ruin. Frivolous conservation edicts were already flying out of the key-stone-cop Congress, but that was not a long-term solution. Maybe he could extend daylight savings time around the clock and stop the earth's rotation so there would always be daylight over North America. That would save electricity.

He knew the American people must wake up and face the music. Conservation only went so far.

"Imagine," the president told the American public during his last televised address, "two people in a desert sharing one canteen of water. No matter how much they ration the contents between them, if they don't get to an oasis eventually, they are both going to be in a heap of trouble." And so it was with America's newest energy crisis. More domestic sources of energy must be found, and fast. Hydrogen fuel cells, solar power, methane from rotting garbage at landfills, and wind power were being applied throughout the country. But the president felt the patchwork of small-scale renewable energies was as effective as a Band-Aid on a severed artery. For example, hydrogen fuel cells mixed hydrogen and oxygen to make electricity and heat. But the challenge of fuel cells was finding an economical way to separate hydrogen from other compounds and store the fuel efficiently and safely. Currently, the main feedstock to produce hydrogen was, no surprise, natural gas. Projects producing methane from waste were limited. Solar power was mostly limited to the Southwest. Wind-power farms had to be gargantuan systems to pay for themselves. Most of the wind blew where people did not live, requiring long-range transmission lines that added to the costs. In addition, wind stations needed backup supplies when the breeze stopped blowing, usually during the hottest days where electricity demand from air conditioning was at its peak.

And Congress was little help. The chairman of the House Energy and Commerce committee, August Doggle—nicknamed "Boon Doggle" by the president—was sitting on the administration's energy bill, while blabbering about "corn fuels," a pork-barrel project for his Iowa congressional district. Doggle's corn-based additive incentives for ethanol authored by lobbyists from the Association of Renewable Fuel Growers would mandate the use of the fuel for all government vehicles. Previously, the Volumetric Ethanol Excise Tax Credit subsidy for producers of ethanol resulted in a tax credit/subsidy about $2.3 billion a year. Doggle proposed that the subsidy increase to $25 billion.

"It's a lot easier to grow a bushel of corn in the U.S.A. than to import a barrel of oil from Islamic Fundamentalists," Doggle bragged to his xenophobic constituents. "Biofuels could replace foreign petroleum not only for vehicular fuel, but also for other uses such as bioplastics."

The president knew what the blowhard Doggle didn't say was that his corn grew with the aid of artificial petrochemical fertilizer, which the United States was now *importing* because the shortage and high price of natural gas put the nation's fertilizer plants out of business. And one scientist, citing that more energy is used to make ethanol that it yields, called corn-fuel production "subsidized food burning." Though ethanol from corn, methane from garbage, methanol from fermenting crop and animal waste, and electricity from sun and wind were all well and good, the president realized what the United States needed was good old oil and gas—the economy's lifeblood—and soon. Freeman was far from an energy expert, but he was learning fast.

"What is the word about Nigeria, by the way?" the president asked his top aide, changing the subject, sort of.

"Not good, I'm afraid. Rebels virtually destroyed the liquefied natural gas cooling plant. There was no explosion, but a fire tore through most of the plant. It will take more than a year to repair—that is, if the rebels don't succeed in toppling the present government. There is another full LNG tanker from Algeria that should dock in Virginia in a few days. The new Islamic Algerian government says so far, a deal's a deal. And they haven't asked our ambassador to leave Algiers … yet. But the shipment will only add a little natural gas into the eastern supply."

The president shook his head. "I warned Congress that depending on imported natural gas from unstable countries was only playing into the hands of our enemies. We've spent a bundle on a fleet of LNG ships to transport these frozen dinosaur turds from the Middle East, Africa, and South America, and our LNG plants are only running at a fraction of their capacity."

"But it's cheap!" Mann said, sarcastically.

Congressional supporters of the LNG industry argued that importing natural gas in its liquid form and then converting it to its gaseous state at massive port plants on the east and west coasts was the answer to the country's energy woes. The U.S. government helped finance the construction of three new terminals with National Gas and Electric Corporation—the nation's largest home energy provider of electricity and natural gas—that would warm the super-cooled liquid fuel back into its gaseous state to flow through its pipelines. Dubbed *Project Frozen Angelfire*, it was another public-private partnership to address the nation's mounting energy crisis. Unfortunately, political unrest in Algeria and Nigeria, the major African countries exporting the fuel, cut expected shipments by two-thirds. The president remembered a quote from some French diplomat about how trade is the secret to peace: *If goods don't travel across borders, armies will.*

"At least we still have our leftist friends in Venezuela," the president said.

"Don't speak too soon. Rumor has it another strike is coming. Both oil and gas operations may be shut down again. In addition, Argentina and Peru are joining Bolivia in playing chicken with the major oil companies by nationalizing their hydrocarbon industry."

The president rubbed his eyes. He saw this coming as a candidate. He knew the United States was at the mercy of hostile governments who could blackmail the great superpower because of its addiction to energy. And Congress still would not end the moratorium of natural gas and oil drilling off the east and west coasts, the Great Lakes, most of the Rocky Mountains, and in the wilderness of Alaska. In fact, even bizarre coalitions were forming to prohibit drilling. Environmental groups were teaming up with ranchers and Native American tribes to sue the federal government to prevent drilling of gas wells on government lands in rich natural-gas regions in the western states. *It was ridiculous*, the president thought. The country was cutting its own throat because of its stupid, antiquated restrictions.

"Doesn't anyone get it?" President Freeman said, pounding his desk with his fist. It was a furious slam from his powerful hand. The forty-eight-year-old was a third-string disaster quarterback for the Navy Midshipman at Annapolis. His weight-lifter frame lost little of his athletic strength and agility over the years. "Even the goddamn Canadians have been drilling for natural gas in the Great Lakes for a half-century, and we can't sink a single hole there. The damn gas under the lake doesn't know an international boundary. It's like two straws in an ice cream soda, and only one kid is doing the sucking!"

"Yep," Mann agreed. "The Canadians drill for gas in the Atlantic Ocean off of Nova Scotia and they used to sell it to New England utilities, but now they are squirreling it away for themselves."

The president heaved an exasperated sigh. "The offshore drilling amendment—any developments?"

Mann scratched his sideburns again. "The major environmental groups, including ANGER, are still tugging on weak links in both parties, claiming that if Congress permits drilling offshore, those in tight districts who vote aye will be toast in the next election. The coalition of chicken-shit coastal state legislatures is backing off because of the public's paranoia about oil-covered seagulls. And Chairman Doggle is insisting on his ethanol amendment while barking that the bill is full of favors for the oil and gas industry."

"We did this to ourselves," the president said, resigned. "We made natural gas the preferred fuel for all applications, including electric generation. It would have made more sense to use coal and nuclear—at least we don't have to buy those fuels from some sheik or mullah that would like to see us all dead. Even the damn French generate 80 percent of their juice from nuclear power. They've traded greenhouse gasses for nuclear waste. Geez, listen to me. I was once a good Kennedy liberal, ran for office as a non-partisan moderate, and now sound like a right-wing reactionary."

"Forget ideology, Mr. President. Think politics."

President Freeman rarely did—he thought policy. Maybe he wasn't cut out for this kind of work after all.

Mann continued. "This is all a personal vendetta. Both the Democratic and Republican leaders are pissed off that an independent president is sitting in the Oval Office and not a member of their political club. First they overrode your veto on that wacky environmental bill proclaiming carbon dioxide a polluting gas, knowing it would double the price of electricity from fossil-fuel power plants. They just want to see the country screwed up enough to get you out of office in two years."

The president feared his chief aide might be right.

Though the United States was the world's largest carbon emitter, it did not sign on to the original greenhouse-gas-limiting Kyoto Protocol. Some scientists said the Earth could tolerate CO_2 levels of about 550 parts per million before facing a cataclysmic collection of climate problems including extreme weather, regional droughts, and a rising sea level. The world needed to cut emissions between 55 and 85 percent. But U.S. politicians complained that China, India, and numerous developing (i.e., polluting) nations were not part of the pact. In China, for example, the county's large coal reserves provided two-thirds of the nation's energy. As a result, the massive Asian nation was home to seven of the world's top ten polluted cities.

But the president's lack of environmental sensitivity combined with high energy prices resulted in his tenable popularity plummeting. The president's dry wit also got him into trouble when he was caught unintentionally on a microphone quipping, "If emitting excessive carbon dioxide is a crime, then several blowhard Congressmen are going to be doing time at Attica." Few found the humor in the statement, especially Congressman Doggle, who felt the comment was directed at him. Now, Freeman was in the midst of a nationwide crisis and the time for joking had past.

"Why not let me take a crack at Doggle?" Mann asked. "I might be able to convince him to come around."

The president frowned. The administration lobbyists were already doing double-time. But Mann was the political genius. He was working backroom deals in the halls of Congress when Freeman was wet behind the ears sitting on the sidelines holding a clipboard during most Navy football games. Isn't this why he asked Mann to abandon sipping mint juleps on his Mississippi beach house deck overlooking the Gulf of Mexico to return to the wretched cesspool of Washington?

"Doggle is a hard nut to crack," Freeman said. "He's already thrown the gauntlet."

"There are ways to convince him," Mann said. "Everyone has their price."

"You sound like Vito Corleone. I don't want any monkey business, Thaddeus. I came to Washington to change politics as usual."

"Mr. President," Mann said. "You are an upstanding leader. But I know characters like Doggle. Let me try to shake his tree a little. Who knows what he's willing to do behind the scenes. We might be able to achieve a compromise."

"Fine, but if you are going to put a horse's head in his bed, I don't want to know about it," Freeman said. And the president knew Mann was not about to tell him.

Freeman spun on his wingtips and made his decision. "I guess the prayers to the LNG *Angel* might not be answered. Well, despite its dubious legality, I'll consider the go-ahead of *Project Hades*," Freeman said. "But first, I need to look the fiend in the eye."

"The lawyers say *Project Hades* is not technically *drilling*, so we cannot be accused of violating the federal moratorium."

"That depends on what the meaning of the words 'is not,' is," the president joked, doing his best impression of one of his predecessors. "I'll see what my buddy Cowboy has to say about that."

That will be the clincher, the president thought. Bruce "Cowboy" Rhodan was an old friend from his early Naval Academy days. The billionaire head of one of the world's largest energy exploration firms was the onsite manager of *Project Hades*—the United States' last chance of turning the energy world upside down. Advocates of the plan hoped it would give the Sheiks, Imams, Ayatollahs, and Mullahs in the Persian Gulf the bum's rush, saying goodbye to foreign energy imports forever. It was a venture begun long before Nate Freeman ever sat in the Oval Office and supposedly as confidential as the Manhattan Project that developed the nation's first atomic weapon. But as far as he could tell, *Hades* could be the light at the end of the pipeline for America's energy woes. Hopefully, the project would be up and running and declared a success long before the American public found out the first thing about it. However, like oil tankers run aground by drunken sea captains, secrets in Washington had a funny way of leaking out and causing a catastrophe.

"It'll work, Mr. President," said Mann. "You will be a visionary who guided our nation out of its greatest modern crisis."

The president's face broke into a crooked smile. "Or I'll be impeached, jailed, and burned in effigy as an alternative fuel."

CHAPTER 14

▼

American Energy was in a Catch-22, the experts told Alexandria Raven. There was an immense natural gas shortage, and even if a new supply could be found, the powerful Washington environmental lobby and their minions in Congress vowed to end the burning of all polluting fossil fuels, even more environmentally friendly natural gas. But the conundrum did not worry her.

"I want that platform clean enough to eat off of," Raven spoke into a hands-free telephone headset perched on her flawless coiffure. "All employees should wear the new uniforms with not one speck of grease. They are green, aren't they?"

One the other end of the line, American Energy's newest senior vice president of corporate communications and Raven's protégée, Danielle O'Day, confirmed American Energy's new thematic color.

"Great," the energy magnate said, her smile growing wider on her face. Her scarlet lipstick accentuated the herringbone-shaped wrinkles on her lips, created from decades of nicotine absorption that she abandoned five years before along with her married name. Though she quit smoking, she remained married. "The tree-huggers love green. And I just approved the new logo—I want it placed on all subsidiary vehicles within two weeks."

Raven's egg-shaped hazel eyes panned her desk like searchlights, locking in on the new design in an advertising packet on her desk. The soon-to-be-unveiled logo featured blue ocean waves interwoven with green sea plants with a yellow sun rising in the background. The advertising firm claimed the image represented the pristine blue waters where American Energy would harvest sea plants to pro-duce clean-burning natural gas that did not pollute the skies—thus the shiny sun opens its unblemished golden eye to a new morning for America. Even though the kelp seaweed that produced methane was actually brown, few would know and no one would care.

"What do you think of the slogan?" Raven asked.

"Clean Energy, Our America," her PR vice-president parroted. "Sounds great."

"I kind of liked *screw the environmentalists and fuck the Arabs*, but it won't fit on a bumper sticker." Raven laughed, a deep throaty smoker's chuckle.

A nervous breath was all that could be heard on the other end of the line.

"We have the DOE energy summit tomorrow in Washington," the CEO said. "I would like to unveil the logo then—you did order the T-shirts?"

"Soy ink on natural cotton," Danielle O'Day confirmed.

"This presentation is critical to the future of American Energy," Raven said. And it was. She was betting the farm on it. "The sale of the company's coal and oil assets raised eyebrows on Wall Street. They don't like us dumping assets that were producing a great profit."

Since coal was America's greatest energy reserve, there was a renewed interest in the dirty fuel that could be used in new clean-coal technologies to produce electricity. But Raven convinced her board otherwise. Coal was so *eighteenth-century*. And in the light of skyrocketing oil prices because of the international boycott, American Energy was accused by fortune-telling talking heads on the cable financial channels of gross negligence.

"They're selling the goose that lays the golden eggs," one boisterous, many said obnoxious, bald-headed prognosticator said on MSNBC.

"Coal and oil are moribund fossil fuels," Raven responded.

Raven was certain that the future was not in the slick, black gold that fueled the industrial world since the dawn of the twentieth century. The future beheld new technologies that might be economically produced, such as nuclear fusion—which combined atoms rather than splitting them—solar and wind generated electricity, and hydrogen fuel cells. "Who knows?" she said, "America might eventually run its cars and heat its homes with peanut butter." But now the present—her real concern—belonged to natural gas. The widespread use of alternative fuels was still many years away in the timeline. Until the real alternative-fuel panacea arrived, the best prospect for domestic security and environmental benefit was natural gas, if enough could be found. And only a select few knew American Energy was sitting on the mother lode discovery of the century.

"I have faith in you," the CEO told her new senior VP. She did have faith in the young lawyer who was rising through the ranks of the corporate energy giant like an oil droplet in vinegar, with a specific gravity that assured its eventual presence at the top. The glass ceiling in the energy business was already shattered. Raven's cuts and bruises were evidence of that. Danielle O'Day was her teacher's pet. When Raven was her age, she was already saddled with three kids—all boys. This bright and vivacious attorney—single and childless—was the daughter she never had. There was something about brainy women in business. They did not get hung up on egotism like men did, brandishing their confidence like a cock on the walk. Women were more supportive, inquisitive, and better listeners. They made superior business decisions in Raven's view as long as they possessed enough intestinal fortitude to back up their ideas. But then again, Raven was a woman and therefore biased. Still, she made her filial-like choice of her rising star just like the old boy's club did for decades. Ms. O'Day better be up to the task.

Despite her confidence, Raven kept her young apprentice in the dark regarding the energy exploration strategy. That was by design. Raven admitted to herself that she was too close to the project to see the forest for the trees. She needed a fresh set of intelligent, feminine eyes to review the operations off the shores of North Carolina to evaluate how their operation would play in Peoria, places like Danielle's hometown, Erie, Pennsylvania.

Raven wished her protégée bon voyage! and ended the call abruptly. She watered her credenza flowers from a lopsided, but decorative ceramic watering jug that was a gift from a grandchild, a project of a second-grade art class. The female energy titan was also an active gardener at her White Plains estate, spending most of her free time digging in the soil, doting over her pansies. Despite spending a good part of her early business career on maternity leave, Raven's University of Pennsylvania Wharton School MBA background, subsequent law degree, instinctive keen business acumen, and aggressive personality helped her climb up the corporate ladder faster than an adrenaline-fueled fireman. Being a woman did not impede her career in the traditional white-male-dominated business. Women CEOs made up less than 4 percent of the Fortune 100 companies, though the top corporate suites of PepsiCo, Kraft, Archer-Daniels Midland, and others had opened their door for the ladies. Because of federal equal opportunity pressures, companies such as American Energy accelerated diversification and appropriately placed women and minorities on the fast track. But it was Raven's aptitude and aggression, not quotas or favoritism, that put her in the queen's chair.

Known as "Alexandria the Consolidate," Raven brought together every link in the energy chain—natural gas production wells, transportation pipelines, and utility distribution systems—adding hard assets to her company while subtracting soft, often human, operational costs. Many managers in the takeover targets were deployed with a golden parachute they could not refuse, and superfluous line workers were showed the door. Therefore, American Energy absorbed incoming producing assets with a minimal amount of human resource expense.

"Pipelines don't need medical plans," she informed the board of directors, "people do." Now, American Energy developed a monopoly in the natural gas business that John D. Rockefeller and his ilk only dreamed of. Three out of four utility consumers on the East Coast were linked in some way to an American Energy pipeline or got their juice from an American Energy power plant. Raven's master plan was to make it four out of four. And she had a plan. It would be hatched in a week when she would stand arm-in-arm with the president of the United States on an ocean platform off the coast of North Carolina.

Five years before, when Raven became president of American Energy, her husband, Douglas Waters, resigned as U.S. Secretary of Energy. The appearance of a connection between the major corporate energy mogul and a cabinet-level leader in charge of policing the industry was inappropriate, Mr. Waters told the press. So he retired to their White Plains estate and their North Carolina Outer Banks beach house to let his wife bring home the bacon. In fact, her $7 million annual salary and generous stock options allowed her to bring the whole hog. But before he left, the White House approved a secret Department of Energy partnership initiative to help reduce the country's dependence on imported fuels. Previously, Congress passed the Methane Hydrate Research and Development Act in 2000, which put federal research funds behind the effort to extract fossil-fuel hydrate— sometimes called "burning ice"—from below the seafloor. The initial law required the secretary of energy to work with the Commerce, Defense, and Interior Departments and the National Science Foundation. The government agencies explored various agreements with universities and private industry to research efficient and environmentally sound development of natural gas hydrate formations, convert the resource to useable fuel, and transport it safely to the marketplace.

Worldwide, industry estimates projected that there were 100 times more gas hydrates than conventional natural gas resources. In fact, more than half of the Earth's organic carbon was made up of methane hydrates. The National Science Foundation and Office of Naval Research initiated study, but other countries, such as Russia, India, Germany, and Japan, were said to be far ahead in applicable research and actual drilling. At least that was what was known publicly. Unbeknownst to the press and Congress, the federal government and private industry were working on a much-advanced hydrate project that could revolutionize the future of energy.

Meanwhile, American Energy won the competitive, sealed bid to develop a kelp-to-methane alternative-fuel project in the Atlantic off the east coast of the Carolinas, known as *Project Blue Sky*. But the green research project to generate natural gas from seaweed below the waters of the Atlantic was only cover for a top-secret strategy to find the world's greatest clean energy supply trapped in frozen crystals below the continental shelf. That covert operation then became known as *Project Hades*, suggesting that the project would seek clean energy supplies as far below the sea floor as Hell itself. The effort sought methane ice buried below the ocean seabed that could fuel industry, generate electricity, power cars, boost the American economy, reelect the incumbent president, and eventually, make billions of dollars for the publicly traded corporation in charge of piping the new found gas: American Energy.

"I believe the power to make money is a gift from God," oil tycoon John D. Rockefeller once said. Alexandria Raven remembered that. And she knew that individual power was fleeting unless it was part of a dynasty. She wanted to pick her successor, and it would not be anyone from the collection of arrogant male dunderheads among her senior officers. She wanted a fresh face, someone who reminded her of herself when she was young, as if she could vicariously live her life again. And Raven believed she needed to do it soon.

PART IV

▼

EUREKA

CHAPTER 15

▼

Atlantic Ocean, 89 miles off the coast of North Carolina

Bruce "Cowboy" Rhodan sat strapped in a modified chair-like device that looked similar to an oversized barber's stool, his four-hundred-dollar snakeskin boots braced against the rail of a $1 billion oceanic platform that stretched as long as two regulation football fields. The United States government financed 80 percent of the cost of the one-of-a-kind steel and concrete mobile research island known as the *China Maiden*. Rhodan founded and had the controlling interest in South-east Exploration, an international drilling company operating as a contractor for the project. As a stiff, tepid oceanic breeze blew in his sun-reddened face, Rhodan was as comfortable as if he was sitting in his living room. In his cattle-glove-covered hands, he gripped a ten-foot deep-sea fishing rod that bent severely from what he just landed on the other end. One hundred and fifty yards out amongst the five-foot swells in the Gulf Stream, an unhappily hooked blue marlin soared out of the surf, shaking its steel-blue proboscis and fanning its majestic rainbow-colored dorsal fin from side to side before crashing into the blue water again.

"Yeehah!" the forty-eight-year-old Oklahoma native screamed, as delighted as a six-year-old darting down the stairs on Christmas morning. The opaque Oakley wraparound sunglasses shielding his eyes from the sun's scintillating reflection off the waters of the Atlantic did not cloak his glee. A five-inch illegally smuggled Cuban cigar clamped between his teeth bobbed up and down, leaving a curly smoke trail like a skywriting plane in a barrel roll. Despite the ocean wind and Cowboy's bobbing motion in reeling in his catch, a tan Stetson balanced on his head did not budge. This was Cowboy's first marlin after angling sporadically for two weeks, catching several blue fish, stripers, and a stingray, which he separated from its spiked tail in ceremonious retaliation for the death of that Aussie croco-dile hunter. Fishing was good in these parts, thanks to miles of giant brown kelp reaching from the continental shelf bottom that attracted numerous species of the fishes. Cowboy knew that casting a line off that platform was probably forbidden under American Energy policy or some anile government regulation. But he was the project director of this multi-million dollar unconventional energy recovery system, so he felt he could do just about anything he wanted. Besides, Cowboy was never one to follow rules. It was one of the reasons he washed out of the Naval Academy. He loved the ocean, but the military contained much too much rigidity for his free-spirit personality. Cowboy was as rambunctious as one of the mavericks on his thousand-acre Oklahoma ranch. Though untamed himself, he did, however, like to conquer other wild things, such as the regal spike-jawed fish he roped in the Gulf Stream. It took nearly an hour, but the nine-foot marlin was finally hauled onto the platform, and the gloating photography session continued for another twenty minutes. Cowboy would have another taxidermy trophy to add to his wall in the den of his rural Oklahoma ranch, which already included the heads and hides from an elk from Manitoba, a crocodile from Venezuela, and a stuffed python from Nigeria. Every locale where Cowboy oversaw an oil or natural gas operation, he collected a prize from the animal kingdom as a memento.

"Must be a 200-pounder, Cowboy," one of his admirers said.

"Just a minnow—throw him back," he replied.

During the backslapping and braggadocio smiles during the picture taking, Cowboy hardly noticed the helicopter that touched down on the helipad of the mobile offshore platform. The whirlybirds were constantly landing and taking off the landing pad that was suspended above deck. The surface structure of the platform was supported by fifteen steel girders connected to a submersible ballast that extended deep below the ocean surface. More than 550 American Energy, Southeast Exploration, and U.S. Department of Energy employees, along with dozens of contract research scientists, geologists, oceanographers, and others in the energy métier were housed on the platform, most returning to the mainland once every two weeks in constant rotation. Sometimes, the vessel's helipad seemed as busy as an airport of a small American city. This latest Bell Aerospace chopper only contained one passenger. The pilot and another crewmember exited the vehicle's cabin and then assisted a pasty-faced and rubber-legged VIP onto the surface of the helipad. The two smiling crewmembers, both former Apache helicopter pilots in the first Gulf War, appeared more than happy to help their guest.

As the passenger awkwardly removed a white flight helmet, Cowboy could tell why. A slender and seemingly attractive woman's long and curly rusty-colored hair blew horizontal from the gusts generated by the chopper's spinning propellers and the steady Atlantic wind. There were plenty of females on the mammoth offshore platform, but Cowboy Rhodan always kept an eye out for fresh legs.

"Woooo, doggie," Cowboy said, sounding like Jed Clampett of the *Beverly Hillbillies*. He winked at one of his many assistants who were helping to suspend Cowboy's huge catch in the air. "Look at the hindquarters from headquarters."

"I think it's that PR lawyer sent by Raven," said Bobby Brogan, a geochemistry manager who was on Cowboy's lead research team. "She's here to do some advance work for the president's visit, remember?"

"Counselor, huh?" Cowboy said. "Well, let's get a look at her legal briefs—what do you think—cotton or satin?"

"Cowboy," Brogan said. "You're a pig."

"Hey, just trying to get under the surface of things. That's what we drillers do."

When Cowboy strode over and greeted the platform's newest visitor, the passenger was as woozy as a losing prizefighter wobbling with a standing eight-count. Dressed in a green uniform with a patch sporting American Energy's new green, blue, and yellow logo on the sleeve, she was still supported by the courteous pilots who transported her from Norfolk, Virginia. She tried to cover her eyes from the blinding sun bouncing off the ocean's endless horizon. Her unkempt, ferruginous strands of hair stuck out in all directions, as if conducting static electricity. Cowboy noted the slender nose, emerald green eyes, and Katherine-Hepburn-high cheekbones. She was a looker, no question about it. Cowboy flashed his most sensuous grin and adjusted his Stetson. *They don't make company men like they use to—thank God.*

"Bruce Rhodan," the platform's director said, holding out a muscular hand in a gentlemanly fashion. "Folks call me Cowboy."

The new arrival reached her white-knuckled hand outward, but it seemed like she was floundering for a life preserver in a monsoon.

"Danielle O'Day, American Energy," the woman said, punch drunk. She shifted on her feet. Her skin was as white as porcelain and her eyes refused to focus on him. Cowboy finally grasped her cold fingers and shook them gently. A silver amulet above the brim of Cowboy's Stetson caught the dazzling mid-day sun, flaring its reflection into the woman's eyes like a laser. Beyond the welcoming reception, the blue marlin hung upside down off a piece of scaffolding on the edge of the platform that had streamers and gonfalons flapping wildly in the ocean breeze. The rounded spear protruding from its snout, which it used to club the fish it fed on, undulated back and forth like a grandfather clock's pendulum. The wet bluish skin reflected a hypnotizing gleam from the sun.

"Is that a … fish?" the newcomer said, her head weaving like a bobble-head doll in the back window of a moving car.

"Blue marlin," Cowboy said, pride beaming from his lighthouse-bright smile. "Just brought her in."

"Don't you need a license for that or something?"

Cowboy raised one eyebrow. "Did Jesus need a license before he became a fisher of men?" Cowboy responded.

The red-haired woman stared dumbfounded, her face vacant of expression. She stumbled on her short, rubber-soled pumps as if tripping on a curb, and then fell forward right into Cowboy's waiting arms—his second big catch of the day.

"Boy, when it rains, it pours," Cowboy said to Brogan and the pilots, grinning at his latest trophy. Then, in the moment she regained consciousness, the stricken woman vomited all over his chest.

CHAPTER 16

▼

Akmed was a child again. He and his pretty younger sisters played a game of tag, burning the fuel that seemed inexhaustible in youth. His mother and father, both pudgy and well-fed farmers, smiled from the vineyard, and then called to them to halt the horseplay and come work. Always fleet of foot, he ran and ran, the giggling girls in pursuit.

In the blink of a dream's frame, he was an adult, sitting in a Gaza café, listening to children playing outside. Two adolescent girls darted through the establishment, evading someone who was playfully chasing them. A slender boy followed, laughing and calling after his playmates. Their eyes met. Akmed motioned the young boy to approach his table. No, he was not just any boy. Slim, tall, though not mature. It was a body-double of twelve-year-old Akmed, wearing a bulky, goatskin jacket. Chestnut eyes, hair as black as oil, olive skin not yet leathered by the sun. The boy grinned, the white of his teeth contrasting to his dark skin like a white shirt beneath a black tuxedo. Akmed smiled back. The boy reached his arms up to his own head, grasping both of his ears. With sudden rage, the boy ripped his head off from its fleshy perch and tossed it in Akmed's lap, veins and blood trailing out of the severed neck like spaghetti in marinara sauce.

Akmed's eyes flung open and he gasped. His heart pounded like that of a terrified rabbit. His short inexplicable catnaps projected nightmares so vivid, he sometimes could not tell when he was awake. The former Palestinian native, now a full-fledged citizen of the United Kingdom, rubbed the black circles under his eyes, the only stains on his otherwise flawless face. The warm zephyr Mediterranean breeze brushed against his face like the temperate caress of a kind woman.

Stubble on his sun-reddened face made his cheeks itchy. He ran his fingers through his jet-black hair that had grown too long once again. He must get it trimmed. Strands of gray were noticeable every time the forty-six-year-old man looked into the mirror.

He never thought he would live to see his hair turn white, like the elders from his hometown of Gaza City. But life is full of twists and turns, including unexpected gifts from God. About a mile off the western coast of the Gaza Strip, four jackup natural gas drilling spars perched on the blue water's horizon like giant mosquitoes on a distant pond. That is what each platform was, after all, a mammoth predator dipteran sinking its metal proboscis into the sea to suck out the lifeblood of the world—fossil fuels. Instead of drawing life-giving blood out of an unwitting host, the derricks were drawing clean-burning natural gas from the willing veins of Mother Earth underneath the Mediterranean Sea. The natural gas rig's legs protruded out of the water like a table, centered on an area known as Gaza Marine off the coast of New Palestine. A 100-foot-high steel derrick protruded out of the drilling platforms like upright Eiffel-Tower-shaped skeletons, holding the heavy drilling string of metal pipe and drilling tools that bored into the sea floor. More than a trillion-and-a-half cubic feet of natural gas lay beneath the floor of the Holy Sea. And the bounty of these reserves was not going into the pockets of the rich capitalists in the West, but rather, to the newly created and deserving state of Palestine. The Palestinian government owned offshore drilling rights on a triangular 10,000-acre tract of water going three miles from the shores of the Gaza Strip. The discovery of natural gas underneath the sea floor was one of the jewels that would provide jobs, energy, and wealth to the poor people of the new country. Yasser Arafat himself called the prospect of natural gas a "gift from God" to Palestine, when he lit a flare off the Gaza Strip field in 2000. *What did the Greeks call natural gas that seeped out of the surface of the ground in ancient times?* Akmed wondered. *Yes, Apollo's breath. God's breath.*

It took several years of haggling with the Israelis, who bought the gas to power their electric-plant turbines to replace less efficient and more costly coal and oil plants, and endless negotiations with the British and American gas companies, which possessed the license to drill and capitalistic motivation to proceed. But finally, the ancient bequest from God was ready to produce nearly $100 million a year from the drilling project, almost half the Palestinian Authority's annual revenues before their official statehood. Akmed's British firm owed him a lot for many years of service of finding oil and gas supplies on behalf of Her Majesty, the Queen, and now the fruit of his efforts were coming home. The Americans owed him as well. But he also performed a great patriotic service to his native land, even if he had not lived there since he was a teenager. Instead of a wanted man, an expatriate on the lam always suspecting an Israeli assassin on his trail ready to gun him down in the street or slip radioactive poison into his coffee, he was now a noted geophysicist, who taught petroleum exploration at Cambridge University. He was an internationally known expert who played a significant role in finding the gas deposits below the Mediterranean Sea. All his hard intellectual work was paying off. Millions of cubic feet of natural gas were now flowing from the offshore wells through underwater pipelines to Palestine, fueling new industry, cooking food, powering electric plants, propelling automobiles … and saving lives. In addition, the ethereal commodity was exported to Egypt and Israel, and in return, hard currency flowed to Palestine. This natural gas was Palestine's key resource replacing its former primary export—despair. Finally, foreign investment was coming to the West Bank and Gaza. Even the Israelis were paying top dollar to reconstruct the long-beleaguered nation, after Israel was assured that the profits would not go to fund terrorist groups. Natural gas demand in Israel was expected to triple by 2025 as oil- and coal-fired stations would be converted to natural gas turbines. The democratic Jewish government was initially worried about dependence on Palestinian energy imports, but the recent creation of the Palestinian state planted hopes of peace based upon trade of energy. The Israelis needed the energy; the Palestinians needed the money to build a stable nation.

Akmed sipped the strong Arabic coffee from a tiny cup served to him at the open-air café. He never warmed up to English tea, but he toyed with his lunch, a fork in his left hand and knife in his right in the British way. Life in Palestine changed drastically since he had left. So much happened. Invasion and twenty years of occupation led to the *intifadah*—the "shaking off" of the Jews. Talks and tanks; revolution and repression. Hundreds of men, women, and children killed, others injured by Israeli tear gas, and then rubber and plastic bullets trying to quell Palestinian nationalism while keeping the death toll down to keep the UN off its back. Many young men and women, much like himself, resorted to killing themselves and as many Israelis as possible. Still, nothing was resolved. But there was finally a tenable, if uneasy, truce with the Israelis, and his people had a land of their own. Palestinian opposition groups clashed for a time, but the internecine struggles eventually faded. Though not a perfect situation, he saw joy on the faces of children playing nearby—smiles he never wore when he walked these same streets.

Akmed was home again. But was it home? He left Gaza in the late 'seventies and lived ever since like a globetrotting Bedouin. He spent more time on ocean drilling rigs than on land in a gypsy lifestyle of performing a little geophysical magic for the local populace and then disappearing. He only returned to his homeland for a few days since. Could he come home again?

Akmed had been on such a long journey. He entered the University of Manchester in 1981 on a scholarship funded by an Arab charity financed by petrodollars. His affinity to science and math propelled him through the school with honors, though he still struggled with the new language. He chose petroleum engineering as a field of study. There were not many lucrative jobs for Arabs in London—only disgraceful slave-like employment. Before he qualified for entrance to the university, he learned that there were great paying jobs on drilling rigs in the North Sea, as the British discovered large reservoirs of oil and gas that would help wean themselves from imports from the Middle East and generate currency in a period of high oil prices. An impecunious immigrant, Akmed needed work—especially if he wanted to help pay his way through university. But there was money to be made, if you were willing to risk your health and safety as a roughneck. Roughnecks were lower-level oil and gas field workers who labored on grimy, hot drilling platforms, hauling huge and heavy drilling bits and screwing metal pipe together. They didn't need fancy degrees for the job, but they could earn up to 25,000-40,000 pound sterling a year. They usually worked twelve-hour days for a week straight and then returned to the mainland for seven days off.

The tall and sinewy Akmed was built for the tough work and he used his time off wisely. He studied English, western culture, as well as petroleum engineering. *Know your enemy*, he was once told. And offshore, he felt at home for he always loved the sea, and he was fascinated by the science of oil and gas exploration. Akmed also proved his courage out on the derrick, where workers were occasionally killed in accidents in the precarious business. He once dove into the bone-chilling sea off the shore of Norway to rescue a fellow worker who fell off the rig after a sudden underwater landslide dislodged the platform from its moorings. But it was his brains, not his brawn, which helped him climb the ladder. Over time, he received a doctorate in geophysics. He searched for oil in Britain, Indonesia, the Caribbean, and even in the Gulf of Mexico. After pioneering several significant finds, Akmed Abram was a widely recognized name in the international energy industry. He became a British citizen. He never returned to the Middle East until recently, when he was selected as the chief geophysicist working in a UN-organized international effort to help the new state of Palestine mine the energy diamonds below the salty waters off the coast of the Holy Land.

Could Akmed become a free Palestinian after all these years? Would he still be hunted from his connections with Fatah if he sought repatriation? His family members remained Gazans. He saw them only briefly during this holy month of Ramadan, during which families are urged to spend time together. He never imagined living anywhere else many years ago. He once hated the Brits and Americans, and especially their lackeys, the Israelis. But now, he dressed in western attire—khaki slacks and an open-collar denim shirt. Years had passed since his aborted suicide-bombing attempt. He was no longer primarily concerned with politics, though he naturally supported the Palestinian cause. He maintained his faith, completing his *zakat*, the giving of alms, by donating much of his earned money to charities that helped the oppressed natives in his land. He even contributed heavily to a scientific scholarship at Bir Zeit, the oldest and most prestigious Palestinian university, established in 1924 as a small private modern and secular school thirteen miles north of Jerusalem. Most of all, Akmed submerged himself in science—maybe that is what Allah wanted him to do. He was not a soldier, anymore. Perhaps he never was.

Akmed sat at a table alone in the café, which was located on the same spot where he used to bus tables in his youth. It was then a decrepit, squalid shack on a cement slab, a haven for weary fisherman. Now it was now a modern seaside restaurant that featured an impressive vista of the open waters. The only other patron of the eatery was a weathered elderly man, who cuddled a ceramic cup half the size of an egg filled with strong coffee—the kind the Westerners said *put lead in your pencil.*

"*Alam Alaikum*, Akmed," a voice broke his meditation, jolting him. "Allah be with you." The Arabic-speaking voice proclaiming "Peace be upon you" was the gravelly tone of an old man.

Akmed was startled by the intrusion. He was relieved his awful nightmare was over and there was no decapitated boy in front of him or bloody head in his lap. But no one knew he was there, not even his Palestinian hosts from the Arafat Energy Company, the state-owned natural gas firm of Palestine. Before Akmed could turn to face the owner of the voice, a wrinkled arthritic hand gripped his shoulder. Suddenly sitting down next to him was a gray, long-bearded man, his head covered with a green tarboosh. A white thobe fell from his shoulders to his dust-laden sandals. Akmed's uninvited guest wore thick, black eyeglasses that cloaked most of his wizened face.

Akmed did not stand to greet the hoary-bearded man. He was still flabbergasted that someone knew his name or knew that he was here.

"It has been a long time, Akmed, welcome home," said the old man.

He must be some type of Hakim—a learned person or a judge, Akmed thought. He looked regal in a way, a cleric, a man of God.

"I am very sorry," Akmed responded in his native tongue. "I am not sure I have had the pleasure of meeting you."

"Has it been that long, Akmed?" the stranger said. He smiled. Only a few teeth remained in the old man's mouth, like withered corn stalks in a harvested field.

Do I know this man? Akmed searched his memory. *Was he one of my teachers in school? A family relative I did not recognize in his old age? How did he know I was here?*

"We are so fortunate to have you back to serve Allah and your country," the aged man said. He swatted a flying insect that rested on the swollen knuckles of his liver-spotted right hand. "What's the matter, Akmed, do you no longer recognize the man who saved your life?"

CHAPTER 17

▼

Danielle awoke in the cramped bunk of the energy platform's windowless sickbay four hours after fainting and puking on deck. Her head throbbed and her mind remained murky. She ingested seasickness pills before the helicopter flight but they obviously did not help much. Though her vision was a bit cloudy, at least her surroundings were not spinning anymore. She never liked amusement park rides much—especially the *Scrambler* her newlywed husband convinced her to ride on their honeymoon—it made her as green as her emerald eyes.

Danielle stretched out on the narrow cot in the cavern-like room. The metal walls and doorways were painted a government-issue dull battleship gray, and the inside of the platform appeared to have the cozy charm of a World War II-era German U-boat. Since the National Oceanic and Atmospheric Administration and the Department of Energy paid most of the freight for the venture, this was not surprising. A total of six cots lined the small room. Nearby, a male nurse attended to another man who looked like he had some type of head injury.

"Welcome to the *China Maiden*," an echoing voice boomed. A large foot-ball-player-sized man barged into the room like he was crashing a party. He was dressed like some western sheriff, Danielle thought. Her eyes rose from his leather boots, up to dusty-brown pants, open-collar cream-colored shirt, tan vest, and western-style hat. Then she remembered. He was the broad-shouldered man she met on the helipad—the loudmouth with the Stetson on his head. Apparently, he never took it off, even indoors. His curly blond hair flowed downward from the back of the hat. He reminded her of paintings of Indian-fighting General Armstrong Custer.

"I feel like I have a hangover," Danielle said. She ran her hand through her frizzy, reddish hair. "My God," she said, strictly to herself, imagining what her hairstyle looked like.

"You'll get your sea legs in a few hours," the intruder said. "Name's Cowboy as you may recall."

"I've been sent here to review the operations in preparation—"

"I know why you're here. Company man—I mean, lady—checkin' up on us bumpkins in advance of the president's visit to make sure that we have swabbed the deck, secured the yardarms, and are not violating any American Energy corporate policy, like fishing for blue marlin in federally protected waters or some such sin."

The pendulous fish came back into Danielle's mind. If there was anything remaining from her crab-cake lunch she ingested before the helicopter ride, it would have crawled sideways up her throat.

"I got sick," she said. "I didn't get you, did I?"

"As good as a drunken old salt after an all-night binge."

"Sorry."

"No problem. I did it myself once on a petroleum minister in Indonesia. One of their rickety floating offshore rigs we were bidding on wasn't anchored well and spun like a turd in a flushed toilet. Needless to say, we didn't get the contract."

"I've never been on the ocean before, or on a helicopter for that matter," she said. "I was a bit dizzy from the ride, and the sight of the ocean was a bit disorienting."

"You just have a slice of vertigo, aggravated by helpings of acrophobia and thalassophobia."

"What?

"You're dizzy because you probably fear heights and the vast plain of the ocean. It's very common."

"I'm not afraid," she said, indignant.

"Of course not—you just need to get acclimated to the territory. When you're up to it, we'll take you on a little tour."

Danielle did not like this man's condescending tone. The cowboy-hat-wearing clod was full of himself. She had enough of arrogant men in the legal offices of American Energy. She was determined to stand on her own two feet. It didn't take Danielle long. She was all business, and would not fail in this PR assignment, however unorthodox. Besides, she wanted to get out of this oil barrel they called the sickbay. In the back of her mind, Danielle was puzzled why she was sent to the offshore operation because she knew little about it. In four days, the president of the United States, along with a gaggle of inquisitive news reporters, curious camerapersons, and other nosy VIPs, would also be on board. Raven told her that because of her vacuous knowledge of the operation, she would pose pertinent questions that curious guests and news reporters may ask. Danielle was forever asking questions—she was good at that. She was told that the platform director would show her the ropes. Everything had to look professional, clean as a newly changed baby's bottom, and most important, leave no peculiar observations unanswered. The costly offshore platform would be under the media's microscope, and it had to look good since the government tossed a bundle of taxpayer dollars into it. American Energy doled out its share as well and hoped to eventually pass the costs along to its millions of customers.

She knew little about the director of *Project Blue Sky*, only that he was a colorful character who, according to her boss, was on a first-name basis with the president of the United States. He was a college buddy or something. And he was filthy rich. She knew his name from industry journals. Apparently, "Cowboy" Rhodan knew more about offshore oil and natural gas drilling in all corners of the world than anyone at American Energy, or in fact, the entire country. His upstart drilling corporation tapped several huge new oil and gas pools around the world, including some prolific elephant fields previously thought exhausted. That, in itself, peaked her curiosity. Why is this oil-drilling expert here? What did American Energy's kelp-to-gas research project have to do with drilling? As promoted in image commercials that portrayed her firm as a progressive "energy" company, rather than a gas or electric utility, this was only one in the cornucopia of government-sponsored alternative-fuel technology demonstration projects in which American Energy took the lead. *Why was this project more significant than the others?*

"I'm up to it," Danielle told Cowboy, dropping her feet to the floor, but bracing her weight on the bunk.

"Well, first, it might help to let me know what you already know of the project," he asked.

"Well, of course, *Project Blue Sky* is the biomass recovery system to recover methane naturally produced from kelp. That's what this is all about, isn't it?"

"Well, there are others."

"Others?"

"Sure, there are three other demonstration electric-generation projects employed here."

"What are they?"

"First," Cowboy began, placing one of his snakeskin western boots on the end of her cot, "partly powering all electricity on the platform, including the juice for our gas compressors, is the offshore wind farm."

"Of course, I almost forgot," Danielle said, feeling stupid. Her helicopter flew over it. American Energy's wind farm in the Atlantic Ocean, constructed with the aid of $5 million in federal tax credits, featured hundreds of towers as large as thirty-story buildings.

"Seagull blenders," Cowboy said.

"What?"

"The 125-foot revolving blades. I used to call them seagull blenders."

Danielle remembered. It was a controversial project. Various conservation groups opposed the wind farm because the visual impact from the coast was less than esthetic and they claimed generators harmed aquatic wildlife.

"But they made improvements," he said. "Now they are made from a fiber-glass composite and spin in a higher arc, moving more slowly than earlier models, allowing the sea pigeons to take evasive action—what a shame."

"What else?"

"There is also an experimental ocean wave electrical generator powered by the underwater currents of the Gulf Stream. And for back-up juice, we employ natural gas-powered hydrogen fuel cells."

"Oh, it's a much bigger operation than I thought."

"Bigger than the Oklahoma sky."

Why was this guy here? Danielle wondered. Surely, the company had contracts with renewable energy experts whose experience wasn't dominated with boring holes in the ocean floor throughout the world. *What else haven't I been told?*

"I have a report due tomorrow, I have to look around," Danielle said, pushing from the bunk, and tentatively testing her balance. It didn't last long, as she gripped the side of the medical cot once she realized her equilibrium was not what she thought it was.

"Are you sure you are okay to walk?" Cowboy asked.

"I'm fine."

"Oakie, doakie," Cowboy said.

Danielle stepped confidently forward and then collapsed on the floor.

CHAPTER 18

▼

Akmed squinted. *How would this help?* His vision was perfect, yet this man was a mystery to him. Or did he recognize, but did not admit, who he saw behind the bloodshot gray eyes of the elderly Palestinian. *Is it?* Yes, how stupid he was. It was his Fatah handler, Omar, who shepherded him out of Tel Aviv when the Israeli police and military were scouring for him after the attempted bombing in 1979. He must be eighty-years-old.

"Omar?" Akmed said. Akmed never knew any other family name of his terrorist mentor. "It has been many years. Please forgive me."

The man he knew as Omar grinned, the sun reflecting off a gold tooth in his sparse smile. He rubbed a bloated blemish partially hidden by his kinky beard.

"Allah has returned you to us to serve *al-Rahman.* God the merciful is great," Omar said. He spoke like a spiritual leader, a Sheikh. "Your country and your brothers are grateful."

"Palestine is a legitimate country now!" Akmed said, in a burst of nationalistic pride. "Recognized by the United Nations. All of your struggles are over."

Why did I say "your"? Akmed thought.

"Over?" Omar said, taken aback. "Our struggle is never over until the Jews are driven from our land, and are sent to *Jahannam.*"

Hell? Akmed thought. *The war with Israel seemed like Jahannam on Earth.* Akmed made a mistake. Though Palestine recently gained its independence as a sovereign nation with its own land, and the Israeli occupation of the West Bank and Gaza ended with a peace treaty agreed to by politicians on both sides and monitored by international peace keepers, he foolishly thought that there would finally be peace in the Holy Land that was host to the world's three great religions, Islam, Judaism, and Christianity—all sons and daughters of Abraham. He thought that the death and destruction of the past half-century may be over. God answered their prayers. These pogroms were over, and economic prosperity was around the corner. He was acting silly. The first thing the Palestinians did when they reclaimed Gaza was burn down the synagogues the Jews built. Akmed thought like a naïve consensus-building, peace-making non-Palestinian. He was thinking like a … *Westerner*.

"After so many years, it is your time to help," Omar said. "It looks like you have been quite successful in the West. You are a man of influence. Now it is time to put your fine work to good use for Allah. All of us of *Harakat al-Muqawama al-Islamiyya* have prayed for you."

Akmed understood the name he mentioned as the Arabic organization known by its more familiar acronym "*Hamas*—meaning "zeal"—that rejected any compromise with Israel over disputed land, and had a long history of conducting horrific terrorism against the Jewish state. Hamas supplanted Arafat's historical Fatah movement as the most popular political force among the plagued people, including middle-class Palestinians, resisting the years of Israeli occupation. And Hamas now received the political endorsement of the people as they had rejected the PLO and corrupt Fatah at the ballot box. Hamas was one of the main terrorist organizations behind most of the suicide bombings in Israel in recent years, but had also negotiated with Israel to consolidate its power. But the radical nationalistic movement politicized Islam and would stop at nothing to impose its version of Muslim beliefs. Along with the Shiite-dominated *Hezbollah*, the Party of God, which led an uprising in Lebanon to create an Iranian-style Islamic State, the adamant military groups were not going to totally stand down though peace was achieved. Despite the creation of the partial-Palestinian state in Gaza and the West Bank, Hamas remained committed to the destruction of Israel and the creation of an Islamic state of historical Palestine. Omar, a good politician, had ridden the tide from Fatah to Hamas. He revealed that he was now a general of *Izzedine al Qassam*, the militant wing of Hamas, along with those leaders in the Al Aqsa Martyrs Brigades. *He lived a long time to watch many others die for Palestine*, Akmed thought.

"What are you talking about?" Akmed said. "I am a scientist. I have helped Palestine. My work helped discover God's buried gift of natural gas for the nation. It will help Palestine become the jewel of the Middle East."

"A jewel that will be stolen by the Jews, like everything else."

"What do you want from me?" Akmed was not the ignorant, hate-filled teenager that Omar and his ilk desensitized to violence and persuaded to put on a jacket full of TNT, ball bearings, and sharp metal scraps. But Akmed was a patriot. He helped his people find a path to wealth. What more could they want?

"The spirits of the righteous martyrs call to you from beneath the hallowed soil of our great land. Their bloodshed nourished our hearts so that our homeland can live. As you know, there is an Islamic revolution sweeping the region. Iraq, Iran, Kuwait, Saudi Arabia, Afghanistan, Indonesia, and several Islamic countries in Africa are throwing the Western puppets out of their lands. Allah has swept his mighty hand from *dar al-Islam* to *dar al-harb*. All leaders of our faith have all been friends of the Palestinian people. They expect us to act, to defeat the godless West, and as commanded by Mohammed, get back our land and toss the Jews into the sea once and for all."

Once a political militant, always a political militant, Akmed thought. He too once separated the world into two camps—the land of Islam (*dar al-Islam*) and the lands of struggle (*dar al-harb*), the West's land of decadence, luxury, and godlessness in which unbelievers predominate. Though tensions remained high between the infidels and the believers, in his travels Akmed did not find the discrimination and ostracism of the Islamic world that was claimed by the rabble-rousers in the Islamic states. He changed so much in the West, though he still kept his faith, and his heart was with his homeland. That was, after all, why he was here. But this bellicose flash could destroy all of this work across the Middle East. The oil and gas rigs in the Mediterranean were full of expertise from the United States and Britain. Didn't the Islamic mullahs know that the West was not going away—oil and gas embargo or no oil and gas embargo? The West and the Arab world could live in peace, if they just gave it a chance, as that long-haired Englishman sang long ago before being gunned down on an American city street.

"You are now internationally known as a geophysicist?" said Omar. "A man who finds fire in rocks?"

"It is my calling from God." *Whose God? The same name of Allah this man evokes every other sentence?*

"You work for this American company, Southeast Exploration?" Omar said.

"I do not work for them. I am an *independent* scientist."

"But you assisted in a project to help America become more energy independent?"

Akmed was silent. Yes, he did extensive research for the Americans. He agreed to work on the mission in exchange for the American and British technical help and financing with the Palestinian natural gas drilling venture. He possessed the expertise, but the Palestinians were short on capital and modern drilling equipment. But no one could possibly know about the American project he was involved in. He was invited to participate by a personal friend who happened to be an American. However, the viability of the project was an American government secret—even he did not know all the details of the operation. No one could know. Or, at least, they shouldn't.

"What are you asking of me?" Akmed said, blankly.

"We are asking that you serve Allah, by defeating the infidels in their quest."

"I am only one man. America is an enormously powerful country. This oil embargo will backfire like it did many years ago. Long embargoes and price increases will only cause the West's money to stop flowing into our land. Oil is not an effective weapon."

"Oil has *always* been a weapon, Akmed," Omar said, breaking out into his toothless grin again.

Yes it was, Akmed knew. In the Middle Ages, when the Crusaders from Europe attacked a city occupied by whom they called Saracens, or the children of Islam, the Arabic peoples' ingenious weapon of defense was fire, an antique version of napalm. The defenders of Jerusalem tossed glass bombs containing naphtha, a derivative of petroleum, soaking the bellicose attacking knights. Then, a burning tree was hurled into their midst, igniting the infidel warriors, burning them alive. Had nothing changed in 800 years?

"We need some of that Western investment," Akmed argued. "Do you not remember when the Saudi OPEC minister said, 'if we force Western countries to invest heavily in finding alternative sources of energy, they will.'"

Akmed's table guest's eyes narrowed. "The Saudi's Western lackey is dead. The immoral House of Saud has fallen. And we do not want the Satan's money from the West. We want its destruction. You sound like the corrupt *Fatah*. Allah spared you many years ago in that market in Tel Aviv, I am sure, for this opportunity now to fulfill His mission. Do you not remember the scholarship that paid your way through university? Did you not know where those funds came from?"

Akmed was confused. He had left this world of war and terror many years ago. He thought he was fulfilling God's quest for him by becoming the best scientist he could be and returning to his homeland to aid in its future prosperity. This was the way to grow in faith and spread the true God's word around the world. But maybe he was wrong. His scholarship? It was intended for Arab immigrants funded by well-to-do Saudis. Did his fellow terrorists bankroll him so they could call in their chits in the future? How is he able to know the will of God? Maybe he did not change. He was ready to die nearly thirty years before, why would he be reluctant now? No, he was ready for death if need be. He had lived an upright life. He even completed his *hajj* to Mecca after teaching at a geophysics conference in Saudi Arabia the year before the Great Revolution that overthrew the long-standing kingdom and established a theocracy. He touched and kissed the sacred Black Stone in the courtyard of the most holy Great Mosque *Kabba* in Mecca, believed by his faith to have been built by Abraham and Ishmael. But after all the suicide missions employed by the Islamic world and the years of *intifadah*, the Jews remained in Israel, the United States grew in power, and the Arab world was still largely ill-educated and deprived. The infidels could wipe out every living soul in the Middle East in a half hour with their nuclear weapons if pushed to the brink. He would give his life to God, but not to a quixotic crusade that had little effect. He was no longer a clueless adolescent, a bilious young man who vowed to seek revenge for his parents' unjust deaths. Akmed demanded proof that there was God's purpose in the strategy.

"I am only a scientist," Akmed repeated. "What can *I* do to stop the Americans in their quest? They are moving away from an oil economy because of the threats of the Arab world. They have many sources of energy—nuclear, wind, ethanol, coal—new supplies are coming in all the time."

"Yes," the old terrorist master said. "They are attempting to bring in more liquid natural gas on ships from several countries to help fuel their evils."

"And what can you do to stop them? South America and Africa are willing to sell to them if we are not."

"You will see very shortly. The Americans will be begging for mercy after our jihad reaches their shores—once again."

Akmed was concerned. What did this have to do with Palestine? He was not a lover of the American government per se, but after nearly three decades in the West, he had many British *and* American friends. He thought the Islamic revolutions simply wanted the materialistic culture and influence out of their countries. Though not as fanatical as he used to be, he observed the decadent West up close. He could understand the Muslim zealots resisting American mores in their own nations. But what more were they planning?

Akmed's head dropped. "Again, what do you want from *me*?"

"Your research, I am told, was integral to the American project. We only ask that you—what is the American expression? Ah yes, *throw a monkey wrench into it.*"

Akmed did not understand how this served Allah. And how did they know about the secret project? He could back away from the Americans—work exclusively on the Palestinian gas platforms. He gave them the best of his knowledge of geophysics to find what they were looking for. He did not even have to go back.

This is where he should be. But he did not want to become involved in the battle beyond liberation of Palestine. He was tired of seeing the death of his people, or any people for that matter. He stared into the cold, gray eyes of one of the deans of terror.

"And if I decline?" he said audaciously.

From beneath his thobe, Omar pulled out a handful of photographs and placed them on the café table. "Your sisters are still very, very beautiful—with many children. Surely you want to see them grow up in a new Palestine—free from the Jews and the satanic influences of the West." The man beamed again with his virtual toothless grin. His few crooked teeth looked like tilting gravestones in a neglected cemetery.

Why bring his sisters into this? There were their photographs, smiling and attractive. And their handsome children. They thought for years that Akmed was dead. *Is this old fool trying to play upon my heartstrings? Or is he ... threatening me? Yes, he is using my sisters and their children as hostages. What kind of a man of God is this who would threaten his brother and his family?*

"Surely, you see that our request is a noble one," Omar said. He licked his lips to remove the dryness and salt from the warm sea breeze. "How you accomplish your mission is entirely up to you, though we have many suggestions. We can meet further with the revolutionary council to discuss them."

Akmed stared out toward the sea. *Was this another bad dream?* So much changed in his life because of the busy Western orientation he adopted. Always in a hurry to accomplish a new goal, conquer a new challenge. Yet, in Palestine, the calendar and clock did not move forward. Their goal had not changed. He pledged his life to his nation, his brethren, and his God. First and foremost, he was a Palestinian. How could he refuse? He lowered his eyes in deference.

"Allah, be praised for you Akmed," Omar said. "You may save our nation from the scourge of the Jews and their nefarious partners in crime. Your name will forever be blessed. Almighty God has spoken the truth."

From a distant towered minaret at a mosque in Gaza City, a muezzin summoned for the faithful to worship for afternoon prayers. Both Akmed and Omar walked from the restaurant carrying their prayer rugs. Akmed, using a GPS satellite phone's compass feature, oriented himself southwest toward the Holy City of Mecca and knelt, his hands stretching over the soil of the new free nation of Palestine.

Akmed prayed. He did not consider himself a fatalist. But he asked what Allah wanted of him. *Insh-Allah*, he prayed. *If God wills.*

CHAPTER 19

▼

Cowboy lifted Danielle O'Day off the ground for the second time in one morning and laid her down on the sickbay cot as gently as setting a newborn lamb on a pile of hay.

"I've done this before," Cowboy said to an attending male nurse, "but the lady is usually semi-conscious."

Cowboy found her attractive enough. That egg-shaped face set on a strong square chin, delicate high cheekbones, alluring green eyes—when they were open—and moist, though pouting lips. He felt her muscular, but feminine frame underneath the drab green tunic as he picked her off the floor. *This girl must spend half her life in the gym*, he thought. The persnickety attorney might be athletic, but she was not a seaman. At the moment, the several-million-ton structure was not anchored into the sea floor like many other offshore drilling platforms. Instead, it floated like the largest of aircraft carriers.

"Takes a while for the land lovers to adjust," Cowboy said absently.

O'Day came to in short order with a quick groan as the nurse put a cool, wet cloth to her forehead.

Cowboy flashed his best charming smile. "Maybe you should sit here and rest a while, young lady."

"My *name* is Danielle O'Day," she said, curtly.

"Certainly, Ms. O'Day," Cowboy said. *Oh, she was going to be one of those! Miss Prissy.* He wanted to ask if her hair was naturally red, or if it glowed like fireplace coals only when she was on the rag. He thought better of it. Though he was the chief operating officer of his own drilling company, Cowboy suffered through all the sexual-harassment lectures and principled-management seminars that

American Energy was famous for—it was mandatory for all major subcontractors. He knew how to play the respect-your-fellow-employee game when called upon. It looked like he had to watch his P's and Q's with this Yankee lawyer. *Why are they so touchy?* he wondered. *It must be those cold Northeast winters chilling their privates.*

Danielle accepted a drink of water offered by the male nurse and presently was again on her feet.

"Let's go," she said.

Cowboy shook his Stetson in a resigned manner, shrugged, and stepped through an oval door hatch of the sickbay, bending his head down so his huge hat just cleared the top of the opening. "Watch your head or you'll end up back here like him," he said, pointing to the man with a new white bandage wrapped around his forehead. The injured worker, conscious, and not appearing to be in serious pain, flashed Cowboy the middle finger of his right hand.

"What happened to him?" Danielle asked.

"He's a roughneck whose neck wasn't as rough as he thought," Cowboy responded. "Got clobbered by a broken piece of gas collection pipe. Broke his hardhat clean in two. By the way," he continued, reaching for an orange industrial hardhat from a shelf outside the sickbay door and handing it to Danielle, "you'll have to wear this while on the *Berg*—company policy."

"The *Berg?*"

"That's what we call this MODU sometimes."

"Modu?"

"Sorry, excuse the jargon," Cowboy said. He grinned warmly at his guest and began striding down a corridor. "Been hanging around drilling types too much. MODU means *Mobile Offshore Drilling Unit*, which is what this platform is. Its official name is the *China Maiden*, but most call it the Berg because it is like an iceberg—only about ten percent of its total structure is above water. And since the surface platform is the size of an Oklahoma cornfield, that'll give you an idea how big the whole vessel is. Once the MODU gets to its designated location, a huge ballast under the structure fills with seawater, and all the hardware is lowered below. It looks like an upside-down pyramid when viewed underwater. But when on the move, the *China Maiden* looks more like a regular ocean-going drilling vessel."

Cowboy picked up his pace, marching down the narrow passageway with his long-legged steps.

"Was it used in China?" she asked, fumbling with the hardhat and trying to keep up with him.

"No, what makes you say that?" His voice echoed down the hollow walkway.

The lady lawyer didn't pursue it; her head must hurt too much. *He shouldn't toy with her*, Cowboy thought. *She's still a little tipsy.* But it was irresistible.

The two followed the low-ceiling hallway through a labyrinth of turns. Danielle finally secured the gaudy orange hard-plastic hat over her unkempt, tangled hair.

"Doesn't this place have any windows?" she asked. She ducked her head as if avoiding imaginary ceiling beams.

"We're below the ocean's surface," Cowboy said. "Not much to see."

She didn't seem pleased to find out she was below sea level. Cowboy read Danielle's distress in her eyes and on her pasty skin.

"Where is your hardhat?" she asked.

"I said wearing a lid was *your* company policy," Cowboy replied, flamboyantly. "I work for Southeast Exploration Company, not American Energy."

"Everyone else I've seen wears one."

"Yeah, that's true, that's an OSHA regulation. And they are wearing those god-awful green uniforms you folks ordered. They look like walking asparagus stalks. But we'll do just about anything to please our customer. But I'm exempt. That is one of the benefits to being the *tool pusher* on this platform—rig manager, I mean. I couldn't trade one of those ghastly caps for my sombrero here—it would ruin my naturally curly hair." He combed a few long blond locks that trailed out of the back of his tan hat with his thick fingers.

Again, she didn't argue.

"As you know," Cowboy continued, "Southeast Exploration is the chief operating subcontractor in this unconventional gas-recovery project. The feds laid out the research dollars, and American Energy financed the pipeline to get the gas onshore to its customers. Southeast Exploration provides the extraction expertise."

The lawyer stopped in her tracks and held a hand up to her lips as if to suppress regurgitation. She either was going to ask him a probing question or she was going to puke again.

"Are you sure you're doing okay?" Cowboy asked.

"I'm fine, I'm fine. I just don't like enclosed spaces."

"You know, claustrophobia is a common reaction inside a vessel like this. It was designed by the lowest bidder and doesn't have many amenities for humans. We all live kind of like moles down here."

Before long, the two entered a more spacious room than the cramped sickbay, furnished with an oblong, modern conference-type table, undecipherable maps on the walls, and a wide computer projection screen. American Energy logo stickers were slapped on the gray metal walls, along with an insignia resembling a drilling rig shaped like a long red isosceles triangle with the name Southeast Exploration Corporation etched along the circumference.

"This is the best place for new guests," Cowboy continued, offering a padded leather chair to Danielle in gentlemanly fashion. "We can give you a virtual tour of the operation from here and you can meet a few folks as well."

"Thank you," she said. She seemed relieved to sit in the chair and be off her wobbly feet. Moments later two white-coated scientist-types entered the room, one male and one female.

"Well, just in time professors," Cowboy said.

"Mr. Rhodan," a petite brunette woman said with formality.

"I told you, you can call me Cowboy," he said.

The woman scientist ignored him. A thick strand of chestnut hair hung in front of her face, seemingly obstructing her vision, but that was a popular hairstyle among younger women. She was the original *Miss Prissy*, Cowboy thought. She was a thirty-three-year-old Ph.D. oceanographer from the University of Maryland now working for the NOAA. She had a triangular jawbone, a thin, hatchet-blade nose and deep brown eyes, the color of "cold alligator shit" Cowboy told others on the platform. The scientist walked with a stiff gait. *She needed a good poke to loosen her up*, Cowboy thought. But he wasn't the person to do it.

"I'm Dr. Samantha Edison, NOAA," the short woman said to Danielle. "My specialty is environmental chemistry, focusing on petroleum hydrocarbons in marine and estuarine systems, and my mission on this project is the monitoring of petroleum-derived contamination in marine environments. I also do marine ecological research, including coral reef and kelp forest ecology, as well as certifying all required environmental impact statements."

"She's like Woodsy Owl," said Cowboy. "She gives a hoot, makes sure we don't pollute, or she'll give us the boot."

"Specifically," the stoic scientist said, "I keep an eye on aquatic environmental fate and effects of petroleum hydrocarbons from offshore operations."

With Edison stood a basketball-player tall, balding African-American man of about fifty, wearing circular John-Lennon-style round glasses. He nodded to the Oklahoman, embarrassed by the ice-like relational snow bank of tension between Cowboy and the female scientist.

"Hi, I'm Cory Roystone," the nerdy-looking man said in a bass timbre. "U.S. Geological Service." He shook Danielle's hand awkwardly, nearly dropping a clipboard full of papers he clutched against his chest. A series of pens were loaded in a pocket protector on the front chest pouch of his white smock. "My area is exploration and production and hydrocarbon fingerprinting in the marine environment."

"Kind of like an oil and gas detective," Cowboy added. He held up his hand to his face as if he were peering through an imaginary magnifying glass.

"Pleasure," Danielle responded, shaking the man's hand, her head still bobbing. *Miss Prissy is going to go down to the mat for a third time*, Cowboy thought.

"Cory Roystone," Cowboy said, laughing. "Bet you can't guess he is a geologist!"

All three looked at Cowboy with blank stares. He frowned. It looked like the scientists and the attorney guest had something in common—no sense of humor.

"Cory?" Cowboy said. "You know, sounds like Quarry? Roy*stone*? You know, like a character with Fred and Barney in Bedrock?" After continued silence, he capitulated. "Oh, forget it."

"Geologist?" Danielle asked. "What does geology have to do with getting gas from seaweed?"

Cowboy raised an eyebrow. *Geez, this broad hasn't been told anything.*

CHAPTER 20

▼

In the congressional hearing room, Glen Bargus could hardly hold his three-martini lunch in his belly. He listened to the canned testimony and gagged at the rehearsed spectacle made-for-television courtroom drama.

"And what happened next?" asked the inquisitive congressman, who already knew the answer to his question.

The elderly woman witness before the congressional committee dabbed her cheeks with a threadbare handkerchief to soak the tears that sprouted from the corners of her eyes, seemingly on a director's command. This was not the first time the old bat testified before government officials. Bargus knew she was a pro.

"They came to my doorstep and demanded that I pay my past due bill, and if I didn't give them the cash right then and there—they had a tool in their hands that would shut my heat off at the street curb," said Olga Stevick, the spokesperson and de facto leader of *Olga's Army*, the nickname of her consumer-advocacy group.

"And what was the outdoor temperature at the time?" asked the chairman of the House Energy and Commerce Committee, Congressman August Doggle. He was an enormous man, who, unlike his fellow congressmen in formal suits, wore a western shirt, string tie, and suede sport jacket. Despite his ample girth, his speaking voice was squeaky as a rusty door.

"It was thirty-five degrees," the old woman said, "but the wind chill made it seem much colder. I don't have much insulation in my home. I've tried to cover my windows with plastic and stuffed old newspapers in some gaps between the walls. But we senior citizens, you understand, have a much more difficult time staying warm."

"Yes, we all know the threat of hypothermia to our nation's older citizens. d what did you do when American Energy demanded payment, or else?"

"I did not have enough money to cover the entire balance. And they said new ılations granted to them by the state allowed the company to shut my heat even in the winter. So, I offered them what I had left from my monthly ___ial Security check—I had to buy some food. I was so hungry—I hadn't eaten in three days."

A collective gasp emitted from the audience in the hearing room. Chairman Doggle tilted his head and offered a sympathetic frown. The television cameras whirred and still cameras clicked like seventeen-year cicadas.

"And when I offered them what I had," she added, "they refused, saying I had to pay at least 500 dollars or they would shut off my heat."

"And did they?"

"They waited a couple of days and came back when I wasn't home—I was at the senior center getting something to eat. And they used their tool. I spent that night in the cold before a neighbor let me borrow an electric space heater. But I caught my death of cold—I was sick for weeks. And then, although my electric bill was just a little behind—American Energy controls the electric as well—they kept sending threatening notices that my electricity would be shut off too."

Stevick glanced back at Bargus, a lawyer-lobbyist for American Energy, sitting in the back of the vast hearing room, his chair tipped against the wall like a gunfighter in a saloon. He was a distinguished-looking, well-tailored man in his forties with a pristine haircut. He rolled his gray eyes. He often crossed paths with American Energy's nemesis in the Capitol Rotunda. They both sought to influence legislation—he with campaign contributions, she with populist clout.

"She should receive an Emmy for her performance," Bargus whispered to another utility lobbyist in attendance, a thirty-one-year-old woman with whom he was having a torrid affair. Both were happily married to non-suspecting spouses when they were away from the seat of government.

Bargus received a six-figure salary for carrying the water for American Energy in congressional halls. He knew Stevick chose to share her well-worn personal narrative of facing service termination for nonpayment of her utility bill for all the drama it offered. And it was working.

"She's a perpetual delinquent customer," Bargus continued. "Her utility service has been turned off and back on for years. She's claimed medical exemptions, changed names on the account to her cat to frustrate collection action, sought court orders ..."

"Many know how to play the system," his female companion said, clandestinely curling her hand in his.

"Now she is using public blackmail to perpetuate her hard luck stories and demonize the big, bad utility out to rape and pillage its customers, including freezing old people to death. She's transformed her small-time gypsy con game into a national reality show."

Sure, Bargus admitted, there were plenty of hard luck stories among senior citizens on fixed incomes. But it was rumored that Stevick drew a huge stipend from her socialist nonprofit group that protested against utility profits and unrestrained capitalism, but no one could prove it. What she did with the money in her eighty-plus years was unknown, but perhaps she only wanted the coast-to-coast fame. After Stevick's crocodile tears evaporated when her claptrap testimony was complete, she would then use her political weight to lean on other members of the energy committee who were not eating out of her hand like Chairman Doggle appeared to be. But Bargus knew the wily congressman was only using her for *his* own machinations.

It was common knowledge among the entire committee that Stevick's act was long on pretense and short on facts, but it helped build the chairman's case, so he allowed it. Doggle was the fossil-fuel industry's number-one enemy in Congress. Doggle attacked the natural gas corporations for profiteering on the price of the product that escalated with the recent energy shortage; he assailed the gargantuan oil companies who exploited the international oil boycott with windfall earnings from their domestic production; and he pilloried the electric and coal industries for creating acid rain and exacerbating the Greenhouse Effect. Although he turned a sympathetic ear to environmentalists who promoted hydrogen fuel cells, as well as wind, solar, and ocean current power to generate electricity, there was only one source of energy that made him warm and fuzzy inside: ethanol—produced by fermented corn, the most plentiful vegetable in his congressional district.

"Big utility companies like American Energy and National Gas and Electric are the catalyst for our nation's rampant inflation and unemployment," Doggle said, glaring at the television cameras over a pair of Ben Franklin rectangular reading glasses perched upon his wide nose like a sparrow squatting on a small rock. "Electric rates have skyrocketed because of higher natural gas prices. People can't afford to heat their homes. Hardworking Americans have been thrown out of their jobs because of companies shutting down because of escalating energy costs. Innocent investors have been swindled. Every energy crisis in last thirty-five years has been followed by an economic recession. The general welfare of our

economy has been assaulted by CEO pigs at the trough with the present administration giving them free reign in the barnyard." He turned his attention to the old
lady sitting at the witness table in front of him. He lowered his voice for dramatic
effect. "I guarantee you, Madam, your testimony will not be in vain. The unrestrained price of natural gas and oil will be harnessed by the power of the U.S.
Congress. The blank check provided to the energy titans back in the 1980s is
about to be torn up."

A hoot of cheers and hearty applause erupted from the citizens' gallery.

"Excuse me, Mr. Chairman," a younger representative from Idaho on the
panel interrupted. Congressman Carl Echo, a freshman who looked like he was
two-months out of law school, received large campaign contributions from
energy companies, even those nowhere near Idaho. "Don't you feel that this *utility* complaint is a state matter, not in the jurisdiction of the federal government?"

The portly chairman sighed, his inhale wheezing audibly over the microphone
like a fat child sitting on a leaking inflatable plastic swimming-pool toy. "Need I
remind the congressman from Idaho that these mega-corporations like American
Energy cross state lines with their wires and pipelines?" Doggle said, glaring over
his spectacles like a surly instructor at an boys' school. "These firms are buying up
independent utilities left and right, eliminating any competition, forming paper
subsidiaries with their iron hand in a velvet glove to hold entire states hostage to
depend on their energy, while polluting the environment all over the country. Do
you think that can be addressed by your state legislature, city council, or zoning
board in Boise?"

Snickers rippled through the hearing room.

"That question cost me about $5,000," Bargus grunted to his paramour, fold-
ing his arms over his immaculate gray suit that smartly matched his eye color. He
attended the Idaho congressman's fundraiser breakfast the week before. "Great
investment, huh?"

"American Energy, for example," Doggle continued in his shrill tone, his
impromptu oration aimed to a national audience, "monopolizes gas and electric
service through the middle-Atlantic states and New England. First they shut off
an elderly widow's gas, next threaten to cut her electricity, and now she has
nowhere else to turn. What's next? The only benefit these greedy corporations
bring is by filling campaign fund coffers of weak-kneed politicians that do their
dirty work."

The deflated congressman from Idaho sat back in his chair, taken to the
woodshed by the bullying chairman once again. He looked toward the gaggle of

lobbyists in the back of the room. Congressman Echo raised his point—enough to prove to Bargus that he defended the energy company's interests.

"Doggle is just warming up," Bargus said, his patience thinning. "Every committee member knows if they left the room right now they would be caught by the major network television cameras. This crap used to be banished to C-Span."

Bargus knew the United States' energy crisis transformed the antics of congressional hearings into the best reality show on the tube. Thanks to America's newest folk hero, Olga Stevick, it was a highly rated show. And Chairman Doggle, a plump, animated, and effeminate congressman from Iowa, took center stage to show his political muscle to the entire nation. Doggle's head was the size of a pumpkin, with curly gray hair bulging out of his temples. To many on Capitol Hill, he reminded them of the famous glowering bust of Ludwig Van Beethoven. Despite his mousy voice, Doggle roared like a lion behind the chairman's microphone in endless soliloquies berating the energy companies, their three-piece-suit lobbyists, and their minions in Congress.

"This nation is in an energy crisis that has been *manufactured* by companies like American Energy. Manipulating prices. Relying on insecure foreign sources. Claiming that the solution is to get the government to allow them to create oil slicks along the coasts of our shining seas in order to profit from the inflated market prices they themselves caused. And the current administration in the White House stands idly by, watching the international situation decay, allowing the selfish to gouge and grab, and the needy to be fleeced and frozen! And they want to grant tax breaks to filthy-rich corporations to pretend that they look for alternative fuels, while they ignore great potential sources like biofuels that can be produced in plenty right here in the good ol' U.S. of A! It's time for an energy revolution!"

A group of more than fifty senior citizen members of *Olga's Army* in the room exploded into spontaneous cheers. Those who could, stood, waving their utility bills in their arthritic hands, shaking their canes or thumping their rubber-tipped walkers on the marble floor. Olga Stevick, the *Grande Dame* of the new and improved Gray Panthers, now sat quiet in the first row after exiting the witness chair, smiling coyly. She looked back at Bargus as if to say, *Put that in your PAC fund and smoke it.*

"I've had enough of that old bag," Bargus said, standing and turning to his lady friend, a devilish gleam in his eye. "Let's go back to the hotel and try page thirty-two," he said, referring to the Book of Kama Sutra.

"I thought you said you weren't double-jointed," the woman said.

＊   ＊   ＊   ＊

After the hearing, the network television reporters did their standup with the angry aged in the background, reporting that if the Freeman Administration hoped to get an energy bill on the floor of the House, it wasn't about to get through Congressman August Doggle's committee with a proposal for offshore oil and gas drilling and tax credits for energy companies to seek new supplies of fossil fuels. One reporter echoed Doggle's words, "The Energy Revolution has begun."

CHAPTER 21

▼

"As you know, my buddy Nate Freeman is going to visit us in a few days," Cowboy said to Drs. Edison and Roystone, name-dropping the president of the United States. "Miss O'Day is here to make sure we are politically correct, OSHA prepped, and every fly on every green uniform is zipped."

Danielle shot a terse glance at Cowboy. He was brash, conceited, and unprofessional, and she was getting tired of his interruptions and insolent tongue. Though she found him brusquely handsome and well built, he was a pompous egomaniac.

"This project, as you know, is a private-public partnership between DOE and American Energy," Dr. Edison said impassively. Danielle noted that her body language, however, communicated her contempt for Cowboy. Edison turned to a console on one end of the room, and punched a few buttons. On the screen, a computer image silhouette of the project platform appeared, and then it phased into a fully detailed depiction of what the facility looked like when not shielded by the water. It looked like the shark fin keel of a large sailboat.

"This mobile offshore platform is the largest of its kind in the world," Edison began. "It weighs forty tons. The main observation deck is 950 feet long, and when its operational parts are fully extended, it protrudes 700 feet below the surface of the ocean. It is powered by four diesel engines when it is moving from location to location at a snail's pace of five knots an hour, because of its overwhelming size."

"Longer than two football fields laid end to end," Cowboy said.

"Mr. Rhodan explained that ballast tanks are filled with water to submerge the platform—like a submarine?" Danielle said.

"Yes, 5 million gallons of seawater are needed to fill the pontoons. If the platform needs to move, a bilge pumps the water out and the entire platform rises. The billion dollar operation has more than 500 workers, 100 different rooms, 50 restroom facilities, and 2 galleys—though, admittedly, the food may not be what you could get onshore."

"Except tonight, we're having blue marlin steaks, grilled over natural gas flames," Cowboy added.

"This platform consumes more energy to run than a major steel plant," the scientist continued in a flat tone like a bored tour guide. But she seemed to know the facility through and through. "Fortunately, we generate most of our own energy through the successful wind farm and the ocean current turbine located on the starboard side of the hull," pointing at a donut-shaped device on the illustration protruding from one side of the massive structure. "The turbine generates thousands of kilowatts of electricity to run the so-called *parasitic power load* of pumps, lights, radio equipment, and other electrical conveniences aboard the platform. Of course, methane gas accumulated as part of the project powers generators and provides the feedstock for DOE experimental hydrogen fuel cells also on board."

"But how does the platform stay in one place?" asked Danielle. "Doesn't the rig attach to the sea floor by an anchor or something?"

"It can, but most of the time the entire facility floats," Edison answered. "Once in place, the platform is kept steady in spite of the Gulf Stream and wind-driven surface waves by a dynamic-positioning system, kind of like how a spacecraft changes its position while in orbit around the earth by firing small positioning thrusters." The unemotional scientist pointed to the computer image, showing cylindrical thrusters all around the platform's sunken hull. She pushed away a wisp of her chocolate-brown hair that characteristically hung over the front of her eyes. "Computer-controlled thrusters and electronic sensors offset wind, wave, and current forces. In addition, three large anchors can lodge onto the sea bottom in case of any electronic breakdown or we need to hold position in rough weather."

"Even a category-five hurricane couldn't budge this tub," Cowboy said.

Danielle pointed to the curved-edged triangular structure that extended below the 100-foot-high hull sunk below the deck of the platform. It looked like some kind of chimerical sea monster. "What's that for?"

"Looks like an upside-down aardvark, don't it?" Cowboy said.

The brainy brunette in the white lab coat continued to ignore Cowboy's gratuitous comments, the lock of hair returning to the front of her face, as if it were a tail attached to the wrong end. "That is part of the gathering operation we can show you in detail later," she said.

"Are those some kind of pipelines?" Danielle said, pointing to cylindrical tubes that could be seen on the three-dimensional diagram extending out of the bottom of the pyramid-shaped structure.

"Yes, there are two major pipelines in the diagram you can see here on the sea bottom, and several gathering lines coming from the processing facilities located on the bottom of the hull."

"What about the kelp? Where does it grow?"

"The kelp is in place," Dr. Edison said, glancing at Cowboy for the first time. Cowboy returned the glare with a shit-eating smile.

"How does kelp produce gas anyway?" Danielle asked.

"This type of giant kelp is not native to this part of the ocean—it actually has been transplanted from the Pacific Coast for this project by NOAA, DOE, and the U.S. Navy. An experimental test farm has existed for years near Laguna Beach, California. It is often called sea otter's cabbage, because of it being a staple in an otter's diet. Its scientific name is *Macrocystis pyrifera*."

"Tastes just like it sounds," the officious Cowboy quipped.

"Kelp is the largest marine algae," Edison continued as if narrating a high-school documentary film. "It is rich in carbohydrates and is normally used to produce vitamins, potassium, algin, and iodine. It has also been a source for potash and even an emulsifier to prevent the crystallization of ice cream. It grows in water up to 100 feet deep on the continental shelf, growing to 200 feet in the adult state, but can get as long as 750 feet. This marine biomass-energy kelp field stretches more than 5,000 acres. Additional site studies are in place in waters off of New York State and other Atlantic Coast areas, as well as the Gulf Coast, Hawaii, and Alaska."

"How does it work?" the quizzical lawyer asked. *This is becoming more fascinating by the minute*, she thought.

"A kelp plant is connected to the sea bottom by a holdfast, and its brown hollow stem has wavy blades or leaves that float near the surface that have hollow gas bladders that produce methane. The plant can grow as much as two feet in a day— it is extremely efficient in absorbing solar energy and nutrients from the ocean environment."

Danielle was spellbound. Her obdurate father would never believe that his job may be preserved and the nation's energy crisis averted by a bunch of seaweed that passes gas. But why would the government transplant seaweed from one ocean to the next? Why not harvest methane off the Pacific Coast? Maybe it was economics. It was like all the natural gas up in Prudoe Bay in Alaska. There was a ton of gas up there under the ice, but no way to cheaply pipe it thousands of miles away at a price many were willing to pay for it. American Energy was footing a large part of this project, and its customers were on the East Coast, not California. After all, those folks were closer to Alaska. Well, in any case, she was a lawyer, and they were the scientists—they must know what they are doing.

"And the gas gathering system, how does it work?" Danielle continued, her curiosity peaked. "I simply find it intriguing that we can collect billions of cubic feet of gas from seaweed that burps methane."

"Well, there is a little more to it than that," Edison chuckled in a sisterly way. "The kelp is harvested by cutting off the top ten feet of the plant, and the self-sustaining plants regrow. The harvested kelp is placed in large airtight containers, called biodigesters. Microorganisms ingest the kelp and convert it into methane. Some estimate that 55,000 square miles of kelp farms could produce 20 trillion cubic feet of methane each year, equal to the current U.S. gas consumption. But admittedly, that's a long way off. Additionally, the solid remains of biodigestion can be sold as animal feed supplements and fertilizer. An added plus is that commercial marine kelp farms will attract a large fish population."

"Next she'll take credit for that marlin I caught this morning," Cowboy said.

Danielle moved right up to the monitor with the three-dimensional image and pointed. "But what is that long spiky cone thing coming from the bottom of the hull? I thought that was the gas gathering system?"

"That's the drilling mast," said Roystone, speaking for the first time since he introduced himself. He looked like a grownup version of the clumsy nerd Stephen Urkel from the old *Family Matters* sit-com, but his full tenor voice was commanding. Cowboy's eyes grew wider at the statement. Danielle's interest perked. She felt like a seven-year-old trying to figure out a secret shared only by her parents.

"Drilling mast?" Danielle responded. "You don't drill for kelp do you? I thought you just collected the gas from the plants."

"We do collect methane from the kelp fields," Edison interrupted, almost stepping in front of her colleague. "Here," she pointed to the side of the diagram. "Much of the kelp is collected by a vacuuming process and after it produces methane, it helps provide fuel for our hot water aboard ship."

"But the kelp gas also goes through the big pipelines pictured here, right?" Danielle asked.

The scientists looked at each other, and then again at Cowboy.

The rig manager cleared his throat, adjusted his pants by grabbing an ostentatious belt buckle cut into the shape of the state of Oklahoma, and spoke in a soothing voice. "I'm afraid that Miss O'Day has not yet been briefed ... fully."

"I'm sorry," Edison said.

"Briefed?" Danielle asked.

Cowboy stepped forward, pushing the brim of his hat back an inch on the crest of his high forehead. "You are under the impression that this facility is for the gathering of methane—the primary ingredient of natural gas—emitted by giant brown sea kelp."

"Yeah, that's what American Energy invested in."

"That's good—the PR is working."

"PR? Is that what this is?" the lawyer questioned like an impatient child. "A public relations ploy?"

"Not exactly," he said. He placed his hands on his hips with the savoir-faire of a ten-year-old and proclaimed proudly, "This is the world's largest and most technologically advanced production rig that will make the United States energy independent."

"Drilling rig? But you can't drill in the Atlantic Ocean—certainly not this close to shore," Danielle protested. "Congress has not lifted the moratorium on drilling off the coasts at this distance. And no states have given their approval. Drilling for oil or natural gas off the Atlantic Coast is against federal and state law!"

"Boy, you barristers do know your laws," Cowboy said. "But, you see counselor, we are not *drilling* for gas—technically. We're *mining* for it."

CHAPTER 22

▼

On the Atlantic Ocean off the coast of northern Virginia

Jean-Pierre Perreaut wiped the Atlantic's briny mist off his binoculars and held the spyglass up to his eyes to see if he could spot the coast of the United States. He was captain of the maiden voyage of the liquefied natural gas storage tanker *Frozen Spirit*, named after the cryogenic state of its invisible cargo. The Americans eagerly awaited Perreaut's shipment. The vessel's double-hulls were filled to the brim with 20,000 tons of liquefied natural gas, or LNG. The enormous quantity of vaporous natural gas was reduced by a factor of 600, as if you shrunk the air inside a beach ball down to that of a Ping-Pong ball. It was not done by compression, but rather by superchilling the gas to minus 160 degrees Celsius until it converted into a liquid state. The leviathan tanker held six spherical vats full of the fuel.

Captain Perreaut piloted LNG tankers since the United States first began importing the energy from Algeria during the 1970s energy crisis. Algeria hosted one of the first gas-liquefying plants built at Arzew, collecting gas from the Hassi R'Mel field in the Sahara. But the efforts of the 'seventies evaporated when the Algerians hiked the price. Later, billion-dollar American LNG terminals, built to warm the frozen liquid gas back into a vapor that would burn in a gas stove, were mothballed in the 1990s because their gas imports couldn't compete with lower-priced natural gas produced in North America. Perreaut scrounged for work ferrying LNG shipments to the Far East. But everything changed when the cost of natural gas escalated in the first part of the twenty-first century to unprecedented levels and were further aggravated by the subsequent international oil and gas embargo.

Energy experts hoped that LNG from western Africa, the Caribbean, and the Middle East would be a critical transition fuel in the long-term quest to obtain secure energy supplies for the United States. Huge supplies of natural gas found in the Arab world in the search for oil were hungry for a market, since the region didn't use much of the fuel for itself. For example, the estimated natural gas reserves of the small peninsula nation of Qatar, adjacent to Saudi Arabia, had 14 percent of the world's conventional reserves of natural gas.

"A natural gas furnace repairman in that tiny Arab nation is as busy as an Eskimo Italian Ice street vendor," said a gas industry official at a ribbon cutting unveiling a new LNG gasification facility on the Virginia coast. "Qatar's reserves could fulfill the United States' energy demand for forty years."

"Which begs the question, when's the invasion," a visiting congressman quipped under his breath.

Perreaut, who overheard the comment at the ribbon cutting of the new American LNG plant, did not find humor in the statement. Perhaps it was his rudimentary knowledge of English.

Until recently, most natural gas found in the Middle East was reinjected into the ground by energy companies to accelerate petroleum production, or flared in the air, wasting billions of cubic feet of the precious fuel. In fact, beginning in the mid-nineteenth century, American oil explorers did the same thing when they mistakenly found natural gas in the search for petroleum. Oil was the *prize*, and natural gas was only a dangerous invisible nuisance that tended to blow up at the most inopportune times. Trillions of cubic feet of methane either burned freely or escaped into the atmosphere, likely exacerbating global warming if there were environmental scientists around at that time to take measurements. But recently, billions of dollars were invested in cooling facilities in major Middle-Eastern countries such as Qatar. Algeria was the second-largest LNG exporter to the U.S. terminals located in Massachusetts, Maryland, Georgia, Louisiana, and the newest and largest LNG port facility in northern Virginia, near the Norfolk Naval Base. National Gas and Electric Corporation, a rival of American Energy, had the controlling interest in the plant.

Perreaut, a portly and grandfatherly man sporting a close-cut white beard that gave him an uncanny resemblance to Ulysses S. Grant, was short in stature, but long in chutzpah. Crewmen who looked up at the bridge window of the top deck of the *Frozen Spirit* could only see the top of his blue captain's hat, and a tuft of white hair underneath. If Perreaut heard any crewmember make reference to his abbreviated height, they would soon find themselves out of a job. Perreaut saw himself as commanding the ocean waters like the most famous of sea captains for he had sailed all over the world. He directed LNG ships under his stern command to destinations as far away as Japan and South Korea, countries that used

LNG as a fuel for years because they had no domestic natural gas supply. He imagined himself on the bridge of the flagship destroyer of the well-trained French Navy, defending the Barbary coasts of Africa from pirates and keeping rouge colonies of his nation in line from the tip of Cape Horn to the South China seas. But in reality, the captain's wanderlust was met by piloting an expensive thermos bottle the size of an aircraft carrier with not much more skill than driving an ice cream delivery truck minus the calliope music. The 1,000-foot-long vessel cost $150 million to build, which was considered a bargain. Thirty-years before, the giant boats cost twice that amount. The ship was lined with three feet of insulation inside its double hull, filled with perlite, a lightweight rock often used in potting soil to retain moisture, and polyurethane foam, similar to that found in the cushions of a shoddy living room couch.

Perreaut raised his binoculars to his eyes again. He stood on the bridge of the *Frozen Spirit*, housed in the stern, four stories above the deck. In front of him the top of the six LNG tanks protruded from the deck like three pairs of bulbous breasts. Like icebergs, the majority of the mass of the cylindrical tanks lay below deck in the hull of the ship.

Perreaut could not be blamed for feeling like he was a military captain on this voyage, however; after all, he received a U.S. military escort ever since leaving the Mediterranean Sea. Navy destroyers flanked the huge cargo ship that also trailed in the wake of a Navy frigate. Though he wasn't told, Perreaut figured that an American nuclear submarine probably swam silently below his hull, guarding its precious contents from potential terrorists. The *Frozen Spirit* was the last LNG tanker to leave the Algerian port before its new radical government shut it down. The New Algerian Reformist Ulama, a group of Islamic religious scholars that transformed the energy-rich nation into a theocracy, now controlled that government. Though the traditional Muslim Algerian officials bragged for years that their natural gas supply was for open sale to the West, the forces behind the latest Islamic takeover, in what seemed to be an intercontinental Islamic revolution, had a different philosophy. Though no blood was shed in the recent coup, the clerics in control told their international natural gas customers they were going to "reevaluate" their sales policy, in thinly veiled collusion with the Middle-Eastern oil embargo. But since this shipment of dire-needed natural gas was already paid for by the U.S. energy company National Gas and Electric, Algerian officials agreed to let it leave port. A deal is a deal. Still, the U.S. government flagged the ship with Old Glory and was ever alert that radical terrorists might target the vessel.

In moments, the U.S. Coast Guard would take over from the Navy and escort the *Frozen Spirit* to the shores of Virginia. Perreaut felt safe with the might of the Americans in front, on the sides, and most likely, beneath him. He dispensed orders from the bridge like a surly, narcissistic admiral. Most of the crew were native Algerians, who most likely resented him, and he them. The natives' umbrage dated back to the French seizing control of the north-African nation in the mid-nineteenth century on the ruse to make it safe from Barbary Coast pirates. A bloody civil war, supported by the Muslim purist descendents of the new government, brought independence in the early 1960s. By the 1990s, the clerics threatened the power of the military-backed government. Now, without a shot fired, the radical Islamists controlled the nation and its vast energy resources. As far as Perreaut was concerned, he would never return to Algiers, the nation's capital. He would miss bartering with merchants in the city's famous bazaars; he was always tight-fisted with his dinars. And, of course, he would probably pine for the veiled belly dancers once provided by his rich Algerian energy company hosts, let alone the ladies of the evening that warmed the chambers of the old Frenchman's heart. But Algiers was not safe for non-Arabs anymore, he thought—not even us French, thanks to the despotic petrostates and the Americans' habit of pissing off every Muslim in the world.

No, the confident sea captain would never return to Algeria. Perhaps he should move to America. There are plenty of young women there that were impressed with his credentials and adventures on the high seas. Soon he would see the coast of Virginia. *Ah yes*, he thought. He remembered the young Italian-American public relations girl who had her silky hands all over him when they met during a press conference promoting National Gas and Electric's new fleet of LNG ships. She would be waiting for him.

Moments before he issued the order to scale back speed of the massive vessel as it approached the coast, a young Algerian galley hand delivered his lunch. Perreaut tasted the crepes. They were bland and he spit them out. He was tired of the galley's incompetence.

"Idiot!" Perreaut shouted at the teenage boy who looked not a day past seventeen. "Get rid of this!"

After shouting and cursing in gutter French—words he thought the galley hand did not understand, the irate captain turned his attention back to the sea in front of him. He never saw, and barely felt, the eight-inch kitchen knife stab through his back, sever his kidney and eviscerate his liver before he gave a weak gasp and fell to the deck of the bridge.

CHAPTER 23

▼

Near the Norfolk, Virginia Shoreline

The seventh-grade school children chattered like the annoying squawking seagulls that circled above them. The tour guide was tired—this was her fifth middle-school group of the day, and she had no patience with children on the pubescent verge of adolescence. Conducting the elementary and middle-school education tours for National Gas and Electric Corporation was the "best birth control device in the world," the twenty-five-year-old Virginia Tech graduate told her girlfriends. The kids drove her nuts.

"Now I understand why some species eat their young," the attractive brunette quipped the W.C. Fields-type line to her supervisor at the large utility company. But all the kids on the tours loved Natalie Sansonetti. She was personable and understanding, and all the young girls were envious of her silken ebony hair and her Mediterranean coffee-tinted skin. And the pre-pubescent boys were absolutely in puppy dog infatuation with her silt-dark eyes, angelic ivory smile, and Coke-bottle figure.

"Now, some of the energy that we use today to cook our food, wash our clothes, and heat are homes is provided from energy colder than the coldest ice cube," Sansonetti, National Gas and Electric's public relations tour guide, said in a droning nasal tone. She did this a thousand times and the novelty of passion long since evaporated from her voice. The group of a dozen twelve- and thirteen-year-old children stood on a platform overlooking a sprawling LNG gasification plant on the shores of the Virginia coast, within eyesight of the Norfolk Navy Base. The massive facility to convert the superchilled LNG to room temperature to produce usable natural gas cost $30 billion, a good percentage of which was coughed up by U.S. taxpayers.

Four enamel-white spherical tanks, resembling bulbous mammoth mushrooms sprouting from a giant's capacious garden, were the anchor edifices of the tank and pipe city. The huge insulated vats could house 126 million gallons of fluid, or 10 billion cubic feet of natural gas, enough to warm 40 million American homes on a winter day. The vast gas storage facility sat on twenty acres of land with huge pipes the size of tubular water slides at an amusement park winding down from the vats. The pipes then traveled about fifty feet underground into a submariner tunnel that led a half-mile off the coast. A long, narrow floating steel dock on the water surface jutted from the shore leading to where the massive LNG carriers parked, after traveling from the coasts of South America, Africa, and even as far away as Scandinavia.

In Texas and Louisiana, there was a love-fest between the LNG industry and the local population as they saw good-paying jobs, an increasing tax base, and economic recovery of the hurricane-ravaged area. Other LNG projects occurred in the Bahamas, with undersea pipelines reaching the southern U.S. LNG was also welcomed in Canada as several LNG sites off of Nova Scotia and New Brunswick imported natural gas from Russia, processed it, and sold the fuel in the northeastern United States. Eastern Canada's lower population density and hunger for industrial development proved a hospitable home for the frozen fuel.

But off the East Coast of the United States, it was a different story. Community protests near the nationally famous Virginia beaches kept construction of the plant as far away from the tourist draw as possible. An explosion at a gas liquefaction plant in Algeria in 2004 killed twenty-seven workers, and injured dozens more, and the NIMBY (Not-In-My-Backyard) opponents used it as fodder.

The Algeria situation was the result of inadequate emergency systems and procedures, and such a disaster could not occur at a modern regasification facility. Converting the liquid to a gas is less hazardous that the initial liquefaction. Those were the stock lines Sansonetti would regurgitate if asked about the tragedy. But many people were infected with "Three-Mile-Island-itis" as one company official put it. Most of Sansonetti's job was to put the safety spin on the general public, especially among the area's children, and her pulchritude and easy-going manner helped.

Although children stood in awe of her, their parents were a harder sell. Some community residents favored a proposal to build a floating facility twenty-five miles offshore, and then sending the vaporized fuel through underwater pipelines so it would be delivered to the shore no different than any other gas pipeline. A $700 million floating terminal for LNG was already in the middle of Long Island Sound. The deal was appealing to environmentalists and anxious Virginians who were not persuaded by the U.S. Department of Energy seal of safety on modern LNG facilities. LNG made them nervous. Citizens flooded public hearings with huge signs that read, "Go modern, Go gas, Go boom!" Unfortunately for the innovative offshore project backers and anxious local residents, Congress balked at the $10 billion price tag. In addition, a floating LNG port would have to be constantly guarded by the Navy from man's wrath as a potential terrorist target, and still be vulnerable to nature's fury through offshore hurricanes. But this LNG certification process was on the federal government's fast track, and nothing could stop its construction. Imports of liquefied natural gas were increasing, and the U.S. was running out of processing capacity. Eventually, the U.S. Navy sacrificed some of its land that buffered the critical port that moored a good portion of the eastern U.S. Naval power. Building such a facility would be incredibly expensive, requiring huge equity and firm long-term contracts. If the plant was successful, it would be a financial boon for National Gas and Electric. After all, LNG was projected to fulfill up to 20 percent of U.S. gas demand by 2025. In 2003, it was only 1 percent of the U.S. supply. But if for some reason the LNG venture was not successful, it would be a boondoggle that could land the large corporation, its pipelines, and markets on the auction block, and maybe easy pickings for a takeover by the firm's largest competitor, American Energy.

In the distance, the young, vivacious boys in the tour group stared at the huge gray naval vessels that seemed to fire their imaginations more than the boring white tanks and tubes that ran all over this industrial site like a canyon full of prehistoric albino snakes. Most of the girls were not paying close attention either, Ms. Sansonetti observed, as they debated the shade of her lipstick. Nearly a half-mile away, an enormous LNG cargo ship sat parked at the T-Bone-shaped dock that stretched from shore.

"This facility will process the invisible fuel that burns in your family furnace," Sansonetti continued, moving her arms with the graceful bend of a flamingo's neck. She displayed the plant in the background Vanna-White style as if revealing a major prize package during a game show. Though she lost her original vivaciousness, she still was pretty good at the tour thing. "The gas comes from thousands of miles away, deep in the ground underneath the African desert or miles below the ocean surface near the coast of South America. Out there off our coast you can see one of the ships that carry the fuel that was once a gas, its molecules cooled and shrunk until becoming a liquid called LNG, which means liquefied natural gas. LNG is pumped off the tankers and the fuel will run through underwater pipelines and vaporized. A teaspoon of the liquid gas expands to the size of a gallon jug as it changes back into a gas at this plant."

The word "jug" elicited a couple of snickers from the boys, nudging each other, eyes wide, gawking at her well-endowed features. She was aware of it, but it did not offend her. The girls envied her Miss-Virginia radiance. The boys were enthralled by the object of their budding lust.

"My grandpa says LNG is dangerous," one of the more aggressive boys questioned. The adolescent, head shaved nearly bald to look like the other toughs on his middle-school football team, badgered Sansonetti the entire tour. She observed that the little brat was early into puberty and decided to flirt through bravado intellectual debate. "My grandpa says a plant like this exploded in Cleveland when he was a little boy and killed a lot of people."

"Well, I'm sure your grandfather is a wise man," Sansonetti said, her beauty-pageant grin not leaving her lips despite answering the hostile question from the pubescent Mike Wallace. She was ready for this one. "There was a fire many, many years ago at a plant in Cleveland that wasn't built with the safeguards we have here. Way back then, a tank leaked because it was made out of substandard metal, because of the steel shortage during World War II. But that was a long time ago. Rest assured, this plant is built with safety in mind and the latest in modern technology. And, all of our storage tanks are leakproof." She knew the answer to the question down pat, but she was surprised at the query from the distrustful little imp who seemed to spend most of the tour staring at her chest. She would not mention a 1973 explosion on Staten Island that killed thirty-seven people or the disaster in Algeria just a few years ago. But if the obnoxious kid brought it up, she memorized responses for those too.

"You can see the big ship docked out in the water now—it came all the way from the Venezuelan coast, and oh, look! We are so lucky—another ship is coming in now—I think this one came all the way from Africa!"

The tour group looked out toward the ocean horizon and emitted a collective "ahhhh!" The large black cargo ship steamed closer to the dock port. The white nipples of its huge LNG vats poked upward from the bow of the tanker.

"It looks like the *Titanic*," one excited girl said.

"What would happen if the ship hit an iceberg?" another asked. "Would it blow up?"

Sansonetti laughed gently. "Well, young lady, there are no icebergs on the route between Africa and Virginia, but don't worry, there is no danger. LNG in its liquid state can't even burn and it is not under pressure. And the ships are safe. They have insulated double-hulled tanks—that is, two containers inside one another that in case of any shipping accident, the LNG would remain safely inside. In fact, there is a story about a Navy nuclear submarine that accidentally surfaced under one of the LNG ships several years ago in the western Mediterranean Sea and cracked the bottom of the vessel. But not one drop of LNG leaked."

"But how does gas burn on the stove if it can't burn on the ship?" an innocent, pony-tailed brunette girl asked.

"Natural gas will only ignite within a small ratio of air to gas mixture. Your stove, furnace, or water heater, carefully controls that mixture and allows natural gas to be used safely in your home to keep you warm and bake chocolate chip cookies!"

"Why do the ships stay way out there?" another child asked.

"For added safety, the ships dock far out in the water and don't come close to the plant."

"Can we go on one?" said the oversexed brat.

"No, I'm afraid not. The LNG ships are only for expert sailors. In fact, I believe that this ship coming into port now is piloted by a famous French sea captain, who has been sailing LNG ships for more than thirty years all over the world." Sansonetti once met the seafarer, Jean-Pierre Perreaut, at a ceremony that christened a new LNG ship partly owned by National Gas and Electric. She knew the captain as a supercilious dirty old man who tried to grab her ass during the festivities.

"Only experts guide the ships," she said. She winced when thinking of the lascivious Frenchman. "After more than 35,000 voyages by LNG ships over more than 70 million miles, no significant accidents have occurred."

"There's a first time for everything," the brat said.

CHAPTER 24

▼

Plaza Hotel, Washington, D.C.

Louis Campbell, a steel-gray-haired lawyer who spent his entire thirty-seven-year career with National Gas and Electric Corporation was not fond of attention-getting parlor tricks, but this one might pay off. The Grand Ballroom of The Plaza Hotel in Washington was full of tension and lots and lots of money. The crystal chandelier above twinkled like a sequined evening gown as it reflected the bright electric candelabra of lights in the cavernous space. Leading Wall Street stock analysts and numerous academics invited to a U.S. Department of Energy summit on the current energy crisis listened skeptically as Campbell proclaimed his company's investment in liquefied natural gas plants as the "Great White Hope" of the natural gas industry.

After the CEO monologue, long on asterisks of "forward-looking" (i.e., cover-your-ass) statements, an analyst asked about the safety concerns of LNG, citing the Skikda, Algeria, explosion in 2004.

"Critics say that leaking LNG can form a gas cloud that is potentially dangerous," the analyst from a leading brokerage asked. "How do you convince investors that it is safe?"

Campbell chuckled. *What a wise-ass*, he thought. *These morons know nothing.*

Campbell's every movement was projected on two large video screens so that every person in the room could see his most innocuous expression. Behaving like a magician in front of children at a birthday party, Campbell placed an ashtray on the speaker's podium, and then held a large thermos over it, pressing a button on the top that released a clear liquid that pooled into the small receptacle. A steam-like mist formed over the ashtray like the cloud over dry ice, and a slick-haired assistant lit a match, igniting the combustible vapor. It did not explode, but held the flame like a lit can of Sterno under a metal pan of green beans in a restaurant buffet line.

"In this thermos is liquefied natural gas," Campbell said, holding the container for all to see. "Not as dangerous as the NIMBY crowd would claim." He snickered again. He poured more of the liquid into a half-filled water glass on the podium. Campbell grinned. *Wait to they get a load of this.* He then drank the water. A few gasps from the analysts were soon replaced by relieved laughter and a couple of clapped hands. "And I am announcing today that National Gas and Electric has placed a $2 billion order for a brand new fleet of tankers to transport LNG. We are staking our company on it."

The black-suited CEO's prominent jowls vibrated like boiling oatmeal as he said the billions of dollars in stockholder and government money invested in its regasification plant in Virginia was money well spent. Campbell's firm now controlled most of the natural gas pipeline and electric grid in the southeastern United States. But he was only one of a number of other energy company executives that sat on the same panel, including his main industry adversary, American Energy's upstart CEO, Alexandria Raven.

"The allowable drilling acreage of natural gas in the nation has dried up, and we have no choice but to depend on imported shipments of LNG," Campbell said. Despite the show-and-tell, Campbell knew his low-key, guttural tones might be lulling the audience into a near comatose state. He would have to pick up the pace.

"The demand for gas, especially for electric generation, has outpaced our ability to supply it," Campbell said. "However, technological advances have reduced the costs of producing and shipping LNG, and our new infrastructure lays the groundwork for a successful future. The U.S. has only 4 percent of world's natural gas reserves. There is much natural gas in Russia, South America, Africa, and the Middle East, but there are no pipelines emanating from Moscow, Trinidad, or Algiers to New York City. We will need 20 billion cubic feet of natural gas a day in five years. We are currently negotiating import contracts with energy firms in Venezuela, Qatar, and Nigeria to meet the need. In fact, Qatar possesses the world's second-largest natural gas reserves, and shares with Iran the single largest natural gas field on the globe. There are abundant supplies of stranded gas in countries potentially open to drilling, which, by the way, isn't the case with oil. For years, natural gas discovered alongside oil in Africa has been flared as worthless, but now countries such as Nigeria and Angola want to find a buyer. More gas on the market will help steady the price—and, it could lessen upward pressure on oil prices. In the end, we need LNG."

He waited for applause, but none arrived.

"You see," Campbell said in his flat-line monotone, "it is just a matter of good corporate social responsibility." He waved his hand toward his demonstration. "LNG by itself doesn't burn. You need a mixture of gas and oxygen in a narrow range." He turned toward the side and extended a hand toward the projection screen. "Here is a larger version of the thermos I just sipped out of."

On the screen, the image of a huge ocean supertanker, with the top of the six giant ball-like, ceiling-white LNG tanks protruding out the deck of the ship. Written on the side of the vessel in bright white Roman letters was the ship's moniker: *Frozen Spirit*. From the side view, the ship strongly resembled a half-dozen eggs sitting in an open carton. Campbell knew all of his eggs were in one basket. He would have to watch that basket.

Campbell said, "This is the future of natural gas."

CHAPTER 25

▼

The assassin, Jamalh Al Dullah, a nineteen-year-old student in an Arabic school run by the new Algerian Reformist Ulama, rehearsed the killing of the captain for weeks, putting up with serving the arrogant old sea salt his crepes and brie like a slave. Only a young adolescent when the Islamic Jihad against the West reached its flashpoint in 2001, Jamalh was proud he was now a man—the one assigned to kill the French pig who fornicated with his nation's women and spit on the beggars in the alleys of Algiers. The snobbish sea captain was now as cold as his crepes. And Jamalh was responsible.

But Jamalh was not alone. Seven other knife murders occurred on the ship within the previous five minutes. Only three actual struggles occurred, and only one ended with an injury—a black eye—to one of the mutineers. Some of the remaining twenty-five people on board the gas-pregnant ship were already willing conspirators, placed upon the vessel by sympathizers with the new radical Algerian government. Others had no idea what was going on. They were not directly connected to the new government—the conspirators made sure of that. The mutineers were a motley collection of fugitive Saudis, Kuwaitis, Egyptians, Syrians, Afghanis, Iraqis, Iranians, and several other smaller Islamic nations who were more than willing to give their lives to attack the United States, who the Iranians many years before aptly nicknamed, the *Great Satan*. Only Jamalh knew that this hijacking of the LNG ship was part of an overall plan to hike the price of the precious environmentally friendly fuel to which the West was now addicted, just as they were with oil. Though oil was the heroin, natural gas was this addict's methadone, and northern Africa had a ready prescription, available at the right price. This individual shipment was not indispensable in the overall energy picture for the oil- and gas-starved Americans, but it would serve as an example that no one in the West could ignore.

Jamalh kicked the lifeless corpulent body of the French captain. A wave of blood suffused the gray metal floor like rose-colored surf on a beach. Jamalh was in command now. The young Algerian did not know how to pilot or dock the gargantuan ship. He and others with a slight knowledge of naval operations kept it on a collision course with a nearly identical vessel parked at the sea dock ahead of him. After all, it was easier than flying a 747 into a skyscraper. Jamalh and his co-conspirators urged his superiors that they were capable to ramming the tanker right into the American LNG facility itself, but the idea was rejected because of the shallowness of the harbor and the heaviness of the vessel that may cause it to run aground. Another suggested plan to crash the ship into the American naval base was rejected as well. Because of the heightened tension resulting from likely terrorist attacks, either the American Coast Guard or the Navy would probably sink any unauthorized vessel if it approached too closely. So instead, the *Frozen Spirit* approached the LNG dock, just as expected. And when it arrived, the terrorists aboard would detonate explosive charges on the numerous thermos-bottle cargo holds loaded long ago at port in Algeria, enough to destroy the $150 million vessel along with its sister ship already at the dock. The ensuing fire fueled by the vaporizing payload would be in full in-your-face view of the American military base that was powerless to stop the impending calamity.

The young olive-skinned man gripped the handset radio of the main bridge of the giant vessel and pressed the button allowing him to communicate with the entire ship.

"Allah Akbar!" the young man shouted. *God is great!*

Natalie Sansonetti did not know that the groping Captain Perreaut was not at the helm of the *Frozen Spirit*, but instead a nineteen-year-old Islamic terrorist who had never ridden on a rowboat before was at the supertanker's helm. And he did not have a pilot's license.

"There is little chance of any leak of LNG," said Sansonetti, continuing her on-the-shore tour, eager to move the children along. "And if there was a leak, there is little hazard. Natural gas is lighter than air, so it would evaporate, vaporizing harmlessly into the air." Sansonetti threw her velvety-skinned arms upward like a fashion model on a runway. "The long and the short of it is—LNG just can't blow up!"

The children saw several small yellow puffs of flame first off in the distance in the water, and like the delay in hearing a fireworks display, an echoing ripple of explosions followed. Then, a brilliant flash and subsequent vibrating concussion blow on the steel observation deck nearly perforated their eardrums, knocked them backwards, and tossed most of them to the metal-slatted surface ass over teakettle. The following aurora of flame seemingly as wide as the horizon itself could be seen for miles. Once ruptured by planted explosives, the liquid gas that would not burn poured out of the severed insulated teats of the *Frozen Spirit* and the other docked vessel. But instead of dumping its contents into the water and dissipating innocently into the atmosphere as Sansonetti theorized, it was instead warmed by the catalyst fire, expanding into its gaseous state once again, making it suitable for ignition. As the experts said, LNG did not lend itself to rapid combustion, but in the right conditions, the fossil-fuel fog became the largest blowtorch humans ever envisioned. The thousands of tons of volatile fuel intended to heat homes, warm water, and bake cookies, now fed an oasis of fire in the pastoral blue waters of the Atlantic like a sea-serpent-sized serving of ocean-tanker flambé.

Sansonetti, her back to the ocean's shore, had no idea what hit her. She collapsed prone on top of the smitten twelve-year-old brat who harassed her with questions a moment before, her large breasts resting on either side of the boy's cheeks. If it wasn't for the excruciating pain inside his ears, the boy may have thought he had died and gone to heaven. And, a half-mile offshore, if reality aligned with the beliefs of the young Islamic militant Jamalh on what used to be the bridge of the *Frozen Spirit*, the freshly dead suicide terrorist was also most definitely in Paradise.

CHAPTER 26

▼

The corporate energy dean of National Gas and Electric declined further questions. Instead, Louis Campbell deferred to the next person on the panel of illustrious energy professionals, Alexandria Raven, who represented his rival energy conglomerate, American Energy. *It is about time that blowhard is done,* she thought. Raven was one of several other energy industry leaders who faced the music before the DOE Energy Summit's attendees. She worried that the LNG dog-and-pony show might try the audience's patience.

After lethargic applause, Raven confidently approached the walnut dais, splashed with "The Plaza" in broad script on the front of the lectern. The elegant and articulate CEO graciously nodded her head of carefully primped platinum-blond hair and beamed broadly at the preceding speaker. Campbell returned a shallow smile. Raven knew Campbell's enmity for her ran long and deep, most recently infuriated by Raven's balking at investing in the LNG plant in Virginia. However, American Energy did agree to share construction expenses of a natural gas compressor station pipeline hub near the coastal Virginia site that would act as a trading marketplace for natural gas coming from the South and offshore to Northeast markets. There, natural gas flowing from National's LNG plant and the Gulf of Mexico would be exchanged and directed to numerous cities served by both firms. It would also accept gas offshore from *Project Blue Sky*. But Raven had no interest in rolling the dice by investing in a big-ticket facility that depended on foreign gas imports for its profitability. She returned the faux grin to Campbell, and nodded to the crowd of gloomy energy analysts. They must be cynical of the rosy picture painted on the energy situation by numerous speakers who knew their industries lay in the crossfire of foreign government boycotts, terrorist threats, and domestic politicians blaming them for the "economic and environmental catastrophe" facing the country. Based on the dim forecast of energy supplies, American Energy's stock price, like most natural gas firms, slid by a third in the previous two weeks. This was despite that the cost of the fuel, which some of their subsidiaries produced, was at astronomical levels. Most figured the price was too high for anyone to afford to consume it. The fortune tellers on the financial cable shows proclaimed that it was certain bankruptcy for the energy distributors.

"Good morning," said Raven in a velvety and energetic tone. "It was suggested to me that one solution to our nation's energy crisis might be to harvest the hot air coming out of this room this morning from individuals such as myself."

A murmur of polite snickers waved across the room.

"But we need a long-term solution. And Mr. Campbell and I agree on one thing. Natural gas was once a neglected stepsister of the global energy industry, but now gas has become the Cinderella fuel. I'm sure all of you are probably weary of our optimism. Therefore, I don't have any prepared remarks, but I would be glad to answer any of your questions."

This statement woke the stock analysts up. Like journalists, they reveled at an opportunity to ask their clever, insightful questions about an industry's prospects just to impress their fellow brokerage houses. Immediately, several hands rose, and Raven nodded to one of the conservatively dressed spectators—white shirt, cobalt-blue suit, and red paisley tie—a well-built, sandy-haired man with chiseled features. He stood confidently and announced his name.

"Dick Mina, Merrill Lynch. Your company has primarily concentrated on distribution and transmission facilities during the past several years, and only a limited amount in exploration and production of natural gas. Now that you have the infrastructure to bring gas to market, where do you plan to get the gas if you frown upon investing in the new LNG supplies?"

"Good question," Raven said. *It was.* In fact, the worry about American Energy's fuel supplies for both its gas customers and fuel for its electric generation capacity was the primary factor pulling down its stock price. She gripped the side of the wooden podium and said assuredly, "I think we have found that depending on foreign oil has been a fool's paradise for many years, and I think depending on foreign natural gas is no different. We are confident that our nation is moving toward new fuel sources and supplies. American Energy has invested in natural gas and numerous renewable technologies, including landfill gas generation and biofuels, and electrical generation from solar, ocean current, geothermal, and wind energy. But it will be a while before those types of power will be either economical or plentiful to meet our increasing demand. For the meantime, we are evolving from an oil-based to a natural gas-based economy. The immediate future is gas—and that's our business."

The stock analyst was annoyed. "But where will you get the gas?"

"We have trillions of cubic feet of proven natural gas reserves within the continental United States. The gas is there. What we don't have yet is the political will to drill for it. But I'm confident our government leaders will recognize that the economic security of our nation depends on becoming energy independent. During the energy crunch in the early 1970s, President Nixon said the United States would be energy independent by 1980. It didn't happen. Likewise, later that decade President Carter claimed our nation could be energy secure by the turn of the twenty-first century. Again, no dice. And so it went for more than two decades. Still, in the twenty-first century, Congress and subsequent administrations have been reluctant to free the nation from the shackles put on us by unsteady foreign governments. Now is the time to do something about it."

"Some in your own industry think that domestic gas exploration is dead," said a twenty-something, brunette woman sitting in the front row, crossing her legs that exhibited her fat ankles.

Raven turned and faced Campbell and smiled daggers. "That's been said before. Natural gas has been with us for thousands of years, but only recently are we waking up to the fact that it can be our primary energy source until nontraditional energies are developed. All of you remember, from grade school I'm sure, the story of the Oracle of Delphi, the Greek priestess who told fortunes based on the mysterious fire that burned on top of Mount Parinisess. That burning spring was most likely natural gas set afire by a lightning strike. But it wasn't until the nineteenth century until entrepreneurs like John D. Rockefeller, George Westinghouse, and Joseph Pew found a way to pipe it safely from rural wells in the Appalachian region to urban industries. And as the natural gas business evolved and expanded in the early twentieth century, adequate supply was always an issue."

Raven now spoke to the entire audience rather than the individual questioner, hoping to put the issue of shortages in perspective.

"For example, back in the 1940s when wartime needs and later, postwar expansion put stress on the available natural gas wells in Appalachia, the predecessor companies of American Energy thought that we would have to go back to the days of dirty coal-manufactured gas to meet demand. But the nascent interstate pipeline industry brought gas from new finds in Texas and Oklahoma. Later, the Gulf of Mexico provided critical supplies. Then by the 1980s, Canadian imports played a significant role. To conquer this new challenge, we have to expand our resource base, like we always have."

Another balding questioner sporting fashionable reading glasses interjected. "If you didn't have pull with the last administration, what makes you think you will be successful with this one? Is American Energy still in bed with the DOE?" More laughter, as everyone in the room knew he was referring to Douglas Waters, the previous secretary of energy—Raven's husband.

She laughed along with them, knowing that the conventional wisdom in political circles was that it was not American Energy, but National Gas and Electric Corporation that had the government's favor since the feds spend millions on the liquefied natural gas plan. The LNG strategy was publicly proposed first by Raven's husband several years before, along with several nonconventional gas resource projects including American Energy's biofuels project to collect methane from giant sea kelp. However, she was no longer in bed with the former cabinet officer. In fact, they slept in separate bedrooms when they had the occasion to be in the same home—they owned four—and their paths did not cross often. But Raven could not reveal that the *current* secretary of energy harbored greater hopes with *Project Hades* off the North Carolina coast, and was urging the endorsement of the president of the United States.

When the laughter died down, Raven flashed her warm, magnetic, dime-sized toothy smile at the analysts and said, "We'll use more conventional lobbying techniques to urge the government to open up offshore drilling. Besides I'm only one person and there are 535 representatives and senators in Congress."

More laughter, and then some uncomfortable sighs as they digested the subtle allusion that the middle-aged, but maturely attractive Raven would be willing, if she had the time, to sleep with every lawmaker on the Hill to get her way.

"Seriously, we are confident Congress will realize the importance of making our nation more energy secure, while at the same time reducing any damage to our environment. The era of oil is over. Natural gas is the next step to fuel our economy, and American Energy is positioned to grow once a secure supply is obtained. Burning natural gas in our electric power plants produces mainly carbon dioxide and water. And for those who still worry about GHGs, that is, the greenhouse gases such as carbon dioxide, American Energy is at the forefront in carbon capture and storage—that is, taking waste gases from power plants and reinjecting them into wells to minimize the release of CO_2 into the atmosphere, and, at the same time, stimulate natural gas production. And that's not all. American Energy owns a lot of acreage throughout the eastern United States, and we are attempting to reforest areas to absorb CO_2, known as *carbon sinks*. Yes, pro-environmentalism and secure, affordable energy can share the same stage."

It was obvious to the assemblage that Alexandria Raven was not only a savvy businesswoman, but she was also a persuasive cheerleader for her company and her industry. This was the speech she declined to give. But, she knew the financial analysts were not swayed by soft talk; they worked in the realm of hard numbers. Clean-energy experiments were goodie-goodie PR projects, but they rarely paid off for shareholders. American Energy was only a good investment if the bread and butter of its business—natural gas—was in ample supply to transport to its millions of customers and fuel its power plants. They had billions invested in metal and plastic pipelines underneath the ground, and unless methane was flowing through them, they were not earning their keep. And given the current stubborn environmental opposition in Congress to additional drilling for gas off the United States' coastal waters, the prospects were not good.

Raven could not reveal her company's confidential offshore partnership with the DOE. She would not dare to hint to the investment experts of the virtually limitless natural gas supply they were about to tap from methane ice beneath the ocean floor. But she never led Wall Street astray before. If on instinct the stock pickers chose American Energy as a strong buy, they would be seen as prophetic as the Oracle of Delphi.

As Raven drew back from the lectern in favor of the next speaker, a curmudgeonly international oil expert turned global environmental cynic who was certain to spell the doom of fossil fuels, several cellphones burbled in the pockets of the audience members. Moments afterward, shrill beepers disrupted the conference like a collection of angry oven timers, and nearly everyone in the room reached either to their belt to read a Blackberry text message or held a pocket phone to their ear. Mumbling among the crowd drowned out the introduction of the speaker, and an aide to the National Gas and Electric CEO jumped on the dais and whispered into the ear of Louis Campbell. Raven, who returned to her seat, watched as the pink pigment of her rival CEO's face drained, and his ruddy countenance was eclipsed by a glassy-eyed and pallid, death-like expression.

"A LNG ship blew up!" a voice from the assemblage shouted.

In moments, a computer projection screen that featured Campbell's graphic computer presentation was wired into a news channel Internet web site by an alert audio/visual assistant. On the screen, a mountain-sized wall of flame was visible off the coast of Norfolk, Virginia, videostreamed live before the collection of analysts and energy bigwigs. The two massive 1,000-foot ships that contained hundreds of tons of LNG were sinking to the bottom of the ocean. The dock facilities, valves, and fittings that connected to accompanying pipelines that ran to shore were mangled into a melded mass. Louis Campbell, whose company invested millions and whose future was tied to the LNG processing facility on the Virginia coast, had to be physically helped from the dais. Alexandria Raven was as shocked as anyone in the room at the devastation that was undoubtedly the work of terrorists rather than some type of accident. But like a NASCAR driver speeding around the track, there was no sense in stopping to view the fatal crash in the wall that took the life of a competitor. There was still a race to be run. And she intended to win. Her eggs were in a different basket.

CHAPTER 27

▼

"This," Cowboy said, as proudly as he was displaying an award-winning steer at the state fair back in Oklahoma, "is the future of American energy, and, by the way, *American Energy*." He delivered the wordplay with a Groucho Marx eyebrow bounce. The theatrics annoyed Danielle O'Day. *This man is so full of himself*, she thought.

The Stetson-wearing drilling expert held a white chunk of a rock-like substance in a large chemistry petri dish as Danielle looked on. She stood in a laboratory, filled with technicians in sterile plastic yellow outfits milling about at computer stations. The dour Dr. Edison of NOAA, and polite Dr. Roystone, the government's chief geologist, also stood by. Cowboy reached into his jeans and pulled out a Zippo lighter with which he regularly torched his stogies.

"It looks like ice," Danielle said.

"It is ice," Cowboy responded. "Frozen crystal methane hydrate, dug out below the sea bottom." He held his cigar lighter's flame close to the top of the rock, and suddenly it ignited into a burst of orange-blue fire, the rock shrinking as it burned. Danielle was amazed. "Behold—ice that burns."

"Hydrates? You mean there is natural gas in that ice?" She knew a little about methane hydrate, which consisted of methane—the main component of natural gas—held within a molecular lattice of water ice. They were created by a combination of natural gas and water molecules under intense pressure. She knew from her pipeline-welding father that hydrates sometimes formed artificially because of high pressure in pipelines and well bores, becoming a nuisance by clogging the flow of natural gas in the lines. But Danielle read that natural hydrates were also found in some permafrost regions and beneath portions of the ocean floor off the continental shelves of North America, Africa, Europe, and Asia. But scientists did not know that much about them—or so she thought.

"Methane hydrates are conservatively estimated to total twice the amount of other sources of carbon to be found on earth, such as coal, oil, and conventional sources of natural gas," Dr. Roystone interjected. He pointed to a large, colorful and three-dimensional topographical wall map that featured the eastern seaboard of the United States and the continental shelf that extended a hundred miles offshore before lowering in steps into the sea's abyss. A large blue triangle appeared on the edge of the oceanic shelf off the coast of North and South Carolina.

"We are floating over a small area of hydrates about the size of Rhode Island in a deep ocean canyon called the Carolina Trough on the continental slope off the coast of Cape Fear," Roystone continued. "NOAA, DOE, and the U.S. Navy acoustic studies reveal it is a significant offshore oil and gas frontier area where no wells have ever been drilled. Another site is the Blake Ridge deposit about 250 miles east of Charleston, South Carolina. Gas hydrate concentrations in deep strata below the ocean floor on the East Coast alone are estimated to contain quadrillions of cubic feet of methane, enough to power the United States for a century."

"Yes," said Danielle, "but I've read in an industry journal that tapping gas hydrates as usable energy is at least two decades away."

"Admittedly, even the latest reports in the energy trades and *Scientific American* are bit behind the times," Roystone said, suddenly taking the didactic role despite his mild-mannered demeanor. "This core sample was taken out of a hydrate formation, using drilling mud chilled to minus eight degrees Celsius so the cores don't melt. Fishermen have even pulled chunks of hydrates out of the sea caught in their nets. But we have equipment that allows us to study the hydrates without actually cutting them out. But in answer to your question, the future is now. This drilling rig you are on is ready to harvest the vast quantities of natural gas and put an end to America's reliance on foreign energy."

"But is this legal? Drilling is prohibited—"

"Mining," said Cowboy.

"Whatever! Has Congress approved this?"

Roystone cleared his throat. The African-American man adjusted his round glasses that had slipped down his nose. "Congress did approve methane hydrate research funds several years ago, and amended the Mining and Minerals Policy Act of 1976 to include methane hydrates as marine mineral resources for the purpose of leasing of Federal offshore mineral rights."

Danielle was not a trial attorney, but she was beginning to feel like one. "But did they approve this project, specifically?"

"Well, not exactly."

"What the hell do you mean not exactly? My job is to protect my company's assets, and if American Energy is involved in some type of illegal operation—"

Cowboy said, "The president of the United States is an ol' buddy of mine, and has given his personal approval."

"The president?" said Danielle, glaring at him. *Now he's name-dropping again.* "I was sent here to review a biofuel methane recovery system from sea kelp in advance of the president's visit. President Freeman is scheduled to come aboard this platform in two days, accompanied by a hoard of news reporters, government officials, and corporate VIPs to see the same thing. Now you are telling me that this is not the purpose of this operation?"

Cowboy lifted a boot and placed his heel on a chair. "Ever hear of the Manhattan Project?"

"I'm not an idiot," Danielle said, contemptuously. "What does the development of the atom bomb have to do with this?"

"Congress did not *publicly* approve a project to build an atom bomb, either," Cowboy said, putting an avuncular arm on Danielle's shoulder, which she shrugged away. "It was wartime. It was a secret weapon. So is this project. If you haven't noticed, we are in a War of Energy. And instead of an offensive weapon like a nuke, this is a defensive weapon to keep us *out* of hostilities."

"But when the media sees this—"

Cowboy suddenly became less animated and adopted a Jack Webb-Sgt. Friday deadpan tone. "What the press sees will be exactly what you have seen up until a few minutes ago. The president is well aware of these operations and he wants to see them for himself—without the scribes, of course. During this part of the president's tour, we'll feed the blood-sucking bottom feeders—otherwise known as the news media—some fresh-grilled blue marlin."

"But what if someone finds out? There are hundreds of workers on this facility. A leak?"

"No one will find out," Cowboy said. "This operation is very secure. Anyway, most of the hydrate operations are well below deck, and you wouldn't know what the hell was happening on the ocean floor unless you had a submarine and even then you probably wouldn't have a clue. Would you have known that this rig is mining for natural gas hydrates if we hadn't told you? Would you ever have believed that ice could burn?"

Danielle yanked on the sides of her fire-red hair. It was an uncomfortable nervous habit. "I believe someone's ass is going to *fry* if this gets out," she said. "If the administration is keeping this project from Congress, there will be hell to pay. Our company has been lobbying Congress heavily to get the drilling ban lifted off the East Coast, but if word gets out that we are involved in a project before the moratorium is ended legally, the shit is going to hit the fan. The president might be impeached. Someone might go to jail."

Cowboy laughed. "Now, now, missy."

"Don't call me missy!"

"Sorry, mamm, no offense." He removed his boot from its perch and stepped toward a computer console, leaning on it like a defense attorney at the jury rail. "Let me ask you this question. If you are rushing one of your family members with a critical illness to the emergency room in the middle of the night, would you wait at a red light if no other traffic was coming?"

"What the hell are you talking about?"

"Our country, Miss O'Day, is critically ill. We have a severe case of lack-of-energy syndrome that is destined to wreck our economy at the least, or cause another world war at the worst. Congress will lift the drilling ban on the country's coasts eventually. But you know those political gents. It takes time and money, of course. But then it will take several years for conventional drilling rigs to produce enough natural gas and oil to get our country back on its feet. Like the red light, it will change, but we can't afford to wait. We have a seriously sick patient that needs emergency assistance now. The president knows that. And I happen to know him personally. He won't wait until a Pearl Harbor, 9-11, or major natural disaster before he takes action. And he is willing to take the risk— and the responsibility—if anything is revealed publicly. But until then, it is *damn the torpedoes, full steam ahead.*"

"Why wasn't I told about this before?" Danielle was embarrassed. She was the pay-grade-leaping, favored daughter of the CEO of American Energy, and now she felt like she was a clueless intern.

"Probably couldn't risk it. Very few people know about this plan as far as I am aware. Even your sycophant board of directors is probably in the dark, along with the financial community. Maybe that's why your stock price is in the tank. It looks like you are betting the farm on a bunch of seaweed."

"Someone will see through this kelp ruse."

"Oh, it is not a ruse," Dr. Edison said, breaking her silence. "The methane collection system is legitimate."

Roystone interjected, "Though it can only produce a fraction of the methane that we are capable of pumping from beneath the ocean floor."

"Don't worry," said Cowboy, pushing his hat up a bit on his forehead. "Once an ample supply of gas is flowing through the nation's pipelines and we can wean our way off the devil's breast of the mullahs in the Middle East, Congress will award us the Medal of Freedom. C'mon, let me show you how it works."

Despite her nay saying, Danielle was a conformist. She always toed the company line. But only if the line was on the straight and narrow. Would she step on a slippery slope if she condoned this activity—this potential illegal conspiracy? The president of the United States involved? She wondered if this was what presidential lawyer John Dean felt like in the early wake of Watergate in 1972. But this wasn't an illegal break-in involving political shenanigans. This was for the domestic security of the country—kind of like the development of the secret atomic bomb during World War II, as Mr. Rhodan claimed. It was well intentioned. But the road to hell was often paved with good intentions.

CHAPTER 28

▼

The president gritted his teeth, but said nothing for several minutes. On the television in the Oval Office, the wall of orange glow of the burning offshore LNG tankers filled the forty-two-inch plasma high-definition widescreen. It looked like you would burn your hand if you touched the flat glass. A befuddled cable news anchorwoman had little idea what caused the catastrophe, but tossed unsupported theories like table-tennis serves to an academic energy expert from MIT the network scrounged up in minutes. He had written a book on the threats to the country's energy system.

"What do you think, Professor Dyers?" the anchorwoman said. "An accident? Operator error? Could it be the work of terrorists?"

"It is much too early to say," the frosty-haired academic said, his hair coifed as if he were impersonating Albert Einstein. The cover of his poorly selling book—so far—flashed on the screen. Tomorrow it would be a best-seller. "But this incident exposes how vulnerable our nation is to imported energy."

In the president's mind, there was little doubt that the inferno was the result of terrorism. The only question was: which terrorists? There was a long line of ignoble Middle-Eastern, South-American, African, Asian, and European groups that would love to shoot an arrow in America's Achilles Heel—energy. The only continents that did not seem to be targeting American interests were Australia and Antarctica. Though if American zoos were attacked tomorrow by exploding dirty nuclear Koala Bears or germ-laden, biological-weapon bird-flu penguins, he would not be the least bit surprised.

"Was it an Algerian tanker or the one from Trinidad that blew up first?" President Freeman asked his chief national security advisor.

"We don't know," said Arias Applebaum, an expert on international terrorism. He was a dumpy man in his late fifties, with a jet-black, wet-look hairstyle, but a ceiling-white band of hair running from the middle of his forehead to the back of his skull, like a racing stripe on the roof of a stock car. His detractors in Congress called him "The Skunk" for obvious reasons. "I would caution trying to pin this on any particular terrorist group or cell. There are a number of nationalities that are crewmembers of these ships. It could be a conspiracy among a number of groups whose only commonality is hatred of the United States. In fact, the detonation could have happened directly on the dock facilities."

"You mean domestic terrorists?"

"Could be. We simply don't have enough information."

The president turned his head toward another in the room. "Condition of the LNG facilities, Virgil?"

The president's secretary of energy, Virgil Priest, a dapper man with a Roaring '20s-era waxed moustache, shifted in his chair uncomfortably. He just toured the LNG facility the week before. "I just talked to the president of National Gas and Electric. Needless to say, he is a little shell-shocked. He says the coastal facilities are not damaged at all. It is perhaps fortuitous that we did not pursue the offshore LNG platform plan—otherwise the conflagration could have destroyed the whole kit and caboodle. However, the obliteration of the docks and accompanying pipelines makes the facility basically useless—at least temporarily. Let alone the destruction of the two tankers—billions of dollars in losses—and of course, the fuel contained inside."

The president paused for a moment resting his head on a triangle formed by the index fingers and thumbs of both of his hands.

"Jerry?" the president asked his secretary of defense, Jerome Van Nostrand. "Thoughts? Who could have done this?"

Van Nostrand was a crusty, balding, and raspy-voiced retired Army general, elected to Congress in Tennessee after he became famous as one of the cable-TV generals during the Second Iraq War. He agreed to join the current administration because the president was a former military man, even if the Commander in Chief was from the Navy, his branch's natural rival.

"I don't think it is a direct attack by a foreign government—at least not officially sponsored," said Van Nostrand. His sea-blue eyes flashed with humor. "The new government in Algeria is not that dumb. They remember Afghanistan."

"Why not?" Applebaum questioned haughtily. "I have warned against this type of thing for years." The president felt Applebaum was a vain man who wanted to cover his behind before he demanded to know how such a calamity could occur on his watch. "That's why I demanded that the LNG ships be escorted by the Navy! Tell me why not?"

"The target," Van Nostrand said, almost as condescendingly as responding to a clueless media type asking him why people get killed during wartime. "One mile into the Norfolk harbor a substantial portion of the U.S. Atlantic Fleet was docked like sitting ducks. The Navy escort of the Algerian ship was broken off— nothing unusual was noted during the voyage. Not that they had the power to notice much aboard ship. And once the Coast Guard took over the escort as the tanker neared the dock, they were unprepared to respond to a sudden suicide attack." The defense secretary looked around the room as if he were addressing the troops. "But if I was a military general wanting to do harm to the United States, I would have rammed that tanker right into the Norfolk harbor full of Navy ships and then blew it up. It would have been Pearl Harbor meets 9-11. Or, if they wanted civilian casualties or general mayhem, they could have run the vessel aground in the middle of Virginia Beach and started a fiery tourist attraction. Most of the people killed were those on the ships, and few of those were Americans."

"Perhaps they were not looking at attacking the military or civilians," the president ruminated. "Any chance it could be accidental, Virgil?"

"Doubt it," Secretary of Energy Priest said. "LNG will not explode like that under normal circumstances. This had to be deliberately set with incendiary devices just to break open the tanker holds. But, once released and vaporized in the atmosphere, any spark could launch an enormous inferno."

"Maybe it was a message," the president said.

"Message?" Priest responded.

The president stood and paced the room in slow, deliberate steps. "LNG received all the press as being one of the keys to respond to the oil embargo from the other nations in the Islamic revolution. More LNG on the market would help steady the cost of natural gas and it could lessen upward pressure on oil prices. This could be a message from our enemies that they have us by the balls, no matter what we do to try to meet our needs without them. Killing massive amounts of civilians or attacking us militarily would undoubtedly lead to a counterattack that would make the wars in Afghanistan and Iraq look like a mild spanking. But if you blow up facilities associated with an American energy company ... who knows ... in today's environment, it could be seen as an accident. Just another energy failure like the great Northeast blackout. And once we are on the ropes and our economy on the brink, the new militant OPEC will lift the embargo to some degree, with oil and natural gas at astronomical prices. And they think we won't have any choice but to pay."

"So," the energy secretary responded, "this isn't an attempt to ruin our ability to permanently import natural gas, it is simply a Mafia-style delivery of dead fish in newspaper?"

"Perhaps," the president said. He moved over to the bombproof glass window of the Oval Office, his hands behind his back. "Still, we must be more militarily prepared. Jerry—put all services on the next highest alert. But we will treat this as an accident under investigation publicly, until we can prove otherwise."

"Aye-aye, Mr. President," Van Nostrand said in lighthearted deference to the president's naval background. Freeman admired Van Nostrand like a favorite uncle. After all, the army general was his senior by twenty years.

"Arias," President Freeman said in rapid-fire succession as he turned to his national security chief. "If we can determine connection with a foreign government, I want to have all options for response before me, diplomatic and military."

"Will do," Applebaum responded.

"Virgil," he continued in his fusillade of orders. "I want room for more press and special guests for the trip to the *Project Blue Sky* energy platform."

"I assumed you would want to cancel that in the light of this," Priest said, twirling the tip of his waxy moustache.

"We'll tour the damage to the LNG docks, but then we will fly off the coast to showcase this new facility. The American people need reassurance that we are doing all we can to address the energy crisis and avoid panic in the aftermath of this catastrophe."

"More press? Special guests?"

"Yes, I was thinking of inviting Representative Doggle and his entourage to give him a close-up look at what we are doing and a get a chance to lobby him a bit on the energy bill."

"In all due respect, Mr. President," Priest said, stiffening in his chair. "Chairman Doggle has no intention on bending on his opposition to offshore drilling, and if I may be so bold—why are you insisting on being perceived as always kissing his fat pandering ass?"

The secretary of defense and chief national security advisor raised their eyebrows at Priest's boldness. Like the coiling of a spring, sudden tension filled the large ovoid room and everyone waited for the recoil.

"I'm not trying to kiss his ass, Virgil," the president responded. "I'm trying to bite it, but I can't open my mouth that wide."

Laughter erupted, breaking the stress.

"Well, how about this," President Freeman continued, returning to his chair. "Instead of Doggle, how about Olga Stevick?"

"What about that old witch?" Priest sneered. "She just wants as much publicity as she can get before she buys the farm. She only came to the White House because it was a good venue to hold a press conference to bite *you* in the ass."

"Then we'll give her what she wants: lots of publicity. If we could woo her a bit, perhaps it could drive a wedge between her senior citizen consumerists and the crackpot corn gasohol supporters that are bankrolling Doggle. And get that Winkle guy too. Once the environmentalists are comfortable with energy coming from seaweed, and there is enough natural gas flowing into the east coast to lower prices and ease spot shortages to relieve consumer outrage, I think we will have enough support in the Congress to get the energy bill passed and begin openly drilling off both coasts. We can publicly announce *Project Hades* sometime later."

"It has to be more appealing than war," the secretary of defense said. Freeman agreed that more than anyone else, nearly every soldier or sailor who has seen combat up close deplored war as the broad-based solution to international disputes.

"You're betting that *Project Hades* will be an unqualified success," Priest said, hesitantly.

"My secretary of energy's future depends on it," the president said bluntly.

Freeman thought about the economic and energy crisis that not only threatened his fledgling administration, but also the safety of the United States and peace in the world. The Arab countries were the world's largest exporters of energy. They were also the greatest importer of arms. Despite the wave of Arab nationalism that led the headlines in leading newspapers around the globe, the president felt that the cauldron of greed and evil would eventually turn the Islamic countries against one another like rats feeding on the same carcass. The history of inter-region conflict was there—800,000 dead and 3 million wounded between the Persian Shi'ites and the Arab Sunnis in the Iran-Iraq war, the subsequent invasion of Kuwait by Saddam Hussein, the constant conflict between Libya and Chad, fighting between the Syrian Ba'athists and Lebanese Shi'ites, the bloodbaths between rival tribal forces of Ethiopia and Somalia, the gangster hits between Fatah and Hamas in Palestine, and later the mutual slaughter between the Kurds, Shi'ites, and Sunnis during the Iraq Civil War. It was not always the Arab states versus the Israelis, or Islam versus Christianity. In fact, the recent Israeli-Palestinian settlement now stood like a bizarre peaceful oasis in the middle of the desert cyclone. The Gulf States not only armed themselves against the

Israelis, but also in protection from each other, not to mention the fanatics in their own nations. Now the rearmed major Arab states were mostly in the hands of bellicose religious zealots. True, the United States could never abandon its military presence from the Persian Gulf. But it would be a lot easier if they were not addicted to the region's oil or natural gas. Junkies do some desperate things.

The president thought of his old Naval Academy buddy, Bruce Rhodan, or "Cowboy" as he called himself. Cowboy washed out of Annapolis, but the president knew back then that his roommate's rakish personality destined him for significant accomplishments. And Cowboy and Virgil Priest assured him that this innovative natural gas hydrate project in the Atlantic had the potential to revolutionize the energy world.

"I hope you know what you're doing," the president said to his energy chief. "If you're right, moving to a U.S.-produced, natural gas-centered economy will result in more domestic security and jobs, and if this carbon sequestration technology also proves worthwhile, it may be a Godsend for the environmental movement. Although I am in favor of free world trade—including energy—that will benefit all societies, just about every American is dying to tell the radical Islamic fundamentalist leaders that they can stick their derricks up their ass and drink their fucking oil for all we care. Yes, Virgil, I'm counting on *Project Hades* will be a *smashing* success."

"And if it isn't?" Applebaum, the national security advisor, questioned. The energy secretary glared askance at him, his waxed moustache twitching.

The president frowned. "If it isn't, I hope war is not the only option we have left."

The final words by the president dropped like a lead curtain on the toes of his supporting cast. The energy business was the second largest industry in the world—and without new supplies, the U.S. would be on the brink of ruin. New energy sources might have to be secured with the help of the largest industry on the planet—armaments.

PART V

▼

A NEW FRONTIER

CHAPTER 29

▼

New York City, the following evening

"You probably shouldn't have come here," said Alexandria Raven, but her counterfeit protest was neutralized by a ripple of pleasure that vibrated up her spine from the center of her groin. She reclined on the bed, naked, her arms perpendicular to her side as if she was crucified, but with her legs also spread wide. Despite her fifty years and the hip-widening wear and tear of vaginal births to three children, her shapely figure was remarkably intact. She half-heartedly cloaked her curves and ample bosom from her associates with business suits. However, private body-pump instruction and aerobic sessions with her personal trainer kept her figure toned. Days on the beaches of North Carolina's Outer Banks, where she owned a three-story, eleven-room beach house with a panoramic view of the Atlantic Ocean, embossed a respectable bronze hue on her legs, arms, and midsection. An exclusive tanning salon in mid-town Manhattan maintained her color during the winter months. Her untanned, milky breasts sat on her chest like two tantalizing bowls of vanilla ice cream with a large butterscotch chip on top. Her hair—previously wound tight in a bun—now draped over a red silk pillowcase and flowed down the side of the king-size bed like shining silver tinsel on a Christmas tree. Undressed, supine, and spread-eagled, she knew her naked body was remarkably appealing.

Her lover did not respond to her weak, disingenuous verbal dissent. Though frequently beset by vaginal dryness since the onset of menopause, there was no evidence of that now. Her moist folds welcomed his gentle touch, for they had not made love in three weeks. He worked in Washington. She lived in New York City. Though not insurmountably distant to conduct a periodic illicit affair, they could not be discovered in the same place often without arousing suspicion. She was not as concerned about being identified as lovers, though that in itself would be a scandal that would upset two marriages, lead tabloid headlines, and cost them their jobs. She was more worried that there would be accusations of collusion between her company and the federal government. That had the potential to abort an embryonic project that took years to gestate, and promised to make Raven, who owned countless thousands of shares of American Energy stock, one of the richest women on earth.

Raven wrapped her legs tightly around her lover's neck, his wide moustache tickling her inner thighs while his remarkably long tongue probed her pleasure zone. After drawn out foreplay, they clawed at each other like cats, creating a pool of sweat on the silk sheets beneath them in a honeymoon-suite hotel bed at the Manhattan Marriott. Afterward, she cuddled in his arms, face glowing and eyes tearing from intense satisfaction. Her husband was not a competent lover, and he gradually desired golf more than her body, despite her tireless efforts to preserve its attractive condition. Her spouse was just a bored, retired bureaucrat—he no longer wielded the political power that Raven craved from a lover. She did not seek a young white-collar stud eager to sleep his way up the corporate ladder, or a washboard-abed gigolo from the gym to make her feel young. She brandished so much corporate muscle herself, she yearned to be dominated—if only sexually— by a mature, vibrant man with the power to change the course of the future.

Things could not get any better for her. She was not only chieftain of her company, she was recognized as the prophetic leader of her industry. She would not flow her shareholders' dollars down the rathole well of LNG imports like National Gas and Electric, and she would soon be hailed for her foresight. She built a huge corporate monolith from a conservative, regional utility company that Wall Street once considered as attractive of an investment as a passbook savings account. But if everything worked out well, she would soon take over her largest rival in the eastern United States. Her company would not only become the most profitable firm since Microsoft and transform herself into a virtual reincarnated Rockefeller, but she also would be seen as the savior of the United States' energy crisis, perhaps averting a potential world war. She might be *Time* Magazine's *Person of the Year*, or maybe, *Decade*. All it took was hard work, determination, and some enjoyable rumbles under the covers. She could not contain her joy—everything was going her way, and she did not experience that thunderous of an orgasm in twenty years. The contented expression on her lover's face conveyed mutual fulfillment.

"Perhaps you should have become the secretary of *love*," Raven said, like a giggling girl scout, fondling her companion's scrotum that he said sent teasing electric post-orgasmic tickles throughout his body. His frame was not that of a body builder, but rather that of a latter-middle-aged desk jockey businessman with a Krispie Kreme-produced potbelly. But he knew how to please her, and he would not give up until he accomplished his mission.

Her lover wiped her secretions from his wide moustache, twiddling them in an effort to return the tips to their waxed curls. She was not sure that he loved her, but he admitted that the relationship provided the most satisfying sex he ever had in his life. Two previous affairs with younger Washington staff members were titillating, he told her, but there was nothing like a mature woman who was an efficient lover. She knew all the right delightful moves and did not waste one twitch or rotation in bringing gratification. And for a gal in her sixth decade, he said she was a fox.

Virgil Priest, the fifty-eight-year-old United States secretary of energy caressed her legs in his. Their mature bodies, both past their youthful prime, melded into the blissful union of young newlyweds. This was a partnership that benefited physical desires, and, Raven felt, the critical needs of the nation. Her lover craved power, perhaps more than her, but no matter. Regrettably, she kept their unions surreptitious and their opportunities for trysts few. But admittedly, the infrequency of their rendezvous increased her carnal craving for Priest, and the furtiveness added a bit to the thrill.

They had been lovers for three years, off and on, of course. And she admired him. Priest lived in Virginia, and had a dedicated wife—a local town councilwoman—and a grown son who was a Ph.D. candidate at Boston University. After a career managing an independent oil company in Texas, he then served briefly as a presidential appointee on the Federal Energy Regulatory Commission. After Raven's husband resigned to avoid a conflict of interest when she took control of one of the largest natural gas firms in the nation, the previous president tapped Priest to become the nation's energy czar. A millionaire several times over, he had nothing to gain financially by joining the president's cabinet, but it did boost his ego the way money could not. He managed the department with his business aplomb, and was a holdover when the new president took control of the White House. She first met him at her husband's retirement party. Their eyes locked for an embarrassing amount of time. He sipped his whiskey sour and dabbed his curly-cue moustache with a cocktail napkin, and she giggled when the white lathery remnants of the drink dripped on his tie.

"Where's the man of the hour?" Priest asked, referring to her husband, once the other guests left the two alone.

"Discussing golf with some career diplomat from the state department," she said, "bragging how much he plans to play at our summer home on the Outer Banks."

They both sipped their drinks.

"And your better-half?" Raven asked.

"Not here," Priest answered. "She detests the Washington cocktail circuit."

"So you get a long leash."

"She knows I'm too old to fool around anymore."

"A virile man like you?"

"I have no interest in immature women," he said, wiping his tie once again from a dribble. "Don't get me wrong. I find the pulchritude of youth as temping as any other man, but involvement with sycophantic floozies is like consuming a colorful peach that is not yet ripe—not as sweet as you think and it results in indigestion."

Perhaps she was the woman of his dreams, she thought. Raven soon surrendered herself to him, and he seemed to relish pleasing her. He would not divorce his devoted wife, however. And neither did she want to split from her golf-addicted husband. Their relationship was perfect the way it was. They would do nothing to destroy it.

Along with the love affair, came business. And Priest's help was critical in the selection of American Energy as the main private corporate partner and potential beneficiary of the federal government's *Project Hades*. But Priest was also a public proponent of the liquefied natural gas plans as well. The president did not want to be held hostage to one potential source of natural gas. And considering the explosion and fire at the Virginia LNG facility, it now looked like a good judgment. But while the LNG promoters would be in check for a while, Raven's company would likely get the go-ahead to test the unproven venture in the abyss of the Atlantic. Priest was under intense criticism by the public, press, and Congress for the dire energy situation in the United States. But he was ready to pull a rabbit out of his hat. If it worked, Raven and her compatriots would become unbelievably wealthy. And who knows, the secretary of energy could transform from goat to national hero who the press might christen as a strong candidate for a future president of the United States. Imagine that, the richest woman on the globe with the most powerful man in the world, secret lovers. *How about that for a Harlequin Romance?* she thought.

The lovers kissed and intertwined their limbs. His manhood was growing again? Must be those little blue diamonds! She would have to invest in pharmaceuticals as well as energy. Tomorrow, together, the clandestine couple would display to the world a public relations dream—clean, affordable energy produced naturally from plants beneath the sea to fuel the future of America. It was as natural, exciting, and gratifying as their experienced lovemaking. The exhibition on the waves of the Atlantic Ocean off the Carolina coast might not be the world's greatest deception since the invasion of Normandy, but getting things done the traditional Washington way was neither effective nor efficient. Like D-Day, a *bodyguard of lies* was necessary for complete success, and Raven must put on a flawless public show. And after tonight's blissful activity, it would not be difficult to flash a bright smile for the cameras.

CHAPTER 30

▼

The odd-looking troika arranged themselves on the points of an isosceles triangle, with the huge walnut desk of the chairman of the House Energy and Commerce Committee at the apex. Congressman August Doggle was not just a power-wielder, he also considered himself a consensus-builder. In contrast to his usual casual tan western sport jacket and string tie, he was now dressed in a tailored Italian suit, bright white shirt, and a silk tie plastered with American flags. He pressed the pudgy fingers of each hand together as if in prayer.

On opposite angles of the desk sat Doggle's guests: the bony, hunched figure of Olga Stevick and the crooked praying-mantis form of Herbert Winkle. Stevick was clad in her Amish-style black dress sprinkled with dandruff that seemed magnified by the contrast of the dark fabric. She stared blankly at the plethora of pictures of Doggle shaking the hands of Hollywood celebrities that littered the walls of the office. Winkle wore black dress pants, brown loafers, white socks, and an ivory, sweat-stained shirt. A plaid jacket buttoned tightly around his potbelly looked like a patchwork quilt cloak worn by a rodeo clown. A permanent scowl was etched on his face.

"There is only so much I can do from behind this desk on behalf of my congressional district," said the congressman. His tinny Truman Capote voice clashed in discordant harmony with the squeal from the wheels on the bottom of his office chair. "The presidency—no matter what dope is in the office—is still a powerful force. We must work together where the rubber meets the road so at the end of the day all of our constituents are content and we save the nation from certain disaster."

Doggle loved waxing his colloquial expressions. He felt it gave him an air of wisdom. Winkle's right eye rolled upward. The environmentalist wasn't buying. The little toad would be a harder sell than Doggle thought. But the congressman could handle him as he had farm animals during his teenage years in rural Iowa. It was up to him when they grazed and when they were slaughtered. And, he remembered, when they had to accept him. He did not wait for the high-school prom and bargain with a dinner and corsage to get a piece of farm-girl ass. He had plenty in the barn. His sheep didn't ask him to take them to dinner before he buggered them, and they didn't nag him about marriage afterward. He had little time for women—they spent money, bitched a lot, and wasted his time. He had things to do, places to go. He wanted to work at the farm bureau. He wanted to go to college. He wanted to run for state representative and then for Congress. And he did it all. Fucking sheep never held him back.

Doggle did not stay on top of the heap in Washington by rolling over and playing dead. He got what he wanted, when he wanted it. Case in point—the evening before. He did not desire sexual gratification like he once did—he was, after all, getting old and his libido was waning. But the old feeling came upon him from time to time. It was not easy finding the object of his desire, but in Washington, DC, everything was possible for a price. And it was such a delicious pleasure. The narrow hips, the smooth skin on his lover's arms, chest, and legs. The little ass he loved to spank and the high-pitched squeal that came out of the pouting innocent mouth. A mouth he loved to kiss. He treated his lover gently for the most part and did the best he could to bring happiness to both of them. What turned him on most was the total lack of pubic hair. So clean, so innocent. And the cute Latin tongue—Doggle didn't speak a word of Spanish. But knew his lover would not say a word in any language. After all, it was a very expensive arrangement. A thousand dollars for a single evening of bliss. Of course, the pimp would pocket nine-tenths he was sure, for this lover was hard to find. But a hundred dollars was a ton of money for a ten-year-old boy, especially one who was in the United States illegally and could be deported back to the Central American slum he came from in two shakes of a lamb's tail.

Doggle stared at the dumpy environmentalist who seemed to have a huge chip on his shoulder. *I'll fuck him like a sheep if I have to*, Doggle thought.

"F-F-Frankly," Winkle said, "I don't see how endorsing corn fuel eliminates acid rain or excess global warming g-g-gasses." Winkle sat still, one eye focused on him and the other seemed to simultaneously peer at Stevick. He looked like a motionless chameleon, eyes rotating, searching for an insect for lunch. It gave the congressman the creeps.

"Mr. Winkle," Doggle said. "The United States did not win World War II single-handedly. We had allies. Without the Russians containing the Germans on the eastern front, D-Day might never have occurred. But we did not all become communists, did we?"

"I don't need a history lesson," Stevick croaked. "The Freeman administration is in bed with an insidious monopoly. This is the robber-baron Rockefeller Standard Oil Trust all over again—a century later. This energy policy of greed and gouge must be defeated. We need to storm the Bastille!"

Doggle smiled at the elderly woman, his lips clenched tight. He was breathing as little as possible since he found the old woman's body odor revolting—it reminded him of spoiled milk. She didn't smell as bad when testifying in front of his committee. Then, they were twenty feet apart.

"I believe Miss Stevick has the right idea," Doggle told Winkle. "There is strength in numbers. I believe we can provide clean energy and affordable prices with the right legislation from this esteemed body."

Winkle frowned, but Doggle knew he could be persuaded. The congressman was not moved by the sob stories of the stinky old lady at the other side of the desk. But she had the media and much of the public eating out of her liver-spotted hand. The environmental movement must bend a little to get enough popular support, and therefore, political power, to pass its agenda. ANGER, the Sierra Club, Greenpeace, and the rest of the enviro-forces could only push so far by themselves. Doggle understood that the American people had a cognitive dissonance with doing the green thing. Americans knew greenhouse gases were anathema to the earth, but were sympathetic to environmental causes only if it didn't cost much money. But get the American consumer behind them, and nothing could stop them. Stevick's geriatric pied-piper tune was also an AARP crossover hit with younger, middle America. She was a star, but might not shine long. Her populist consumer movement could be used to further his agenda. With enough government regulations controlling the pollution sources and enforcement of price controls on clean sources of energy, everyone could be happy, with the possible exception of the energy industry. Yes, he knew it smacked of socialism, but he was no communist.

Doggle backed slightly from his desk, the wheels under his chair whining under the undue stress they bore. He was trying to accomplish two things—first to signal that the meeting of the minds was about to be concluded, and second, to get out of olfactory range of Stevick's Limburger aroma.

"The president wants us all to be part of the seaweed-gas show on his Department of Energy garbage scow, a $1 billion sinkhole I might add," said the congressman. "I, regrettably have duties that restrict me to the Capitol."

Stevick and Winkle squirmed.

"But I think it would be advisable for both of you to accept his invitation," said Doggle.

"That is playing right into the p-p-president's hands," Winkle protested.

"There is no better place to throw a monkey wrench into his silly PR machination than from the inside," Doggle counseled. "Play the game—learn what you can. See if you can uncover the folly of the effort. Frustrate him at every turn. Then, we can expose the Golden Fleece for what it is—a total misuse of public funds that would be better spent on developing alternative fuels, and," he said, winking at Stevick, "providing energy assistance to senior citizens. And once the president's sacrificial lamb is exposed, then it can be ... slaughtered." He almost said, *screwed*.

"He can't fool an old fool," Stevick cackled. "This grandmother will take him to the woodshed if he can't prove that this will control the energy power trusts."

"And r-r-reduce carbon dioxide emissions," Winkle added.

"Go, and remember to take Dramamine," Doggle advised. "I bet the president's little project may not be too seaworthy."

After offering the two keychain trinkets with the seal of the U.S. House of Representatives, Doggle dispatched his disciples like the Wicked Witch of the West sending off her flying monkeys to do her bidding. Hopefully, they would return with red ruby slippers in hand, with or without their owner attached.

CHAPTER 31

▼

Danielle O'Day's tour of the world's largest offshore drilling rig was interrupted as Secret Service agents arrived on a Marine helicopter to conduct their security advance work in preparation for the president's visit. She was disappointed with the delay; she was just getting intensely interested and finally over her seasickness. But it was a relief to get away from Cowboy's advances.

The Secret Service briefly interviewed each major official on the platform about the logistics of the itinerary, the schematics of the MODU, the route of the president's planned tour, and the identities of project staff who would come in close proximity to the president. Although a drilling rig nearly a hundred miles offshore in the ocean was more contained and controllable than an open limousine motorcade through the downtown streets of a major city, the security inspection was more than routine. The president attracted as many assassination plots against him every day as there are bomb threats in New York City.

Despite the popular reputation of the agents' persona as unemotional robots, there was much jocularity between the federal bodyguards and the *Project Blue Sky/Hades* staff. The officers in charge of the president's safety did not wear their game face all the time—only when it counted. The Secret Service was generally satisfied with the plan and already reviewed the backgrounds of every person aboard the drilling facility, so there were few questions or suspicions. That was until the latest helicopter touched down on the platform—one that was not in the logbook. The aircraft had one passenger, a copper-toned-skinned male flown in from a connection in Bermuda on a French-made chopper owned by a British firm. He was a British citizen, possessing a viable passport. The crew immediately recognized him on the helipad, and greeted him with smiles and handshakes.

Danielle's curiosity rose as she peered out at the deck observing a tall newcomer who was seemingly lionized like a rock star by adoring groupies. He moved deliberately, his legs moving like stiff stilts, like a star basketball player who just exited a cramped bus to sign autographs. Beyond the glad-handing scene on the deck, the bright blue sky that stretched from horizon to horizon when O'Day arrived had turned into a hazy gray and the Atlantic breeze had picked up.

"Who is Akmed Abram?" asked Robert Sempran, the lead Secret Service agent of the advance team. He thumbed through the passport and eyed Cowboy. They sat in a conference room adjacent to the control room of the platform—called the "doghouse"—that towered two levels above the vessel's main deck. She sat silent in the room, sipping a cup of steaming coffee, and stared through the window at the dark stranger who appeared to be known by everyone aboard. Another agent informed Sempran that the visitor needed to visit the privy to relieve himself, understandable after the long chopper ride from the Caribbean island that served as his connection from London.

"Without Akmed Abram," Cowboy said, "we wouldn't be out here in the middle of the ocean right now."

Danielle's emerald eyes lifted upward from her white Styrofoam coffee cup, inquisitive.

Cowboy continued. "Akmed is one of the world's leading petroleum geophysicists. It is his research that led to the realization that we could find infinite quantities of recoverable fossil fuel off the continental shelf of the United States, as well as along the shores of Norway and China. And," Cowboy emphasized, "along with the president, he is one of my very best friends."

Danielle found Cowboy's name-dropping obsequious, but then again, he did know the president. Her boss told her so. Maybe not bosom buddies, but perhaps more than a casual acquaintance.

"Hydrates were discovered off the coasts decades ago," Danielle said. "That man does not look very old."

"He does look good for someone that long-in-the-tooth," Cowboy admitted. "Must be all that goat's milk. But no, he didn't discover the hydrates, he pioneered a new three-dimensional sonar technology that could distinguish between loosely held hydrates in small concentrations that are basically useless and thick clusters of hydrates that can be economically recovered from below the ocean floor. He's been a consultant to my company for years."

"Mr. Abram's name is not on the list of employees working on the platform submitted by the DOE or American Energy," the assiduous silver-haired Secret

Service agent said, flipping through several papers in a folder. Sempran didn't seem suspicious, just efficient, Danielle thought.

"Akmed is not an employee—he is a contracted scientist. He is the brainchild of the sonar-imaging apparatus on this platform. Most of his work is completed and he currently is involved in drilling gas wells in the Mediterranean. That project is now producing, and he asked whether he could return here to observe the first active methane-recovery test. Since he is our contractor and my good friend, I told him he was welcome anytime."

"But he is a British citizen?"

"Yes. He was raised as a child in Palestine, but he has spent his entire adult life in England. He even joined me in Houston for a few years when he was involved with several Southeast Exploration ventures. You should have seen the looks on his face when I took him to this redneck bar ... Well, I've worked with him on numerous projects throughout the world."

At that moment, the lanky Palestinian-born geophysicist appeared, bending his head to avoid the short, metal bulkhead doorway into the control room. He raked his oil-black hair specked with gray, blown askew by the unrelenting Atlantic wind. His high cheekbones dominated the features of his long, Lincolnesque face. The Arabic man's protruding brow, prominent nose, and lantern-shaped jaw projected a countenance of determination, maturity, and strength. Danielle found him stunningly attractive and confidently strong, but unlike Cowboy, somehow humble by his slow, methodical gait.

"Akmed!" Cowboy hollered, standing to greet the man as if he were a long-lost brother. He kissed the coffee-skinned man on both hollow cheeks and hugged him firmly, his Stetson bumping into the man's forehead.

"Cowboy," Akmed said with a baritone and distinguished Omar Sharif British-Arab accent. "Why are you so happy to see me when you owe me fifty dollars from our last wager?"

"Akmed, Akmed, is that any way to greet someone in your debt?" Cowboy laughed, and the tall Arab man smiled, revealing a rack of perfectly aligned and impeccably white teeth.

"Mr. Sempran, Ms. O'Day," said Cowboy. "This is Akmed Abram, Professor of Geophysics at Cambridge University."

The polite Palestinian native was charming and demure, bowing and shaking the agent's hand and then, with more deliberateness, Danielle's. His large hand was callused, but clean, warm to the touch. His midnight-black eyes enchanted Danielle, though when he bowed he avoided direct eye contact. Unlike Americans, Danielle knew, many other cultures found direct eye contact rude.

The Secret Service agent tapped a pad he was holding. "Professor Abram," Sempran said. "I am from the United States' Secret Service."

"Yes," Akmed said. "You protect the president of the United States. I am honored." He nodded respectfully.

"Likewise. However, we had no idea you were going to be aboard this platform. I'm sorry, but I'm going to have to get confirmation of your status if you are going to stay here during the president's visit."

"Of course," Akmed said. "I am sorry. My decision to come here was made at the last moment. I'm afraid I took advantage of my friendship with Mr. Rhodan and asked him to allow me to board. I should have realized that there might be a security question. Again, I apologize."

"I'm sure everything will be fine," Sempran said. "We just need to get confirmation from Washington."

The courteous agent promised to return the passport in short order, and he left the room.

"Well, Akmed," Cowboy said. "He thinks you're a terrorist."

CHAPTER 32

▼

Hilton Hotel, New York City

"Let's face the facts, Louie, National's stock is going to tumble and you know it," said Alexandria Raven.

She did not want to gloat. She did not want to say, "I told you so." She wanted to seal a business deal and strike a good bargain for both sides.

Louis Campbell seemed to have aged ten years in a day. He sat on the edge of his bed in his twenty-seventh floor hotel suite in the Central Park Hilton. It was a beautiful room, with walnut paneling, a lavish black-leather couch, an adjoining bedroom with a king-size mattress, and a spectacular view of Manhattan below. It smelled of cigars, Campbell's gaudy cologne, and stale booze. Raven, repulsed by the barroom odor, nevertheless did not reveal her discomfort. Her unannounced visit to her fellow energy company CEO might not cheer him up, but it could keep him out of bankruptcy.

Raven understood that the destruction of the LNG ships off the coast of Norfolk was not a catastrophic loss of assets. Campbell headed a big company and it had pockets deep enough to absorb the initial hit. But it meant a tremendous interruption of future gas supply that may cause havoc in that firm's twenty-state-wide natural gas and electric distribution system. LNG ships would likely be banned from the high seas until stricter security measures could be enforced. It would hit the LNG importers the same way the airline industry was devastated by 9-11. It was unfortunate, but that's life. In the meantime, factories in National's service territory might have to be closed and schools may have to shut down until warmer weather. Only so much emergency gas could be diverted from other areas of the country. Campbell was in a serious pickle. State governments would point the finger at National Gas and Electric for not having a secure supply of fuel for its customers. They would slash the firm's utility rates—

destroying its profitability. National's electric plants would also be slammed and brownouts and blackouts were on the horizon. They were now more dependent on gas than coal or nuclear. Layoffs would follow. The stock would drop further. An endless maelstrom of fiasco. Raven foresaw this scenario. National Gas and Electric would not go bankrupt today, but unless something positive happened, it might be inevitable. They needed a white knight. They needed a fire sale.

"The pipelines coming out of your Norfolk facility have not suffered damage, correct?" Raven asked her energy rival. Campbell stared out into the mirror of his hotel room, seemingly seeing nothing. His eyes were glassy with the effects of Benadryl he ingested for allergies, tobacco for stress, and alcohol for depression. Raven felt as if she were a grief counselor.

"No damage to the pipelines," Campbell repeated lugubriously, as if under hypnosis. His tie hung low around his open collar. *He's been drinking for a day,* she thought.

"So that's not too bad," Raven said, sitting next to him on the bed. Her arm slipped around his shoulders like a sister providing comfort.

"But no gas to go through them. The shortfall will be colossal."

"What if I can get some of American Energy's gas through those lines?"

Campbell seemed to come back to sobriety and consciousness. He snorted a laugh.

"American Energy gas?" he said. "And where are you getting this methane from—imported sheep droppings from New Zealand?"

"Now Louie, have faith in me. We have new supplies ready to come on line." She stood and moved away. His scotch and cigar stench was disgusting.

"You're not serious about your seaweed gas, are you? Everyone in the industry knows that's a red herring. A goodie-goodie PR project with the DOE to cozy up to the feds. It's not a large secure supply. Get real."

"What else are you going to do with your pipelines, Louie?"

Campbell was reticent and his head slumped forward.

Raven first met Campbell at an International Gas Association conference in Houston several years before. As a senior vice president of American Energy, she sought to glad-hand major industry CEOs like Campbell, who had led National Gas and Electric for some time. She remembered the meeting with delight. Campbell was supercilious and demeaning. Laughing at some ribald joke, Campbell halted his old-boy network discussion when a *woman* tried to enter the conversation.

"Whose wife are you little lady?" Campbell said, drink in hand and half in the bag with several drilling and pipeline company executives. "Or are you taking drink orders. I'll have a Chivas Regal."

Raven smiled and shook Campbell's hand, "I'm the wife of the keynote speaker over there," she said, pointing to the major guest of the annual conference, the president's nominee for U.S. secretary of energy.

Campbell was embarrassed, and then further taken aback when Raven was named American Energy's CEO a couple of years later. Though her company was smaller than National's and no obvious takeover threat, he always gave her the cold shoulder. She knew he didn't like her. He was one of the many in the tired old-boy network in the energy industry who did not warm up to women running part of the show. Ladies were for assuaging irate customers in phone centers or holding cooking demonstrations, not for making decisions about assets.

She overheard snippets of his sexist ranting before the energy summit got underway. "I started my career in the ditch," he boasted to the group of industry heads. "I worked my way to the top ... bitches running gas companies ... It's a joke." *She who laughs last*, she thought. Now it came to this. Louis Campbell, energy industry titan, drunk and despondent, and a little *damsel* his knight in shining armor.

Campbell stood, wavering a bit, but once he stabilized his stance against a high dresser in the hotel room, he regained some of his business chutzpah he was known for.

"Look, Alexandria," he said. "I know the Feds have been sitting on your own pipeline proposals because of a lack of proven supply. But if you want to lease pipeline space from us, that can be arranged. I still don't know what you are going to be pushing through those lines other than hot air. This industry may have to go back to synthesized gas from coal—let me tell you something from my forty years of experience in the business: domestic natural gas looks like it's finished. There just isn't enough in the ground to go around. Our only hope is increased imports."

"You let me worry about gas supply, Louie," Raven said. "We might even be able to secure some for your company's customers."

Campbell laughed again, this time heartily. "Fine, Alexandria—I won't hold my breath. But you can lease the whole damn capacity of our lines if you want." He slugged down the dregs of a drink in a whiskey glass.

"I didn't say anything about lease."

"What?"

She rose and approached him. "I want to buy your interstate pipeline subsidiary, Louie. Not lease the space. American Energy wants to own it."

He turned his back to her. "That's ridiculous—it's not for sale."

"Look at me, Louie," she said.

Slowly, but obediently, he did.

"What are you going to do with the lines, Louie—convert them to waterslides for an amusement park? If you don't have gas, you can't serve your retail customers. I'll get the gas supply and can bail you out. The lines are the only hard assets you can easily unload to come up with cash to pay National's debt. Don't count on the government to bail you out. There are no more Lee Iacoccas."

"This accident is just a temporary setback—LNG shipments will resume soon."

"Accident Louie?" Raven smiled. She reached for her old cloth handbag on the hotel room's desk. It looked like something a grandmother would carry, but she liked it. "This is no accident, Louie. This is war. Your shipments from the Middle East are over. And Russia's gas is going to China and Europe at top dollar since Moscow has abandoned its capitalism energy experiment—it's not coming here. And the leftists in Venezuela, Mexico, and the rest of Latin America are going to take a siesta until the price is so high, you won't be able to afford it. We have to find our own. And you have to show Wall Street some positive cash flow. You have serious debt payments on that LNG plant, Louie. The bills are coming due—where are you going to come up with the cash unless you unload your pipeline assets?"

He said nothing. His liver-spotted hands started to shake. "It's hot in here," he suddenly blurted. Campbell staggered toward a mini-bar on the wall and poured himself another scotch on the rocks, spilling several ice cubes on the floor.

Why don't you have a few sips of LNG, Raven thought. *That should cool you off.*

"Even if you get your drilling bill passed," Campbell said. "It will take years to get supplies on line." He slammed down the scotch with one gulp.

"You let me worry about that, Louie. Sell us the lines. We'll give you a fair price. And we'll transport gas for your end users and power plants. We'll bail you out. It's your only choice."

"Those lines will be needed when the LNG shipments resume."

"*If*, Louie ... *if* the shipments resume. *If* they do, then you can certainly lease capacity space back from us. But in the meantime, if you don't sell your pipelines, your stock will be in the tank, you won't be able to attract any investment to pay your debt, and your customers are going to get mighty cold this winter."

Raven sauntered toward the suite's exit and grasped the doorknob.

"I'm really sorry about this shotgun marriage Louie," she said. "But I'm your only date. I'll wait to hear from your lawyers, but you better act quickly. When the markets open tomorrow, you won't like what you see on the big board."

Louis Campbell was silent. Raven knew she had him by the balls, but she did not want to incapacitate him. She just gave them a gentle squeeze. Just hard enough so that he knew she was there and had a firm grasp to do whatever she wished with them. They could be tickled, or torn off.

"The quicker the sale, the less of a hit National Gas and Electric will take," she said.

Raven left. As she closed the door, she heard the CEO of National Gas and Electric hurl his empty whiskey glass and ice cubes against the walnut-paneled wall and curse, "Bitch!"

That's right Louie, she thought, walking to the elevator, an effervescent smile widening on her face. *And this bitch now controls most of the major interstate pipeline capacity in the eastern United States.*

CHAPTER 33

▼

"Akmed, it is truly good to see you. *Alam Alaikum,*" Cowboy said the traditional Arabic greeting to his old friend.

"Peace be with you," Akmed said in the King's pristine English. "And what is happening with your bad, bad self." He high-fived Cowboy like a fellow basketball player at a New York City playground. Danielle was puzzled. The Secret Service was questioning. Cowboy was bragging. And joking—a terrorist? *Who is this stranger?* she wondered.

Cowboy turned to Danielle once more and introduced his close associate, the proclaimed world-renowned geophysicist.

"Akmed and I go way back—in fact, I once stood up for his honor in a London pub at the tender age of twenty-one."

"Yes," Akmed said. "But I managed to get the worst of the deal as I recall. I was struck on the face by a juvenile delinquent and then forced to listen to Cowboy's ranting for hours. Hell on earth."

"I think I know how you feel," Danielle said.

Cowboy avoided the barb by talking. "Akmed and I met in England back in— when was it? Oh yeah, 'seventy-nine—and I suggested to him that the oil biz was a good racket to get into. I was just shooting the breeze. Little did I know that he would take me up on my suggestion. Before I knew it, he had a sheepskin in the trade while I was covered with salt and sludge as a tool-pusher back in the Oklahoma oil fields. We hadn't seen each other for ten years and then we met on a drilling rig in the North Sea where Akmed was directing some sonar work looking for gas formations below the sea floor. His crystal-ball discoveries earned British Petroleum some beaucoup pound sterling, and then he became in high demand all around the world. When I went out on a limb and formed Southeast Exploration, I enlisted Akmed's expertise in the deep waters in the Gulf of Mexico off the Louisiana coast. We discovered a gusher of natural gas that helped pay off my gambling debts. Well, not really, college loans and a few other things. Let's say he has the Midas touch when it comes to divining rods when looking for oil and gas."

"Mr. Rhodan exaggerates," Akmed said, his eyes lowered to the floor, not looking Danielle in the eye. She wasn't sure if he was shy or if in the culture in which he was raised it was improper to stare at a woman. "It is the new seismic technology that allows such discoveries. In fact, we are using the latest three-dimensional seismic, that is, sound waves, to find great natural gas reserves off the shores of my native country."

"Palestine?" Danielle asked.

"I am now a British citizen. But I was born in Palestine."

The word Palestine sent shivers up Danielle's spine. She did not know why. Palestine was now a sovereign state, and purportedly at peace with its long-time nemesis—Israel. Perhaps it was all the other Mid-East conflicts that put her on edge. Maybe that's why the Secret Service agent raised his normally placid eyebrows when this man showed up unannounced. Then again, maybe she was painting every Arab person with a broad brush. Was she as bigoted as her pig-headed father?

"What are you doing here?" Danielle asked, as innocently as possible.

Cowboy interjected—nothing unusual about that. He couldn't go thirty seconds without talking for himself or someone else.

"Akmed led the 3-D seismic search that discovered the huge formation of clustered natural gas hydrates in the Carolina Basin. Without his work, as I said before, we wouldn't be here. I invited him back to the rig to celebrate in the President's visit—he is dying to meet him."

Danielle tried to meet the averting eyes of the towering Arab. *There were a lot of people from the Arab states who would be 'dying' to meet the President, with an AK-47 in their hands or a jacket full of C-4 plastic explosive.* She caught herself again. *Why am I so prejudiced and mistrustful? I am not my father!*

Akmed nodded politely to Danielle. "Mr. Rhodan assures me he is your president's personal friend, and I am hoping to receive the honor of a handshake, and perhaps an autograph."

"Hell, Akmed, when the gas starts flowin' through the pipeline, you might get a night in the Lincoln bedroom and a Rose Garden ceremony."

Danielle finished her coffee and placed the disposable foam cup down. "Perhaps you can show me how the gas hydrate is extracted?" she asked, restraining her impatience.

"Of course," Cowboy responded. "We were right in the middle of a dog-and-pony show, Akmed, please join us."

The three left the meeting room on the platform's surface and scaled a submarine-like ladder below deck. Prominent signs on the doors read "AUTHORIZED PERSONNEL ONLY."

"This operation is not too much different than a traditional drilling rig," Cowboy began, as they walked a circle around a forty-foot wide tubular structure that, he explained, held the drive motor of the drilling apparatus. "It is a traditional hydraulic motor, powered by a natural gas generator—the natural gas produced by the seaweed gas recovery program."

"At least the kelp's being used for something," Danielle said.

"This spar is the largest of its kind in the world, capable of drilling in ultra-deep depths, up to 30,000 feet below the ocean floor. It costs more than $200,000 a day to operate when it's running. Fortunately the federal government is picking up most of the tab and your company is financing the $1 billion underwater pipelines. Southeast Exploration couldn't do it for a week without the subsidy; we've already mortgaged our entire world-wide operation to pay for our investment in construction of this drilling equipment."

The numbers stunned her. How could American Energy finance such an operation? It was a large company, but was no General Electric. Despite its recent acquisitions, it was still a lesser Fortune 100 company, according to Wall Street rankings. It was already relying too much on debt than equity to finance all its purchases.

"How much gas is being produced?" Danielle asked.

"Actually, we haven't produced a single cubic foot for public consumption yet."

"Why not? The price of natural gas is at record high levels."

"We are waiting for the final go-ahead from the president," Cowboy said. "That is part of the reason for his personal visit. He wants to see the operation in person before approving production."

"When he does—if he does—how much gas will be produced?"

Cowboy shrugged. "We're not sure, but we are confident your company's pipeline will be at full capacity."

Danielle was skeptical. Maybe the whole project was kept under the hat because it may not even pan out. "If you haven't produced any gas yet, how do you know it is going to work?"

"It will work," said the bass, rock-steady voice of Akmed, entering the conversation for the first time. She drew to him like a magnet to steel. So much of Cowboy's ranting could be written off as braggadocio. This man sounded like someone of authority and trust.

"Professor Abram," Cowboy said with an erudite British accent, "why don't you brief our attorney friend on how this operates?"

"Certainly," the tall, elegant man replied. "I'm sure you know, Miss O'Day, the organic theory of organisms, where oil and gas deposits are thought to be ancient microorganisms and plants covered by sediments such as mud, silt, sand, and lime flowing from rivers into the ancient seas, compressing over millions of years in alternating levels. Most of the continental shelves are terraces, sometimes as many as six, continuing to build up sediment from rivers to the ocean."

She nodded. "You mean oil and gas are thought to be the remnants of dead dinosaurs and plants. Even we attorneys remember some high-school geology."

"More plant than animal, though the teeth of mastodons and mammoths have been discovered off the East Coast continental shelf in water up to 500 feet deep and eighty miles offshore along with that of prehistoric giant sharks, forty- to fifty-feet long. Today, the shelves are teeming with life, from microscopic photoplankton, in turn eaten by zooplankton—pinhead-sized animals, and subsequently up through the food chain to swordfish and tuna. About 90 percent of food from the ocean comes from the shelves—along with much of the world's fossil fuels. The intense pressure squeezed the oil out of the mud or shale and into the porous sandstone and limestone, kind of like the way a sponge holds water. As you know, besides oil, conventional natural gas reserves have been mainly found in the United States in Appalachia, the Southwest, the Rocky Mountains, Alaska, and underwater in the Gulf of Mexico. And, likewise there are great quantities of oil and gas that can be reached by ocean-based drilling operations on the continental shelves."

"The Canadians drill in the North Atlantic," O'Day said. "But offshore development this close to the coast is currently forbidden by the U.S. federal moratorium."

"Because our congressmen are a bunch of pansies," Cowboy quipped.

Akmed continued as if not hearing the banter. "Methane exists not only in conventional deposits in its gaseous form in these regions, but also in a frozen, lattice-like crystal known as hydrates."

"Yes, I saw the demonstration of burning ice," Danielle said. She inched closer to Akmed as they walked, stepping in front of Cowboy. When Akmed spoke, it was in a relaxed, classy, almost hypnotic tone, not the haughty bragging of Cowboy that irritated her. Akmed reminded her of the affable Jacques Cousteau, whose television specials she would watch as a kid, except with a British-Arabic accent rather than the French.

"Very good," the elegant geophysicist said. "There are estimates of billions of tons of methane below the ocean and continents—several countries are researching them—including Russia, China, Norway, and Japan. For example, I was involved in a hydrates find in the Indian Ocean off Java's southern coast that was formed when gigantic slices of earth crust collided some 10 million years ago. The U.S. National Science Foundation has also studied this for years. But we recently discovered this major hydrate zone that was previously unknown."

"How did you find it?"

"Through the latest seismic technology," the Palestinian native replied. "Kind of like a MRI of the earth's subsurface. Sonar high-frequency sound pulses are emitted from a device towed behind a ship. The sound pulses reflect back from the sea bottom to the sonar instrument, producing a three-dimensional geological map of what lies below the seafloor. Hydrates form where temperatures are near the freezing point and the pressure equals the weight of three to four kilometers of water above it."

"And you can verify that what you discovered was hydrate?"

"Yes, the velocity of sound in hydrate is very high. To confirm, test well core samples are withdrawn. We have found hydrates in different concentrations, from individual hydrate grates in sedimentary rocks, to nodules, layers, and veins of hydrates within sea-floor sediment."

"Akmed found a huge frozen gusher," Cowboy said.

"We call it a *massive* hydrate zone, more than forty meters thick. One cubic meter of gas hydrate can produce up to 200 cubic meters of natural gas. These types of hydrates may have been formed by microorganisms living in a frigid, anaerobic, high-pressure environment that produce methane as their waste byproduct."

"We call 'em *fire-ice* worms," Cowboy said, elbowing between the two.

Get lost, Danielle said with body language, doing her best to ignore the impudent Cowboy. She stared into the dark eyes of Akmed, who suddenly returned her gaze. Something stirred within her, like the internal burn of a shot of alcohol on an empty stomach.

"Yes, fascinating new species have been discovered," said Akmed.

"How do you get the hydrates out?" Danielle asked, eyes still locked on him.

"As you know, Miss O'Day ..." Akmed stopped suddenly, "I'm sorry, or is it Mrs.?"

"No, Miss is fine," Danielle said, smiling coyly. She did not mind this man knowing her marital status. He was handsome, intelligent, and polite. Besides, it might piss off Cowboy.

"Yes, Miss O'Day. Reservoirs of oil and gas are found in porous sandstone or limestone trapped in voids that have porosity."

"They have tiny holes in the rock," Danielle said.

"Exactly. You are most knowledgeable."

"Thanks," she said. She could not hide her grin now. Cowboy stood behind her and groaned like someone cut off in a queue for popular concert tickets.

"Effective and efficient wells are also permeable," said Akmed. "That is, the pores are connected so the gas or oil can flow freely up the well hole. Previously, most known hydrates were located in clay-rich sediments with little or no permeability. Therefore, it has not been thought until now that hydrates could be economically exhumed. Proposed methods include heating and/or depressurizing the reservoir. In this case, we use a combination, but primarily, depressurization. But that has to be conducted safely."

This was thrilling, Danielle thought. A few weeks before, she was stuck in a New York City office building, her eyes nearly bleeding reviewing environmental compliance briefs, and now she was out on the Atlantic Ocean involved in a confidential government project that could solve the energy crisis and probably mean big bucks for her company. And she was hobnobbing with a dignified, world-famous scientist who was attractive and by examining his left hand, unmarried, though she couldn't be sure. Maybe in his culture men did not wear wedding rings. In any case, this PR job might be more of a bargain than she thought. She couldn't wait to unveil this to the public. Then, her cautious attorney's mind registered what Akmed had just said.

"What do you mean *safely?*" she asked.

Akmed's jaw tightened slightly, but he continued in a pedagogue tone.

"Hydrate molecules are more densely packed than in conventional gas pockets. Drilling through gas hydrate cemented strata must be done carefully. Often sealed underneath is free gas in what is known as a *trap*. Drilling through the hydrate causes a reduction in pressure, resulting in a breakdown of the hydrates so they can be easily extracted. However, the freed gas has the potential to ... well ... disengage most severely."

"You mean explode?"

"Yes, and unstable hydrate layers could cause shifts in the continental ... what is known as an underwater landslide."

"Landslide?"

"He means an earthquake." The scary phrase made her jump like the sound of a dropped tray of china. It came from Dr. Edison, who just entered the room. Danielle had forgotten all about her.

"Is that dangerous?" asked Danielle.

"It could be cataclysmic," Edison said. "Unstable hydrate layers could cause a tsunami that could swamp the eastern coastline and kill thousands of people."

"Oh, welcome back Miss Sunshine," Cowboy quipped.

Danielle said, "I guess *that's* why we haven't issued a press release."

CHAPTER   34

▼

Off the coast of Norfolk, Virginia

The degree of devastation was not conspicuous to the naked eye. To millions of TV viewers, there was nothing but a blank slate of blue water. The LNG tankers and the docking facilities in the waters off the coast of Norfolk, Virginia, were shrouded by waves, submerged, as buried beneath the Atlantic waves as the H.M.S. Titanic. With the help of terrorists, the country's premier energy import site struck an iceberg of its own design, and the supercooled natural gas along with the millions of dollars to buy and transport it from across the ocean either burned or vaporized into the atmosphere, adding to the greenhouse gasses the environmental movement railed against. Molecule per molecule, methane, the environmentalist talking-head Herbert Winkle noted on the cable news shows after the disaster, is a much more powerful greenhouse gas than carbon dioxide. That's why some felt cow emissions were thought to be a bigger cause of global warming than SUVs.

"M-M-Methane has a residence time of about ten years in the atmosphere before it is oxidized into carbon d-d-dioxide," said Winkle on a CNN talk show. "And as methane emissions increase, handling excess CH_4 in the world's atmosphere gets more d-d-difficult. M-m-methane in our atmosphere has doubled in concentration since the pre-industrial period. That is why the pursuit of fossil fuels, even the so-called miracle fossil fuel natural gas, which is composed primarily of methane, is a dead end for the p-p-planet."

"What do you think of President Freeman unveiling a methane biofuels facility in the Atlantic Ocean?" the suspender-wearing interviewer asked.

"It's a f-f-fraud," Winkle said. "A p-p-publicity stunt for the president and his cronies in the energy industry." Even if the project produced natural gas, Winkle told the cable newsman, it would be like bailing out a sinking cruise ship with a Dixie cup.

Environmental concerns were on President Freeman's mind as well, as were economic issues that usually determined how voters make their choices. However, the last thing from his thinking was any inkling of being reelected two years from now. He knew that no matter what the United States did regarding the hemispheric energy shortage—from war to rationing—it would likely translate into a one-term presidency. But that did not worry the president too much. He really never wanted the job in the first place, but he was drafted and persuaded to accept, so here he was.

On the deck of a Coast Guard cutter nearing the site of the terrorist attack, the president bowed his head toward the waters, along with several other dignitaries as if they were looking down at the sunken battleship *Arizona* below the black waters of Pearl Harbor, with its eternal drops of oil still bubbling to the surface from the bowels of the graveyard ship sixty-five years after it sunk from Japanese bombs and torpedoes. Perhaps leaking natural gas out of the two LNG tankers bubbled up ethereally as well, but it was difficult to tell without a match. Only twelve Americans at the docking facility perished in the calamity, and only three U.S. citizens were aboard the other tanker from Trinidad. Still, the occasion was as solemn as other terrorist attacks that took the life of innocents on American soil. Information was still sketchy on the parties responsible for the calamity, but CIA informants pointed at various radical Islamic groups working in cohort against their sworn enemy—the United States of America.

Though it was not the president's original intention, the horrendous occurrence might work to his political advantage. From the deck of the Coast Guard ship he would fly directly via helicopter to the offshore platform nearly 100 miles from the shores of North Carolina for a media event to cut the ribbon on the federally funded project that would harvest natural gas from sea kelp. Much to his advisors' chagrin, tagging along with him on the next leg of the trip, in full regal escort, was Herbert Winkle, the leading ANGER environmentalist lawyer and bandleader that banged the green drum on Capitol Hill warning of imminent human-created climate catastrophe. Accompanying him was Olga Stevick, America's favorite senior-citizen consumer advocate, carping against corporate greed.

The president's policy regarding the cross-eyed attorney and cantankerous octogenarian was containment, like quarantining a computer virus. However, he worried the two political adversaries had every intention of infection on a worldwide scale.

*   *   *   *

"God damn camel-jockeys," Dan O'Day muttered, glaring at his television as if the electronic device was his sworn enemy. He wasn't the biggest fan of LNG, knowing that his company's future natural gas supply and the viability of his retirement funds might have to depend on some Mullah in an Arab desert. But now, terrorists again arrived at the United States shore, bringing with them hate, death, and destruction.

"Nice mouth," his wife Maureen said. She sat on a kitchen stool clipping grocery coupons from the Sunday newspaper.

"Don't you understand?" he growled. "Depending on these sons-of-bitches for our energy is a losing game. We haven't learned a damn thing since 1973. They had Nixon by the balls with oil, and now more than three decades later, these ivory-tower assholes in the gas industry walked right into the same trap."

"Your daughter works in one of those ivory towers," she said.

Not today, O'Day thought. He was not only inflamed by the terrorism that threatened his job, but he was also thinking about his daughter Danielle. She was on an offshore platform in the Atlantic Ocean. If energy facilities less than a half-mile off the American coast were infiltrated by murderers, who says she is safe? But his worry must not reach the surface where his wife could read it. As scenes of the LNG fire replayed over and over on the news channels, flames of worry burned in his mind. His wife would pick up on his thoughts—she always did. She came into the room and he quickly clicked the remote to change the station.

"You don't think Danielle is in any danger on that project out on the ocean do you?" she said.

"No," he said curtly. "I'm watching the weather channel."

The tropical forecast was on. Tropical Storm Zeta may become an official hurricane.

"Good news for Florida, bad news for the Bahamas," the female weathercaster said. She was very pregnant, O'Day noted. "Tropical Storm Zeta has took a turn for the north and fortunately will miss the Florida coast, but instead our storm track has it heading north through the Bahamas and possibly toward the Carolina coast."

Out of the frying pan and into the fire.

"Oh dear," Maureen said.

What channel should I switch to now? O'Day wondered.

CHAPTER 35

▼

"Tsunami? You mean like the killer tidal wave that occurred in the Indian Ocean?"

"Tsunamis are technically not tidal waves, but the results could be the same," said Dr. Edison as monotonous as a coroner muttering into a microphone suspended over a stiff. "Tsunamis are usually caused by deep earthquakes or volcanic eruptions which disturb the water above them causing a massive, high-speed wave front. That's what brought us here in the first place."

Danielle shook her head, perplexed.

"Oceanography studies of ocean depths discovered landslide scars, what we think are cracks on seafloor slopes where normally we wouldn't expect them," Edison said. "These mysterious scars are near the top of the hydrate zone on the ocean floor off the Virginia coast, on a twenty-five-mile stretch of the continental shelf east of Chesapeake Bay. Blowouts have blasted holes in the shelf slope up to three-miles long and 165-feet deep, probably caused by the breakdown of hydrates at the base of the hydrate layer."

"These *blowouts* Dr. Edison refers to," said Akmed, "have the potential to trigger a landslide that can cause a tsunami, and could pose a threat to boats traveling in the area. Some theorists suspect some *Bermuda Triangle* mysterious disappearances of some ships may have been caused by methane blowouts that caused swamping waves."

"Missing ships and boats?" Danielle said. "The tsunami in the Indian Ocean killed thousands, swamping entire seaside villages."

"That's what I mean by catastrophic," Dr. Edison replied. "About a dozen tsunamis have been recorded over the past century or so at intervals between five to fifteen years. Suddenly, the sea begins to heave and churn without warning, sometimes receding to the point of the ocean floor, or rising far beyond normal tide. The name is from the Japanese—*tsu*, meaning harbor, and *nami*, meaning sea. Many can be minor, and are observed in some areas in the Pacific as an oceanic curiosity. But you have seen when some who ignored large underground earthquakes paid the price with their lives when the waves hit the shores of Indonesia and other nations from the 2004 Indian Ocean tsunami."

The thought of tsunamis on the East Coast was as foreign to Danielle as snowstorms in Miami. "And you're telling me these blowouts pose a threat to the mid-Atlantic shore as well?" she asked.

"Potentially," Dr. Edison said, tossing her frontal loop of hair to the side with a nod of her head. She seemed almost intrigued by the idea, Danielle thought. "Depending on the velocity and mass of the waves, there could be significant impact and kinetic energy. At sea, a tsunami is hardly noticeable though it travels fast. A tsunami of 4,000 meters deep will bounce off the continental shelf, and various damaging waves and horizontal water movements can strike low-lying areas. Though a tsunami wave weakens as it spreads, its pernicious power increases as it slows down when it reaches the shallows, creating waves between two- and forty-times normal crest levels. Such landslides could send twenty-foot waves across the beaches in Maryland, Virginia, and North Carolina, and could also lead to severe flooding in places like New York City and Washington, D.C. As I said, that's what first brought us here, to study the potential seafloor shifts. At first many scientists thought these underwater cracks were caused by fault lines, but we now know, in this case, they are caused by massive blowouts of gas."

"In other words, these blowouts could be killers," said Danielle. "A tsunami on the East Coast? Just a couple of years ago, I couldn't even pronounce the word."

"Before the well-known Indian Ocean incident, a tsunami in Chile in 1960 killed 5,700, injured 3,000, and caused millions of dollars in damages," Edison recited as if from an encyclopedia.

"Dr. Edison is a heartwarming expert in the Apocalypse," Cowboy quipped.

"Another in 1964 destroyed fishing villages in Japan, Hawaii, and struck by the light of a full moon in California, 1,200 miles away," Edison continued. "Long before the infamous Exxon Valdez oil spill, that tsunami destroyed the old town of Valdez, Alaska, causing a Union Oil company tank to rupture and ignite in a fire that finished off the few structures that survived the initial thirty-foot waves. It killed about a hundred people in Alaska and several others as far away as Crescent City, California. Six-foot waves caused a half-million dollars worth of damage there again from a 2006 underground quake near Japan. Yes, I guess you can say they're killers all around the world. No one is immune."

"They are a threat to normal drilling operations as well," said Akmed, expressionless. His composed voice tone reminded Danielle of the Mr. Spock character on *Star Trek*, disinterested in the potential peril, void of surface emotion, but somehow benevolent beneath. "When pumping hot oil from great depths underneath the earth, it can cause warming of sediments and the dissociation of hydrates, freeing great quantities of methane, which can dislodge from highly pressured pockets. I was working on an oil-drilling rig in the North Sea when a blowout caused a landslide under our platform." He paused as if reliving the event. "Fortunately, no one was seriously hurt."

"But then isn't this drilling program just asking for disaster to strike?" Danielle said, excitedly. "If you know the danger is here ..."

"Well, as I said, that is what brought NOAA here in the first place," said Edison, ever the stoic scientist. "We've noticed these blowout scars and have been researching how we can avoid such a disaster. This is not just a drilling program to get natural gas. It is a way to not only prevent future landslides, but also to prevent a potential worldwide catastrophic climatic event."

"Worldwide climatic ... huh?"

Cowboy sighed impatiently. "More from Miss Sunshine. Film at eleven."

Edison stared at Danielle and said deadpan: "Virtually all of the scientific community feels the gradual warming of the air and oceans is a growing danger."

Danielle nodded.

"Well, there is a growing body of evidence that suggests that huge *natural* releases of methane from gas hydrate deposits may have had devastating effects on the Earth's climate more than once in its geologic past."

"You mean like wiping out the dinosaurs or something?" Danielle asked.

"Well, one theory postulates that mass extinction of half to two-thirds of significant marine fauna 55 million years ago at the Paleocene/Eocene boundary was caused by a huge and abrupt release of methane from natural gas hydrate deposits worldwide, triggered by rapid warming and/or depressurization at the sea floor."

Akmed added: "It's what is sometimes called an ocean *burp* of methane. Methane is a greenhouse gas, ten to twenty times the threat of carbon dioxide in causing global warming."

"Great, from killer tidal waves to global climate devastation—the news gets better and better," said Danielle. "I think I prefer an energy crisis instead."

"Chicken Little lives," Cowboy said.

"We want to ensure that something like that doesn't happen again," said Edison.

"But won't drilling under the sea floor potentially cause such a catastrophe?" asked Danielle.

"The risk exists," Edison admitted.

"But it might occur naturally anyway," Akmed added. "A huge quantity of oceanic methane hydrate has existed since the Silurian Epoch—millions of years ago—deposited by abundant terrestrial flora. Organic particles eroded into the ocean and deposited on the continental shelves. According to the theory, it may have been suddenly released into the atmosphere."

"How?"

"Well, we are not exactly sure," said Akmed.

"CNN wasn't in existence then," Cowboy gratuitously added.

"Maybe a volcanic event or similar natural catastrophic occurrence," Edison suggested.

"Yeah," Cowboy said, "like one giant cow fart."

The group turned their heads to Cowboy after the vulgar statement.

"Hey," Cowboy said. "The UN says methane emitted from cattle is causing more global warming than all those humvees out there. Look it up!"

"How can this be avoided?" Danielle asked, trying to raise the level of conversation again. "It seems to me that we would be better off to leave these hydrates alone."

"Let sleeping dogs lie?" said Cowboy, unable to restrain his comments to drive-by wisecracks. "After the horrid predictions by Miss Gloomy Gus here, I don't blame you for feeling that way. But that's where Akmed comes in. He is an expert in undersea impact predictions related to offshore oil and gas developments. His 3-D seismic profiles not only found the massive hydrate deposits, but he's developed a solution to the hydrate instability and occurrence of landslides. He developed a process that can restabilize the hydrate zones, while at the same time, recover the lion's share of frozen natural gas in the area. This dog can hunt."

All eyes turned toward the stately looking Arab. He spoke modestly while looking at a computer screen. On it a series of wavy colored lines depicted the underground formations. Another screen looked like a close-up photograph of a tweed jacket, with a large coffee stain in the center.

Akmed cleared his throat. "The production of natural gas from hydrate deposits will not only enhance energy supply but could also mitigate a potential long-term environmental hazard that has global consequences," he said. "The process is not as complicated as you might think."

Akmed held up a laboratory model of a crystal hydrate that lay on a nearby table. It was a tinker-toy contraption like a molecule mock-up you would see in a chemistry classroom. It was shaped like a three-dimensional spider's web made out of wooden blue and white marbles connected with small sticks, with blue-colored marbles in the nucleus of the model.

Akmed launched into a detailed, arcane delineation of how the process worked:

"This elementary model demonstrates how water molecules, the white balls on the outside, trap gas molecules, the blue marbles inside, in a cage, a structure known as a *clathrate*. There are three obvious methods of freeing the hydrates from this structure to produce a usable gas. First, it can be heated—as I mentioned before, that can occur unintentionally by oil drilling. Second, you can free the hydrates by injecting an inhibitor, like methanol, or, more effectively, glycol to decrease hydrate stability."

"That's how our field pipeline workers thaw freeze-ups in our pressurized pipelines or in gas wells in the winter," said Danielle, glad to vocalize her limited knowledge to show she was not a total dope when it came to the operational side of the natural gas business.

"That is correct. But both of those methods, heating, and thawing with chemicals are expensive ways to *melt* the hydrates. Instead, this operation uses the third method by reducing the pressure of the hydrate equilibrium, allowing the methane to release from the clathrate." Akmed motioned with his hand as if he were cracking an egg on a frying pan, and pulled the child's tinker toy apart. The blue balls released from the inside sticks fell toward the floor and Akmed seized them with his free hand like a magic trick. "The gas is free, but the clathrate in the underground formation is now unstable."

"But how do you restabilize it?" asked Danielle.

"Many years ago," Akmed continued, sounding like a tribal chief spinning a well-worn yarn to mesmerize the younger generation, "geologists found a way to reinject gasses into the earth as easy as they withdrew the gas originally, using the porosity and permeability of the gas-bearing rock."

"Of course," Danielle said. "You mean natural gas storage. That has been around for nearly a century—using depleted wells to hold critical wintertime supplies. Our company now has the nation's largest gas storage capacity in former gas fields from Appalachia to Texas." She sounded like she was bragging, reading the public relations pap in the company annual report.

Akmed flashed a movie-star smile and nodded. "Yes, you are astute and knowledgeable. Well, this process works much the same way. As we remove the natural gas hydrates from underneath the sea floor, sometimes the shelf formation destabilizes, similar to how a coal mine could collapse during deep mining. But, if a similar hydrate is injected into the shelf, it actually will not only replace what has been withdrawn, but also will act as an adhesive—a frozen glue to restabilize the weakened underground formation and hopefully avoid further underwater landslides and blowouts."

"What would you inject?"

"Any gas that forms a stable type of hydrate when under pressure would do. In this case, we are going to use carbon dioxide since it is freely available and benign to the environment below the sea in a frozen state. And it is significantly more stable thermodynamically than methane hydrate."

The lights went on in Danielle's head.

"Of course," she said. "Carbon sequestration. American Energy is involved in several carbon sequestration projects to inject carbon dioxide into old wells to get into compliance with individual state greenhouse-gas legislation."

It was all making sense to her now. Until recently, the EPA lacked any regulatory authority under the Clean Air Act to address climate change, so states and municipalities developed their own climate programs. She worked on the permits when in the legal department of the company. But before the latest Clean Air Act amendments passed Congress, she had been transferred to oversee the company's communications functions as part of the policy of cross-training top managers.

"It was going to cost us a fortune to comply with the new federal emissions restrictions," Danielle said, snapping her fingers. "Carbon sequestration might be the answer."

"You can kiss your greenhouse-gas problem goodbye," Cowboy said. "You can call this carbon *sea* s-e-a-questration. We'll pump trillions of cubic feet of pressurized CO_2 under the ocean floor like the world's biggest fire extinguisher preventing the gas from causing further global warming—if it ever did in the first place. The tree-huggers will be buying your company's stock like it was latte at Starbucks."

"But how does drilling in the ocean contain waste gasses from a power plant on shore?"

"You asked earlier why there were two pipelines running from the mainland to this rig," Cowboy said, pointing at the two large underwater lines on the schematic of the large drilling operation on the wall. "Now you have your answer. One underwater line sends natural gas depressurized from hydrates a hundred miles to a compressor station on the Virginia coast, and the other funnels carbon dioxide produced at several East Coast power plants out to us to be pumped underground, under the sea, never to be heard from again—I call it the *Jimmy Hoffa* plan."

"That might be convenient," Danielle said. "But it sounds a little like science fiction to me."

"Science fiction often becomes science fact in time," Akmed said. "About 40 percent of the carbon dioxide emitted by industrial nations comes from power plants. This method will revolutionize the energy-generating industry. When you burn natural gas, you produce heat, carbon dioxide, and water with few pollutants. Therefore, there would be no shortages of fuel to generate the power, and few emissions by burning the fuel. When it comes to generating power, there need not be nuclear power plant waste, poisoning polluting gases from coal, or even greenhouse gases like carbon dioxide."

"America gets clean-burning natural gas to fry eggs and power computers," Cowboy said, "and your company will far exceed its EPA guidelines for carbon dioxide emissions."

"But it is untested," Edison suddenly added.

Danielle, caught up in the excitement, ignored the devil's-advocate comment from the NOAA scientist. This was groundbreaking. Would it be Danielle's job to help sell this new injection system to federal regulators, or perhaps, since she was now heading the company's PR efforts, to the general public?

"What do you think counselor?" Cowboy asked.

"I think this is a very impressive project that from what you say will be a quantum leap in the energy world," Danielle answered. "What I'm wondering is why is it such a big secret?"

CHAPTER 36

▼

The ocean of stars shimmering in the coal-soot sky was once the sprawling road-map of ancient mariners. For Cowboy, it was just another pretty night that women often found romantic—moonless, cloudless, with countless diamond-like points of light emanating love. The slight, but persistent ocean wind pushed back his hair around his Stetson. An occasional puff of smoke billowed from his cigar like the stack of a steam locomotive. The drilling manager leaned on the steel rail of the edge of the rig, gazing upward, listening to rhythmic nighttime waves slosh against the sides of the *China Maiden*. Though the activities on the center of the platform were as well lit as a city highway interchange, the edge of the deck was peaceful in the shadow. Though no astronomer, he was familiar with all the major constellations in both the northern and southern skies, spending more than one evening surveying the heavens from the deck of a drilling platform either off the warm coast of Venezuela or above the chilly waters of navigable parts of the Arctic Circle. And many of those times he had his arm around a new female acquaintance, usually a young petroleum geology graduate student on a semester-at-sea looking for a few nuggets of knowledge from an experienced hand. Thanks to his expertise in geology and romance, it was mutually beneficial. Tonight, alone, he spotted the constellation Dorado, the Swordfish, twinkling from above. The arrangement of distant suns reminded him of his valiant, fighting sea prize.

The stars of the sky are all our dead relatives of years' past, a childhood friend once convinced him at the I'll-believe-anything age of six. The brightest star in the sky then, the young Bruce Rhodan deduced, must be that of his own father. He told everyone who would listen that his dad died in a rodeo accident when

Cowboy was a toddler. By the time he was eight-years-old, he knew that not to be true. His father died of a knife wound in a bar fight in an argument over a woman. He heard his mother and aunt discuss the issue late one night when he was supposed to be sleeping. However, he would not spoil the image of his father's bright star. It was too beautiful. Cowboy would often tell his theory to his graduate student of the moment before closing in on a kiss.

Other than that, he wouldn't reveal much detail of his past. His father did own a firearm business, and after his father's death, his mother wanted nothing to do with it. Cowboy took care of her the best he could, earning money as a ranch laborer, and then finally working as a roustabout in the oil patch on his uncle's drilling rig. After experiencing life on an offshore platform, he fell in love with the sea. His uncle financed a college degree, and with the help of a local congressman, Cowboy was off to the Naval Academy. However, the stringent structure of the armed forces could not break a mustang like himself. After a few short months, he washed out. But not before he became life-long friends with another midshipman who eventually found himself in the White House. Back on his own, Cowboy's meager investments in speculative wildcat Gulf of Mexico oil and gas wells resulted in big payoffs, and he was able to start his own independent drilling firm and provide his aging mother with a plush retirement. However, like a sailor wed to the sea, he never returned to land long enough to settle down. There was always another well to sink, another significant discovery waiting for him.

Cowboy reached into his leather jacket and slipped out a whisky flask, unscrewed the top, and took a swig of Southern Comfort. Though one was always on duty on a drilling rig, the rules relaxed after dusk, at least for the boss.

"What's in there?" the voice of Danielle O'Day broke the tranquillity of the night like a shattering pane of glass.

Cowboy didn't flinch, though he was startled.

"Gatorade," he responded. "Want some?" He offered the flask to Danielle, who approached him from behind. Her arms were folded tightly around her body as if she were cold.

Cowboy gave her the once-over. The prissy attorney had traded the green tunic she donned earlier during the tours of the rig for more relaxing attire. She was now clad in tan corduroy pants and an Icelandic sweater, an import she probably purchased in a trendy Manhattan boutique, Cowboy guessed. Her reddish hair was tied behind her head and tucked into the thick collar of the bulky sweater. Despite the oversized waterproof wool and her closed body language, she could not completely disguise her feminine curves. Her figure caught Cowboy's attention as much as her Irish-green eyes did when she first set foot on the rig. He motioned with the flask again.

"No thanks," she replied.

"You sure? It provides some real *southern comfort.*"

"I don't think it would agree with me—I admit I'm still a little woozy from the helicopter flight."

"Suit yourself," he said and took another swig. "You look like you're ready for a nor'easter with that sweater."

"I'm a little chilly," Danielle said, reaching the steel deck rail and surveying the water beyond, an endless vat of undulating ink in the moonless night. "It's this constant wind."

"I thought you were a native of northern Pennsylvania—this should seem like the tropics to you."

"I've always hated winter," Danielle said, looking away from his gaze. "I was cold most of the summers too. That's why I don't live in Pennsylvania anymore."

"That asphalt and concrete heat island of Manhattan is much warmer, I suppose," Cowboy said. She didn't respond. "Still," he said, knocking back another nip before returning the flask to his jacket, "the sweater is quite fetching."

She refused to look at him. *Hard to figure this filly out*, he opined. *Miss Prissy!*

"So what brings you on deck long after hours?" he asked.

"I couldn't sleep. My stomach ..."

"Insomniac, claustrophobic, agoraphobic—you are a walking medical condition. Sure you don't want a drink?"

"I'm not an alcoholic, however," she said, glaring at him. "What are *you* doing out here?"

"I do my best thinking at night here looking over the endless plain of ocean. It reminds me of Oklahoma."

"The ocean reminds you of Oklahoma?"

"No, not the ocean. The peace. It's like home on the range and all that stuff, 'cept without nature's beautiful creatures ... horses, that is."

Strands of Danielle's red hair that weren't tied down flapped against her temples in the night wind, like streamers from a child's bicycle. "I find it comforting as well," she said.

"You do? With all your phobias and what not?"

"I'm also near-sighted and I don't have my contacts in," she said. "I can't see a damn thing farther than three feet away. As long as I don't see that I'm floating in the middle of the friggin' ocean on an oversized steel raft it doesn't bother me a bit."

Cowboy chuckled and gazed out at the sea that was as black as an oil slick.

"Have you seen Akmed?" she asked, tentatively.

Huh, he thought. *It figured. Miss Prissy is stuck on my dark, handsome buddy already. It happens all the time. That damn Akmed. Some guys get all the luck. But as far as he knew, the guy never seems to take advantage of his lady-killer magnetism.*

"Sometimes the sea is friendlier at night, sometimes not," Cowboy said. "Akmed loves to be on deck of any oil and gas rig during the daytime, but he wouldn't be caught dead out here at night."

"Why?"

"He doesn't fear the vastness of the sea when he can see it, but on a moonless night like tonight, he feels like it will swallow him up. Goes back to an accident when he was much younger while working as a roughneck on a small British Petroleum oil platform in the North Sea."

"Yes, he mentioned that—about an undersea landslide. That seemed to bother him a bit."

"Yeah, but he didn't brag about his heroics," Cowboy said, placing his free hand in the front pocket of the leather western jacket he wore, as if he were suddenly as cold as Danielle. "He doesn't brag about anything." *The Prince of Cool,* Cowboy thought.

"What happened?"

"Akmed was working the night shift—a pitch-black night like this one. He was on the rig floor helping to put drilling pipe down the rathole, when the rig partially collapsed."

"Rathole?"

"That's a shallow hole drilled off to the side for temporarily storage of the Kelly. As I said, the rig—"

"Kelly?"

"That's a thirty-foot-long part of the string of pipe that rotates the drilling bit." Cowboy gave up on the drilling vernacular. "The names don't matter. It's all heavy equipment, that's why they call these well workers *roughnecks*—that's how Akmed earned his sinewy physique. Anyway, the entire rig tilted thirty degrees when underwater supports broke on one side of the superstructure. The string of pipe pinned him against the mast of the spar and it became partially submerged. He blacked out and nearly drowned in the frigid, forty-degree water, but was able to free himself and crawl back onto the rig floor that remained above the surface. The piece of pipe broke his leg in two places—that's why he walks with a bit of a limp."

"I hardly noticed."

"He hides it well. Despite his injuries, he dove back into the black water and retrieved two other drilling workers who were unconscious and drowning. He suffered from hypothermia by the time others pulled him out of the cold ocean. He was honored by the British government for his heroism."

"Impressive," said Danielle.

"I'm the one who told him to look for some honest work in the oil and gas industry. And he did and it almost killed him." He took a puff on his cigar. "But as Nietzsche said, 'that which does not kill us makes us stronger.' A few diplomas and several oil and gas wells later, he's now world famous." *And he has a hot babe after his bod*, Cowboy thought.

"That Secret Service guy seemed to be a little concerned," Danielle said. "But Akmed seems like a nice man."

Damn, Cowboy thought, *the cute redheaded lawyer already seemed bewitched.* Akmed had that effect on many women, but he was always too consumed with geophysics to go on the prowl. Cowboy thought he himself could win the attractive lawyer over. The driller worked women like gas wells, steady, and one foot at a time. Yeah, she was a bit prissy, but she was a lynx.

"What about you?" he asked. "What's a nice corporate attorney like you doing on a drilling rig like this?" Cowboy asked.

"You already know."

"So you are Alexandria Raven's personal emissary?"

"She is my boss."

"Yeah, the former energy secretary's wife. She worked her way to the top, but never stepped on a drilling rig in her life."

She turned to face him. "You have a problem with women in authority, don't you?"

Cowboy's jaw dropped. "Now why would you say a thing like that?"

"It's written all over your wrangling boots and blue jeans. The way you spoke to Dr. Edison, the NOAA scientist. And you obviously have a chip on your shoulder regarding the president of American Energy. If it were a man who headed the company you would be swabbing the deck before him. Because she's a woman, you are calling her a bitch."

Cowboy held up his hands in surrender. "I never said such a thing."

"Not in so many words."

Cowboy smiled and tossed his withering cigar over the side of the rail. He put his hands back in his pockets and leaned back on the rail of the drilling rig like he was leaning on a fence post of a corral. Danielle unfurled her hands as well, and pulled out what looked like a big cell phone, but it was some kind of electronic device the size of large television remote.

"What do you have there?" Cowboy asked. "A cellphone? Don't see any cellular towers a hundred miles out at sea."

"It's a satellite phone," she answered.

"Well, I'll leave you alone if you need to make a personal call to a boyfriend or something."

Danielle glared at him. "I need to file a report with my company."

"Sorry, I wasn't insinuating anything."

"You do spend a lot of time in bars, don't you?"

"Excuse me?" Cowboy said, as innocently as a Hollywood superstar accused of killing his wife and chainsawing her body into small parts to dispose of in a sewer.

"First you compliment my sweater, next insult my boss, and then you go fishing around in my personal life. I am here on important company business Mr. Rhodan. I'm not at a singles' bar."

"Until a few minutes ago, I was out on deck enjoying the weather … alone. Let me assure you Ms. O'Day, I can be as professional as you want me to be. But it is in my nature to be courteous and sociable."

Danielle dropped her guard and let out a long breath. "I'm sorry," she said. "I've been under a lot of stress lately and I'm a little sensitive." She began pressing keys on the satellite phone.

"No problem. Use that thing a lot?"

"No. Birthday present from my father. A two-way global positioning system device, if you can believe it."

"GPS—sweet."

"Weird present, huh?"

"Beats a Chia Pet. Actually, we use them all the time out here—looks like they are getting smaller and smaller."

"I'm not even sure how to use it. My dad said that when I turn it on, he can track wherever I am within five meters through this website he subscribes to, and he told me that I can figure out wherever I am by holding it up to the Southern sky—wherever the hell that is. It's so damn black out here I can't tell North from South without a compass."

"Sounds like you need a little *sex*tant," he said, slightly stressing the first syllable of the last word of his sentence.

"Excuse me?" she said, flatly.

"A sextant—an instrument that sailors have used since the mid-eighteenth century to determine their latitude and longitude by measuring the relation between a star and the horizon."

"Oh."

"But folks that work on offshore oil and gas rigs don't need fancy computerized dead-reckoning gadgets like that to figure out where they are; they use the *naked* eye and the stars." He turned and faced the dark ocean, grasping Danielle on her elbow, a politically correct touch of the opposite sex he learned in one of those management-development classes. Danielle followed his lead better than Ginger Rodgers waltzing with Fred Astaire. "If you look way into the horizon there," he continued, pedantically, "you can see the front stars of the Big Dipper's cup. Up in Pennsylvania that would be almost directly over your head this time of year." He pointed with his leather-sleeved arm, aligning it not far from Danielle's cheek. "Now follow an imaginary line running through those two stars on the front of the cup to the next star that is visible. That's Polaris."

"The North Star," Danielle said, suddenly cooperative.

"Right. So now you know where north is." Cowboy rotated and pointed in the opposite direction with his other arm. By doing so, he put his arm around Danielle's back, leaning into the side of her head close enough to inhale the subtle scent of her flowery perfume. "Now if you look the other direction, you can see the Southern Cross."

"Nice try," said Danielle, spurning him, and escaping from his artifice embrace. "I think I'll use the GPS from here."

She walked away toward the deck's operating center, known as the "doghouse" to the crew.

As Cowboy stared at her ass as she sauntered away he said almost in a shout, "Real sailors don't need satellites!" He smiled. He knew that she played along to see how far he would go. She didn't see the North Star. She was virtually blind without her contact lenses—or so she said.

Me thinks she doth protest too much, Cowboy thought.

CHAPTER 37

▼

The ghostly blue TV light in Dan O'Day's living room in the pre-dawn hours glowed like an apparition in a coal mine. O'Day woke everyday at five a.m., a habit he picked up from his father who reported to the job as a construction fore-man at the gas company well before seven, punched the clock, and then returned home to a full, home-cooked breakfast prepared by his dutiful wife. O'Day didn't have the same routine—today's clock-watching bean counters would never allow such a habit. But he still rose early, habitually snapping on the Weather Channel to see the temperatures and precipitation forecast not only for his neighborhood, but also the entire world. He sat in a clean pair of his gray-green dungarees he wore to work and a white T-shirt, drinking unsweetened black coffee and swal-lowing chunks of a cheese danish. It was a morning ritual. He rose ahead his wife to enjoy the peace of a quiet house before he set off to the company garage to bear the noise of rumbling trucks, clanking metal tools, and hungover men complain-ing about the on-the-field performance of the Cleveland Browns, Buffalo Bills, or Pittsburgh Steelers. Since Erie was equal distant between the three major NFL cities, football rivalries ran deep. When it wasn't football season, preseason, or draft week, most of the male construction and service personnel then grumbled about their bosses or ex-wives. In any case, the shop was full of strident sounds, and O'Day appreciated the solemn tranquillity of twilight in his TV room before the storm. The news channels were too depressing to watch with all the problems in the world, so he relaxed watching cold fronts, high-pressure systems, and thun-derstorm warnings.

O'Day was lulled into a trance by another pregnant meteorologist waddling across the screen. The weather lady's protruding abdomen was eclipsing most of the southeastern United States, as she stood left-center before a graphic of the East Coast. A late season tropical storm brewed into a hurricane south of Bermuda and was wandering in the Atlantic, undecided whether it would strike land. *Great*, O'Day thought. He was scheduled to go to Virginia the next day as part of union negotiations with American Energy. And his daughter was somewhere out on the ocean, perhaps in the path of the impending storm.

"This is quite unusual in late November, though the hurricane season does not officially end until the thirtieth of the month," the bulbous-bellied woman said, with as much excitement as if she was already having contractions.

O'Day liked to watch the "weather ladies" as he called them, and marveled that many of them spent half their television career with child, only pausing to pop out a kid and returning to work the next week to talk about the big white blob of lake-effect snow off the Great Lakes, or the warm Santa Ana winds fanning forest fires in southern California.

"Zeta is now a full-fledged Category One hurricane, the twenty-ninth named storm of the season, a record," the expectant forecaster said with shocked glee as if she just found out she was carrying twins. She explained that Atlantic storms were named after Greek letters after the alphabet names ended at "W." In the Pacific, whose storms were named differently, tropical storm "Zeke" was chopping at the Baja Peninsula.

O'Day heard stirring in the kitchen. His wife was up now and rearranging pots and pans as quietly as marines on K.P. at a Paris Island mess hall. "Honey?" he called in the kitchen. "You hear from Dannie?"

"Yes, she called last night after you went to bed," Maureen answered. "She was using your satellite phone from the ship. I didn't recognize the number at first."

"The number constantly changes as a security measure," he said. "The only way to find the number is to check the website and punch in a secure ID."

"Whatever—you know I'm computer-challenged. She says she's nearly a hundred miles out in the ocean. And to think she used to be afraid of the water."

"Why didn't you let me talk to her?"

"I told you. You already went to bed."

O'Day growled. But he knew if his wife did wake him up, he probably would have complained about that too.

He glanced back at the heavy-with-child television weathercaster, sweeping her arms upward toward a large red conical arrow that showed the possible route of the season's late storm. Its projected path touched the shore of the southeastern United States from Georgia to Virginia.

"If she calls again, I want to talk to her," he said, almost a warning. He did not want to discuss the hurricane. "Can you get me some more coffee?" he barked. He wasn't trying to be churlish or dominating. He just didn't want his wife to look at the weather report. Mothers worry, fathers brood.

He picked up the cable remote and clicked to another channel. More video of the disaster in Virginia of the liquefied natural gas explosion and fire. The president of the United States was touring the ruins. *News stories like this make hurricanes look good*, O'Day thought. He shut it off—he didn't want Maureen worrying about that too. Before he went to work he booted up his personal computer and surfed to the global positioning system website. He paid $39.95 per month for the service that claimed to locate the GPS signal on the remote unit he gave his daughter within five meters. He entered in the code for the remote phone.

After an interminable wait, he read the message that popped up: *The GPS locator you are seeking is either not operational or the system is busy.*

"Jesus Christ," O'Day muttered to himself. "Just like a goddamn cellphone."

His daughter was somewhere out on the Atlantic Ocean—what difference did it make exactly where? *She always hated the water*, he thought. *Damn sissy was afraid of the backyard pool. Now she is floating on trillions of gallons of it.*

CHAPTER 38

▼

Danielle O'Day rolled out of her guest bunk on the *China Maiden* and promptly struck her head on the steel-gray bulkhead. The pain was numbing. At five-foot-eight, Danielle never considered herself tall, for she always looked up to her father, literally, if not figuratively. Though her modest apartment in Manhattan was not as capacious as her father's suburban three-bedroom ranch in northwestern Pennsylvania, it was roomier than the six-by-eight bunkroom awarded her on the *China Maiden* that was no bigger than a train's sleeping compartment. She did not have much luggage other than her overnight bag and laptop computer, which was a good thing because there was no place to put anything. What annoyed her most was that the tiny room on the behemoth rig was an insulated steel box with no windows. She refused to embark on her honeymoon cruise because of the diminutive "roomette" sleeping chambers on the Carnival pleasure ship that was nothing more than a glorified closet. It was a prelude to disaster. The marriage was just as claustrophobic. Why she married the smooth-talking stockbroker ten years her senior, she could never figure out. It wasn't for love. It wasn't for security. Was it his perfect teeth? Maybe it was just to move beyond the shadow of her parents. Her husband was an exquisite bore who imprisoned her with paranoid suspicion. In any case, it was over and she finally had a clear mind to concentrate on her career.

She missed the ample vista of Central Park and the Manhattan skyline from her apartment window, a steaming cup of black coffee from her espresso machine, and the comforting crooning of Josh Groban singing Italian songs on her stereo. She made her daily commute by cab, rather than subway, since she did not relish spending time below ground in a worm tunnel with drunken, lascivious old beggars in urine-soaked pants standing next to her on the platform. She would rather pay an overpriced English-challenged cabby named Muhammad for the trip to American Energy's New York office near Rockefeller Center. At least she could look out the window and see daylight.

She didn't sleep well. The bunk was as confining as lying in a casket. After showering in a bathroom the size of a broom closet—the head, as they called it on the vessel—she brushed her imperfect teeth. She applied a conservative amount of base make-up to hide her Irish freckles on her strong cheekbones and enough lipstick to plump up her thin upper lip. Still, she could not hide the sack of fatty skin underneath her chin that she inherited from her mother. Her father called it her pelican pouch. It made her cry at twelve and she wished it would go away. She glared at the microscopic mirror perched over the shoebox-sized sink and scowled. What did she care what she looked like on this drilling spar? She would be wearing a hardhat all day with her long reddish-brown hair tied in a bun underneath. She donned her forest-green American Energy tunic and reexamined herself. She kept the top two buttons of the shirt unfastened and sprayed the top of her chest with a mild, strawberry-scented perfume. She pushed her collar to the side, displaying a small crucifix on a thin gold chain, wondering whether her low cleavage could be noticed if she bent over at the waist. Her breasts were not large, but she wasn't flat either. What was she doing? Was she trying to look professional, or alluring? For whom? That chauvinistic, vainglorious, Neanderthal Cowboy? Maybe for the mysterious geophysicist? For someone she had yet to meet? *You've got to be kidding,* she told herself.

She walked down the corridor toward the galley. Passing a narrowly ajar oval door several rooms away from her own, she heard a murmuring that stopped her in her tracks. It was a deep voice, muttering softly, not singing, but not conversation either. She leaned her head toward the door. It was a foreign language. Repetitive phrases, spoken almost reverently, louder, and then softer. She leaned farther, nearly touching the metal doorjamb with her head as the voice faded away. The oval door suddenly thrust open. Danielle's head snapped backward and she let out a gasp.

"Can I help you?" the sonorous Boris-Karloff baritone of Akmed Abram said. His six-foot-four sinewy frame filled the much shorter entranceway like a huge bear climbing out of its winter's lair. He stood stiffly in the doorway, sandals on his feet, wearing nondescript khaki pants and a beige long-sleeved T-shirt.

"You scared the devil out of me," Danielle said, covering her small exposed neckline with her hand.

"Please accept my apologies," Akmed said, genteelly. "I thought I heard some-one near my door. I did not intend to frighten you."

"No, no. It's just your door was open and I thought I heard voices and I stopped to see if I knew who was there. I'm sorry too. I did not mean to eaves-drop."

"No apologies necessary. Living aboard this vessel in such close quarters one never gets much privacy."

"You can go back to your conversation," she said. "I'm on my way to break-fast."

"I was not speaking with anyone."

"Sorry, I thought I heard—"

"I should have shut the door, but the ventilation in the room is not opti-mum."

Akmed stepped into the hallway to avoid the short header on the doorway. Danielle peeked into Akmed's small room, the layout identical to hers. On the floor lay a two-foot-by-three-foot ornamental rug parallel to his bunk. He was praying.

"Oh, I am sorry—you were in worship and I disturbed you."

"My morning prayers, yes. Don't worry Ms. O'Day. I do it five times a day. I do not suspect that God will condemn me to damnation for one abridged ses-sion."

"No," Danielle said. Silence followed.

"That was a joke," Akmed said.

Danielle forced a laugh. "Of course!"

"You said you were on your way to breakfast?"

"Well, I guess, but I'm not sure if I remember the way to the galley."

"Perhaps you can wait a moment and I can show you. And if I am not intrud-ing, we could dine together, yes?"

"Why, I … yes, of course, sure."

"I will only be a moment," Akmed said. He retreated into his quarters, and reappeared less than a minute later in a similar American Energy issued-tunic, though it was brown with matching leather loafers. Akmed was clean-shaven, and his oil-black hair was carefully combed in waves. *He was eye-catching*, Danielle thought. His muscular arms were woven with a forest of black hair, and his cof-fee-tinted chiseled features were magnetic. He didn't smell of cologne or deodor-ant soap, just a natural redolence that she found alluring. His manner of speaking was innocent and charming, yet confident and charismatic. And his manners were as exquisite as a British nobleman. Everything her ex-husband and that boob Cowboy was not.

In the nearly empty dining area, a galley hand promised to bring them breakfast in short order, filling two large plastic coffee mugs with the ship's own brew. Akmed stood until Danielle sat, and then joined her.

"You are a devout person?" Danielle asked, wincing bringing up the uncomfortable topic of religion with one who was obviously not Irish-Catholic like her parents. She couldn't even discuss her faith with them, let alone someone who was alien to her upbringing. She felt like she was asking an African American how it was to be black.

"I know that worshiping God cannot hurt any of us," Akmed smiled, as if trying to ease her into a more relaxed state.

"And you seem very spiritual." She kicked herself again. "Well, I mean, your Muslim faith is important to you."

"Yes, I am a child of Islam, and the key to Islam is simply submission to God. But we are all children of God are we not?"

She looked around the galley as if he were speaking about someone else.

"And you are too, Miss O'Day," he said.

"Me?"

"A child of God." He nodded to her, suggesting there was something marking her as a religious person. She looked down toward her chest. The small gold cross on a chain that circled her neck dangled below. It was a confirmation gift she received more than a decade earlier.

"From my Mom," Danielle said, stuffing the crucifix under her tunic. "Irish-Catholic. But I must admit it's been quite some time before I said Hail Marys before breakfast."

Akmed smiled disarmingly. His ink-black eyes glimmered with the shine of polished onyx. Characteristic crow's feet jutted out of the sides of his eyes like river deltas.

"One could argue there are more similarities between our faiths than differences," he said.

"Really?"

"Certainly. For example, the word *Allah* for God is used by Arab Christians as well. Allah is the creator and judge of mankind, omnipotent, compassionate, and merciful. Like Christianity, Islam is monotheistic—there is no god but Allah. Islam recognizes the same prophets of history that you do including Adam and Abraham. Of course, we recognize Muhammad as the last and most perfect prophet of God."

Danielle shifted in her seat. "I'm more comfortable discussing law than religion."

"Yes, I'm sorry—perhaps I should discuss geophysics instead?" He smiled again, his huge white teeth dominating his appearance.

Danielle was silent.

"That was a joke, too," Akmed said.

"Sorry."

The galley hand, a boyish, crew-cut man in his early twenties wearing immaculate white slacks and a matching buttoned, collarless shirt, walked over and greeted Akmed and Danielle.

"What will it be this morning? You are the first in—early birds get the eggs benedict—except we have a limited menu today: eggs, pancakes, cereal—we've got to prepare for the president's entourage. It will be a zoo in here later on."

"Do you have something high-protein?" Danielle asked.

"Yes, mamm, an Atkins fruit-flavored shake. Several folks are on that low-carb diet thing," he said. She nodded affirmatively. "Anything else?"

"That is all for me, thank you," she said.

"And you Mr. Abram?"

"The usual," Akmed replied.

"Righto," the galley hand said and walked off.

"You've spent a lot of time on this vessel, I see," Danielle said.

"About five months—that is a long time in those spacious rooms we enjoy."

"I don't think I can handle it for a week."

"Oh, you get used to it."

"I don't know."

"You are on a special diet?" Akmed asked.

"Just the woman thing. Do you have special dietary restrictions?" she asked.

"Some," he replied, "but the breakfast cereal here is, what is the expression in English? Oh yes, to die for."

Danielle's lips broke into a forced smile.

"So, what do you think of the project so far?" Akmed asked.

"It wasn't exactly what I expected."

"Yes, Mr. Rhodan told me the purpose of this facility was not revealed to you until after you arrived."

The galley hand returned—the fastest service Danielle had ever seen. She was used to the frenzied languor in the New York City eateries she frequented. A large glass of a grayish-brown fluid was placed before her. It looked like dish water. Akmed was delivered a large bowl full of yellow nuggets of cereal.

"Sugar Pops?" she said, her eyes widening.

"Is that what this breakfast is called?" he replied.

"It was when I was a kid. Now I think they call it Corn Pops, as if they are fooling anyone about the high-refined sugar content. I thought you had dietary restrictions?"

"I do. I only eat what tastes good. And since trying this on the *China Maiden* last year, I have had it every morning I've been on board."

Danielle laughed. "I think they taste like sugar-coated Styrofoam packing peanuts."

He raised one eyebrow. "I thought it was a specialty on this vessel only."

She grinned revealing her less-than-perfect teeth. Akmed was polite, handsome, adorable, and in many ways, naive as a boy.

"Perhaps you would like another tour of the platform after your breakfast to see how the gas will be transported to the American mainland," Akmed asked her between crunches of milk-soaked cereal.

"I'd love that," she said, enraptured. But then she doused her zeal to not appear overeager. "If we can find time."

Akmed was mysterious; perhaps that was his allure. Other than his strict adherence to his religion, he said little about himself, leaving a cloak of shadows over his objectives. Her ability of reading men's sincerity was never that sharp, anyway. Akmed's striking countenance controlled her like a puppet on a string, and she did not like that feeling. Well, she liked it, but thought perhaps she shouldn't.

CHAPTER 39

▼

"Strengths, weaknesses, opportunities, and threats," said Alexandria Raven. "SWOT analysis reveals why we must move from an oil economy to natural gas."

"I've read the executive summary of the report," President Freeman said. "I'm not sure the nation needs to put all of its eggs in one basket."

Here come those eggs again, Raven thought. She had a golden opportunity, sitting in Marine One next to the president of the United States. She had approximately twenty-five minutes of face time of the most powerful lobbying on earth. They were speeding across the Atlantic Ocean waters to *Project Blue Sky/Hades* and would be greeted by a score of news reporters on deck of the *China Maiden*. She was sure the press would be impressed by the kelp-methane collection system and the president would be intrigued by the initial tests of the hydrate extraction. She didn't need to persuade him of the value of obtaining domestic sources of natural gas in the midst of a serious energy crisis. But what she needed to do was convince him that the heyday of oil was over, and the United States must transform its prime energy source from petroleum to natural gas.

"Our industry has always suffered from its historical ties with oil," Raven told the president, whose attention appeared to focus on her like a laser beam. "The public cannot separate the fossil fuels from one another. They think natural gas pollutes or we are running out of it. But natural gas is this nation's environmental and strategic strength, not its weakness. *Project Hades* will prove that. The increased use of natural gas for electrical generation will clean up our skies. When it burns, all that is produced is carbon dioxide and water. And for those who are concerned about global warming, virtually all of our converted electric-generating plants can eventually be linked into carbon sequestration pipelines into the hydrate formations. This will help the U.S. meet its greenhouse gas limits without destroying the economy. But an additional, even more exciting, opportunity comes with vehicular transportation."

"Cars and trucks fueled by natural gas?" the president said.

"It's the icing on the cake, Mr. President. When the test proves successful and the hydrate supplies come on line, I believe our problem will be not a lack of supply of natural gas, but what to do with the surplus. If there is not a market for this clean fuel, it most likely will be wasted. We've made that mistake in the past. Natural gas has always been under-appreciated. We cannot miss the opportunity this time."

"And the weaknesses of natural gas as a vehicular fuel?"

"Our only weakness, if I may be so bold Mr. President, is the lack of political backbone to drill for it, transport it, and use it in more applications."

"But your industry has plenty of competition—the ethanol lobby for example."

Raven smiled bewitchingly. "Ethanol is an open joke among economists."

"Yes," Freeman said, glancing out the window of the chopper. "But governors from thirty-three states and some influential congressmen and senators are pushing it rather hard."

Raven did not miss a beat. "It is not in favor with the environmentalists and requires more energy to produce than it yields. Even the refining industry doesn't like it because it requires a different type of gasoline stock for blending and it can't be shipped through oil pipelines."

"But it's a domestic fuel," the president countered in the dance of persuasion between the two.

"Sir, if I may be frank—the only reason the ethanol industry exists is because it receives more than fifty cents per gallon subsidy by the waiving of its federal and state fuel taxes. It will only add to gasoline bills. God put natural gas in the ground for us to use as fuel, and he planted corn for us to eat."

"Now, you've got God on your side." Freeman chuckled. "I've read that many other countries use compressed natural gas for vehicles—but it has never taken off here. That appears to be a weakness. Can you teach that old dog new tricks?"

The president was no fool, Raven thought. He played the devil's advocate role well. She must try harder.

"True, until now, engine-conversion costs have hurt us because of low oil prices, and now, high natural gas prices," Raven said. "We've been in a Catch-22. Detroit is not willing to build natural-gas powered vehicles unless there is a demand for them. There is no demand because of a lack of infrastructure—no place to fill up. But we are advocating something totally different. And that is the opportunity."

"And that is?"

"GTL. Gas to Liquids. Technology that dates back to World War II Germany."

"Synthetic fuels from coal?" the president observed.

"You know your military history as much as anyone," Raven said.

"It's what powered the Nazi war machine on the eastern front."

"Yes, but this alternative fuel would not be from coal. Instead the source is natural gas. Plants in the Middle East are already producing a clear liquid fuel that has the high efficiency of diesel, but without the pollutants. We've been involved with compressed natural gas since the 1970s. Unfortunately, people have always been uncomfortable with compressed gas, even though it's safer to use than gasoline. But, unwittingly, most people are comfortable with liquid fuels. It is already used in buses in London and Shanghai, and is for sale in Germany, Greece and Thailand. It even powers a fleet of delivery trucks in California. And with a gasoline station tank infrastructure already in place, nothing changes, except for the type of liquid fuel put into the cars and trucks. You remember how the hybrid craze caught on a few years ago. There were not enough of them to go around. Likewise, Detroit may not be able to crank out enough natural gas diesel vehicles to meet the initial demand. But if they want to stay out of bankruptcy, they'll start making them. Like leaded gasoline, eventually oil-based gasoline will fade away—you don't even need legislation to phase it out. Our company is willing to invest in major production facilities in the United States. But that's not all. The oil producers and refiners will jump on it—the majors already have invested in GTL plants around the world where natural gas is plentiful. Who will need Mid-East oil when people can fill up with diesel produced by American natural gas? Clean, efficient, domestic. As wholesome as baseball, hot dogs, and apple pie."

The president displayed a poker face that was tough to read. "A bold proposal," he said. "But what about coal? It will be tough to take on the farm states and corn fuels let alone add the twenty-plus states that support increased use of coal. There are political realities I must deal with."

"I understand. Ninety percent of the coal in the country is used to generate electricity. We will continue to use it with new clean-coal technologies. They are expensive, but if the government guaranteed recovery of costs, coal can be integrated to some degree. And even the ethanol industry can fulfill some role. But as you know, Mr. President, nothing can replace America's dependence on oil, unless an equally convenient and familiar fuel for the family car can supplant it. And Mr. President, think of the future. Natural gas can be the primary fuel for future fuel cells—the *hydrogen* economy."

"What about the last component of your analysis—*threats*? What if there turns out to be a problem with the hydrate extraction—how can we bet the farm on natural gas if that doesn't work?"

"Well, Mr. President, there is always importing more liquefied natural gas."

The president frowned.

"The better question may be," said Raven, "what is our nation's *larger* threat? It is the enemies of the United States and the hoarders of the fuels they think we can't do without? Do we have any other options? Let's face it, the public won't accept massive increases in nuclear power because of perceived hazards and the problems of disposal of wastes. Use of coal pollutes and clean-coal technology is expensive. Oil isn't clean either and we are dependent upon unstable foreign sources. Imported natural gas is better, but again, much comes from areas that are not friendly to our interests. Until we discover a magic alternative-fuel bullet, natural gas hydrates are our best bet. But if we harvest that crop ... *when* we harvest that crop, we need to be ready to use it for all that it's worth."

A presidential aide appeared in the small cabin's door. "Landing in one minute, Mr. President."

The president nodded. "Well, Ms. Raven, I appreciate all of your insights."

"Thank you, Mr. President," she said.

As a good politician, the president was inquisitive and appropriately skeptical. He did not reveal his hand and would not until he made a decision. She couldn't read him. But Raven felt she hit a home run. It was slow-pitch with a target as big as a beach ball. The president had two choices. Either he puts all of his chips on the potential of natural gas or he goes to war for oil. It seemed like a no-brainer. She knew the president owed her nothing. She didn't have to bribe him with political support. He would do it for the betterment of the country. All the planets were aligned. Citizens would be able to afford their most prized possessions—affordable heat for their homes, electricity for their gadgets, and fuel for their cars. The government would collect plenty of taxes. The air would become more breathable. The United States would reduce its greenhouse-gas output meeting international demands, quieting the chicken-little environmentalists. Temptations to war with oil-rich nations would be eased. The heart of the sea would pump clean, cheap energy throughout the United States. And much of the nation's lifeblood would travel through the veins of Alexandria Raven's pipelines.

GE, Microsoft, ExxonMobil—move over. American Energy would become the most successful company in the history of the world.

All of this would happen if the hydrate extraction proved successful. *Not if*, she thought again, *when*!

CHAPTER 40

▼

Deep below the main deck of the *China Maiden* Akmed Abram led Danielle O'Day with a nod of his head. She was close enough for him to touch her lightly on the elbow, and she welcomed it. But he kept his hands to himself. Akmed pointed to a wall of computer monitors that registered pressures of inert gases that filled the pipelines than ran underneath the deep-sea waters all the way to the United States' coastline. Akmed was as polite a tour guide as Danielle had ever seen. The geophysicist gestured with his long fingers like a relaxed television weather forecaster.

"I believe they are testing the flows of nitrogen through the pipelines, testing for leaks or obstructions in the lines," Akmed told her. "I understand this is the longest underwater pipeline in the world."

"It's also a marvel of modern pipeline technology, baby," came a gratuitous comment from behind the couple.

Danielle turned. The voice came from a short, stocky man massaging a large bald spot surrounded by unkempt blond hair. Dressed in tan dungarees and work shirt, he held a yellow hardhat under his arm as he rubbed the top of his head as if he had fleas. He smelled of grease and soap.

"Mr. Sheldon, always a pleasure," Akmed said with little emotion. But Akmed said most everything with little emotion, Danielle noted.

"Yeah," Sheldon said.

Akmed turned to Danielle and made an introduction. "This is Roger Sheldon, chief engineer and your firm's contractor that manages the ship-to-shore pipeline project. And Mr. Sheldon, this is Danielle O'Day, senior vice-president at American Energy."

"My pleasure," Sheldon said curtly, not showing even courteous recognition that a high-flying company executive was present, though he seemed to eye her as an attractive member of the opposite sex. Danielle put that out of her mind, however. All of the drilling and pipeline personnel looked rough around the edges. Except for Akmed, they seemed unimpressed, almost contemptuous, of corporate types. Sheldon cleaned his fingernails that were laced in oil and barked a couple of orders to assistants who were in the room. Danielle thought she recognized Sheldon from the deck of the platform when she vomited on Cowboy. But she had double vision then and could not be sure.

"I am here as part of the preparation for the president's visit," Danielle said.

"I'm just a lonely subcontractor for the big operation, baby."

Sheldon's use of "baby" was not a condescending reference to Danielle, she figured, but a speech mannerism that she found particularly annoying—like that bombastic college-basketball announcer.

Akmed interjected, "Miss O'Day, Mr. Sheldon's firm, Universal Pipelines, is the contractor that built the underwater lines."

Suddenly, Sheldon's pentagonal face looked up at Danielle as if in sudden recognition. He raised his bushy blond eyebrows, the right one separated by a thin white scar that perhaps looked like the result of a boxing injury or a bar fight. He was clean-shaven, with a wide face and pug nose. His lips were as wide as a frog's mouth, making his grin span from cheek to cheek. As he spoke, his Adam's apple bobbed up and down the front of his neck like a large cork in ocean waves.

"O'Day ... O'Day," he said. "Do you have other relatives at American Energy?" He hunched his shoulders together as if he were shoring up a backpack.

"My father works for the company on the operations side—he's a local union president." She said it as if she were ashamed, like talking about a relative with mental illness.

"Any relation to Dan O'Day, the pipeline pioneer?"

Danielle sighed. A hundred miles out on the Atlantic Ocean, she runs into someone who heard of her family's legacy. The shadow she was trying to escape so she could bask in her own light kept following her like a rain cloud no matter where she went.

"A great uncle, I think," she answered lethargically, as if cornered on a witness stand. "But, that has nothing to do—"

"Wow, baby, glad to meet you," Sheldon said. His voice tone turned whimsical. His bulbous Adam's apple seemed to bulge under his skin as if it were a large rodent slithering under a thin blanket. "Daniel O'Day was the original master. John D's right-hand man. It was his idea to pipe natural gas over long distances."

Sheldon was as giddy as a pointed-eared Trekkie in a polyester tunic meeting Captain Kirk at a *Star Trek* convention.

"You know about Daniel O'Day?" she questioned. She thought only her father remembered her ancient uncle and talked of him as if he were Paul Bunyan or Johnny Appleseed.

"Sure. Dan O'Day was the *man*, baby. One of Rockefeller's main lieutenants. The gas industry has him to thank for its initial development. He was, like Elvis or something, y'know, for us gas pipeline guys. Whoa, baby."

"Elvis?" she repeated, incredulous.

"Well, maybe more like Mozart. They used to say, pipeliners were so close, if you stuck one with a needle—"

"They all bled, I know," she said, believing prior to that moment it was a statement her father made up. "How do you know all this?"

"I wrote a book on the early pipeline industry. It's my avocation. Didn't sell much, but was interesting as hell if you ask me. You know the first gas lines were made out of wood, believe it or not—hollowed out Canadian white pine logs. Leaked like a submarine with screen windows, baby. But we've come a long way."

"Perhaps you can explain how this new line works," Akmed suggested, patiently tolerating Sheldon's historical rant.

Without acknowledging Akmed's request, Sheldon complied. "A bit more complicated than sticking a hole in the ground—those rock hounds and pole plungers think the job is done when they hit a sweet spot." Danielle wasn't sure whether he was kidding the foreign-born geophysicist or insulting him. Sheldon continued. "But after a successful well has been hit, that is when the real work comes in. In the early years of the industry when pipeliners first started using metal pipe instead of wooden pump logs, they were also kind of dangerous. The lines were screwed together, leaked like a sieve, and couldn't handle high pressures that came out of the gas wells. That is until folks like O'Day got on the job."

Neither Danielle nor Akmed seized the opportunity to interrupt Sheldon's lecture.

"Today's underwater pipelines are ten times more technologically involved than what is buried in a trench on land," he boasted, displaying a lack of rhetorical sensitivity that might reveal that he was boring his audience to tears. *What Sheldon lacks on social graces, he makes up in pedantry*, Danielle thought.

"Stronger pipe is necessary to handle the crush of 10,000-foot waters and possess the ability to handle high pressures. We use flexible composite steel fiber material that features smart technology. Natural gas must flow a long distance through pipelines laid through near-freezing seawater along the ocean bottom. Therefore the new pipelines must control temperature and humidity, moisture and heating content, impurities, specific gravity, and inner and outer pressures. It is like securing a spacecraft, baby. If consumers only knew what it took to get their energy to them, maybe they wouldn't be bitching about it so much."

Sheldon moved to an illustration on a computer screen that sat below the numerous round pressure dials and temperature monitors on the wall, and punched a few keys. A diagram of one of the underwater pipelines appeared on the monitor. It looked like a cross-section of an earthworm or a long cylindrical spaceship with many hulls.

"We've advanced a bit in the few years since the oil and gas industry began working in extreme water depths. On land, the various threats to pipelines include being ripped up by a careless backhoe operator from the outside, or once, I saw a pressurized plastic line near a creek chewed clean through by a beaver. Needless to say, it created a nasty hole and blew out a ten-foot-wide section of ground—never found a trace of the beaver." He laughed at his own humor. "Underwater, we use flexible pipe that is lighter than standard rigid pipe and neutrally buoyant. It is installed in less time and at less cost. It has bending capabilities that allow it to move with the *China Maiden* from hydrate site to hydrate site. One great thing about the system is that it can be put in place and removed in a matter of hours. The pipeline can also be lifted closer to the surface for inspection and repair work. We haven't had any underwater line breaks—I don't know if beavers can swim that deep, baby." He laughed equally as hardy as before.

"What threats does an underwater line face?" Danielle asked.

"On land, the main non-mammal culprit is electrolyte corrosion—basically the metal pipe rotting. Underwater we face the corrosive effects of salt water and we have to ensure the line's integrity under the great pressure of deep-water regions. We inspect the line on the outside with the bathysphere."

"The bathywhat?"

"It's like a little disk-shaped submarine, about the size of a hotel bathroom. I've been along the entire stretch of the line twice. It can be controlled as a ROV—Remote Operated Vehicle—but it's more fun to dive in it personally. It's kind of like riding in a little MG sports car in the ocean. A nice easy glide, baby," Sheldon reached out an arm and braced his weight against the wall next to O'Day and leaned in a bit closer. "I'll take you for a spin sometime if you're interested."

"No thanks," O'Day said, stepping back from his advance. "I'm claustrophobic enough."

Sheldon backed off his body language. "Well, once we are satisfied with the outside review, the real concerns are inside the line. Like in the winter on land in northern areas where ice and gas hydrates can form inside the line, blocking the flow of gas."

"I'm familiar with that," Danielle said. "Hydrates in pipelines form underwater too?"

"At extreme depths it is a nightmare," Sheldon answered, scratching his bald spot again. "In shallow water, hydrates cause a problem called *flow assurance*, which can be hydrates or paraffin that can build up in the line—kind of like cholesterol clogging in your veins from eating too many Big Macs over time."

"And do you use chemicals like methanol or glycol in insulated pipe to keep the hydrates from forming?"

"Well, deep water requires a different approach," the pipeline expert huffed like an arrogant professor annoyed by a know-it-all neophyte student. "The high pressures and near-freezing water cause constant hydrate formations. A blocked pipeline means lost money. And using chemicals would be too expensive for the amount that would be needed. We've developed more economical ways to keep the veins open." He pointed to the cross-section of the pipe on the computer screen that showed several layers of a cylindrical tube. "In shallower water, we still use some compounds called *kinetic hydrate inhibitors* that melt hydrate formation in the line—kind of like rock salt on your sidewalk in the winter—but in ultra-deep water, we need both a pipeline that will withstand the enormous water pressures outside and prevent hydrate formation inside the line. We transmit electricity to heat the inside of the line that prevents buildups."

"You heat the entire pipeline?"

"We heat as necessary, depending when the hydrates begin to collect. We remedy the situation long before the hydrate buildup blocks any flow of gas, keeping the pipelines as clear as Richard Simmon's veins."

Danielle couldn't help herself. She laughed.

"Who is this Mr. Simmons?" Akmed asked.

"He's an effeminate health-nut guy who used to be on TV," Danielle explained with a chuckle. "He jumped around and clapped." Akmed stared stoically. "Well, it's not important," she said.

"Well," Akmed said. "In any case, the pipeline system is not 100 percent reliable in preventing hydrates."

Sheldon scowled at the erudite geophysicist like he was a rival, one of the drilling guys versus the pipeline guys. "Yeah," he admitted, "there still could be blockages." He continued pointing at a layer of the pipeline that looked like tightly wound thread around a tube. "But we use fiber optic technology to monitor the entire project to regulate the current along the line to pinpoint the formation of any obstructions."

"And then what?" Danielle asked.

"That's where Arnold comes in."

"Arnold?" Danielle asked.

"I'm not sure if you are old enough, but do you remember Arnold Ziffle, from the 'sixties TV show *Green Acres*?"

"Arnold … the pig?"

"Actually, our Arnold is a high-technology porcine cyborg terminator," Sheldon said, slipping into a poor eastern-European accent impression of actor and politician Arnold Swartzenegger.

"You mean 'pigging' a pipeline to clean it out?" Danielle said, using the industry vernacular.

"Yep. Ever know how cleaning out a pipeline got called 'pigging?'"

Akmed spoke up. "Does this have something to do with the television pig Mr. Simmons?"

This time, Sheldon laughed. "Akmed, you slay me. Pigs root through the dirt looking for things to eat, like truffles right? So pipeline pigs root out dirt or other obstacles through the pipeline. They're mechanical devices—in this case a metal mandrel scrapes the pipeline's inner wall free of deposits. And, by the way, when you shoot them through a pipeline, sometimes they squeal like a hog at a slaughterhouse. Follow me."

Sheldon led the two through an oval doorway into a large chamber filled with various colored piping and round valve controls that looked like metal truck steering wheels. Technicians milled about with palm pilot devices, checking dials and monitors on the various valves where the pipes joined. Though the area was immaculately clean, it had the aura of an auto-repair garage. Two huge machines the size of diesel train locomotives dominated the center of the room. Danielle recognized them as gas compressors that pumped natural gas through pipelines.

"This is Adam and Eve, our compressors," Sheldon said, pointing at the machines. "Ten-thousand horsepower a piece—the largest in the world. One will pump natural gas out of the bottom of the ocean and the other will pump carbon dioxide back into the formation."

"They're not running now, are they?" Danielle asked.

"Oh no. When these suckers start up, baby, you can't hear yourself think in here." The trio walked the length of the machines to two round openings, four feet in diameter. They reminded Danielle of bank vault doors.

"This is our access point to the major underwater pipelines," Sheldon said. Leading into one of the openings was a short metal railroad track. At the end of the track, Danielle noticed a ten-foot long, flat-nosed, bullet-shaped metal vehicle, about the same diameter as the round doors. The outside circumference of the device was lined with dozens of metallic wire brushes. On the back end of the mechanical missile, a technician sat on an attached metal scaffold, looking at the control panel of the device. Two black ovals were painted on the blunt front end of the machine. They looked like huge nostrils.

"This," Sheldon said, "is Arnold. The latest technology in pipeline cleaning and inspection. Arnold is powered through the pipeline either from pressurized gas, or it can run on its own internal battery. It has just enough charge to tunnel its way through the underwater pipeline a hundred miles to shore, x-raying welds, checking for weak spots through magnetic imagery, and cleaning obstructions such as dirt, impurities, and methane hydrates, all at the blistering speed of fifteen-miles-per-hour."

"That's one big pig," Danielle responded. She never saw a pipeline pig before, even a small one.

"It is a *smart* pig too," Sheldon said, slapping it on the side like a faithful dog. "Some of the same technology as NASA's Mars rovers. It can even do internal repairs thanks to a robot arm and digital magnetic imaging. It may look like an early Russian space orbiter, but she ain't no bag of bolts—it cost seven million bucks."

"It's not piloted by a person is it?" Danielle asked, pointing at the technician in a white suit pushing buttons and pulling levers on the back of the machine.

"No, Smitty over there is giving Arnold a once-over. It just came through the mainline in a final cleanout before the test of flowing gas from the hydrate well. He's sitting on what we call the caboose of the pig. I never thought about it, but I guess you could hang on the end with a deep-diving suit and flow through the vein of pipeline like one of those miniature underwater subs in that old sci-fi movie *Fantastic Voyage*. I'm not claustrophobic, but sailing through a four-foot-wide tube five- to ten-thousand feet below the water's surface for a hundred-mile stretch doesn't appeal to me, baby."

Another white-suited worker approached Sheldon and whispered into his ear and handed him a slip of paper. His neck bulge quivered, his eyes sparkled, and his bleached-white teeth and thin lips erupted into a banana-wide elliptical grin.

"Gonna have to cut this short folks—I'm told the president's tour will be on its way shortly. The Secret Service is on its way down to secure the area." He flashed his broad Jack-Nicholson Joker's grin at Akmed. "I don't know if you are cleared for this, Akmed; I have a list of those that are permitted in this area during the president's tour and I don't remember seeing your name."

Again, Danielle could not read whether he was conveying concern or insolence. Akmed, poker-faced as ever, nodded his head and shook Danielle's hand.

"Yes," Akmed said graciously. "I will have to bid you farewell for now. The tour was most entertaining and informative. Mr. Sheldon, I am grateful."

"Yeah," Sheldon said.

"I'll join you," said Danielle.

"No," Sheldon said, interrupting with force. "This message regarding the tour comes from Alexandria Raven of American Energy. You Ms. O'Day, apparently are to join the president's tour as soon as possible on deck."

Danielle stood transfixed. Akmed bowed politely like Jeeves, the English butler, and left.

"You know Akmed the Arab very well?" Sheldon asked Danielle, once out of Akmed's earshot.

"Not really, I just met him."

"Thinks he's the cat's ass," Sheldon said. "I don't know what he's doing here now. With all this terrorism stuff going on, he gives me the creeps."

CHAPTER 41

▼

After departing the Coast Guard ship, a flying motorcade of passenger helicopters approached American Energy's sea platform like a flock of giant mutated steel dragonflies, using the parking-lot-sized helipad surface to land one after another. The first to unload were advance personnel and Secret Service agents—both plain clothed and others in full military regalia including body armor and automatic weapons. Next came a gaggle of journalists—print and broadcast with their electronic accoutrements. And finally, a helicopter touched down full of several other VIPs, lawmakers, energy department staffers, and the president's personal guests. They included the irascible aged consumer-activist Olga Stevick, and the cross-eyed attorney Herbert Winkle. The two Freeman adversaries disembarked from their maiden ride on a chopper into the wall of wind on the deck of the *China Maiden* with all the grace of hillbillies at a Hollywood black-tie affair. Though not attempting to suavely lobby the two mighty Lilliputian citizen lobbyists, the president wanted to show them the dignified respect usually reserved for a foreign head of state on a White House tour. Stevick and Winkle, allies against what they called the "axis of corporate evil," (i.e., companies like American Energy), did not necessarily conspire on their government-lobbying strategies. But they were sympathetic to one another since they shared the same nemesis. By escorting two of his largest unelected political foes, the president hoped to convince them that his administration was not at odds with American consumers or those sympathetic to alternative energies. Exceedingly circumspect, but at Congressman Doggle's suggestion, the curmudgeonly consumer-activist grandmother and the unsympathetic environmental barrister warily accepted.

Having his public critics at his side did not please many of his political advisors, but the president allayed their fears quipping, "Better to have them on the inside of the tent pissing out, than outside the tent, pissing in."

About an hour after the press and other guests arrived, the president stepped off the whirlybird Marine One—any flying vehicle the president boards assumes the prestigious designation of Air Force or Marine One—dressed in a naval flight jacket and pants. Since the president was a decorated Navy captain during the first Gulf War, few criticized him when he donned military outerwear. Accompanying the president was Secretary of Energy Virgil Priest, twirling his waxed mustache at the president's heel, and Alexandria Raven, who kept to the rear with other lesser-known dignitaries. Much of the crew from roughnecks to scientific technicians was piped on deck, standing at-ease as well as any Navy seamen. The president waved to the onlookers and shook hands with several dignitaries, including the director of the rig, his ephemeral Naval Academy roommate, Bruce "Cowboy" Rhodan. Seeing his old buddy gave the president a sense of security he had not had in quite some time.

"Mr. President, an honor to have you aboard," Cowboy said. Neither the rotor blades of the helicopter nor the brisk Atlantic winds that tossed numerous baseball caps off of TV cameramen's heads nudged Cowboy's Stetson one centimeter.

"Cowboy," the president said, "it's great to see you again." A broad grin broke across both their faces, and the media, already stationed for the embarking president, caught the greeting and broadcast it live across the world. A recorded speaker on the deck of the offshore platform blurted out "Hail to the Chief."

"Looks like you've done okay for yourself," Cowboy said to his old friend. "The last time I saw you, I think you were conducting business leadership seminars and riding coach."

"Well, I still had to take a pay cut," the president answered, "but room and board are included."

Though the television pictures beamed back to the mainland illustrated ceremonious glad-handing, all was not well in the Atlantic. The National Hurricane Center, tracking the late season hurricane rotating in the Caribbean, was still uncertain of the storm's eventual path. Preliminary forecasts projected that the eyewall could head straight for the Carolina coasts, but if it veered eastward into the Atlantic, it might chart a course toward the gas recovery platform nearly 100 miles offshore of North Carolina. Still, the problem was days away, and the president's visit would only last hours. But President Freeman had a premonition that he would have to return to the Atlantic Coast before long to survey more damage to life and property.

The first leg of the visit was kept topside, as there were ample video opportunities as the president surveyed the miles of white pipes, red gridwork, and yellow ladders snaking around the above-deck section of the floating derrick. Platform workers wearing smart green uniforms and burnt-orange hardhats buzzed around their stations of responsibility and tried to avoid the stare of the television cameras. But streams of rig workers waved their hardhats to the president as they tended to a multitude of tasks. While the president shook hands, top officials of American Energy Corporation, including CEO Alexandria Raven, trailed inconspicuously behind. The president wanted to keep Raven's presence under the radar. Otherwise, the media would be tempted to identify President Freeman as a tool of powerful energy industry interests rather than a public servant attempting to solve the country's energy crisis in the interest of Joe Lunchbucket.

The president delivered a speech on the deck of the spar calling for passage of the administration's $47 billion, 1,500-page energy bill that would result in not only more nontraditional sources of energy such as the methane-producing kelp farm, but also the most controversial provision, the lifting of major offshore drilling restrictions to ease the country's dependence on foreign energy.

"In 1973 when the first Arab oil embargo hit and Americans waited in gas lines, only about a third of the nation's oil was imported," President Freeman proclaimed in appropriate sound-bite fashion. "Today, that share is up to three-fourths. Meanwhile, we now import nearly one quarter of our natural gas, which was once strictly a domestically produced energy. But *Project Blue Sky* will harvest nature's gift of energy from the sea to keep our homes warm, our lights on, our air clean, and our nation secure. But it is not enough. We must not only improve our energy efficiency, we need to produce more energy in our own nation."

The friendly audience aboard the *China Maiden* cheered.

"So that's the dashing president?" Dr. Edison said, more a deadpan statement than a question.

"Never saw him in the flesh?" Danielle asked.

"No."

The two women stood in a receiving line, waiting for the president of the United States to shake everyone's hand. The nation's chief executive, by all reports, was personally charming, even if you disagreed with his politics. Danielle never paid much attention to the political world. Though American Energy coerced all of its executives to contribute heavily to the firm's PAC fund, it was just another payroll deduction that palled in comparison to their salary and extra bonuses. But meeting the president was not something humdrum.

"He's even better looking than on TV," Danielle said. Then she felt stupid.

Edison expressed neither excitement nor anticipation.

"Do you think he'll give the project the green light?" Danielle asked.

"If there is a success with the initial extraction test," Edison said. Again, Danielle observed no emotion in the NOAA scientist, but Edison's eyes were also focused on the handsome president, whose broad smile appeared to mesmerize each person as he clasped his hands in theirs.

"You seem cynical," Danielle said.

"Success sometimes is more troubling than failure," was the scientist's cryptic response.

Danielle finally turned her full attention to Edison. "What do you mean?"

Edison glanced downward at her shoes. "We are all addicts, you know."

"Addicts?"

"Of energy. All us Americans can think of is consuming more. More energy to power our cars, our computers, our toys. More energy to build more stuff. More energy to get richer and richer without concern over global consequences."

"Well, I guess you're right," Danielle answered. "But we are in a crisis. Without the promise of this project, what are we going to do?"

"How about consuming less?" Edison said, her sea-blue eyes almost tearing. "How about not exploiting the earth every chance we get?"

"I didn't realize you were such an environmentalist."

"After I got my Ph.D. in oceanography I spent three years studying the effects of Japanese over-fishing in the Arctic. Then, I volunteered as a researcher for a Greenpeace vessel observing changes in ocean temperatures. The warming oceans can affect all life. For example, satellite photography shows that the oceans are getting bluer."

"Isn't the ocean supposed to be blue?"

"It is primarily blue because of how water filters light. But phytoplankton that reflects green near the surface is declining, and that can have serious effects on the ocean food chain. Also, phytoplankton absorbs carbon dioxide from the air and in turn provides about half of the oxygen we breathe."

Danielle didn't follow up. Every time she did she exposed more of her ignorance.

"I joined NOAA to get into government to see how science could impact public policy," Edison continued. "You know, stop complaining about things and revolutionize them from the inside. Think global and act local and all that. Now this." Edison flipped her hand as if she was disgusted.

Danielle thought maybe this was why Edison harbored total disdain for Cowboy, the *damn-the-torpedoes* oil-and-gas guru who seemed hell-bent on drilling despite any environmental consequences, just like he was looking to dip his wick into every attractive woman he met without worrying about knocking her up or catching the clap.

"But don't you think if this project works, it will help eliminate the need for using more dirty coal and oil, and end up reducing carbon-dioxide emissions?" Danielle asked.

"Do you think that's why we are out here?"

"Well," Danielle fumbled. "Yeah."

Edison shook her head and smiled like an adult not sure how to explain the birds and the bees to a child. "All of us at NOAA came out here to see what we could do to study the potential catastrophe of underground earthquakes on the continental shelf, and before we can publish one study, it turns into a commercial-energy project. This isn't about saving the environment; it's about money. You from the big energy company should realize that." Edison nodded her head at the president, who was edging closer to them in the line. "For him it's about political power and votes."

Danielle stood silent for a moment, stone-faced. She took everyone involved in the project at face value. Drillers wanted to drill. Scientists sought to discover new frontiers. Business people desired to earn revenue. And consumers demanded to improve the quality of their lives. And some politicians did aim to solve problems *and* stay in office. If it all took energy, so be it. That's what makes the world go round. She never thought it was a moral issue.

"Do I want the project to succeed?" Edison asked rhetorically. "For starters, I want to prevent these knuckleheads from causing an underwater earthquake that could destroy part of the United States' East Coast. If your company gets rich at the same time, that's part of the price. But second, realize this. No matter how much gas flows onshore, before you know it, it won't be enough because of our insatiable greed for energy. We'll want more and more and the cycle will never end until we end up destroying ourselves by our own gluttony."

Before Danielle could answer, her right hand was in the grasp of the bear-like warm paw of the president, who flashed his hypnotic smile at her.

"This is Danielle O'Day, an attorney from American Energy," said Cowboy, who apparently appointed himself official greeter.

"I'm glad you could be here," the president said. *He was dashing*, Danielle thought. He was good-looking, confident, and smelled great.

The president then moved on to Dr. Edison, and shook her hand just as graciously. Cowboy did not make an introduction.

CHAPTER 42

▼

"This is n-n-nothing but a lapdog media-stroking s-s-session," said Herbert Winkle, poking at German potato salad that was amazingly perfect as if it were dished out at a Germanic festival in central-Ohio. "A d-d-dog and pony show for these asinine lackey j-j-journalists."

"Are you going to finish that?" Olga Stevick said, her plate as clear as if a hungry St. Bernard licked it clean. *There are starving children in China*, she wanted to say to him, but she kept her powder dry. They sat in the galley of the *China Maiden*, among three-dozen journalists, cameramen, and audio engineers from the nation's top news outlets engaged in spirited discussions and massive consumption of a free lunch. The menu featured fresh tuna steaks and soft-shelled crab, broccoli au gratin, and white table wine from New York's Finger Lakes region (a powerful member of the House Energy and Commerce Committee from Rochester, N.Y., was in attendance). The salad bar also contained edible kelp, though few media types tried it. White tablecloths, fresh flowers, authentic china, and crystal candlesticks adorned the stainless-steel tables that usually echoed with the clang of plastic plates and insulated coffee mugs of the rig's hungry workers.

"W-What?" Winkle responded.

"Are you going to finish your potato salad?"

"B-B-Be my guest," Winkle said, moving his china plate toward his elderly companion. Stevick ate like a college linebacker, and she was proud of that. Her metabolism had been high since nearly starving to death as a kid during the Great Depression. Winkle appeared to not have an appetite. The cantankerous lawyer opposed from the start tagging along on the visit to *Project Blue Sky*, or whatever the hell it was called. But Stevick knew a good opportunity for media coverage. They did not have to play along with the president's PR ploy. They could make their own news.

"Damn f-f-fascists," Winkle said. "That's all they are. M-M-Mussolini couldn't be prouder—the seamless joining of government and c-c-corporations."

As she continued to devour the lawyer's German potato salad like a starving wolf, Winkle stared at the White House press corps that contained familiar television faces and more obscure print journalists known primarily by their bylines. Stevick felt the group made their living by trailing the chum dropped off the presidential communications' yacht. The award-winning reporters gobbled up the free eats subsidized by the taxpayers like performing organ-grinder monkeys. They would hold out their tin cups and hope that a highly placed White House official might drop something in it. A scoop. An exclusive. Life revolved around an unnamed source on background leaking someone's diabolical plans. However, in Stevick's opinion, the media were nothing but cheap whores. The press was full of charlatans masquerading as professionals doing the people's business. They *were* the establishment—part of the problem in Washington. In her opinion, what the nation's capital needed was a good enema.

"I would give anything to eavesdrop on Freeman's meeting with these s-s-scientists," Winkle stammered, almost to himself.

"Oh, fiddlesticks, I left my purse on that God-awful helicopter," Stevick said, ignoring him. "I must have my Tic-Tacs."

"You think this is a p-party?" Winkle admonished. "W-w-w-e should be right on Freeman's tail and you are worried about breath m-m-mints?"

"Well, go and demand that we be admitted to the president's private meetings," Stevick said, dabbing the last of the bitter vinegar sauce off her lips with a cloth napkin. "That's what I'd do."

"F-F-Fat chance," said Winkle. "Look, the doors to this galley are guarded by federal g-g-goons." His wild eye bounced erratically from side to side like the silver ball in a pinball machine.

Stevick surveyed the exits of the eating area. Yes, Secret Service agents, Navy, Coast Guard, and other security personnel shielded them. They were not protecting the horde of journalists from an unknown enemy. They were making sure no scribe or photo jockey slipped off the reservation and became curious.

"Well, I think it is high time we find out what our dear president is up to," Stevick said, standing. "Care to join me?"

"You c-c-can't leave the formal t-tour," Winkle said. "N-n-not with those jack-booted thugs there. You're just an old l-l-l ..." He held his stuttering tongue.

"An old lady?" Stevick said. "That is correct young man. Some things must be left to those more experienced. Leave it to your elders."

The spunky consumer activist pushed away from the table and hobbled toward the door like a crippled crab, her rubber-tipped wooden cane reaching in front of her like the proboscis of a blind ant. Stevick didn't always use the walking stick, but it was a handy prop when the senior citizen wanted to appear pitiful. She approached a suit-clad Secret Service agent and a military type with U.S. Coast Guard insignia on the uniform. His nameplate read "Ensign Bradley Kelly."

"May I help you madam?" the Coast Guard officer said in a polite tone. He was a handsome man in his early twenties, with military-cropped blond hair and a southern accent, perhaps from Mississippi, she guessed.

"Oh honey," Stevick said in her most disarming old lady tone. "I need to find a ladies' room."

"There is a women's room on the other side of the galley," the Secret Service agent interjected, as respectful as he could. He was a distinguished African-American man of about forty-five, with patches of gray in his closely cut ebony hair.

"Oh, sir, I don't think I can use that one," Stevick wailed in a melancholy pitch. "It is much too close to the eating area. I am too modest, for you see, I have some intestinal problems that can be quite ... oh, I don't know how to say this ... well, boisterous."

The Secret Service agent's eyebrows rose.

"I don't want to be too close to others within earshot—it can be embarrassing for an old lady. And, besides, the odor sometimes—"

"Sir," Ensign Kelly, the Coast Guard Officer, offered. "There is another facility on an adjoining deck, away from any major traffic. It is not very far. I would be glad to escort her."

"Fine," the agent relented. He was uncomfortable with the talk of noisy bowels and, if his skin pigment allowed, would have turned red on the spot.

"Thank you young man," Stevick said. "You are so kind." She began a hobble toward the exit as if she knew exactly where to go. The president's protector shook his head in amusement.

Ensign Kelly escorted Stevick down a short hallway and through a metal door and down the stairs to the adjacent deck. When approached by one of the rig's deckhands explaining that the area was closed off for the VIP tour, Ensign Kelly waived him off.

"The old lady needs to use the head," he whispered, though she heard him.

Once closing the door behind him, Ensign Kelly pointed toward the end of one hallway and started to speak. Stevick ignored him, and walked in the other direction, appearing aimless, but in reality checking out what she could see.

"No, mamm, this way," the Coast Guard officer said, gently steering her shoulders the opposite direction.

"Oh, thank you honey," she said, as defenseless as a defanged, declawed kitten. "You are so sweet."

"I'll just wait here at the end of the hall," he said.

"That's fine, honey." Stevick ambled down the narrow, gray-floored corridor and slowly stepped through the metal door of a cramped, one-hole, but more private toilet. After several moments of quiet, Stevick dragged the rubber tip of her cane against the toilet stall door, making a muffled, vibrating sound that she hoped would resemble serious flatulence.

"Oh, young man!" Stevick called in a pathetic whine, echoing from inside the metal room.

"Yes, mamm?" Ensign Kelley said.

"Oh, honey, I forgot my purse. It has my suppositories in it and I must use them. Would you be so kind as to get them from my son and bring them here?"

"Uh," he said uncertainly, "okay."

"Just open the door to the toilet when you come back and place them inside— I'll retrieve them."

"Yes mamm," he said.

After a few moments when Stevick was confident the Coast Guard chaperone was gone, she placed her ridged, ankle-high, thick-soled orthopedic shoes inside the toilet stall where they might be noticed from the doorway. She then exited the room in her thick wool socks. With a surprisingly agile gait, the old crone scampered up the hallway with the aid of her cane and down the opposite corridor in order to see what she could see.

CHAPTER 43

▼

"From all your detailed reports, I can see you've done a fine job," Alexandria Raven told her protégée.

Danielle O'Day looked dumbfounded. She felt she did nothing. Still the words from her boss rejuvenated her. If she could only get such accolades from her father. Well, her mother always praised her, but despite her heart of gold, she was clueless. Danielle could be promoted to the head Girl Friday of the secretarial pool and her mother would brag the news all about town.

They sat in the small conference room where Danielle initially learned the difference between the publicly acknowledged *Project Blue Sky* that involved the production of methane from seaweed and the secret *Project Hades* that would extract natural gas from methane ice.

"I'm just a little concerned about all this press here," Danielle said. She did not know much about the modus operandi of national journalists and she was far from an expert in public relations, despite being in charge of it for American Energy. But she wanted to make the corporation look good. Still, she knew there wasn't much to look at on board that was not confidential. The reporters would likely get bored. *Idle minds were the devil's workshop*, she thought.

"Oh nonsense," Raven said. "The president is an expert with the press; they love him. Remember when he was the press secretary in the previous administration? He had those hacks eating out of his hand."

Danielle was still dressed in the drab green wardrobe of the *China Maiden* platform. Raven, on the other hand, was smartly clad in a sea-blue business suit that concealed her creeping matronly poundage while allowing her enough feminine curves to attractive admiration. Cream-colored flats matched her blond hair.

Her hazel eyes and herringbone-lined lips shaded with firehouse-red lipstick conveyed a stylish, yet executive presence. She smiled disarmingly and placed her firm hands on her hips, admiring Danielle as if she were one of her own children. Danielle felt Raven's delight and she did not object to being the teacher's pet.

"I'm not sure what PR role I have," Danielle said.

"You don't need to do anything—this is the president's show. We are laying low. I didn't tell you much about the project here because I needed an unbiased opinion of what the operations looked like. And you have provided that. But being here puts you on the ground floor of what will be our company's greatest achievement."

"It is impressive," said Danielle. "Still I have some concerns how all of this would play if it was made public."

"There is nothing to worry about. The first test has yet to be conducted. Everyone is on a need-to-know basis."

Danielle was not sure why she was on the list of *need to know*. "Yes, but I'm wondering about the ramifications of this project. From my judgment, this could be considered drilling on the continental shelf within 100 miles of the coast, something that violates of the nation's moratoria on such activity."

"Don't worry," Raven said. "This project is backed by the president of the United States."

So was Iran-Contra and the search for Iraqi weapons of mass destruction, she thought. *Well-intentioned policies that ran amuck.* Danielle was reluctant to challenge the CEO of the firm. She had been beaten down enough by her father when she bit the hand that fed her. But she felt obligated to offer her legal opinion. "Yes, I know, but I have a feeling that a few congressmen might have another assessment. And, there is this thing about environmental risks." She paused and looked at her mentor for acknowledgement.

"Go on."

"The recovery of natural gas hydrates on a large scale has never been attempted before. According to the NOAA scientist I spoke to, there is a serious risk of upsetting the continental shelf and causing an underwater landslide that could have, well I don't know ..." —she was speaking so rapidly she began to stammer— "... d-d-disastrous effects."

"You are beginning to sound like that Herbie Winkey character," Raven said, her hazel eyes sparkling when she laughed.

"Well, as an American Energy risk management attorney and now corporate communications officer, I need to give you counsel to protect the company's assets and reputation."

Raven smiled again. "And so you have, and that's exactly why you are here. I need to hear these things. That's why you have a bright future at American Energy, Danielle."

All Danielle could think of to say was, "Thank you."

The parlay was interrupted by one of the president's aides who informed the two American Energy officials that the president's private tour without the horde of media was about to begin. Moments later, a coterie of suited figures entered the small room, including several presidential aides, Cowboy, Edison, and other key figures of *Project Hades*. Finally, President Freeman and Secretary of Energy Priest entered the small room, making the elbow-to-elbow congregation reminiscent of the comedic overcrowded stateroom scene in the Marx Brothers' *A Night at the Opera* film. Danielle swallowed a large breath to avoid the claustrophobic feeling the room now possessed.

Priest shook hands formally with Raven and Danielle, and as the secretary of energy said, "I'm honored," a demur smile settled underneath his waxed moustache. He seemed sophisticated and charming, Danielle thought, though a bit too intimate. The president, vigorous and vivacious as his reputation, was eager to see the tour begin. Though Edison and Roystone formally conducted the walk-through of the natural gas hydrate recovery operation, having the president's ear as a personal friend, Cowboy continually interjected.

"Hey, somebody get a hold of Akmed," Cowboy ordered one of the project's underlings. "The president should meet the brains behind this operation." Several of the president's aides looked at one another, indecisively.

"Akmed?" President Freeman asked.

"Oh yes, Mr. President," Cowboy said. "He's the geophysicist whose pioneering work in freeing hydrates led to the techniques we will be using on the rig."

"Then, by all means," Freeman responded.

As the entourage moved out of the conference room and toward the hydrate laboratory, the president's aides and other project officials scrambled to find Akmed Abram.

In his Langley, Virginia, office at that moment, the Director of the Central Intelligence Agency, Gen. Edwin Wells, a retired Marine Corps officer, answered his telephone. His counterpoint in Mossad, the Israeli Intelligence Agency—also an ex-military general—was on the other end of the line. Even though there was peace with the new state of Palestine, the Israelis never let their guard down. DCI Wells knew the Israeli spy chief for years and they swapped pictures of their grandchildren as well as human intelligence. They first met when Wells was deployed to help secure Patriot missiles to protect Israel from Iraqi Scuds in the First Gulf War.

"Akmed Abram, the geophysicist," Isaiah Ludium said.

"Yes?" the DCI said.

"We believe he may have terrorist connections."

"But I understand that he is actually working on a United States government project. He's been cleared by the Secret Service."

"I would be very, very careful," Ludium said.

"We have an agency informant close to him. He can watch him." Actually, it was an ex-informant, a pariah of the agency, Wells realized.

After more details about the subject's recent activity, albeit sketchy, Ludium and Wells shared a discussion of how their families had grown. After the DCI hung up the phone, he then realized time was of the essence. He must get word to the Secret Service aboard the *China Maiden*.

CHAPTER 44

▼

When Coast Guard officer Kelly arrived back at the galley, he nodded to the Secret Service agent at the door and scanned the diners, looking for the old lady's son. The agent turned to see that the old woman was not trailing the officer.

"Hey, Ensign," the agent barked. "Where's the old woman?"

"She's in the head sir. Said she forgot her purse. She needs some medication or something."

"You left her there all alone?"

"She's just in the can, sir. Fartin' up a storm. Walking down there with her, she smelled like she shit herself yesterday. I told her I'd bring her purse."

"For crying out loud!" the federal bodyguard said. "Hurry up!"

Seeing the rumpled Herbert Winkle sitting alone at a galley table looking annoyed, the Coast Guard officer assumed he was the son in question.

"Sir, your mother says she needs her purse."

"M-my m-mother?" Winkle said, irritated.

"Yes sir, she said she needs her medications."

"M-m-medications … My mother?" Winkle looked around and seemed to mumble something. "She needs her T-T-T—"

"Tucks, sir? Yes, I think so, sir. She said she needs her …" Ensign Kelly paused, and then whispered, "*suppositories* in her purse."

"Suppositories!" Winkle moaned, without a stutter. "Her purse on is on the hel-hel-helicopter."

"Oh, shit," Ensign Kelly said.

*   *   *   *

Olga Stevick ambled down the corridors of the *China Maiden* as clandestinely as possible, but with no more direction than a rat's maiden voyage in a maze. Fortunately, she did not encounter any of the rig's personnel. They were either at lunch enjoying tuna steaks and potato salad, or perhaps the area was cleared by the Secret Service. The lower deck of the spaceship-sized facility was eerily quiet. Stevick stepped silently in her stocking feet on the metal floor like an Indian stalking game. She had no idea where she was going, or what she was looking for, but she was not afraid of being caught. After all, she was a kooky old lady who could easily wander away and get lost. And besides, she was eighty-one-years-old and had nothing left to fear in life. She made a right turn at the end of a corridor and approached a sealed metal door with a glass window. Etched on the window were the words, "Hydrate Testing Lab." She crept toward the door and turned the lever. It was locked.

She was suspicious. This vessel was supposed to be a natural gas collection facility that absorbed methane from sea kelp. What in the devil was something called a *hydrate-testing lab* necessary for? She didn't even know what it meant. There was a snake in the woodpile somewhere. Inside the room, Stevick could see two lab technicians dressed in canary-yellow plastic-looking outfits and fabric helmets resembling the kepi caps worn by the French Foreign Legion. They featured a see-through visor in front and a plastic havelock draping over the back of their necks. No doubt they were sterile uniforms typically used in a germ-free lab. Next to Stevick was a spacious open closet with several of the yellow uniforms draping from plastic hangers. When she glanced back through the window, one of the technicians rose from a large computer console and darted toward the door.

The snooping elderly consumer advocate jumped backward with the reflexes of a cat in its prime and stepped into the adjacent open closet, attempting to bury herself behind the collection of yellow plastic garments. The lab worker punched buttons on a keypad and unlocked the door.

As it opened, Stevick heard one of the other workers holler from a distance, "Where the hell are you going?"

"I gotta take a crap," said the lab technician.

"The tour is supposed to be here in just a couple of minutes!" the muffled voice said.

"That friggin' potato salad at lunch gave me the Hershey squirts," the frantic man at the doorway responded. "I gotta go!"

The technician raced out of the lab, not looking left or right, leaving Stevick in her banana-colored camouflage safely concealed. The technician scuttled down the hallway in rapid, but short steps, like a man running on stilts. As he ran, he could not contain the expulsion of intestinal gas that launched in a fusillade of sputtering bursts with each abbreviated leg movement. Moments before the lab door closed, Stevick stabbed her old wooden cane out of the closet like a rapier and it lodged in the entranceway, preventing the door from automatically closing and locking.

If this was easy for me, Stevick thought. *God forbid I was a terrorist or something.*

CHAPTER 45

▼

"Mr. President," Cowboy said, "Meet Akmed Abram, the genius behind methane-hydrate mining."

"An honor to meet you," the president said.

President Nathaniel Patrick Freeman held out his large college-football quarterback's hand to the man who once attempted to blow up a Tel Aviv marketplace. The American leader was nearly as tall as the towering Akmed, and their gazes locked. Akmed stared at the piercing, steel-blue eyes of the leader of the free world. All those years ago, the thought of catching a glimpse of the American president was akin to meeting an alien from Neptune. In his youth, he believed the U.S. president had devil's horns, a forked tongue, and nuclear-missile-tipped fingers if the European newspaper editorial cartoons and political posters on the Arab street were to be believed. And here he was, yes, many presidents later, but weren't they all the same? Wasn't the American government led by imperialists, capitalists, and Zionists, who would no sooner see his native Palestinian people disappear like an annoying swarm of gnats? Here he was, the paragon of western power, the satanic focus of hate in the Islamic world, offering his hand in congratulations and friendship.

He shook the president's hand.

"If we can tap this supply of natural gas," Freeman said, "your efforts might single-handedly result in a quantum leap in solving the energy problems of the free world."

Free world? What would *Omar* tell him to do right now? He could lunge directly at the tall man, and despite the American leader's strength and his heavily armed bodyguards, Akmed could bite into his sinewy neck and rip a hole through his carotid artery like a starving vampire. Death would be quick. An assassination by human incisors. What was he thinking? *Who am I?* the Palestinian thought. He was a noted petroleum geophysicist who was helping to bring energy and prosperity to Palestine. Was it so bad that America would benefit from his life's work, too? Without Cowboy's help and his industry friends, funding for the Mediterranean Sea exploration may not have occurred. Despite all this, the fanatics in Palestine wanted him to be an attack dog. A human bullet. A walking improvised explosive device. *Am I what they say I am?*

"Thank you," Akmed said. "It is truly an honor for me as well."

"Maybe you can give me some idea how this project works?" the president asked.

"Yes, Akmed, you're the expert," Cowboy said. "Let's move next door to the hydrate-condensation lab."

If Olga Stevick's geriatric hobble was not enough to frustrate Ensign Kelly, Herbert Winkle's dilatory gimpy limp sent him over the edge. The Coast Guard officer tapped the toes of his well-polished shoes several times while waiting for Winkle to negotiate the stairs from the vessel's galley and shuffle across the deck of the *China Maiden* to the helipad where the chopper dropped the guests off. After watching him stop to rest twice, adjusting his thinning, greasy hair in the wild ocean breeze, and leisurely cleaning his Coke-bottle spectacles of the ocean's salty mist, Ensign Kelly volunteered to retrieve the old woman's handbag himself, despite Winkle's objection. After verifying the ratty handbag's identity with the short, limping man, Kelly flew down the stairs heading to the hallway where he last left Stevick in her intestinal distress. *How could one old woman become such a pain in the ass?*

CHAPTER 46

▼

"The greatest obstacle in harvesting frozen methane hydrates—otherwise known as *gas-ice* or *burning ice*—is finding a way to economically free the natural gas molecules from the water molecules, as well as preventing subsea blowouts that potentially could leave part of the continental shelf unstable," said Akmed, lecturing the president and his assembly. Danielle stood in the back of the group behind Raven and Secretary of Energy Priest. *Akmed seemed to be at his professorial best*, Danielle thought. They stood in the laboratory where experiments were being conducted in condensing the frozen hydrates into usable natural gas that could then be piped to the mainland. All had donned sterile shoe covers and were asked not to touch any equipment. A series of small glass decompression chambers held samples of the hydrate material inside. A control panel filled with computer screens, toggles, switches, and lights covered the middle of the room like a massive island cooking range in a mansion's cavernous kitchen. Three technicians staffed computer stations, dressed in bright yellow suits and caps. A fourth computer station was empty, faced by a vacant chair. One of the president's security detail paced through the room briefly, checking the only other entrance into the room—it was secure.

"These hydrate deposits were likely formed when huge plates of the earth's crust collided more than 10 million years ago," Akmed continued his learned address, pointing at the two-foot by two-foot cylindrical compression chambers that resembled some aquatic zoo container in a science-fiction movie. "This particular methane hydrate region was first discovered by NOAA researchers, including Dr. Edison here, working with funding provided by the National Science Foundation."

"And how did you find them Dr. Edison?" the president asked, turning to the brunette scientist.

Dr. Edison cleared her throat, combating her nervousness in the warm, but intimidating stare of the handsome president. She swatted at her lock of hanging hair over her forehead like it was a hovering bee.

"Well, initially NOAA was investigating cracks in the continental shelf that may have been caused by underwater landslides," she said. "Our investigations picked up after the Indian Ocean tsunami. During our monitoring of this site, we found abnormally salty seawater."

"Isn't all seawater salty?" the president asked, innocently.

"Well, when gas hydrates form quickly, the salts in the seafloor sediments do not have time to diffuse, thus the water here is saltier than ordinary seawater. And, in addition, methane-marked fluids were leaking from the sea floor in this location. We've known about this for some time, but the challenge is, as stated by Professor Abram, finding a way to safely extract the hydrates for study, let alone widespread use."

"That's when Akmed rode in like the cavalry," said Cowboy, adding his Oklahoma homespun lingo to the scholarly discussion. Danielle thought he sounded like Jethro Bodine of the *Beverly Hillbillies*.

"And how is that?" the president asked.

"Along with several colleagues, I have been studying ways to extract hydrates in various parts of the world," said Akmed. "Hydrate formation is common off the coasts of China, Indonesia, Russia, as well as the east and west coasts of the United States. Unlike traditional land mining, hydrate extraction is different since it is thousands of feet underwater, adding to the cost dramatically. And similar to land mining, you have the problem of cave-ins, which, unfortunately, are not localized to the areas where the blowouts occur. Such an underground disturbance can have a ripple effect, potentially causing a tsunami, like those that occur naturally around the world."

Danielle flashed a glance at Raven. *See, I told you so,* she wanted to say with her eyes, but Raven wasn't looking at her. Instead the head of American Energy whispered something into the energy secretary's ear.

"Along with my colleagues at Cambridge University, we have developed a technique to sample the hydrates in their native state—that is, frozen and under pressure from the thousands of pounds of seawater above. Previously, 3-D seismic technology could demonstrate where likely strata of hydrates are, but not their precise composition. We had to dig out a core sample and bring it to the surface in order to study it, often changing its chemical and molecular composition, and possibly causing a gas breakout because of pressure reduction. But our new technique is unique, giving us a true picture of what lies beneath the subsurface. Therefore, with this process, we can determine where the rich layers of hydrate are, without disturbing a great deal of sand and bedrock, decreasing the need for numerous wildcat or random wells, and reducing the chances of causing unintended blowouts of free natural gas below the sediment that can cause the subsea landslides."

"What assurances do you have of avoiding any potential gas blowouts or landslides as you call them?" said Virgil Priest, exercising his cabinet-level authority in a deep, melodious voice. He sounded like a talented trial attorney, Danielle thought, but good attorneys did not ask a question of a witness without already knowing the answer.

"Unfortunately, as with most things in life, one can never eliminate every risk," Akmed responded. "But the experiments we have conducted so far have not only avoided gas blowouts by extraction of the methane, but also we have successfully injected frozen carbon dioxide into the hydrate formations that cement the surrounding area, virtually strengthening the already fragile composition of sediment below the seafloor."

"Do you mean that the underground formations are actually stronger once you extract the gas?" the president asked.

"Well," Akmed said, "removing the methane and injecting the frozen carbon dioxide has the same effect as, if you excuse the analogy, a healing broken bone becoming stronger at the point of the initial separation.

"And the carbon dioxide won't escape?"

"No, not unless some natural occurrence frees it, but it is certainly no less safe than the hydrates in their original formation."

"And we have plenty of carbon dioxide to inject, Mr. President," said Alexandria Raven. "Greenhouse gas that would otherwise be released into the atmosphere. Our onshore reinjection testing so far has gone well."

The president was quiet for a moment, looking at the computer screens, blinking lights on the control panels, and vibrating needles on the various monitors of the laboratory. The windowless room was calm, with only the accompanying sound of humming electronic equipment and the soft shuffling of fabric-covered shoes of the dozen individuals on the tour. The president's confident features morphed into a quizzical mien that made Danielle wonder what he was thinking. She knew the decision to move ahead with *Project Hades* rested with him and him alone.

It was risky—no one could truly know what the negative effect could be by disturbing the hydrate layer below the ocean floor no matter what these scientists said, and the worst-case scenarios were catastrophic. But the payoffs could be enormous and the benefits unlimited. What were the alternatives to the country's energy crisis? What were the consequences of another deadly world war over energy? Danielle remembered her history—German U-boats sunk American oil freighters in these same waters as they transported petroleum from the Gulf Coast to the Northeast during the Second World War. The government built emergency oil pipelines that ran from Texas to New Jersey costing millions to secure energy for the wartime factories making planes, ships, guns, bullets, and bombs. Sure, American oil companies benefited. But only the government could address a national emergency concerning energy, the lifeblood of the American economy and war machine. Today, American Energy stood to make millions by transporting the new energy supplies—if it worked. They were not profiteering; they were in the risk business. Who cares if American Energy's stockholders would reap the benefits of the federal government's decisions financed by oodles of taxpayer dollars? American Energy owned the pipelines and took the risk of providing much of their own capital. Public-private partnerships were necessary for the nation's economic health. Most mutual funds included plenty of shares of oil, gas, and utility firms like American Energy. Everyone would benefit—from the wealthy CEOs and their coterie of executives to the smallest investor whose retirement funds were tied up in a 401K. The critics called it fascism. *But American capitalism was always a bastardized coalition of public and private interests*, Danielle mused.

"What are the estimated reserves that could be extracted from this drilling?" President Freeman asked to no one in particular.

"This is not exactly drilling Mr. President," interjected Raven.

"Drilling, mining, whatever. How much can we take out?"

"Well," Akmed said. There is no precise estimation, but we surmise that there could be more than 20 trillion cubic feet of natural gas in this location alone."

"What does that mean in terms of energy consumption, Virgil?"

"That is a comfortable figure," the energy secretary said, flicking his curly moustache as if to fling a fly off the end. "That is the total U.S. consumption for approximately eight years. Of course, if this project proves successful, there are many other hydrate zones on the continental shelf that could be exploited."

Danielle winced. What a choice of words.

"Extracted," Raven said.

"Yes, of course, extracted," Priest said with the air of a browbeat husband.

"Mr. President," Cowboy volunteered. The president nodded. "Excuse me for buttin' in here, but I want to point out something."

"Go ahead, Cowboy," his old roommate said, "you rarely can go a minute without saying something."

Everyone on the tour laughed. No matter the actual degree of the president's humor, Danielle thought, an obsequious laugh track followed any obvious attempt at levity by the nation's Commander in Chief.

"Everyone seems to be dancing around whether this is natural gas drilling on the continental shelf or a high-school geology trip to collect a few rocks," said Cowboy. "Once we start sucking out the gas in this here hole in the ocean and the price of heating an American home drops in half because of the new supply, and clean-burning natural gas fuels power plants, vehicles, and even provides stock fuel for hydrogen fuel cells to wean ourselves off the teat of OPEC—excuse the expression—there ain't going to be nobody who cares *how* we are gettin' this gas out."

"Let's hope you're right, especially mother earth," the president said. Silence followed as the group pondered Freeman's rumination.

The sudden crash and rattle of a metal clipboard on the steel floor of the laboratory startled everyone in the otherwise tranquil room. The initial cymbal-sounding noise did not sound like a gunshot or explosion, but the bodyguards did not take any chances as it was alarming enough. Two Secret Service agents leapt forward in front of the president, pulling automatic weapons from under their well-tailored suit coats faster that Marshall Dillon in Carson City. They both looked toward the opposite side of the room, where another exit led to a hallway. A row of humming electronic devices stood next to the door, each about a foot wide and five feet in height, topped with small computer screens. The president was quickly shielded from any line of sight from the direction of the sudden noise. One agent hustled the president behind the control panel, as the space-suited technicians dove to the floor on each end. The other agent waved an automatic machine gun, searching for a target, finger on the hair trigger.

CHAPTER 47

▼

Ensign Kelly rapped on the restroom door with terse, but apologetic knocks, Olga Stevick's purse in hand. He held his breath. *God, it smelled.*

"Miss, I have your handbag," Kelly said in a nasal tone. "I'll just place it right outside the door."

The horrific smell of bowel permeated the entire hallway like rotting garbage. Kelly heard the booming echo of sporadic expulsions that resonated against the metal walls of the john. *She wasn't kidding*, the Coast Guard officer thought, gagging on the miasmic fumes. He moved to the end of the hallway out of gentlemanly courteousness and olfactory necessity. After a couple of drawn-out minutes, syncopated with intermittent muffled flatulence and splashes clearly audible from twenty feet, the toilet flushed. After a pause, another flurry of semi-liquid spatters and gaseous eruptions ensued followed by obligatory flushes. Next the splash of sink water ran for a minute. Eventually, the door opened, the hard metal latch emitting a loud clunk. Another effluent wave of unpleasant bathroom bouquet wafted past Kelly like the stream of a sewer.

Keeping his back turned modestly at the end of the hallway and attempting not to breathe too deeply, Kelly asked, "Did you get your purse okay?"

"Yeah, but it doesn't match my outfit."

It was the unexpected voice of a man, the bass timbre filling the hallway as complete as the reeking stink.

Kelly's facial features dropped as if stricken with a sudden stroke, the blood draining out his cheeks. He spun sharply to see one of the rig's scientific technicians, dressed in his Tweety-Bird-yellow suit, sans flexible helmet, standing in the narrow hallway holding an old woman's bulky, moth-eaten canvas handbag.

✳   ✳   ✳   ✳

"Get down, get down!" President Freeman's personal bodyguard Frank Carter hollered to the touring group. He was a twenty-year veteran of the Secret Service and this was the first time he drew his weapon outside of a drill. From behind the row of electronic devices, Carter saw what he did not want to see, a hunched human figure holding a long cylindrical object the approximate size of a rifle barrel with what looked like some type of silencing device on the end sticking out of one side of a metal monitor.

"Drop it or you're dead," Carter yelled out toward the dim light at the end of the room. His automatic weapon focused on the blue-steel cover of the computer-type machine, his finger nearly squeezing the trigger that would send twenty rounds a second through the machine and whoever crouched behind it. Carter would not wait one more moment before blowing the inanimate and animate figures away. Unlike the local police or FBI, the Secret Service's first concern was not centered on claims of constitutional rights and the threat of potential lawsuits.

Before Carter emitted another thought, the rifle-resembling cylindrical object he spotted was tossed out from behind the row of computer machines and it rattled on the metal floor of the lab. Now in better light, Carter recognized the item. It was a rubber-tipped walking cane that settled next to a fallen clipboard that apparently was the cause of the initial clatter.

"What the ...?" was all that came from the Secret Service agent's mouth.

"Excuse me young man," came the scratchy voice of Olga Stevick as her osteoporosic silhouette hobbled into open view. "Can you direct me to the cafeteria? I seem to have lost my way."

CHAPTER 48

▼

The security breech on board the *China Maiden* was egregious, the Secret Service admitted, but not a word of it became public. The remainder of the private tour, including viewing the pipeline operations was abruptly cancelled, and the president returned to the platform's deck to be observed by the press touring the kelp-methane extraction process. The technician with the irritable bowel was reprimanded severely, with little sympathy for his bodily necessity. *When you gotta' go, you gotta' go* was not a good excuse for leaving his station when he was told he could not move from his seat, his supervisor said. "Better to shit your pants than cause an incident where someone could have been killed, including the president of the United States." Ensign Kelly was relieved from his current duty for his complete neglect of proper protocol and immediately dispatched from the spar to where he thought he would likely spend the next year—supervising a garbage scow or equivalent service. The Secret Service agent on duty in the galley who permitted Kelly and Stevick to leave the corral of journalists and guests would also say *au revoir* to the presidential protection team and prepared for tedious counterfeiting investigations in the heat of the Texas-Mexico border for the remaining years of his career.

Meanwhile, Olga Stevick, apparently glassy-eyed and confused, was dispatched back to join the journalists on a formal tour of the kelp-methane collection system, which featured the president holding up a wet clump of brown seaweed as if it were a record seawater catch, posing for the network video cameras and wire-service shutterbugs.

"How much do you think she heard?" the president later asked Virgil Priest, as they took off on Marine One from the deck of the *China Maiden*.

"She seemed clueless to me," Priest responded. "Nothing to worry about."

"I don't know," President Freeman said. "She is a master manipulator and the greatest golden-age actress since Katherine Hepburn. I've got a feeling she did not get in there by accident."

"Well, let's thank God it was not a real assassin."

The president said cryptically, "Time will tell whether that's a blessing or not."

After the president was safely away, Secret Service agents detained Akmed Abram and questioned him on board the *China Maiden*. He was cooperative and unfazed, though Cowboy put up an indignant fuss. The United States had no specific intelligence regarding Akmed's activities other than unsubstantiated claims by foreign agents. The Palestinian-born geophysicist did nothing to create suspicion. He shook the president's hand and gained his confidence. After unsuccessfully finding out anything new, the Secret Service broke off the interview and thanked the British citizen for his understanding and patience.

The next day, the *New York Times* led its editions with a banner headline claiming that the Freeman Administration might be conducting test drilling off the coast of North Carolina, flouting a congressional moratorium on such activity in place since the early 1970s. The newspaper's unnamed main source was most likely Congressman August Doggle of the House Energy and Commerce Committee, who had his own mole "deep within the Department-of-Energy operation." The informant revealing the drilling operation was an eighty-one-year-old woman who innocently claimed to have a lack of orientation and incontinence. After reading the comprehensive article quoting a generous list of shrill environmental activists, Chicken-Little-cautioning scientists, and outraged congressmen and senators, the secretary of energy had his own bout of diarrhea.

CHAPTER 49

▼

Roger Sheldon chucked a food tray against the wall of the galley. He dug furiously into the undersides of his fingernails. His swollen Adam's apple pulsed as if it was an alien creature ready to burst out of his thyroid. Cowboy gawked at the ill-tempered pipeline chief's tantrum, knowing Sheldon was piqued he did not get to meet the president of the United States. Sheldon's pipeline operation was the next stop on the classified tour, and he wanted to shake the hand of the president. *Boo-hoo-hoo*, Cowboy thought. No one outside of the testing lab knew why the tour was suddenly called to a halt, but rumors raced from deck to deck: *Freeman wanted to avoid the press. A "security problem" caused the cancellation. The president had diarrhea.*

Cowboy tried to avoid Sheldon's attention, but he couldn't avoid laughing at the idiot's antics. Though he was a pipeline construction expert, Sheldon was a self-absorbed pain in the ass—a six-year-old in a forty-year-old body. Cowboy turned to leave, but Sheldon confronted him and demanded an explanation.

"Well, the president saw what he needed to see," Cowboy told Sheldon. The Secret Service instructed Cowboy to keep the incident with Olga Stevick under his hat. He agreed. Nothing ever came out from there.

"I had an elaborate presentation ready," Sheldon said, exasperated, his wide lips turning into a huge frog-like frown.

"Sorry," Cowboy shrugged, trying to break away. Sheldon was boorish, puerile, and pompous. Anyway, well drillers did not hang out with pipeline guys. *Especially ones who were assholes.* "You know how those political folk are. Always changing plans."

"But how will the president understand our elaborate procedure for getting the gas to the mainland? It is critical to the entire operation."

Cowboy tried to keep from staring at Sheldon's oscillating Adam's apple that pulsed like a beating heart and bounced like he was attempting to swallow a tennis ball. "Don't worry, Roger, American Energy as well as the DOE have total faith in your ability to move the product. And it looks like we will be starting soon, so you better get ready."

"The project test has the go-ahead? Without touring our complete operation?"

"They were mainly concerned with extraction, not transportation. Don't worry, Akmed put on a great show—completely wowed them."

"Akmed?" Sheldon asked, shocked. "How did that damn Arab get security clearance from the Secret Service?"

"I vouched for him," Cowboy said, walking away.

No one on board the *China Maiden* had any idea Akmed was detained by the Secret Service, other than Cowboy. And he wasn't going to let anyone else aware of it. What did Sheldon know of Secret Service protocol? *Sheldon was just jealous,* he thought. *What a callow, egotistical schmuck.*

"Fucking raghead," Sheldon said. "That sand-nigger has no business being on this rig."

Cowboy turned on a dime, reached forward, and grabbed Sheldon by the front of his collar. He shoved him against a wall with the force of a pile driver. Sheldon was an independent contractor in *Project Hades* and did not report to Cowboy's drilling company. Therefore, the Oklahoman didn't feel that he had to be politically correct. He could kick his ass without facing a harassment charge. Assault, maybe, but not harassment. He moved his face close to Sheldon's and spoke quietly, "I'd advise you to change your terminology if you would like to preserve your present dental work."

Sheldon swatted Cowboy's hands away and laughed. "What's the matter, Cowboy? Has Ahab the Arab been drilling his tool into the little lawyer chick who won't drop her briefs for you? The word's out all over the rig, baby. She's given you the cold shoulder and is all over the sheik like white on rice."

Cowboy clenched his fists. *Was it worth it?* At that moment, the tall, princely Palestinian entered the galley, still talking with the smiling and adoring Danielle O'Day. Cowboy knew she was smitten with his strong, ordinarily taciturn friend, who now seemed to be a garrulous tour guide. This appeared to be one marlin the broad-shouldered Oklahoman was not going to land.

"Fuck off, Sheldon," Cowboy told him. "And stay the hell away from me or I'll stuff your ass through your pipeline all the way to shore."

Cowboy turned and stared at his friend with the attractive young attorney. He had to admit it. He was jealous. *Well, there are many other fish in the sea.* But he couldn't seem to sway this woman. Despite Akmed's handsome mien, he rarely talked about women, and Cowboy occasionally wondered whether his friend was gay. But no. Akmed was not a homosexual, he concluded, but rather, Akmed was deeply committed to his faith and his work that left little time for female dalliances. The prissy lawyer will have a tough time getting Akmed to swoon over her. Cowboy always found time for both work and play, a multi-tasking talent he was proud of. Though he was not willing to admit defeat in the conquest of the saucy American Energy exec yet, he cast an impatient glare at Akmed and bolted the galley to lick his wounds in private.

When Danielle entered the room, Roger Sheldon's truculence radiated everywhere. A tray of food lay scattered on the floor. He now was berating one of his white-suited compressor operators. Other workers in the area cleared away. Cowboy abruptly left the room, and soon Sheldon was in her face. However, his ire focused on Akmed, a man he obviously did not care for.

"Well, it seems like you two are getting along famously," Sheldon said, in a gratuitous manner, interrupting the discussion between Akmed and Danielle as they sat down at a table. "You apparently have used your new contact to squeeze past the Secret Service to get an audience with *our* president."

For Danielle, it was difficult to tell whether Sheldon was incensed that Akmed upstaged him, or if he was some type of paranoid, xenophobic racist. Still, Danielle was not one to mince words.

"I beg your pardon?" Danielle said, slipping into a less-than-gracious tone.

"So, Akmed," Sheldon continued in a condescending manner, "the president's tour got cut short a bit—that didn't spoil any long lectures on your geophysicist genius or disrupt your cell's plots, did it?"

"Mr. Sheldon," Akmed said, maintaining his magnetic equanimity as steady as a compass. "If you would like to have a discussion with me, I would beg of you to do it in private and spare others the tediousness of our professional dialogue."

"Oh, how you've mastered the English tongue," Sheldon said, contemptuously. "Must be that Cambridge book-learning. There appears to be no limit to your prophetic brilliance."

"Excuse me," Danielle said, her body temperature rising and her heart banging on her ribs as if she were on the edge of the school pool again with someone threatening to push her in. "We were having our own private professional dialogue here, and I don't remember inviting you to partake in it."

"No offense baby," Sheldon said. "I'll leave you two love birds to yourselves. But I would watch your back. Some say that folks like him have no regard for human life. Not even their own."

Sheldon spat a prolonged irate stare and then skulked away. The remaining diners in the galley slowly returned their attention from the apparent imbroglio to their meals.

There was complete silence between the two for a few moments, until Akmed lowered his eyes.

"Please accept my request for forgiveness," Akmed told Danielle. "This is unfortunate."

"What the hell is it with that guy?" she said.

"Please forgive … I'm terribly sorry," Akmed reiterated in his Arab-English dialect, a habit of apologetic discourse he picked up while living in England where everyone used the phrase *I'm terribly sorry* before making the slightest request such as *please pass the salt.* "There is a long-standing … how would you say … *feud* between Mr. Sheldon and myself, one which he apparently does not want to fade away. This is most embarrassing as any conversation we may have is not meant to injure your ears."

"Don't worry, I've heard worse than that. You haven't met my father."

"Still, I am most shamed."

"Don't be. What's up his craw?"

"Craw?"

"You know, why does he have a bug up his ass for you?"

"Bug?"

She shook her head. "Why doesn't he like you?"

Akmed remained silent for a moment, and then motioned Danielle to follow him down an unoccupied hallway, where they could have more privacy.

"Well, many years ago, Mr. Sheldon and I were working on a drilling spar in the North Sea. His pipeline company was proposing to pipe oil to the English island, and I questioned the specifications of his firm's plan to move the oil by pipe rather than by tanker. I feared that his pipeline design was unsafe and subject to breakage in the rough waters. Though I was responsible only for the identification of oil reserves, the British oil company heeded my reservations and concerned that a major oil leak may cause unprecedented damage to the environment, let alone the company's reputation and finances, they backed off Mr. Sheldon's design. It caused much consternation and, I'm afraid, a loss of a large amount of money for Mr. Sheldon. Thus, you can see how he resents me."

"I guess so," Danielle agreed. "But what about now, do you think the current pipeline that Sheldon's company built for this project is faulty?"

Akmed's eyes widened. "Oh, not in the least. His firm made great improvements in pipeline technology. They are worldwide innovators. And I vocalized that as well to Mr. Sheldon directly and many others involved with this project. However, Mr. Sheldon's resentment runs very deep. I am very, very sorry."

"No, I'm sorry, on behalf of all Americans," Danielle said, "that Sheldon used ethnic slurs against you. That is not what our country is all about."

"I understand. You do not have to apologize. I know many Americans fear Islam because there have been horrible deeds committed by those in the name of Allah. They too, do not represent what most Islamic followers believe."

"I know that," Danielle said in an unintentional patronizing way as if to say, *Some of my best friends are Islamic fundamentalists.* Akmed still would not look her directly in the eyes. He was not being deceitful. That was his custom, a sign of respect. Besides, when he was humble, almost sad, as was his whole demeanor, he was compellingly attractive. She grasped his hands in hers. He backed off from her ever so slightly, not in repulsion, but in modesty.

"Many Americans paint the Muslim faith with radical fundamentalism," Akmed said. "The radicals see western modernism as corrupt and atheistic, but let me assure you, that is the minority viewpoint in the world of Islam."

"Let's be friends and we'll ignore the ugly American," she said. Her crooked smile of bright white teeth lit up Akmed's face as he finally met her gaze. "But I want to understand one thing."

"Yes," Akmed said.

"How in the world did you ever become a bosom buddy with that arrogant, macho, self-important Cowboy character?"

Akmed offered a polite smile. "Long ago, I wanted to get to know America. And at the time Mr. Rhodan was my first opportunity for observation."

"You should have gone to a zoo, instead. I hope you haven't judged everyone in the United States based on your contact with Mr. Sheldon or that egotist Cowboy."

"Let's say," Akmed mused. "The jury is still out."

"Perhaps you could consider this argument," Danielle said, embracing Akmed lightly and placing a kiss upon his cheek.

When he looked quizzically at her, she decided to underline her point by planting a sustained kiss upon his lips.

CHAPTER 50

▼

The girth of the chairman of the House Energy and Commerce Committee filled the blue-fabric colonial guest chair across from the president's Oval Office desk like a triple-decker ice cream scoop precariously balanced on a narrow sugar cone. President Freeman gritted his teeth. He could barely stomach this man in his office.

"It is entirely possible, over my objections of course, that Congress will demand hearings to investigate these serious charges," Congressman August Doggle said, frowning like an oppressive elementary-school principal hovering over a ten-year-old caught smoking in the boy's room. "Some individuals in your shoes have faced, dare I say it, *impeachment*, for much less."

"Is that a threat, congressman?" the president asked, deadpan.

"Absolutely not!" Doggle wheezed. "As a loyal leader of the Congress, I would defend the president of my party to my last breath on the House floor."

"But I was elected as an independent as you may recall. I would think you would be at the head of the line calling for my head if your serious allegations leaked to the press by hearsay were found to be accurate in any way." *That senile crackpot consumer-activist obviously went squealing right to Doggle*, the president scolded himself. *Chalk another one up for my brilliant PR moves.*

"Oh, but Mr. President," Doggle pleaded with disingenuous passion like a smarmy snake-oil salesman, "you were once a great party spokesman. We know where your allegiance lies. You and I, sir, will always be allies. Besides, in this time of national crisis—"

"Cut the crap, Doggle. What do you want?"

Doggle smiled like the fat cat who swallowed a twenty-two-pound canary. His smugness was repugnant.

"I want what is best for the American people," Doggle squeaked.

"Uh-huh."

"And especially, those who live in my economically disenfranchised congressional district."

"Go on."

"The energy bill that is being seriously debated in my committee …"

"You are sitting on it, congressman."

"Let's say we are debating the unintended consequences of such bold proposals. We do not want to throw out the baby with the bath water."

The president rolled his eyes. He wanted to throw Doggle in the middle of the Atlantic, but the corpulent congressman was such an oily character, the ensuing slick might be declared an environmental disaster and the offshore drilling provision in the energy bill would never become law.

"There is some room for compromise," Doggle hinted, pushing the tips of his fat fingers together.

"Let me guess—corn fuels," the president said, as if he were the *Green Acres* city-lawyer Oliver Douglas just swindled by the backwoods suspender-wearing Mr. Haney into another worthless purchase.

Doggle's eyes lit up like gas lamps on a foggy night on a nineteenth-century London street. "We could insert a provision in the energy bill that reclassifies what is occurring out in the Atlantic deep as *limited exploratory hydrocarbon extraction* and not, heaven forbid, environmentally damaging drilling for oil and gas to benefit these soulless, multinational conglomerates who repeatedly line their pockets with the hard-earned cash of the working poor. We must harbor our domestic energy sources wisely and protect the interests of the common man."

The president thought of reaching across his walnut desk and grabbing the chairman of the House Energy and Commerce Committee by his string tie and yanking his corpulent face to his. *This is about averting a national economic catastrophe,* he wanted to shout at him. *This is about avoiding the next world war where hundreds of thousands of American troops, and who knows, thousands, if not millions, of civilians in the United States faced death or mutilation with biological, chemical, or dirty nuke terrorist retaliation all because blowhards like you are too goddamn lazy to get off your fat duff and walk to the grocery store rather than drive a hundred feet in your gas-guzzling SUV!*

But the president said none of that.

"One should never watch laws or sausages being made," the president repeated the oft-turned political phrase.

"But we need both."

"I was thinking of becoming a vegetarian."

"The many growers of fine vegetables in my district would not be disappointed with that."

"I'll see what I can do, congressman," the president said formally. "We need to get that energy bill out of committee, passed by both houses and on my desk soon. Or we will end up becoming a third-world country."

"Mr. President, you are a patriot," Doggle said.

Mr. Doggle, you are an asshole, the president thought.

After Doggle left, the president called the secretary of energy.

"Virgil?" he said. "Go ahead with the test."

"Yes, Mr. President," Priest said on the other end of the line. "But what about Doggle? I hear he plans immediate investigative hearings. Indirectly, he'll bang the drums for impeachment."

President Freeman thought about his job. *Splendid misery*, John Adams and Thomas Jefferson called it. And then, he paraphrased the supposed famous words of Benjamin Franklin during the drafting of the Declaration of Independence.

"Virgil, are we going to hang together or hang separately?"

CHAPTER 51

▼

The Coast Guard received the news first, and then it was passed on to the NOAA manager on the *China Maiden*, Dr. Samatha Edison. They might have to evacuate. The christened category-three storm, Hurricane Zeta, was traveling due north from the Caribbean off the coast of the United States at twenty-five miles-per-hour. A hurricane watch alerted the eastern Carolina shore, and the president demanded that the seaboard state governors evacuate coastal areas. After the misery brought by Hurricane Katrina, neither politicians nor level-headed coastal residents took any chances. However, meteorologists now believed the storm would not veer left into the United States mainland with its most powerful wrath.

Though land may be spared, the whirling storm now would likely swipe its lethal vortex through the path of the *China Maiden*. The spar was designed for such events, however. Being a mobile platform, with enough notice it could empty its ballast and steam away at the ferocious pace of fifteen miles-per-hour. But because of its limited speed, it needed plenty of lead-time to evade the path of the raging seas kicked up by the storm. They had waited too long already. Since the bulk of the *China Maiden* was underwater, its designers claimed once anchored to the sea bottom it would not be damaged by the most vicious of surface winds and waves. And there was a slim chance that the vagarious hurricane would stall or alter direction out to sea away from the platform.

Preparation for the first major test of *Project Hades* was only hours away. The president signed an executive order approving the withdrawal of hydrates from below the ocean floor, converting the methane ice to usable natural gas to be pumped to the shoreline, and replacing the hydrates with frozen carbon dioxide emitted from electric power plants that would otherwise be blown into the atmosphere.

Danielle O'Day retreated to Akmed's cramped cabin, not only absorbing his human touch, but also trying to evoke a response from his impalpable soul. She found him soft-spoken and endlessly fascinating. He also made love with feverish fury. And that was not easy in a twin bunk. She achieved an orgasm not once, but twice. Danielle had only shared herself with three lovers: a drunken college one-night stand with a frat boy that stole her virginity; her awkward courtship and marriage to the self-absorbed stockbroker; and another no-commitment ephemeral relationship on the rebound afterward with a man she met in her health club. She did not consider this spur-at-the-moment liaison a symptom of creeping promiscuity. She simply reeked of too much pent-up sexual energy and this opportunity was too deliciously mystifying to pass up. She liked Akmed. She lusted after him. Akmed was divinely unselfish and devilishly handsome. Danielle thought the latter quality should be least important, but she couldn't help herself. At the point of his climax, her new lover collapsed into sleep while still hard inside her as if struck by a silver bullet of fatigue. Surprised, but not hurt, she cradled his sleeping body in her arms for hours. She was smitten with the olive-skinned hunk, who lay next to her like a warm masculine-perfected statue of Apollo, silent but magnificent. His only blemishes were faint scars that crisscrossed his back in a herringbone pattern. They looked like the marks of whips. He was the antithesis of most other men she knew. If they weren't grabbing power, they were grabbing asses. She felt threatened by most men, but not this mild-mannered scientist with coal-black, magnetic eyes. She extinguished the potential of relationships since her quick Mexican-style divorce, but everything rekindled on this drilling rig in the Atlantic.

When Alexandria Raven left the offshore facility after the president's tour, she permitted Danielle to stay on the *China Maiden* to supervise the first full-fledged test of the hydrate extraction. Danielle had much to learn about the new natural gas industry in a short period of time, and Raven told her this was the best place to cram. As a result, she would be leagues ahead of the mushroom senior officers of the company who were kept in the dark about the entire affair. Danielle found herself a quick study, especially with a teacher like Akmed. Her passion perhaps clouded her thinking, but she could not leave him—not yet.

Akmed was not involved directly in the test, but like Danielle, played the observer, and they joined Edison, Roystone, and other DOE scientists in the hydrate-testing room as they reviewed the final operating procedures. Roystone explained the process that was about to occur in steady terms, like a sports play-by-play announcer. Cowboy supplied the gratuitous color.

"There is a remote-controlled ocean-bottom station for continuous monitoring of sea-floor stability," Roystone said. "These multi-dimensional seismic images of oceanic hydrate deposits you see on the monitor are obtained by using the seafloor seismometers. This allows us to reveal the sediments and the accompanying hydrate layers to see how they are structurally organized. We review their mass and determine the methane content in the average hydrate through perflourcarbon tracers."

"That's a fancy way of saying we like making sure we have 150-proof southern mash," said Cowboy. "No watered-down stuff blowing out of our still."

"Next," Roystone said, tweaking his round bookworm eyeglasses, "we conduct an examination of the methane recovery through a dynamic flow test."

"May I?" Akmed asked Roystone.

"Certainly Dr. Abram."

Akmed picked up a portable headgear device that looked like bulky binoculars and placed them over his head. He bent forward and reviewed the materials in a rectangular glass block that ran from the floor to the ceiling. Through the clear glass-type container, a crystal lump of hydrate first converted to slush and then dissolved into a milky liquid.

"What's that?" O'Day asked.

"A high-spatial computed tomography spectrometer," Akmed replied.

"Those are X-ray glasses, Miss O'Day," Cowboy quipped. "Rumor has it that if you hold your hand up to the light, you can see finger bones, and maybe, through layers of clothing."

"Most assuredly not," Akmed said.

"Well, heck, that's what the ad in my *Spiderman* comic book said."

Roystone continued, "The chronograph device he is looking through enables us to study the structure, chemical bonding, thermodynamics, and kinetics of gas-hydrate formations. We can examine the hydrate being extracted to ensure that it contains only methane, and not other contaminants or sediment particles that can further aggravate the structure of the underground formation."

"What's the status of the Drake?" Cowboy said.

"Proceeding as planned," the geologist said, surveying a monitor that showed a three-dimensional image of a snake-like device and a plethora of indiscernible mathematical readings on the side of the screen. "Engaging the pressure transducer."

"The Drake?" Danielle asked Cowboy. "What's that mean?"

Cowboy smiled. Perhaps he was pleased she asked him a question for a change.

"That's what we call one of the three drilling stem probes that actually does the boring into the sea floor," he answered. "Named after Edwin Drake, the driller of the first oil well."

"Oh, of course," she said. She did know a bit about the origins of the oil and gas industry born in her backyard in western Pennsylvania. "Drake's well was drilled in Titusville, Pennsylvania, in 1859, just an hour from my parent's house."

"Yep, we figured he should be the first to penetrate the virgin sea floor here, so to speak. And we are prepared to drill all the way to China. That, by the way, is why this MODU is known as the *China Maiden*. Drake started the first commercial oil boom and this probe will extract the first natural gas hydrates for commercial use. This little baby is a pioneer that will suck out a gold mine in gas."

"Yes, and after drilling the first oil well, Drake ended up penniless and depressed just a few years later," Danielle said.

"Don't you worry none, counselor. Our second drilling probe that injects the carbon dioxide is named after that fine environmentalist, John D., as in Rockefeller."

"Environmentalist?"

"Well, he saved the whales when he developed the kerosene industry from oil, didn't he? *No more blood for spermaceti. Ahab lied, people died* and all that hoo-hah."

She shook her head in exasperation. "And the third drill?"

"Well, we haven't named that one yet—just known as drill number three," Roystone mused. "The first two drilling devices—Drake and John D.—are what we call *smart drills*. They are flexible, moving like earthworms through the soil, following the hydrate formation without disturbing much of the surrounding sediment."

Roystone nudged his glasses farther up his nose as if he had to scroll down on the screen of his brain to explain more. "The two smart drills contain numerous well-logging data monitors that measure the progress of drilling, including a high-resolution laterolog, azimuthal laterolog, resistivity log, induction log, sonic log, neutron log, Zeta ray log, nuclear magnetic resonance, and full wellbore imaging. We can actually watch on the monitors as Drake extracts the methane, and John D. reinjects the carbon dioxide."

"It's like liposuction," Cowboy suggested.

Danielle understood little, but continued to ask questions. "But what does the third drill do?"

"The third drill is just a standard drill to be used only to relieve any unsafe underground gas pressure in an emergency," Roystone said. "It can drill quickly and effectively to help prevent a blowout that can cause a rupture in the sea floor. The third drill doesn't have the sophisticated equipment."

"It's just a *dumb* drill," Cowboy said.

"Perhaps we should name it *Cowboy,*" Dr. Edison said dryly.

Cowboy fired a *that's so funny I forgot to laugh* face at Edison.

"How do you know if there is unsafe underground pressure?" Danielle asked.

"The extraction device should penetrate areas that contain only hydrate-bearing rock," said the equable Roystone, "but it also measures the structural strength of the formations under the sea floor as it proceeds. It produces geological models of hydrate deposits and studies seafloor stability and safety. As the hydrates are extracted, the frozen carbon dioxide replaces the hydrates as needed, maintaining the structural integrity of the formation."

"In other words," Cowboy said. "We don't want any blowouts to occur on our watch."

"In addition," said Roystone, "there is a series of valves and seals called the BOP—a blowout preventor—attached on the floor of the ocean."

Once preparations were made and various safety checks were reviewed, Cowboy gave the signal for drilling to begin.

"Let's roll," the master driller said.

"You've tested this process, correct?" Danielle asked. "It works right?"

Cowboy looked at her, a wily grin erupting at the corner of his mouth. "Sit back and watch little lady and we'll find out."

CHAPTER 52

▼

The director of the CIA was embarrassed, but resolute. General Edwin Wells tread in the footsteps of numerous other DCIs who only saw their reputations destroyed by the ghastly errors of field agents and mid-level analysts. But the sixty-six-year-old martinet-trained bureaucrat was a patriot. He could care less what the press or congressmen might call him in the future. He had a job to do. But the mistake in intelligence was more than embarrassing. Everything Langley told the Secret Service before the president's trip about Akmed Abram was true. But assembling intelligence was like putting together a jigsaw puzzle. The most obvious parts are snapped together first, usually around the edges. In this case, the middle of the picture was crystal clear, but the edges were missing until it was too late.

The subject was a Palestinian refugee who left the war-torn land in 1979 for England without a pence in his pocket. He was now a British citizen, a famous geophysicist no less, who was widely respected. But the agency had a dearth of information about Akmed Abram's activities before he left Palestine. That is when the sudden call from the Israeli intelligence agency jolted General Wells out of his chair. The Israelis alleged that the subject met with a major Hamas terrorist leader days before he headed to the *China Maiden*. They also received an unconfirmed rumor that Akmed Abram left Palestine after his involvement in a failed suicide-bombing attempt at a Tel Aviv marketplace in 1979. The perpetrator in the incident was never caught, but records indicated that the attempted assailant somewhat matched Akmed's description. The Israelis kept an eye on him in London for some time, but interest eventually receded.

General Wells groaned. The subject—a potential suicide terrorist—shook the president's hand. *Jesus!* But the president was now back in Washington, safe and sound. Perhaps the haunting reports were wrong. A case of mistaken identity. But the subject was still involved in a confidential government program. There was little concern now that the president's safety was now secure. But the CIA head was livid. Who was going to follow up? Terrorist threats are not just against high public office holders. This supposedly was a classified operation, though the director himself was not up to speed on the precise activity. The Company had its own spook on the platform. Well, not an agent, but a former informant. He was often unreliable and demanding, so his handlers recommended that he be cut off. But he was potentially the best source at the agency's disposal. Wells picked up the phone and called the White House.

Danielle was led into the spacious main operational center for the extraction operation, which she had not seen before. A row of computers and switchboards lining the room reminded her of a recording studio. Huge video monitors spread across one wall. It looked like a cross between a sports bar her ex-husband once dragged her to and the bridge of the Starship *Enterprise.* But instead of football games on a 100-inch screen or visions of stars whipping by at warp speed, rainbow-colored designs and mathematical figures filled each of the displays. She gazed open-mouthed. *The government must have bankrupted Medicare to pay for this,* she thought.

The drilling already commenced, and the serpent-like flexible drilling bits buried themselves into the sea bottom like earthworms. Most of the monitor screens were bluish at the moment, something Roystone explained registered the ambient pressures and temperatures that existed in the sediment.

"Some are infrared cameras, others are temperature and pressure monitors that reveal downhole readings," Dr. Roystone told her. The African-American's deep melodious tone amongst the frantic activity in the control room soothed her like a Bach cello solo by Yo Yo Ma in the midst of a rap concert. "The monitors reveal what's happening by the colors on the screen—kind of like weather radar—when the pressure in the hole changes, the colors will change."

Each technician on the floor of the operation center wore a slim headset, and presumably had a specific responsibility, Danielle thought. Though it resembled Mission Control in Houston, it wasn't the launching of the space shuttle after all. It was only a drilling operation. Still, the technology appeared to be tantamount to rocket science. The only person who did not wear communication equipment was Cowboy, who, of course, wouldn't remove his Stetson to put one on.

Instead, he paced the room like a football coach on the sidelines, giving instructions through clenched teeth that clamped an unlit cigar. One person now absent from the room was Akmed. *Where did he go?* No one seemed to notice, except Danielle. *Why wasn't he here?* It was like missing the first step on the moon. *Why did he disappear at his moment of triumph?* She wanted Akmed close to her, to see his bright smile, hear his consoling voice, and inhale his earthy-scented skin. She ached for him.

"Once the hydrates are reached, the depressurization process begins, unlatching the methane from the ice particles," Roystone said.

The colors on one monitor suddenly changed from mostly hues of blue and purple to yellow and orange.

"Okay people," Cowboy said. "We're going in—let's round up some little frozen doggies and rope us a cash cow. Yeeeeee—hah!"

Akmed saw the shining chain holding the crucifix around Danielle's neck as he slipped behind her. She didn't see him. He walked as quiet as a cat. The chain seemed thick and strong as it encircled her nape. Her neck slender and delicate. As he crept closer, she turned to him, the cross above her breasts gleaming in the blinking lights of the control room. Her broad smile was alluring. He reached his hands around her white neck, grasped the necklace and ripped it backward. He twisted and pulled bending her body until she fell to her knees. There was no sound coming from the woman. Just her open mouth in a silent gasp. The friction of the necklace tore into her throat as easily as through the skin of an overripe peach. A trench of red tissue oozed around the circumference of her delicate neck. With one final tug, her entire head tore from her body and toppled to the floor below.

Akmed hit the floor of his quarters as he rolled off his bunk.

Dear God. No more nightmares!

He pulled his legs up and was on all fours, bending down in submission. The sweat poured from Akmed's forehead and dripped on the floor. He knelt on his prayer rug in his modest cabin, murmuring, "Allah akbar, Allah akbar, Allah, akbar," praying for guidance. *The One and Only, the Constant Forgiver, I will do your will. There is no God but Allah and I submit to you.* The room was unlit, but he was in the dark in more ways than one. He received no instructions aboard the *China Maiden*. But Omar promised. The moment that he postponed in his own mind might never come. Was he just gathering intelligence? Or would someone tell him at the last moment that he must stick a knife into his best friend? Or kill the lovely woman he just made love to? Did his physical satiation fill a void in his spiritual quest? Kill her? What would happen to him if he did? What would happen to his sisters and their children in Palestine if he didn't?

He chanted again, asking for God to relieve him of this dilemma. How does this serve Him? Akmed never embraced the life of the West. He only wanted to endure it, to understand it. His faith was rock solid. After Palestine, Akmed felt his purpose was only to heal, to aid the less fortunate of his land by pulling from the earth the bounty that Allah kept below it to better their lives, clothe the naked, assuage the sick, feed the hungry, and comfort the oppressed. What was his great sin? His action as an ignorant teenager was an effort to serve God. What was God's purpose for him? How could he ascertain the true path? If his youthful actions were not right, so be it. No one was killed. If his attempt to kill was right to defend Palestine from the Jews, how can he be blamed for its failure? He was in a moral gray area. He now walked the path he believed was illuminated for him. For some reason, he remembered Adam, who suffered for his disobedience. He thought of Abraham and his test of faith by his willingness to sacrifice his own son. He contemplated the teachings of Muhammad, the most perfect prophet, to sacrifice and give alms. Finally, he envisioned the Christian scripture of Jesus in the Garden of Gethsemane on the Mount of Olives. *Let this cup of suffering pass me by*, the prophet of peace asked. *But not my will, but God's will be done.* But what is Allah's will? He raised, and then lowered his head once again. "Allah akbar, Allah akbar, Allah akbar." What happened to the prophet Jesus next, according to the Christians? It came to him. His destiny was betrayal.

Virgil Priest was handed a short message at his desk in the Executive Office Building adjacent to the White House. It was from the National Hurricane Center. The deputy director of the department of energy, Regis Lief, stood by waiting for both Priest's reactions and instructions. Hurricane Zeta, now with category-four gusts of 120 miles per hour picked up strength from the warm Caribbean waters and was heading due north in the Atlantic. It was now not expected to strike the Carolina coast at all. FEMA and most of the 500,000 people who evacuated their coastal homes would be relieved. But Priest was not. The eye of the powerful storm was heading right into the path of the *China Maiden* and *Project Hades*.

"Damn," he said.

"The most powerful winds are expected to hit the area within twelve hours," Lief said. "Instructions?"

"Have they begun drilling yet?"

"I'm not sure sir."

"Well, shit, we don't have any choice either way. We have to evacuate."

Priest knew that if the operation started, the mobile drilling unit would not have time to disconnect and move out of the hurricane's path. That was okay, the spar could handle high winds and waves—it was a state-of-the-art ocean platform designed for severe weather. However, all personnel must be evacuated. No one's life could be jeopardized. It would take several hours to move the entire crew by a stream of helicopters. They must start now. He wanted no human casualties to cause an interruption to the drilling activities. They would have to wait until the storm passed and start over again. What would Alexandria think? Priest would do anything for his lover. *Was that a sign of love or vulnerability?* He gave his deputy the order.

Priest reached for the phone, picked it up, and then placed it back on the receiver. He wanted to tell Alexandria about the decision, but thought better of it. She would find out through other means. She would not be pleased. He might be able to manipulate the president of the United States, but as of yet, he couldn't control the weather.

CHAPTER 53

▼

Two of the snake-like drilling stems edged closer to their target, massive hydrate zones approximately eight-feet thick. This was the moment everyone was waiting for. Cowboy shifted the cigar clenched between his teeth with his tongue and swallowed some saliva. To Danielle, he seemed to be drooling.

"As every good driller says," Cowboy said to the group, "go down one more foot."

"Depressurizing Drake," a wiry male technician said, pressing several buttons on his control panel. There was no sound, just a change of color on the downhole monitor of the Drake drill. The colors on the screen morphed from bright yellow and orange to an explosion of cherry-red, blossoming like a rose.

"What's happening now?" Danielle asked Dr. Roystone, whom she seemed to be suddenly clinging to like a piece of lint. *Where was Akmed? Was it time for his late private prayers, vespers or something?*

"The hydrate is basically melting by lowering the pressure in the formation as measured in ppi—pounds per square inch," Roystone answered as he surveyed a monitor. "As the formation pressure decreases, the pressure inside the Drake drilling stem increases as the hydrate is withdrawn."

"Withdrawal pressures?" Cowboy asked again.

"Now 300 ppi and climbing," the technician said.

Cowboy leaned over one of the main control monitors and flicked a switch. He spoke toward a microphone.

"Sheldon, we're at 300 ppi, okay to open the seal?"

"Been waiting on overtime, baby," the voice of Roger Sheldon squawked over everyone's headset. Cowboy held an earpiece up to the side of his head. The pipeline director was the only major operation figure not in the room. There seemed to be no sign of the antagonism Sheldon displayed earlier. It was all business. He was a professional, after all. "Once at 500 ppi we'll open the line and begin pumping."

The monitor reflecting information from the second drilling stem also flowered into view as bright red pressure bars on the monitor on the side of the screen shot upward. Unseen below the platform, the flexible diamond drilling bit tore through the ocean bottom, wriggling, boring, and searching for its quarry like a high-tech mole.

"Sheldon, start building up pressure in the CO_2 line," Cowboy said.

"Just called on shore," Sheldon said over the speaker. "It's on its way."

"How long until you reach 500 pounds?"

"Approximately three hours."

"Why does it take so long?" Danielle asked Roystone.

"The withdrawal of the hydrate and the insertion of the replacement gas cannot happen simultaneously," the scientist answered. "We need to withdraw the hydrate through depressurization first, and then at a certain point, pump in the frozen carbon dioxide."

"But won't the formation become unstable?"

"Not for that short period. We believe as long as the stabilization gas is inserted shortly afterward, no structural destabilization will occur."

"The Drake is now at 500 ppi," the technician said.

"Let 'er rip," Cowboy said.

"We're opening up the line and priming the pump," said the technician. "Withdrawal commencing."

A phone on Dr. Edison's belt buzzed. She pulled it off and answered.

"What?" she said in disbelief, loud enough to catch the attention of everyone at the monitors.

"But they've already started," she said into the phone. A pause. "Very well." She clicked off the phone and returned it to her belt.

No one said a word, but all eyes were on the NOAA scientist.

"The hurricane has veered north. We have orders to evacuate."

Two decks below, Roger Sheldon barked orders to subordinates. The seal on the main pipeline to shore was secure and valves were opened sucking the pressurized gas from underneath the sea floor. Monitors revealed the increasing pressure in the line as the first natural gas from frozen hydrates flowed through the four-foot diameter pipe.

"Ain't she beautiful, baby," Sheldon said, staring at a video monitor blinking with multi-colored pressure readings. He was downright giddy. But he had an uncomfortable, prescient feeling as if someone was watching him. The hairs on the back of his neck stood erect.

Sheldon turned around to find Akmed Abram staring at him with the dead glare of a zombie.

"What the hell are you doing here Sheik?" Sheldon asked him.

"Damn it all," Cowboy said. "Nothing like a case of drillus interruptus." He felt it was worse than a hotel maid walking in his room to make the bed while he was hammering a foxy cocktail waitress. Though the woman beneath him would be horrified, he wouldn't mind banging away no matter who was watching. And just when his feet began to twitch, Miss Sunshine had to spoil the party.

"The Coast Guard will handle the evacuation," Dr. Edison said. "We will follow the drill as exercised last week."

"We have to leave?" Danielle asked.

Hmmm. Miss Prissy sounds like a kid who doesn't want to go to bed, Cowboy thought.

"Government regulations require regular evacuation drills on all offshore drilling rigs," Edison said. "This is no different."

"Do we have to move the MODU?" Cowboy asked. He hated to do that. The rig was now tethered to the sea bottom with ultra-heavyweight anchors as it withdrew the hydrates.

"No," Edison said. "There is not enough time. This will only be a human evacuation. Believe it or not, that includes you. Everyone must leave via helicopter."

Smart ass. There was nothing Cowboy could do. Nothing in his bag of tricks of rule bending could keep the process going. He was on the verge of his victory, the greatest drilling discovery since Spindletop, the Texas gusher that really opened up the oil age in 1901. His glory would have to wait. It was like pulling out a couple strokes short of busting a nut, perhaps the most painful image he could imagine. They would have to stop.

"Okay, pass the word," Cowboy conceded. "Grab your gear and line up."

"What will happen to the drilling operation?" Danielle asked.

"Nothing," Cowboy said. "As long as we balance the pressures before we leave, there will be no problem. This rig is designed for huge ocean swells." *A little blowjob from Mother Nature won't hurt it.* "However, people can't stay on board.

In fact, all non-operating personnel should be on the first chopper. So, you, Akmed … by the way, where the hell is Akmed, I told him to be here."

"I haven't seen him," Danielle said as if she were denying before the cock crowed.

"Well, don't worry your little heart about it. He knows the drill. This ain't the first time we've had to evacuate a drilling spar."

Cowboy stood up on a chair.

"Okay people, all of you know what needs to be done, so let's stabilize the pressures."

"Mr. Rhodan," a female engineer interrupted.

"Honey, I wasn't finished …"

"Chemical sensors reveal high levels of sulfur present in the sample gas."

"What?" he asked, moving closer to that technician's monitor. He reviewed a few numbers of chemical analyses of the gas produced by the hydrate. "Son-of-a-bitch," he said, drawing out each syllable as if he were first learning how to read.

"What's wrong?" Danielle asked.

"Looks like we hit a patch of sour hydrate," Cowboy answered. I've run into this before in many an oil well. Oil and gas drilling often produce sulfur—there's a ton of it in the Gulf of Mexico. Not bad stuff if you are making sulfuric acid or stink bombs, but we don't want it here."

"What can you do about it?"

"It's nasty stuff—it's corrosive as hell to the pipelines. We can extract what has been collected and the particles in the gas can be solidified for disposal. But we'd like to avoid that. Sulfur dust can spontaneously burst into flames and it smells like the devil." He puckered his lips like he just ate the stuff. "We can reinject hydrogen sulfide gas back into the reservoirs, but the best thing to do is withdraw and find another hydrate formation nearby that is not contaminated and we'll leave this stuff where we found it."

Cowboy pointed at a technician. "Tell Sheldon to stop the outbound flow."

"We need to take samples for analysis to measure potential environmental contamination," Edison said.

There's old Woodsy Owl, again, Cowboy thought. "Sure, go right ahead, but don't let that dead skunk leak out inside this rig. Perhaps it's a good thing we have to stop—we would have to back out of this formation anyway. We'll go fishing in a different spot."

CHAPTER 54

▼

Maureen O'Day kissed her husband good-bye and gazed into the bear-like man's eyes. He knew his wife could be persuasive if she looked him in the eye. His plane for Washington, D.C., left in two hours and even after siphoning gasoline from his lawn tractor, he wasn't even sure he had enough fuel in his truck to get to the airport. He should have called a cab but they were few and far between these days and not reliable. The IGW union and management negotiators were scheduled to meet at a hotel across the Potomac in Virginia later that day to discuss a new contract. American Energy was attempting to force concessions it previously browbeat on other company unions. O'Day thought about his task. It was up to this less-than-stellar high-school grad and former welder to beat back the Harvard-educated labor lawyers. A more daunting task, however, was to assuage his worrywart wife.

"I want you to call Danielle the first chance you get," she said.

"We're going to be tied up in negotiations and I don't think the union nor the company would look favorably upon me talking with someone in higher management right now," said Dan O'Day, doing his best to avert her gaze.

"For Pete's sake," his wife said. "She's your daughter, not some enemy spy."

"She is a senior vice president of the company that is screwing our union."

"Dan O'Day," Maureen replied. Her tone was not affectionate. She was now the matriarch laying down the law. She didn't do this often, only when he acted oafish. "You know Danielle has nothing to do with your labor-management squabbles. She's just a lawyer who is trying to build a respectable career."

He rolled his eyes and glanced at his watch.

"I just saw the weather report again," Maureen continued in a lachrymose tone. "That hurricane is heading right up the eastern seaboard in the path of where our little girl is. They have evacuated a good part of the Carolina coasts. Get your company to contact her or something. You damn well better call her on that fancy satellite phone and make sure she is safe. She is our only child, Dan O'Day."

O'Day gripped his wife with his burley arms and flashed a mitigating smile.

"Of course I will," he conceded. "She probably won't talk to me, but I'll check on her."

She hugged her husband back.

"I'll call you as soon as I land," he said.

"Don't worry about me," she said. "I don't want to hear from you until you find that our daughter is safe and sound."

He kissed her and promised again. He did have Danielle on his mind as well. He didn't want to outwardly express concern. He was the rock of the family and if he showed any type of fissure, Maureen would crack. He jumped into his Ford pickup, throwing his single luggage bag on the passenger seat. He turned the key. The engine refused to turn over.

"Maureen! Call me a damn cab!"

The sun was scorching for a late November day, and despite hurricane winds a hundred miles offshore, the breeze moved in light, pleasant gusts on the frothy beaches of North Carolina's Outer Banks. It was eerily quiet. Perhaps it was the paucity of human activity, Alexandria Raven thought, for the narrow beach-lined islands were virtually deserted. The previous day, traffic on the narrow two-lane causeway linking the islands with the mainland was jammed packed with the vacationers and permanent residents who were urged by the Federal Emergency Management Agency to retreat inland. The National Hurricane Center had expected Hurricane Zeta to glance off the resort islands off the coast of North Carolina and wreak havoc on the multi-million dollar beach homes.

Raven and her husband elected not to fight the traffic and leave their shore-front beach house, because if the storm was going to hit, an American Energy helicopter would retrieve them in plenty of time, and sweep them away over the less fortunate citizens who endured the bottleneck on the bridges. However, the storm turned and headed straight north in the Atlantic. She brooded over how this might affect the hydrate project.

Raven enjoyed the ocean, the impeccable white-sand beaches, and the gleaming southern sun during the summer months. The Outer Banks, once a refuge for pirates, were home to many of the rich and famous. But this late in the year, the temperatures usually were not warm enough for her to stretch out on the sand in a swimsuit. Today, however, the massive storm offshore did drag with it tropical air with temperatures into the eighties. After the successful presidential tour offshore of *Project Hades*, Raven felt she deserved a short respite. She was drained from twelve- to fourteen-hour workdays. She needed rest. Unfortunately, she could not spend it with her lover. Virgil Priest returned to Washington to help meld a compromise on the president's energy bill. There were complications, he told her. Congressman Doggle's allies on board the *China Maiden* knew something of the hydrate extraction project. Doggle probably would not blow the whistle on the project if he received what he wanted in the energy bill. In short, he would extort the president. Still, Priest told her not to worry—the president will give the natural gas hydrate extraction his blessing, no matter what. So instead of passionate sex with her secret paramour, she would settle for reclining on the upper deck of her $5 million beach house with the company of a good J. D. Robb mystery.

But it was not to be.

"We need a fourth, hon, come on and join us," Raven's husband said.

Douglas Waters wanted to play the island's posh private golf course, but only had three players. He wanted to round out the foursome. The fatuous man was always so rigid. He was dressed in bright yellow slacks, bleached white shoes, and a neon-green golf shirt. He looked like a flag from some African country, Raven thought. Once a trim man in his youth, his indolent lifestyle resulted in a prominent potbelly after leaving the president's administration as secretary of energy. He did golf a lot, but always took a cart. The only exercise he engaged in was swinging his light graphite clubs and bending his elbow after completion of the round in the country club's bar. His face was reddish-brown from endless afternoons on the virtually treeless island course, and his nose was cherry from a liquid diet of Crown Royal and cola. Once a mover-and-shaker in Washington, D.C., he now was a golf bum and a drunk. Raven couldn't remember the last time she even kissed, let alone fucked him.

"The entire island is empty," Raven replied. "How do you have *anyone* to play with?"

"The pro is still at the club, and Senator Stevens is still hanging around, since the hurricane threat is gone. Good guy to get to know." He sloshed back the drink in his hand and came over and put his arms around her.

She recoiled, but not with obvious revulsion—this was her husband after all. The former secretary of energy was on a first-name basis with many in Congress, played golf with them, and *that* she found useful in pursuing American Energy's legislative agenda. Senator Lance Stevens of North Carolina *was* on the important energy committee.

"For Christ's sake Douglas, you know I don't like to play golf," she said.

"Oh Alex, you are a natural athlete—you can stand it for a couple of hours—humor me. You can bend Senator Stevens' ear if you like. Besides, we haven't spent any time together in months."

That was true. Raven worked every waking hour, constantly on a sojourn, and when forced to occupy the same household with her husband, she spent it as far away from him as possible on the phone making business calls, burying her nose in a book, or tending to her garden in White Plains. They were wealthy beyond reasonable imagination, and they both had their own interests. Hers, business and adultery, and his, golf and booze. He did not raise one eyebrow of suspicion that she might be having a torrid affair with his successor in the president's cabinet. He rarely could maintain an erection and showed no desire to ingest modern medications to improve the situation. Perhaps she should play golf with the lush. It sure beat fucking him.

"Very well," she consented, putting her novel down. "Just the eight holes."

"Nine," he said. "There are nine holes on the front—eighteen total. Haven't you learned anything about golf?"

"Whatever," she said like a disgruntled teenager. *Eight holes, nine holes, what's the difference? It's a waste of time.* She had no interest in the game and didn't know a hook from a slice or a bogey from an eagle. Now sex was a sport she enjoyed—but not with her husband, who was a loser in that arena. But she refused to discard him because he was still useful in other ways. She must submit to him from time to time. But time was something she did not have a lot of.

CHAPTER 55

▼

"Hurricane" Herbie Winkle was on the warpath and he wanted the press to know it.

"H-H-Hurricane Zeta is the sixteenth category-three storm or higher of the s-s-season," he shouted into the microphones in front of him. "H-H-Human-induced global warming is the leading cause of greater storm wind speeds and their increased destructive p-p-power."

The environmental advocate waved a scientific paper that had just been published in the journal *Nature*. He explained that with every increase in hurricane category, the destructive capacity of the storm increased by ten times. "Here is p-proof that greenhouse gases are destroying the earth in numerous ways. Now the president is creeping toward a natural gas economy that will increase greenhouse gases and add to the p-problem."

Winkle was determined that Congressman August Doggle would not get all the press on opposition to the president's energy bill. And he had his fill of that twit Stevick.

"In addition," Winkle warned, "d-d-drilling off the Atlantic can cause massive environmental damage from accidental oil slicks damaging wildlife and property and destruction of the coral reefs and the aquatic life it s-s-supports."

Whatever the degree of verisimilitude in the recent scientific study of climate research, to every reporter in attendance, it rang true. It *was* another horrendous hurricane season. Though the amount of storms were approximately the same in recent years, the devastation caused seemed to be growing. Whether it was the path of the storms hitting the United States' East and Gulf Coasts or the fact of massive building of homes on the coasts added to the overall dollar figure damage, no one could agree. But the video pictures of collapsed homes resembling broken *Monopoly* game pieces and yachts dumped onto land like discarded bathtub toys were powerful images.

"The increase in global ocean and air temperatures is increasing the energy of ordinary hurricanes into *s-s-superhurricanes*," Winkle said. "Increasing fossil fuel use will only add fuel to the f-f-fire."

The only additional ammunition Winkle needed for a slam dunk was for the latest hurricane to strike the Carolinas with full force, but it now appeared that would not happen. Still, it looked like the president was in for rough seas anyway. Pressure from the politically active hoi polloi would mandate that additional global-warming legislation fly through Congress and the offshore plans would be scuttled. And Winkle, who envied the public adoration and softball treatment of that wrinkled old witch Stevick, was convinced that this opportunity to pile on the Freeman administration would result in his recognition as the greatest public advocate since Ralph Nadar.

The line of military passenger helicopters landing on and taking off of the *China Maiden* reminded Cowboy of video of the evacuation of the American Embassy in Saigon in 1975. MODU personnel, their personal belongings, and any portable equipment were moving with haste, but precision, according to the emergency plans. But with each landing helicopter, the pace quickened. In three hours, approximately 95 percent of the platform's workers were off the spar, retreating to inland points on the Virginia coast. However, Danielle O'Day and Akmed Abram were not among the evacuees, and that was disturbing Cowboy, who was ultimately in charge of everyone's safety.

The wind picked up on deck and the summer-like sun present a couple of days before was missing. The sky was thick with multiple levels of clouds, all various shades of purple and pewter. The pastoral blue sea was now a dark gray undulating mass with thousands of whitecaps leaping upward like claws. "I want you off this rig now," Cowboy said to the American Energy lawyer, both of them standing on the deck, the wind lashing down upon them.

"I want to observe the complete evacuation," Danielle said. "It is vital that we communicate to the public that this offshore operation is safe and that the concern for the employees and scientists on board are taken with utmost importance."

"For crying out loud, counselor, this is a routine event. Drilling spars are abandoned all the time in the Gulf whenever a tropical storm hits."

"Then I guess I present no risk by staying."

This obstinate bitch! To think I wanted to give her a poke—maybe with earplugs. The winds were picking up, and between the roar of air and the thumping of helicopter rotors on the deck's helipad, the ambient noise forced anyone speaking to shout. A helicopter pilot jogged over to Cowboy and they reviewed the emergency evacuation list. There were still a few missing who should have departed, including Sheldon, Edison, Roystone, the prissy lawyer, and Cowboy's buddy Akmed. The helicopter pilot explained that only two more helicopters were accepting passengers, his and another yet to arrive. At that moment, Dr. Edison appeared on the deck, without her yellow duffel bag full of personal belongings that most crewmembers lugged with them. Her signature lock of black hair that usually hung in front of her eyes now flew perpendicular from the side of her head in the wind like an erect black flag.

"Edison," Cowboy said, impatiently. "Aren't you taking anything with you? Your helicopter is waiting. And where the hell is Roystone?"

"We have a problem," Edison said.

"What?"

"The withdrawal valves are not sealed. There is still gas being depressurized from the hydrate coming from the formation."

"I ordered it stopped," Cowboy said.

"We can't stop it until the pipeline is sealed—if it isn't, backup pressure could potentially blow apart the hydrate formation."

"Well, what the hell is the matter with Sheldon? Tell him to seal the line."

"We've called him repeatedly—there seems to be some communication malfunction at the compressor deck. He doesn't answer."

Cowboy shook his head, holding onto his Stetson so it wouldn't blow off his head in the storm. "Jesus Christ, I'll go down there myself."

"Dr. Roystone already has, but he hasn't returned yet."

"Shit. By the way, where the hell is Akmed—did someone reach him?"

"I'm not sure," Edison responded. "We've been so busy trying to figure out why the valves haven't been closed."

Cowboy ran for the stairwell leading down to the first lower deck. The two women followed him. He turned back and pointed his finger at them. "You two have to leave this rig—I'm ordering it—get on that helicopter now. There is only one more whirlybird on the way and the last one is for Sheldon, Roystone, Akmed, and me. I don't really wish to have you sit on my lap. I can't have people missing in action when I take off." The helicopter on the platform suddenly lifted into the stiff ocean wind and turned away toward the mainland. As soon as it did, another transport helicopter landed to take its place. "Damn it—that's the last one," Cowboy groaned.

"We have to seal that pipeline—there is a danger of a pressure blowout," Edison said firmly.

"I'll take care of it," Cowboy said. "Now get your stuff fast and get on that chopper—and hold it until I get back with the stragglers. As commander of this rig, that's an order."

A sudden gust of wind nearly knocked the three of them off their feet. As they struggled to regain their balance the women looked at him as if he were someone else. Cowboy clasped both of his hands on the top of his head that was as bald and white as the cartoon floor-cleaner trademark—*Mr. Clean*. His few blond locks hung from the back of his skull like tassels on an ornamental curtain. His Stetson bounced across the deck of the drilling rig like tumbleweed down a ghost town's main street.

"Shit!" Cowboy growled, and he tore down the stairs below deck, hand over his naked skull.

After Cowboy left, the two women looked at one another and laughed in unison. It was the first time Danielle saw Edison with a genuine smile on her face. And it was about time the vain gas driller got his due.

"Let's get our luggage, and I'll meet you back here in ten minutes," Edison shouted over the howl of the wind. She turned toward the helipad and held up ten fingers toward the pilot.

"Sure," Danielle said. "What about Dr. Roystone and Akmed?"

Edison was already walking away. "They'll take care of themselves," she said.

That answer wasn't good enough for Danielle. She decided to find Akmed herself.

PART VI

▼

TREACHERY

CHAPTER 56

▼

Cowboy stomped his wrangler books in fury as he bolted into the compressor room. When he found who was responsible for this, heads would roll. The facility was vacant—no engineers, no technicians, no Sheldon. The driller glared at several monitors that measured pressures in the pipeline. The output line registered at 550 ppi, meaning a huge volume of gas was flowing from the underground formation. Why it wasn't shut off was beyond him. Sheldon was a stupid conceited cuss, but he was a professional. He followed procedures meticulously and crucified any of his staff who didn't follow his orders. If Sheldon received word to close the valves, he would have done so. He would have been the last person out of this section of the rig and would not have left his station without shutting the valves. Something was seriously wrong.

Cowboy's eyes shifted to the input monitor that gauged carbon dioxide pressure flowing back into the formation. He tried to comprehend the hundreds of numbers and colored blinking geometric shapes that represented open or closed valves. On the output pipeline monitor, the triangular shapes that represented various valves glowed a deep blue, which meant they were open allowing gas to flow out of the formation. However, the valves on the pipeline bringing the replacement carbon dioxide back into the formation were all pulsing fire-engine red. They were closed and the pipeline had no pressure of replacement carbon dioxide at all. There was something amiss. Worse than that, another console looked like it had been beaten to a pulp with a crow bar.

"What the …?" he said. He glanced inside the compressor deck operational floor. Several tanks of compressed air stood along one wall. They included samples of the hydrate withdrawn for analysis purposes. Several of the tanks were strewn on the floor. *Fucking Edison and her environmental samples*, he thought. He wanted to put his carbon footprint up her ass. Moving his attention beyond the tanks, Cowboy noticed that the input pipeline was wide open as if it were undergoing maintenance. The pipeline pig was sitting at the entrance to the open shaft. The input line that was supposed to contain the carbon dioxide was open like a tin can of beans, let alone not operational. If nothing was flowing back into the formation, it *might* become unstable. This was ridiculous. Where the hell was Sheldon? *When I get my hands on that idiot …* He turned to leave the area and felt like he stepped into the path of a swinging baseball bat. A crushing force hit his shoulder and the side of his head. His body flung backward against a computer station. Before the rig manager fell to the floor, he saw in his last moments of consciousness a four-foot long adjustable metal wrench crash to the floor next to him with a ringing clatter.

Danielle quickly retrieved her yellow duffel bag, tossed her scant belongings into it, including her bulky satellite phone. She dug out her useless cellphone and paused before tossing it in thinking it useless. Instead, she slipped it into a breast pocket of her tunic. She then ran to Akmed's cabin, breathing rapidly, her heart in her throat. She rapped on the metal door and heard nothing. She called his name, but again, no response. She grasped the latch and the door was unlocked. Inside, the few personal effects of the geophysicist were undisturbed. Akmed's prayer rug was rolled up neatly on his bunk where they had made love the night before. A copy of the Holy Qu'ran sat on the made bed. So was a small, dog-eared paperback copy of the King James Version of The New Testament. Wherever Akmed was, it appeared that he wasn't packing to leave.

After retrieving her belongings, Dr. Samantha Edison slung her duffel over her back and scurried to the compressor operations center tracing Cowboy's steps shortly before. Entering the compressor control center, she saw the computer stations vacant. Everyone had evacuated. There was no sign of any of the compressor operators, including Sheldon, and no trace of Cowboy who claimed to be investigating. As she walked through the compressor room, without notice the entire drilling rig lurched to one side with a violent jerk. Edison toppled sideways as if struck by a passing car, toppling over a chair in front of the console. She struck her forehead against the metal seat, and she saw a fireworks palette of colors—red, blue, yellow, orange, and an assortment of combined hues that resembled a tie-dyed T-shirt studded with polished jewels. Then, all she saw was black.

CHAPTER 57

▼

Danielle didn't know what to do. Should she scour the hallways of the rig look-ing for Akmed, or should she return to the deck as she pledged to Dr. Edison? If the helicopter on deck was the last ride, she shouldn't take any chances. She never walked through the rig without a guide. She would end up getting lost in the nar-row hallways and labyrinth of staircases. Akmed, Cowboy, Edison, and Sheldon knew the rig backward and forward, and no matter what the problem was in seal-ing the well, she was sure they could figure it out and get on deck in time. She must return.

She turned on her heels to exit Akmed's room and ran directly into another person, who grasped her by her arms. She let out a vociferous cry of surprise and fear.

"Sorry," Roger Sheldon said, easing up on the grip he had on her arms. "I didn't mean to startle you."

Danielle gasped and tried to catch her breath. "Why did you sneak up behind me like that?"

"I didn't mean to. I was coming down the hall and I heard someone milling around in here."

"Did you see Akmed or Mr. Rhodan? What is wrong with the drilling opera-tion?" She wasn't sure which question she wanted answered first.

Sheldon rubbed his eyes. "No, I haven't seen Ahab the Arab or Deputy Fester, but we have to leave the rig ASAP."

"Where are they?" she said.

"We don't have time to talk about this now," Sheldon said, again grabbing her firmly on the elbow and leading her out of Akmed's quarters, "our lives are in danger."

"What are you talking about?"

"There is nothing we can do."

"About what?"

"The project—it's been sabotaged. Akmed's just what I suspected—a terrorist."

"That's impossible," she said, the pit of her stomach suddenly heaving.

Sheldon started down the hallway toward the stairs that led to the main deck. "We don't have time to have a trial, Miss O'Day. You have to get the hell out of here if you want to save your life, now come on." The pipeline manager reached a yellow-painted metal stairway and began his ascent two stairs at a time. Danielle decided to follow.

When they reached the deck, the ominous sky was becoming more black than purple. A helicopter pilot wearing a flight suit and helmet stood on the helipad. He was waving desperately to Danielle and Sheldon with the clipboard he held in his hand, its papers blowing wildly. The rotors of the large transport helicopter were spinning in the now steady wind that uprooted anything not secured on deck. The hurricane must be approaching faster than anticipated.

"Where's Edison?" Sheldon said. "I thought you said she'd meet you here."

"Mr. Rhodan said he wanted to check the compressors," Danielle said. "Maybe she followed him."

"It's too late. The input pipeline is damaged and Akmed is still on the loose down there. He attacked me after my staff evacuated. Son-of-a-bitch swung a four-foot-long monkey wrench at me. He destroyed some of the consoles. I barely got out of there alive."

She was perplexed. *Akmed a terrorist?*

"I told Dr. Edison that I'd meet her up here," she said.

Sheldon was lost in thought for a moment, and then spoke. "Look, we have to get on that chopper—with this storm kicking up I don't know if the Coast Guard will be willing to send out another one."

Danielle looked at the pilot and then back at the stairway that she climbed from below deck. She didn't like helicopters, oceans, or dimly lit mole-sized hallways under the deck of floating drilling vessels. How the hell did she get here? Why didn't she leave with Raven? Before another thought crossed her mind, both she and Sheldon were falling. The entire deck of the drilling rig seemed to buckle as it just dipped in a huge ocean wave. Neither could find their footing and they crashed to the deck, hands reaching out, grasping vainly at air to get a grip on something. As they slid across the tilted deck as if they were traversing down a playground sliding board, the helipad could be seen at a queer angle. The elevated structure seemed to bend downward. The helicopter's blades continued to rotate as it dipped off the collapsing helipad. It crashed on the edge of the deck, flipped over like a child's toy, and tumbled into the sea.

Sheldon and Danielle continued their slide, with nothing solid to catch hold. Ropes, wires, towels, buckets, and sundry other unsecured items rolled along with them as if they were heading down a coal chute. They were tumbling toward the side of the deck. If they had already boarded the helicopter, they would be now sinking into the sea. But that wasn't much comfort. Danielle screamed. Her ultimate fear was fast approaching—the edge of the platform and the water below.

Sheldon was the first to stem his uncontrolled slide by striking the side safety railing, bouncing off the hard metal rungs. He was able to grab hold of a vertical cross section of railing with the crook of his arm, which halted his precipitous descent into the sea. Danielle did not have such luck as she was sliding right underneath the bottom horizontal rail, ready to topple into the waves below. She attempted to break her momentum by thrashing out her arms and grasping the bottom rail like she was reaching for a fallen limb over a swift river before she was swept over a waterfall. Her arms struck the metal rail, but she could not hold on. Her legs were now dangling off the edge of the rig and her center of gravity pulled her downward off the side of the structure. She felt the rage of the wind-driven choppy waves below as spittle of sea spray soaked her from the open violent mouth of the devouring ocean.

CHAPTER 58

▼

Akmed's head swam. Still, he limped forward, his bad leg aching, dragging Cowboy's unconscious body up a stairwell. Then without an inkling of warning, the entire MODU shifted, throwing him off the metal stairs and into a gray-painted wall. He lost his grip on Cowboy, but the Oklahoman's limp body merely shifted to the side, lodging between the stairs and the railing. Blood trickled down Akmed's forehead—he must have struck something sharp. His vision blurred and his consciousness was cloudy as well. He detected the copper smell of blood in his nose and his long-ago-injured leg throbbed with pain. The rig was now cockeyed at a forty-five degree angle, so he saw what appeared to be a slanted-V corridor merging into a wall instead of a hallway. He tried to remember what he was doing before the rig apparently collapsed. He was first puzzled why the MODU was tipping. There must have been some type of explosion, like a depth charge hitting a submarine. Perhaps a blowout. That's it. An underwater landslide that probably ripped the anchors out of the sea bottom, rocking the drilling spar.

Then he saw we he most feared. Water. Seawater raging down the hallway, threatening to encapsulate him. The rig was seriously damaged, punctured like a torpedo struck it. Perhaps there was an internal explosion. He could not remember. The MODU was sinking. He must escape. Akmed shot an anxious glance at Cowboy's motionless body. If he wasn't dead already, he would surely drown in moments.

Danielle could do nothing but pray that the raging sea would suddenly become halcyon. And just as she was slipping toward certain death, the powerful grip of a warm, strong, male hand clamped on her wrist. In an instant, she was pulled upward and under the rail of the deck once again. The rig then partially corrected itself. Whatever rocked the massive offshore platform nearly to its side mysteriously disappeared, and the surface was almost as level as it was before. Back on the deck Danielle continued to bellow gasps of shock, her head between her legs. She did not look at who saved her.

"Are you okay?" her rescuer said.

She looked up. It was Roger Sheldon.

"Yes," she said, trying to collect herself. Sheldon saved her life. She would have surely fallen over the side and drowned. She owed this irascible antihero everything.

They both stood, a bit wobbly, and looked at the helipad. The helicopter, pilots and all, were gone, sinking to the bottom of the ocean.

"Oh my God! Will there be another one?" Danielle asked, exasperated.

"I'm not sure," Sheldon said, now breathing just as heavily as her. "We have to get word to shore. Let's get to the doghouse."

They both ran to the operations center on deck to call the mainland Coast Guard.

"What the hell happened?" Danielle asked as they ran.

"There must have been a blowout—a fucking undersea landslide by not sealing the hydrate formations. One of the MODU's anchors must have dislodged."

They reached the communications center and scaled the canary-yellow stairs awkwardly as they were slightly skewed to one side. They found chaos. Computer equipment and consoles were overturned with their contents eviscerated, and half of the room was crushed from the collapsed helipad that landed on it when the vessel lurched. Equipment from an upper deck also crashed through the ceiling after the MODU tipped to its side. Sheldon struggled to reach a communications handset on one of the undamaged consoles, picked it up, pressed a button, spoke some nautical parlance, and waited for a response. Nothing. He tried again, and then noticed that the handset's wires led to nowhere. They were ripped from their casing, and only bare copper wire dangled from the bottom.

"Shit," he said. "It's destroyed."

"The landslide?" Danielle asked. "My God, did it create a tsunami?"

"A what?"

"A tsunami. Dr. Edison said that undersea landslides can cause a tsunami—a massive tidal wave."

Sheldon scanned the horizon. "Hell, I don't know. I can't see anything out there but a fucking hurricane coming."

Danielle did not understand how cavalier Sheldon was about the tsunami. *Did he not know of the danger?* She looked out into the western sea herself. She did not notice anything out of the ordinary. Then again, from what she was told, the tsunami wave in the deep ocean was a long, slow, and gradual one. It was only when it approached the shallow waters did it pick up speed, height, and deadly destructive power.

Sheldon panicked and tossed the handset to the floor in frustration. "This isn't going to work."

"Can we ride out the hurricane below deck?" Danielle asked, her thoughts shifting from one potential calamity to another.

Sheldon thought, his eyes wandering. "Yes, but who knows what damage the MODU suffered. This son-of-a-bitch may be sinking for all we know. We've got to contact the Coast Guard and let them know we need another helicopter."

Danielle looked out on the deck of the *China Maiden*. Items that broke loose because of the sudden upheaval now lay strewn across the deck, some blowing toward one side in the gusts of wind, aided by the slight slant of the off-kilter platform. She saw a yellow duffel bag rolling past the doghouse on the lower deck. It was her belongings.

"My bag!" she said.

"Can't worry about that, for crying out loud," Sheldon said. "We've got to go below deck and find working communication equipment."

"But I have something—I have a satellite phone in the bag."

Sheldon paused and then bolted from the room. "Come on!"

CHAPTER 59

▼

As if the president didn't have enough problems. During the past twenty hours, President Freeman witnessed one of the greatest evacuations of the East Coast, as the Federal Emergency Management Agency and the National Guard of four coastal states assisted island and beachfront communities from Georgia to Virginia in abandoning their homes in fear of the approaching category-four Hurricane Zeta. Then the National Hurricane Center, like the late *Saturday Night Live*-comedienne Gilda Radner's Emily Litella character, said, "Never mind." The storm changed its course like an errant football field goal attempt on a windy day. This would be another knock against his administration. Not willing to see damage and death like the storm that destroyed New Orleans, he commanded the states to empty the coastal regions by federal decree and federalized the states' National Guard to get the job done. Though most people cooperated, the military units were not going to drag obstinate people out of their homes. However, they promised to shoot looters on sight.

"The damn National Hurricane Center must have the same intelligence as the CIA," President Freeman told his chief-of-staff, Thaddeus Mann, who stroked his curly sideburns like a pet cat.

"FEMA recommends we sound the all-clear," the wizened aide said.

The president was about to do just that, but his personal secretary interrupted him. She said the secretary of energy was demanding a palaver with the president.

As the president picked up his desk phone, the chief-of-staff's own cellular unit buzzed on his belt. He retrieved it and moved to the opposite side of the room.

"Virgil, what lump of sugar do you have for me now?" the president said jovially.

"Sir, there has been some type of accident with *Project Hades*."

The words hit Freeman coldly like the bone-chilling words, "Houston, we have a problem," or worse, "America is under attack."

"What problem, Virgil?" the president said cautiously.

"The hurricane sir, we've evacuated most of the crew and there were just a few personnel left. But the Coast Guard lost touch with the last chopper sir. It might have taken off because we can't reach anyone on the rig itself. But the chopper is missing, Mr. President."

"How many on it?" the president asked.

"Not sure sir—we are making a count of personnel as they land at Norfolk."

"Okay, Virgil, keep me informed."

"Excuse me, Mr. President, there's more, sir."

"Yes?"

"We are receiving natural gas from the hydrate formation sir."

"Well, that's good."

"No sir, it isn't," Priest said in an ominous tone. "The command was given to shut in the well because of the impending hurricane and evacuation, but according to the compressor station onshore that accepts the gas, it is still flowing from the rig to the mainland. And the gas apparently is contaminated with hydrogen sulfide. But worse than that, the outflow of carbon dioxide is not operational."

"And?"

Chief-of-staff Mann interrupted the phone call by approaching the president's desk. Freeman did not hear his secretary of energy's answer.

"Mr. President!" Mann said.

Freeman felt like a father being pestered by two teenage kids, one telling him he wrecked the car and the other informing him he would soon be a grandfather.

"Jesus Christ, what?" Freeman said.

The president looked up into the terrified face of his confidant, his reassuring elfish countenance now registering sheer terror.

"We've just got word from NOAA," the president's aide continued. "There has been some kind of tremor in the Atlantic. They are not sure of the cause, but there are emergency monitors going off throughout the outer continental shelf."

"Monitors?"

"Tsunami monitors, sir. There may be a high-powered tsunami wave approaching the Carolina coasts. According to NOAA, it could have a surge as far south as central Florida and as far north as Washington, sir."

The hydrate test, the president thought. *It not only was a failure, it caused the catastrophe he was warned of.* "How much time?" the president said, deflated. The secretary of energy on the phone receiver now on his lap kept talking away, but Freeman was no longer listening.

"Not sure, sir—half hour tops."

"FEMA? What have they—"

"The emergency broadcast system is in operation—they are getting the word out. But people won't have much time to react. But, thank God you demanded the states to clear their coasts for the hurricane, sir. That will save thousands of lives."

That was reassuring, the president thought. He felt he just accidentally ordered a nuclear strike against lower Manhattan but was told he was lucky it was a Sunday when not too many people were at the office.

President Freeman buried his head in his hands. "Christ, what have I done?"

The rig *was* sinking. Even though the sudden lurch to one side soon stabilized almost to vertical, Akmed knew that the MODU experienced irreparable damage. It was tethered to the sea bottom and part of the formation must have collapsed in a landslide, pulling it to one side and perhaps ripping a hole in the hull. On the surface, there were impending hurricane force winds, and the evacuation of the offshore rig had to be nearly, if not totally, complete. Cowboy should have been gone, but somehow he returned, heroically, to see if he could stop the hemorrhaging of the hydrate layer. *That stupid cocksure man.* But Cowboy arrived too late. There was nothing to be done.

Akmed noticed the decks below the surface were flooding with alarming speed. He spotted a doorway through which he might escape. After scaling the stairs around Cowboy's unconscious body, he reached for the doorway's heavy latch and pulled. It did not budge. Repeated attempts with all the strength in his arms and the force of his shoulder against the steel door did nothing. Something must have collapsed on the other side, or perhaps bent the locking mechanism that jammed the door latch. He could not leave this way. Even if he did, would there be a waiting helicopter? He thought methodically, without panic. He did not know the layout of the *China Maiden* completely, but he knew there was another possible exit. But it didn't lead to the deck.

CHAPTER 60

▼

Danielle clutched the satellite phone in her left hand, and furiously punched buttons with the right, trying to get the device to work. Mustering up all the strength she possessed, she retrieved her duffel moments before it rolled off the side of the slanted deck, nearly giving her enough vertigo to vomit and pass out. But she held on. Next, she grabbed the phone out of the bag and stood on the tilted deck, a gale-like wind flailing against her, forcing her to lock her legs around a stairwell railing to keep her balance. She didn't know if the device would work if they went below out of the wind. Sheldon tried to help her, but he was unfamiliar with the device. Danielle did her best to remain calm in the panic, but she was failing. After all, she nearly fell into the choppy ocean with neither lifejacket nor competent swimming skills. She had never come so close to death. Not in the high-school swimming pool, and not in the helicopter crash practice tank. The last helicopter to the mainland was now in Davy Jones' locker. She was fortunate she missed that bus. And neither she nor Sheldon had any confidence that another helicopter could fly in this wind, or if it could, whether it could even land on the damaged MODU.

The phone registered battery strength by the green bars on the three-inch screen. But she could not get a connection with American Energy headquarters on shore, or the Coast Guard emergency number already programmed into the device. Was it the approaching storm? What was wrong? She even tried to dial her home in Erie, Pennsylvania, and her father's cellphone, but didn't get a connection before it failed.

"Look," Sheldon said, attempting to feign some patience. "We have to find another solution. Let's go below deck; we can find some other equipment."

Danielle conceded and followed the pipeline expert down a stairwell. Below one deck they ambled through a cockeyed corridor leaning against one wall like they were in an amusement park funhouse. Danielle wasn't sure, but it seemed like the slant of the platform was increasing again. It didn't seem this hard to walk on deck before.

"We should be able to hail the Coast Guard from the conference room facilities," Sheldon said.

There was no trace of Sheldon's talkative self Danielle observed the first time she met him. Neither was there the impish professional jealously he exhibited around Akmed. He was nervous and terse. His previous sangfroid must be all bravado. He was in the time of crisis a worm of a man. But he was her only companion and she was under his aegis. How could she be critical? He saved her life.

When they turned a corner the entire MODU shifted again, this time like a clunking elevator coming to a halt. The slant in the hallway increased. They could see the door to the conference facilities ahead of them. Sheldon, who must have feared the worst, picked up speed despite the angle of the hallway. He reached the door first and turned the latch. The door did not seem to swing open; it blew open with an explosive deluge. And behind the door came a cataract of water, ice-chilling seawater, flinging Sheldon backward in a rush as if in a cartoon. Danielle turned to flee, but it was like outrunning a train. The torrid rush of fluid swept them both down the corridor like they were rats in a sewer during a flash flood.

The union bargaining with American Energy was a bust. Dan O'Day felt he was not cut out for negotiations—he was a field guy, uncomfortable around stuffed suits. But he followed orders. He was president of the International Gas Workers local and consented to be on the negotiating team. The union was imploding and they were running out of members who were willing to deal with management—all silver-tongued New York lawyers. He flew from Erie to Philadelphia after it was diverted from Washington because of the impending storm, waited in gas lines to fill up his rental car, and paid $25 a gallon for gas at a rip-off state-sanctioned highway service station on the way to Alexandria, Virginia. He was furious. Union funds for such excursions were running low. To top it off, the team of three hired guns from American Energy never showed. The pussy lawyers feared their flights would be cancelled because of the impending hurricane and might not be able to retreat to their Manhattan ivory towers. They might be marooned with a group of union negotiators in a suburban beltway hotel. Horrors!

Now, there were no negotiations and he was in Virginia with two other union buddies with nothing to do other than sop up some suds at the hotel bar. Perhaps he could drop by the White House and ask the president how he and his daughter Danielle got along.

O'Day knocked back a Yuengling in the hotel bar, glassy-eyed, watching CNN on a wall-mounted screen. The weather dominated the news, with reports of orderly evacuations of shoreline areas along the East Coast. The threat of a direct hurricane hit on the mainland passed, but the storm surge was expected to plague low-lying areas. He thought of Danielle. Along with all other personnel of the offshore platform, she surely would have been evacuated by now. He attempted the satellite phone upon arrival, but of course, only received another error message. Hurricanes and tropical storms were regular occurrences in the Gulf of Mexico, and the oil and natural gas industry was ever efficient in clearing the offshore rigs affected by the severe winds and waves. For all he knew, his daughter was probably back in her Central Park apartment gabbing on a landline with her mother.

Suddenly, the happy talk between a weather forecaster and anchor was broken with the words "Breaking News" in capital letters flashed across the screen. O'Day looked up. He could not hear the news reader, but the abbreviated headline below the talking head told him all he needed to know: *Helicopter Missing from Offshore Platform.*

O'Day put down his beer and reached for his cellphone again.

CHAPTER 61

▼

Number four was the island course's signature hole, a par-four dog-leg left with an elevated tee that offered a spectacular view of the Atlantic off the left rough, and North Carolina's Pamlico Bay on the right. Oncoming battleship-gray clouds were pushed by the periphery of the hurricane, hiding the late morning sun. The wind picked up a little during the round, but it provided a little relief from the unusual November heat. Alexandria Raven was a natural athlete just like her husband said. She knew it. She drew a slow and steady backswing and took a powerful sweep at the golf ball propped up on the anti-slice tee her husband provided for her. Still, her shot was a banana ball that cut into the weeds on the right, out of bounds. She grimaced with sudden pain, her hands reaching across her chest. *Such a stupid game,* she thought. She couldn't wait for the excruciating experience to end. Still the view of the ocean from the tee box was breathtaking. The powder-white sand beaches, vacant from the hurricane evacuation, were august from her vantage point as those on an Oceanic island. It must be low tide; the beaches were wide and seemingly stretched forever. Most likely the effect of the hurricane's rip tides, she thought. No time for swimming. The rest of the foursome already hit their balls and she climbed into her husband's electric golf cart. They drove down the fairway to the approximate spot where her ball disappeared. There, in a swell about 100 yards down, she could no longer see the ocean.

"Just drop one anywhere you want," her husband said. "And try to keep your head down. Your swing is great hon, but you don't seem to want to watch the club hit the ball."

Douglas Waters was always locked-and-loaded with gratuitous advice. That was another thing she hated about playing golf with him. But she could not concentrate. Her body ached. And her mind was on the hydrate test. Her cellphone was on the fritz too, probably because of the weather. She wanted updates every hour on the progress of the hydrate extraction, but hadn't heard a thing all morning. Somebody's ass would be in a sling for this. She was sure it was not Danielle O'Day. She followed in step perfectly. It was whoever was next in the communication chain at corporate headquarters in New York. Why hadn't Virgil called her? Hell, she knew why. He was always careful about contacting her. More between them was at stake than two loveless marriages. She would place her own landline call to American Energy headquarters once this interminable game was over. The U.S. Senator and club pro sat silently in their cart across the fairway. They were gentlemen and offered praises when she hit a decent shot and maintained silence when she duffed one. She lined up her second shot and mimicked a practice swing.

It hurt. She was accustomed to the pain. But she was tired. When she first saw her doctor three months ago with complaints of shortness of breath, her meticulous physician ensured that it evolved into a full physical examination.

"Did you notice this lump?" said her doctor as she methodically massaged her breasts. The physician was a mature woman general practitioner who treated her for years.

Raven had, but ignored it. A fatty cyst existed in her right breast since her teenage years. She thought nothing of it. The exam led to blood tests and an MRI. Two weeks later, she was back in the doctor's office for a biopsy based upon the dubious results of all the tests. In another two days after a biopsy, the boom was lowered.

"I'm sorry, Alexandria," Dr. Amanda Kerry, an oncologist, told her. "It's cancer."

Raven did not react; she just stared blankly without emotion.

"We are not sure if it has already moved into your lymph nodes," the cancer expert said. "We have to begin radiation and chemotherapy immediately after a radical mastectomy."

The way the doctor said it, it sounded like she was to undergo the surgery and chemical poisoning like her car was getting an oil change.

"And then what?" Raven asked Dr. Kerry. "My hair falls out, I puke every day, and then I die anyway, right?"

"Well, there are no guarantees; the cancer is very far along. But if we don't do something ..."

"We? Since when is it we? And if *we* do do something, I am basically paralyzed for months, incapacitated with poison in my system, too weak to get out of a chair, unable to keep down food, wasting away."

"I don't like to give survival percentages, because they are almost always wrong," the doctor said flatly. "There are great new drugs out there. But if you don't take action, you will certainly die."

"That is the only certainty we all share," Raven said. "How long can I live a normal life if you don't cut my breast off and inject me with chemicals?"

"I'm not sure. It depends on your pain tolerance. I'm surprised you haven't had more pain already."

Three months? Six months? It might be enough. Enough to say goodbye to her children. Enough to find her successor at American Energy. Enough to reach her goal of assembling an empire that would be envied for generations if it wasn't broken up by a group of capitalist-hating regulators in the federal government. Could she endure?

"I think you should talk to your husband," Dr. Kerry said.

Husband? Raven thought. *That pompous, self-absorbed ass. I need to talk to my attorney to keep that son-of-a-bitch from getting my shares of American Energy after I'm dead. My company.* She knew no one lived forever. But her legacy might. She would stick it out—get the job done, and then maybe consider the medical community's concept of torture for cancer victims.

"Just throw your hands to the hole," her husband said with clenched yellow teeth. He was puffing on a large cigar.

She glanced at him with an infuriating eye. *I'd like to throw you in the fucking ocean,* she thought. She lined up her shot again and drew her club backwards. Just as she began the downward motion toward the ball a siren blared in the distance. Her club came forward and struck the ground six inches behind the ball and she twisted in agony.

"What's going on?" she cried, doubling over with the pain.

"I don't know," her husband said, his head rising to the clamor. "Sounds like the siren they blow if there is lightning on the course." They looked skyward and despite the ominous clouds from the outstretched radius of the hurricane, there was no evidence of an electrical storm.

The club-pro's cart drove over to them, but he was void of answers as well.

"Perhaps the hurricane changed direction again, or a tornado," guessed the pro, a slim man in his late fifties, with a snow-white mustache that matched his ashen hair. That's when they heard it. A roar like a train in the distance rising in crescendo. But in the depressed swell of the fairway they saw nothing except the elevated tee behind them and the elevated green in front. They could not observe the receding surf on the beaches or the emptying of the ocean's basin along the shore. Neither could they see a thirty-foot black wall of seawater as long as the horizon itself approaching the island at a high speed. When the two golf carts climbed out of the swell in the middle of the fairway, the tsunami wave was less than 100 yards away and approaching at a mercurial clip.

"Jesus Christ!" Douglas Waters said, his cigar dropping out of his mouth. "What the fuck is that?"

Alexandria Raven did not answer. Her last conscious thought was how much she really hated golf.

An avalanche of water swept the foursome away, clubs, balls, carts, cigars and all, in the worst water hazard on any golf course in the world.

CHAPTER 62

▼

President Freeman's eyes were riveted to the large television screen in the Oval Office along with thousands, if not millions, of Americans who were watching the major networks during the daytime hours. The president was concerned about panic. He pictured a mad dash of people on the East Coast of the United States rushing inland as if they were fleeing an incoming asteroid. The event would undoubtedly cause injuries and death. A colossal human stampede. How could he avoid it? Then again, it may not happen. The suddenness of a tsunami would not allow for most people to know that disaster was impending. True, the Carolina coasts were more or less evacuated because of the threat of the powerful hurricane offshore. But since the storm careened northward over the ocean, people were champing at the bit to return to their precious seaside escapes. The other uncertainty was the breadth and width of the tsunami wave. According to NOAA, there was no certainty among the scientists that observe such phenomena about how high the potential deadly wave would reach, how wide a swath of shoreline would be affected, or how deep inland it might penetrate. There might be minimum impact if the energy of the wave dissipated before reaching shore.

When the estimated time came, the president held his breath. He was tackled by 250-pound linebackers when he played quarterback for the Naval Academy, wounded by an Iraqi Scud missile in Dhahran in Saudi Arabia during the First Gulf War, and shot in the Kevlar-covered vest he wore by a would-be assassin during his presidential campaign. But none of that scared him more than the unknown, unseen force of nature, which could wield unimaginable ruin. And he may have caused it from an action he ordered from behind the comfort of the highly polished Oval Office desk. *The road to Hell was paved with good intentions,* he thought once again.

Coast Guard and network news helicopters hovered over the shoreline from Virginia to Georgia. To the naked eye, there was not much discernable as the initial undertow increased the width of the beaches on the oceanfront. The surf was high from the winds on the outskirts of the hurricane. There was no deafening roar like an oncoming tornado; the approach was almost silent from a bird's-eye view. The rush of water toward the coast would be barely noticed from above. The underground earthquake was localized the experts told him, only affecting a couple-mile length of the continental shelf—only a little hiccup compared with a natural earthquake. Or so he hoped.

No dunking in a swimming pool or helicopter safety-training exercise prepared Danielle for this. The water rushed over her like a crashing Big Kahuna wave on a Hawaiian beach, tossing her like a wind-blown leaf down the angled corridor. With the tilt of the drilling platform and the cascade of water pouring over her, she had no idea which end was up. The water was numbing cold, paralyzing her attempts to thrash to the top. She prayed for the grip of a lesbian gym teacher to pull her out of her worst nightmare.

When the force of the water struck the end of the hallway, it ricocheted and Danielle swallowed a mouthful of salty seawater. She choked and coughed. Her eyes stung. Her nose burned. She thought she would surely die. After the water filled part of the corridor, it quieted as if it reached some kind of equilibrium and now was settling.

"You okay?" Sheldon asked.

He was standing behind her, also soaked to the bone. Hearing his voice reassured her. Maybe she wouldn't die. At least not yet. The water was only about three-feet deep, allowing Danielle to regain her footing. But it was cold. Paralyzing cold. She thought of the movie *Titanic* she saw many years before where the hero and heroine waded through hip-deep water of the sinking ship like they were in their backyard pool in August. Only in the movies. This was the mid-Atlantic, not the iceberg-floating North Atlantic, but the water was still shockingly frigid. She must get out. She was already losing feeling in her legs as the pins and needles were fading.

"Yeah," she said, almost breathless, gagging. Saltwater up her nose made her sneeze and her nostrils stung. There was a bit of an undertow of flowing water, but fortunately not enough to suck them down the hall.

"This rig is sinking!" Sheldon said.

Perceptive, Danielle thought. She did not have much faith in Sheldon, but he was all she had. "What do we do?" she asked. She tried to keep panic out of her voice. Sheldon appeared to have enough for both of them.

"We have to get out!" he said.

No shit, Sherlock. "We are a hundred miles from shore. What are we going to do, swim?"

"The bathysphere," he said. "We have to get to the bathysphere."

She remembered the little submarine Sheldon told her about. "Can we reach shore in that?"

"No, but it has communication equipment and a GPS locator. The Coast Guard can get a helicopter to us."

"But the hurricane …"

"That's the chance we have to take. If we stay here, we drown." He moved ahead of her in the water-filled corridor. "Let's hope we can get there."

An hour after the tsunami's impact, the president received good news. By the time the wave spread and lost power, in most areas, the rush of water was slightly greater than the surge caused by a powerful tropical storm. Yachts were upended, docks were damaged, some seaside residences flooded, but for much of the coasts, the worst was avoided. However, the Coast Guard reported that a wave with a twenty- to thirty-foot crest pelted the thin islands of the Outer Banks of North Carolina from Cape Hatteras to ten miles north of Kitty Hawk, swamping the pristine beaches and pounding the famous lighthouses with a steep wall of water. After the wave receded, however, the towering landmarks stubbornly stood their ground. But the cresting rush of seawater pummeled the multi-million dollar beach homes on the precarious environmentally delicate archipelago. Casualties were reportedly light, though the next summer tourist season would be in doubt. By the time the wave engulfed the narrow islands, the power of the surge was stemmed. The sand dune Outer Banks acted as a natural breakwall, preventing the incredible power of the tsunami from lashing the mainland with any considerable force. There was damage, but human casualties would be low because virtually everyone evacuated because of the hurricane threat.

The president exhaled when the Coast Guard relayed damage reports on the East Coast. He would live to breathe again. The source of the tsunami, however, if identified to be caused by the hydrate-extraction activity, would mean the death of his administration. He might be impeached, removed from office, and jailed. At this point, he did not want the job anyway. *Damn the know-nothing scientists. Damn the insatiable energy companies. Damn the kooky environmentalists.*

Damn the opportunistic politicians. Damn the gluttonous American energy consumer. Damn the oil and gas Islamic fascist dictators of the Middle East. Damn John D. Rockefeller for getting us hooked on the stuff in the first place. Freeman would rather kill more whales than drill another hole in the ground. He was playing a no-win match. And the game was over.

CHAPTER 63

▼

"C'mon baby," Roger Sheldon grunted. Sweat mixed with seawater dripped from his face.

The pipeline expert twisted a circular handle on the middle of a door that opened into a bay he claimed housed the submersible craft that was used to inspect the underwater pipelines. The door mechanism seemed to be jammed as Sheldon groaned as he strained to open the hatch. His Adam's apple pulsed as if it were a huge pimple come to a head and ready to burst. Danielle stood behind him a couple of paces away, soaking wet and beginning to shiver with incredible chills. Danielle's intestines cramped. She had not eaten much since coming on board, but whatever she ingested seemed to demand to depart one exit or another.

"Is it stuck?" she said, her teeth chattering.

"Tighter than a rat's rectum," Sheldon said, gritting his teeth as he struggled with the wheel.

Danielle was barefoot in ankle-deep water, her flats lost in the deluge a few minutes before. She could no longer feel her feet and her soaked clothes chilled her from top to bottom. The straps of her wet bra chaffed her skin. She braced herself against the wall, ready to bolt the best she could if another cascade of water blew through the door when it was opened. She thought how inane that idea was. She could not outrun the discharge of seawater and what was the point of running? If the two stranded survivors could not escape through the bathysphere, they might as well experience a quick death. Drowning—perhaps her worst fear of the kiss of death—stared her right in the face with lips pursed.

Danielle did not summon bravery from within. She was too tired. She was too cold. She was too numb.

The door latch emitted a hollow clunk and Sheldon flashed a furtive glance at Danielle before he pulled open the heavy steel door. He turned his face away as if to ready himself for an onslaught of water. But nothing happened. He opened the door wider and nothing entered the corridor but relief. In the bathysphere bay, everything was dry and quiet. The little baby-shit-beige submarine could be seen on the other end of the bay, sitting like an obedient Labrador Retriever waiting for its master to throw a stick.

"Thank God," Danielle said.

"Thank me," Sheldon said, his ego-driven confidence returning.

They rushed toward the small underwater craft that was their savior. Sheldon dashed to a computer console and looked over several monitors. He flicked a few switches and waited for visual responses. Lost in the flooded corridors below the deck of the MODU a few moments before, he suddenly looked in his element.

Danielle was shocked at the small size of the escape craft, which looked not much larger than a disk-shaped port-a-potty. "We're both going to fit in that?"

"Unless you plan on swimming," Sheldon said. "Everything seems to be working. We can exit the bay from controls inside the bathysphere."

"But then what?" Danielle asked. She hated to sound like a dissatisfied customer, but she was always playing the devil's advocate. "Where the hell are we going to go in the middle of the friggin' ocean in an oversized tuna can?"

"Hey baby, I know what I'm doing," Sheldon said. "This little sub has state-of-the-art communications on board and it has a bit more range than a jet ski. We can travel out of the path of the storm, send out a distress signal and be picked up by the Coast Guard in calmer waters."

She peered into a small window of the escape vehicle. The sub was more oblong than round, and larger than she thought after peering at it from a different angle. It had air tanks, a little larger than what a scuba diver would strap on his back, attached to the rear of the vehicle. "How long can we survive in that thing?"

"There is plenty of air for both of us for ten hours. That is, if you don't start breathing heavily." He winked at her.

Danielle was startled by Sheldon's abrupt change of personality—from fraidy cat to a boorish cad. *If the only way to get rescued was by this vile creep …*

Sheldon cracked the seal of the hatch to the bathysphere, which popped with the expulsion of air from inside like the opening of a soda-pop can.

"Leaving so quickly, Mr. Sheldon?" The voice was deep. Resonant. And it scared the hell out of Danielle. Her guts twisted again like she consumed tainted oysters. Both spun to see the Lincolnesque frame of Akmed Abram standing about ten feet behind them. His face was taut, drained of emotion. His princely dark eyes that Danielle fell for now seemed as lifeless as a shark's dead stare. In his hand, the Palestinian geophysicist carried the largest wrench Danielle ever saw—it was the size of a bass guitar. Akmed—an infiltrating terrorist according to Sheldon—brandished the four-foot-long tool like a double-bladed ax carried by a Middle-earth dwarf as described by J.R.R. Tolkien.

Dan O'Day waited as patiently in a public reception area of the shoreline compressor station as he did in the gasoline line back home in Erie, Pennsylvania. He paced the room, fuming, firing glances outward at the helipad site to see if another helicopter landed. There was nothing. Nothing but mud and small pieces of debris. It looked like the hurricane storm surge hit American Energy's compressor station and soaked it with sludge, flotsam, and jetsam.

"What the hell happened here?" O'Day asked a compressor-station worker, who gave no answer. The station was manned by a skeleton crew because of the hurricane evacuation. However, such an important energy facility could not be totally abandoned. But no one was giving him the time of day.

The facility, co-operated by American Energy and National Gas and Electric, was the main natural gas compressor station in southeast Virginia that would accept fuel coming from the offshore kelp-to-gas project. It was only an hour drive from his Alexandria, Virginia, hotel. He called Danielle's satellite phone again, but he still could not get through. *What a waste of a thousand bucks*, he thought. Then, O'Day contacted a union official at the compressor station and found that most of the evacuees of the offshore platform were being brought there. The facility looked as if it were still under construction. The station contained just a few innocuous blue-steel buildings that housed the compressor engines that would push the new supply of gas to the marketplace. Several rows of large pipes and bulbous valves stuck partially out of the ground like half-buried fingers of a giant's curled hand. Still, compared with the sprawling LNG facility a few miles away with its leviathan LNG storage tanks, it looked like a Popsicle stand by the side of the road. Though a half-mile inland, it appeared as if an ocean wave just broke over the grounds and then receded. The air smelled of salt and burnt matches.

Moments before, O'Day berated another worker demanding to talk to someone in management at the facility. When an official-looking shirt-and-tie representative of the company entered the room, O'Day pounced on him.

"Where the hell are the remaining evacuees? Where's my daughter?"

"Excuse me, who are you sir?" the man answered. He was about forty, with greasy black hair and a hooknose that supported oval, librarian-style, plastic-rimmed eyeglasses. He wore a plastic name badge listing his name and position with American Energy. He was a supervisor named Howard Allen.

"Dan O'Day," he said. "President of the IGW in Erie, Pennsylvania. My daughter was on that offshore rig and I was told she would probably be on the next chopper. I've been here an hour and I haven't seen anything land on that pad out there."

"Sir," the foreman said, looking at a sheet that contained some kind of list. "All hourly personnel have been accounted for. She must be here someplace."

"She's not hourly personnel. She's not in my union, she's an American Energy senior vice president." He said it not with his usual contempt for management; he said it with a tone like *My daughter attends an Oxford College on a Rhodes' scholarship.*

"Oh," Allen said. He glanced at his list again that he cradled like a baby. "There are a few people who have not arrived as of yet. According to the Coast Guard, there is one helicopter that has not returned."

"Well, where the hell is it? The TV news says there's a chopper missing—what gives?"

"We aren't sure sir. There seems to be some type of communication problem. We've had an unusual storm surge from the hurricane that knocked out our primary power. We're running on generators."

O'Day looked outside. The wind blew with gusts that ranged from thirty- to forty-miles-per-hour, he guessed. He glared at the supervisor—his eyes were shifty. They looked away from his stare. There was something he was holding back.

"Hey buddy—I've got friends who flew choppers in Iraq. They can't fly safely in this kind of weather. Are you suggesting that it crashed or something?"

"Oh no, sir," Allen said. "We don't have any information of the sort. The helicopter may have picked up its passengers and headed somewhere else to land because of the weather."

O'Day again looked outside. *Where the hell were they going to land that wasn't affected by the storm? This place is a disaster. If it was this bad on shore, what was it like off shore?*

"Where?" O'Day asked.

"I can't give you any more information sir, we just don't know. We haven't even received any confirmation that the passengers were even picked up."

"You mean to tell me they may still be out there in the middle of the fucking ocean in a hurricane?"

"I'm not saying anything sir, I just don't know." The supervisor's walkie-talkie burbled. He answered. "A what?" Allen said into a phone.

O'Day perked up, hearing the shouting voice on the phone as clear as day.

"That wasn't a storm surge, there's been a fucking tsunami."

CHAPTER 64

▼

"Akmed," Sheldon said with false bravado. "Are you ready for your final instructions?"

Who is this guy kidding? Danielle looked at the geophysicist with a mixture of trepidation and relief.

"Akmed!" she said. Her voice was burning with tenderness *and* fear hoping to placate Akmed. She trusted him. He cannot be evil. "What's going on?"

Akmed inched forward toward the two of them, gripping the mammoth metal tool in his hands that was ordinarily used to manually open pipeline valves.

"You cannot leave in the bathysphere," Akmed said, his voice low and controlled.

"Oh I can't?" Sheldon said. The pipeliner's tone was arrogant, annoyed. "Well, I just got word that Allah says you can't either. You were waiting for your final instructions from your buddy Omar, so here they are."

Danielle stared at Sheldon, confused. *Omar?* She had no idea what Sheldon was talking about. Sheldon moved in front of her, suddenly chauvinistic and courageous.

"Get in the hatch," Sheldon said. "I'll take care of him."

Danielle did not want to go. She did not understand. There must be a mistake. Akmed cannot be who Sheldon says he is. But if he was, how could the pipeline manager confront him? Akmed was wielding a makeshift weapon, an immense one that certainly could crack their skulls like a sledgehammer on walnuts. Sheldon was unarmed and acted like a pansy a short time before.

Sheldon reached inside his tan work vest and unveiled a small steel-blue semi-automatic handgun. Danielle recognized the square-ish design from her father's weapon collection that she detested, but learned the names of anyway—it was a SIG-Sauer—compact, rectangular, with a short butt handle, supposedly a favorite sidearm for police SWAT teams and government agencies. Sheldon pointed the weapon at Akmed, directed his voice to Danielle, and spoke in a terse, authoritative tone.

"I'm with the CIA," Sheldon said to her in a whisper. "I'll protect you, but you must get in the bathysphere now." He turned toward the Palestinian. "I'll handle Akmed."

"The woman stays here," Akmed said, his voice louder than before, again creeping forward as if to listen to the whispered speech between the two, his piercing eyes locked on Sheldon. Danielle froze. She was paralyzed by confusion. Everything was happening too fast. She always acted on impulse. Her proclivity to make snap decisions almost always turned out better than the ones she agonized over for months. It took her a year of inner-debate to decide to marry the Wall Street broker. It was a fiasco. She decided to leave him on a whim and it was the best thing that had ever happened to her. She had no evidence, no basis for trust in this mysterious foreigner who bewitched her. He looked fierce now with a deadly weapon in his hands, seemingly not afraid of death. But she felt she possessed some power to cure whatever went wrong. She could fix the misunderstanding with reason, with compassion, with love. *I am turning into my goddamn mother!* she thought.

"If you want to live," Sheldon shouted at her, "get in the fucking sub!"

"If *you* want to go," Akmed said only to Sheldon, "then go. But the woman stays with me."

Sheldon grabbed Danielle, roughly, pulling her toward the hatch of the bathysphere. It didn't feel like a protective action. It felt like the perfidious pipeline director seized her as a hostage.

Danielle thought of her Tae Bo fitness classes and basic self-defense training at her health club. A single woman in Manhattan must know how to defend herself or be fresh meat for the wormy wackos that slithered through the streets of the Big Apple. The instructors demonstrated defending oneself against guns and knives, but the weapons were made of rubber then. Her heart drummed like a power-riveter. A kick in the knee, shins, or instep will immobilize the strongest attacker. *Don't go for the groin,* her instructor lectured. Men instinctively protect that vital region. It's now or never. She kicked as hard as she could at Sheldon's instep with her bare heel. It worked. Sheldon screamed in agony, his leg retreating backward and his torso tipping forward, losing his grip on Danielle. Then, with both hands clasped together like a hammer, she chopped Sheldon's right forearm with every ounce of force she could muster with her flesh-and-bone tomahawk. The SIG-Sauer flew out his hands like a football fumbled by a blindsided quarterback, clanking on the metal floor and sliding under a console, out of sight. Danielle knew how to handle guns—her father made sure of that. But she wanted no part of it. She exhibited enough daring for one moment. Besides, at a cursory glance, she had no idea where the discarded weapon went. She darted toward Akmed, her heart in her throat. The geophysicist raised the wrench and Danielle braced herself. *Why did I do this?* As she reached Akmed, he shifted the wrench on his shoulder and seized Danielle against the side of his body. She hugged him, hiding her head, preparing to receive a deadly blow.

Sheldon seethed, furious, almost insanely jealous rather than worried for her safety.

"Aren't you getting forty-plus virgins in Paradise or something for this Akmed?" Sheldon said. "What do you want with her now?"

"And what are you getting?" Akmed said. "Did you sell your soul for forty pieces of silver?"

"Yeah, Akmed, a lot of fucking silver, my friend. And I thought until a minute ago, a few fringe benefits. But you can have the bitch for your trip to Allah's Motel 6. She's a cold fish anyway."

Danielle hugged Akmed and he struggled to hold the heavy wrench with one arm while gripping her with the other. He had not struck her. Now he shielded her with a fatherly caress. It was the touch of a man she so much desired. Sheldon looked frantically for his weapon, and then gave up.

"Okay, Akmed," Sheldon snarled, "Here's the rub, baby. Your mission is to stay right here. You don't have to do anything. You don't have to wrestle with your conscience. You don't have to lift a finger or strap a bomb on your back and blow up a bunch of school kids like the rest of you fucking cowards. You are to be a loyal captain, Akmed. Your mission is: *go down with the ship.*"

Akmed returned a bitter glare at Sheldon, feet steady, but hands fumbling with the heavy wrench. Danielle never saw his eyes like this. They radiated hate like laser beams.

"Don't you want to know why, Akmed?" Sheldon said.

Akmed said nothing, but pushed Danielle behind him as if Sheldon were going to discharge a weapon and he wanted to catch the bullet.

Sheldon sported a miscreant's grin. "Omar wants proof so they can take responsibility. Omar wants to show the West that he has them by the balls. But he didn't trust you and neither did I. He felt you would chicken out at the last moment, and he was right. But what Omar doesn't realize is that he underestimates the West. Just like your buddy Osama. Once this gets out the U.S. government is going to blow all you fuckers off the map. There will be war, just as Omar wants. But you know what, you stupid raghead? America doesn't lose wars that affect its vital national interests." Sheldon laughed like he heard the funniest joke in the universe. "This ain't Vietnam or Iraq. Just ask the Germans. Ask the Japanese. Ask the fucking Sioux, Cherokees, and Apaches. The United States doesn't negotiate with enemies to its existence—it eliminates them. You morons think the Israelis are tough? Does the name *Hiroshima* mean anything to you? How about *Dresden*? Okay, that was the Brits, but you get the idea. I hope you are happy with your homeland once it is turned into radioactive dust. And no matter how many LNG tankers you blow up or how many offshore platforms are sabotaged, there will always be more. My pipelines will still be intact after this dump sinks to the ocean floor and I'll move them along to the next job. Now, if you would excuse me, I have a sub to catch."

Sheldon vaulted through the hatch of the bathysphere and slammed the door behind him. In a moment, there was a buzzer sounding, almost like a truck backing up. A conveyer belt under the bathysphere lurched into action, and the hockey-puck-shaped submarine crept backward toward the flooding chamber.

"You have to stop him," Danielle said to Akmed, pulling at his shirt. "That's our only way out!"

"I do not believe he will get far," Akmed said quietly. He said this dispassionately, without a hint of emotion.

Danielle gazed into Akmed's eyes that she once thought so alluring and compassionate, but now were the shady color of death. Akmed turned her around to exit the bathysphere bay. And there she saw the sprawled body of Cowboy lying near a doorway, unconscious, if not dead. Then, she saw another figure. It was face down on the deck of the room, a pool of blood surrounding the upper torso. Though Danielle could not see the face, it was easy to tell who it was. It was the tall, soft-spoken African-American scientist, Dr. Cory Roystone. The side of his head was caved in and scarlet blood and white brains oozed out everywhere. Danielle felt vomit crawl up her throat. She trusted her instincts and now was in Akmed's control. She gambled on her guts that he would not harm her. Maybe she bet wrong.

CHAPTER 65

▼

"Mr. President," said General Wells, the DCI. "There is a security problem aboard the offshore platform."

"No shit," the president replied.

"We have an informant on board, and his last transmission reveals that the platform may have been sabotaged."

"I think your intelligence is a bit tardy," President Freeman responded. "We suspect the offshore vessel and perhaps your informant is on the bottom of the ocean."

The DCI stared, openmouthed. "That would be unfortunate."

"Quite."

The CIA chief appeared embarrassed. This was only the second time since becoming the head of the spy agency he addressed the president in the Oval Office. Freeman almost felt sorry for him. The president was never friendly to the agency, and despite the Company was now run by a military man, he wasn't warming up to it now. Several others in the room remained silent including Freeman's head national security advisor, chief of staff, and secretary of defense.

"And the saboteur?" the president asked.

"We can point the finger at none other than the geophysicist, Akmed Abram. According to Israeli agents, he recently met with Palestinian terrorists bent on scuttling the new Israeli-Palestinian peace. They are in league with the loose coalition of Islamic militants who are controlling several Mid-East governments. Probably the same ones who blew up the LNG tanker."

"How did this happen?" Freeman said, pounding his desk as if answers would splat out from under his hand.

"I can't answer that," the CIA chief said.

The secretary of defense cleared his throat. "But there is one unquestionable fact," said Jerry Van Nostrand in his hoarse army-general voice.

Freeman stared at him.

"This, Mr. President, is an act of war."

"And who do we retaliate against?" the president said. "A dead terrorist at the bottom of the ocean? Or should I just lob a cruise missile at Mecca during Ramadan and call us square?"

The defense secretary was silent. Now, the national security advisor spoke.

"Mr. President," said Arias Applebaum. The president looked at Applebaum's shiny black hair with its distinguishing band of white weaving through it. He did look like a skunk. "We have always known it would come down to this. The free world is powered by energy. Oil fuels 95 percent of cars, trucks, and planes. Our military is propelled by fossil fuels. Our economy is dependent on affordable oil and gas. We have paid out the ying-yang for the Arab's oil for a half a century. We've given them money. We've given them weapons. Our soldiers have died to preserve their backward regimes. They must understand that we will not tolerate blackmail and extortion any longer. Look what they've done to us!"

The D-Boys at the Pentagon may not be fond of conducting war, the president thought, *but they seem to love to plan them.*

"We have brought this upon ourselves," Freeman said, standing and ambling toward a window in the legendary office. "We've meddled in the petro-states since World War I and what has it got us? Most of them still live in the fourteenth century but soon all will have twenty-first-century weapons. We've done what we could to help these decentralized tribal states modernize and show them the light of democracy. At the same time we have become addicted to their only worthwhile natural resource. We literally stole it from them for years until they wised up in the 'seventies and refused to be taken for granted anymore. Unfortunately, we didn't wise up as well and now are pressured to either kick their ass in all-out war, or put up a wall like the Israelis and somehow survive on our own in a glass bubble. Now we've seen how that has turned out."

He flung his arms in futility, and then returned to his desk. He spoke directly to his advisors' faces.

"In our shrinking world, we can do neither," the president said.

"We must defeat our enemies, Mr. President," the defense head said flatly.

"Yes," the president said. He thought of the terrorists. He pondered his domestic rivals in Congress like August Doggle. He shook his head when he reflected on the environmental kook "Hurricane" Herbie Winkle and the self-serving consumer advocate Olga Stevick. He dreaded judging the military plan he would be presented by the Pentagon that spelled out the seizure of oil and natural gas fields in the Middle East, Africa and Caspian Sea, indiscriminate bombing campaigns, and the death of young intrepid soldiers thousands of miles away. He thought of Cowboy, who always had something to prove, and now may be a victim of his own adventurism.

"Yes," the president repeated. "But we first need to determine not who are enemies are. But who our enemies aren't."

Danielle broke from Akmed's side and leapt to the fallen gas driller. She touched Cowboy's shoulders, gingerly at first, and then attempted to roll the body over to see if it was still warm and breathing.

"What did you do to him?" Danielle shouted.

"I hit him and knocked him out."

"Why?" Danielle said. "Why are you doing this? You said you were a peaceful man, Akmed. You convinced me you were sincere. And I believed you. I made love to you!" She started to sob, angrily.

"And I am," Akmed said. He dropped the large metal wrench and it crashed to the hard floor with a piercing clang. Behind them, doors closed in front of the bathysphere and the launching chamber filled with water. Danielle started to stand as if to make another attempt to flee, but Akmed grasped her shoulders with his long, powerful fingers. She pointed at the dead body of Dr. Roystone. "Did you kill him?"

"No," Akmed said. "I did hit Cowboy, but it was an accident. But Dr. Roystone was dead when I arrived here."

"What?" she said. She did not know what to believe anymore.

"Sheldon attacked me. I had just recovered consciousness and I was confused. I mistook Cowboy for Sheldon. I-I have never seen Cowboy without his hat on for years."

Danielle turned to the still body of Cowboy. He was hatless, balding, and was dressed in colors similar to Sheldon. She remembered the gust of wind that tore the Stetson from Cowboy's head and how she and Dr. Edison laughed about it. The swashbuckling gas explorer now looked pathetic without it like Samson minus his hair.

"Who are you?" Danielle asked Akmed. "Who is Omar?"

"There are many things I want to tell you," Akmed said. "But there is no time. This facility is damaged beyond repair and will probably sink. We have to get you out of here."

Cowboy's silent body stirred. He moaned.

"We have to get both of you out of here," Akmed added.

"Is it true?" Danielle said. "Is it true what Sheldon said about you?"

"Mr. Sheldon is a traitor to your government, who has accepted money to destroy this project. And he has succeeded."

"But who are *you* Akmed?" she said, touching her fingers to his face, staring into his eyes, that still after all this time, were reluctant to return her gaze.

"I am your friend," he said. "But I have done evil things in the past. And I will face Allah soon for my sins. Now help me with Cowboy. We must find our way to the deck for your rescue."

"I don't think that's going to work," Danielle said. "The winds are too strong, the helipad is destroyed—the last helicopter fell in the sea. I don't think anyone else will come."

"They must come," Akmed said.

"I couldn't reach anyone on my satellite phone, and when Sheldon and I tried to reach the surface again, the halls were flooded."

Akmed shook his head, seemingly looking for a solution in his brilliant mind that somehow eluded him.

"Is there another bathysphere?" Danielle asked.

"No."

Akmed sat on the floor, with obvious ennui.

Danielle thought. Was their victory over Sheldon a Pyrrhic one? Out of the frying pan and into the fire, or in this case, water? She always came up with a solution on the job. It was one of the reasons for her meteoric rise in the company. Snap decisions in a blink. For her, they were always the best ones. Yes, they wanted to promote women, and maybe she was being manipulated because her father was a big shot in the union. Maybe Raven and her ilk thought they could use her to soften up the union boys. If she did, Raven underestimated her obstinate son-of-a-bitch father. But she was smart, damn it. She cursed at herself. *So think of a way to get out of this one. C'mon you bitchy descendent of Daniel O'Day, the great pipeline pioneer.*

That is when it hit her.

"Akmed!" she said.

He raised his head. He looked like a lost dog.

"The pipeline!" she said. "It's still intact, right?"

"Yes."

"Can't we get out of here through the pipeline? It runs all the way to the shore, right?"

"But how?"

"That contraption, the pipeline pig. Dr. Edison said the line that was supposed to bring the carbon dioxide wasn't being utilized. Sheldon said it was possible to go all the way through the line with the pig and we could fit on the back of it, just like he said."

"Underwater? Well, I guess that could be physically possible if the line was raised closer to the surface. You cannot travel on the sea bottom—the pressure would be too great."

"So let's bring it up—Sheldon said it could be raised."

"If the process is still operational, yes."

"Do we have some breathing apparatus on board? It might get a bit stuffy in there."

"Yes, we could find some, I'm sure. You could not survive without it. But how would you get out of the line?"

Danielle reached down to the satellite phone on her belt. "With this. Once we travel to the shoreline, we can call for help. We'll be at or near ground level and this phone should then work. It has a GPS on it as well. According to my dad, rescuers would be able to locate us within five meters. They would be able to get us out somehow."

Icy water suddenly streamed over their feet. They both directed their attention to the doorway, which was now the mouth of the cold river flowing into the room. The sinking rig was filling up with seawater. Cowboy's moribund frame suddenly flipped over like a reeled-in fish on the bottom of a boat, apparently revived by the chilly water washing over him.

"Ohhhh," he moaned. His eyelids flickered and he was partly conscious.

"Cowboy?" Danielle said. "Are you okay?"

Cowboy mumbled something like he was talking in his sleep and then said clearly, "Get that son-of-a-bitch with the wrench."

PART VII

▼

REDEMPTION

CHAPTER 66

▼

Roger Sheldon's hands gripped the large rubber-tipped joystick that controlled his fate. He piloted the bathysphere on numerous occasions in the past, inspecting the underwater pipeline for corrosion, damage to the linings, and stress cracks. Usually he functioned as a glorified copilot with a professional nautical engineer at the helm—safety regulations. But the bathysphere was as easy to navigate as a go-cart, his pilot confessed to him. He gave Sheldon the joystick to drive himself most of the time.

The transfer tank rapidly filled with seawater and once equal pressure was obtained, the outer door to the launching bay opened. Sheldon pressed a lever in front of him that dislodged the lock that secured the bathysphere to the bottom of the bay and then guided the joystick backward like he was carefully backing out of his two-and-a-half car garage in Houston in his Lincoln Navigator. Sheldon regretted not having the other seat in the subsea vehicle filled with the derrière of the redhead lawyer whose butt he had been eyeing for days, but he had to cut his losses. *Stupid bitch*, he thought. *She would drown with that idiot Akmed. The world lost a nice piece of ass. But there were other fish in the sea.* He would be so rich thanks to that dunce Omar and his brethren, he would never have to worry about rejection by women again. He could marry and divorce a different woman every week and afford the alimony for the rest of his days.

Sheldon rationalized his actions. He was not anti-American. He was not a foreign spy. He could care less about Mid-East nationalism or Islamic extremism. He was for free trade. America was trying to disrupt the petro-states from achieving economic progress. The hydrates project would only make a few corporate heads rich while destroying the worldwide oil industry as a result. Those nations would only be stable as long as they had a commodity to trade.

Sheldon spent seven years as a CIA operative, passing along what he felt was critical intelligence to the U.S. government when he worked in Arab countries designing and building pipeline systems, including the Palestinian gas pipeline in the Mediterranean. Then, Langley cut him off. His handlers felt the information he provided was inane. They needed real intelligence, not someone who echoed the formal proclamations of OPEC ministers they could glean from CNN. The Company promised him much, but didn't deliver. The real reason they let him go, he surmised, is that he questioned orders. He disputed government policy. The numbskulls at Langley didn't know the first thing of how to deal with the Arabs, Sheldon thought. *Those ignorant bastards.* They ignored him. Then a mysterious Palestinian with plenty of cash in hand approached him, and then he decided to come in from the cold. Dumb fucks at the Farm should have killed him, not fired him. He thought they might try anyway. Sheldon decided to give the CIA one last tip as instructed by Omar, revealing there was a terrorist on board the *China Maiden*. Sheldon knew that the terrorists would accomplish their goal one way or another. With millions of dollars in his pipeline construction company tied up in projects in the Middle East, the hydrate project not only threatened the future of petroleum, but also his livelihood. War or not, Sheldon decided to place his bets on both sides of the table.

And then came Akmed—the jerk who cost his company millions of dollars back in the North Sea *dash for gas*. It figured that he was linked to the terrorists. But he knew the princely Palestinian had a yellow streak in him, and he couldn't carry it out. He was ready to head out of the compressor room when Akmed confronted him. They argued.

"You must allow the carbon dioxide line to run at full capacity," Akmed told him.

"Akmed—it's the hurricane—the pipeline is not operational," Sheldon answered. It was a thin lie, and the Sheik wasn't buying.

"It will destroy the test—it could cause destabilization. It is dangerous."

"It's time for me to fly, Saheeb."

The Palestinian looked at him like a dumb mutt.

"Get out of my way or else," Sheldon said. He retrieved a huge pipeline wrench off the wall to take the pusillanimous terrorist out, and what did Akmed do?

He fainted. He just plain passed out like the chicken of the sea he was. Omar told him as much ahead of time. *Don't count on Akmed—he is not a soldier.* So

Sheldon left him there—*the stupid sot*. He should have bashed his brains in right then and there like he did that meddling nigger Roystone. But he didn't expect the MODU to be damaged so quickly. If it wasn't for the hurricane, there would be no plans for evacuation. Coincidences.

As the bathysphere cleared the hull of the *China Maiden*, the only light that Sheldon could see was from the two bright halogen headlights of the oblong craft that glowed eerily through the dark, greenish ocean. He moved away from the mother ship as quickly as possible in case the rig collapsed with another landslide on the sea floor. With the hurricane churning up the surface, he would have to remain underwater for hours. Still, Sheldon turned on the GPS locating beacon that signaled a SOS. He wanted to inform those on shore that he was alive and well. After several minutes aboard the bathysphere, Sheldon unbuttoned his shirt. He felt stuffy and warm, probably from the excitement of his escape. He looked at a temperature monitor on the helm. It read ninety-two degrees. No, it wasn't just him. It was stifling hot inside the cabin. The air was dank, almost moldy. He coughed. There was no airflow at all in the craft. No oxygen was being fed into the bathysphere. He was breathing the stale ambient air inside the small sub and now was sucking in his own breath like his head was inside a big balloon. He became light-headed. Where was the air? He reached for a dial on the control board that regulated oxygen from the outside tanks on board. It was turned off. He flipped the dial on the airflow mechanism. A loud hiss emitted as pressurized air was released from tanks attached to the rear of the craft. Sheldon breathed deeply. It was not oxygen.

"What the hell?" Sheldon choked.

Whatever pumped into the bathysphere was not meant for human lungs. Sheldon gagged. It was sour, choking, bitter air. It smelled like a burning match. It tasted like the flavor of Hell. Sheldon coughed on the acrid air. It was not oxygen flowing into the airspace, it was a noisome stench that stung his eyes and burned his throat. It was sickening. *Sulfur*, Sheldon thought. *How can this be?* The burning, strangling gas pouring into the airspace—hydrogen sulfide—made him feel as if he were eating fire.

Sheldon opened his mouth to scream, but he no longer had breath to expel. His hands grasped his aching throat and the moist flesh inside felt as if it were melting. He fell backward in his chair, his feet kicking the control board ahead of him. He tried to turn off the airflow with a sweeping move of one hand, but he missed, his vision cloudy and fading. He stumbled off the chair and onto the floor of the small craft, writhing and kicking in his last throes. His lurching leg kicked the joystick of the bathysphere forward, leading the subsea vehicle into a plunging dive. Sheldon vomited over and over again and his strength soon drained. His vomit now became filled with bright crimson blood heaved over himself and the floor of the craft as he slipped away from consciousness.

The bathysphere continued its descent with no one at the helm, led by two bright, but lifeless eyes, tumbling deep into the abyss.

"To what do I owe this honorable visit?" said Congressman Doggle, almost snorting.

Thaddeus Mann, the president's chief of staff, sat across from Doggle, thumping a legal-size manila envelope in his hand. Mann knew the powerful legislator since the Iowa politician was first elected. They were old comrades in the Congress, though he never really liked him much. But it was the time for rapprochement, not contention.

"Congressman," Mann said, an air of dignified respect in his voice. "The president sends his best and he hopes we can find agreement on this energy bill that seems to be keeping us all up at night."

"I sleep like a baby," Doggle said.

"With the terrorist attack off the Virginia shore, I'm sure you know the intelligence agencies, Department of Homeland Security, FBI, and CIA are working overtime."

Doggle looked irritated. Mann knew the congressman was a direct person and did not like his time wasted.

"What does this have to do with the energy bill?" Doggle asked.

Mann slipped a photograph out of the manila envelope and held it up to Doggle. "You, of course, know this gentleman."

It was a picture of Herbert Winkle.

"Of course," Doggle said. "He's the environmental advocate. Thinks he's the spiritual son of Ralph Nadar and Erin Brokovich. What does that have to do with me?"

"The FBI has been investigating foreign influence in domestic social and environmental movements, specifically, following the dollars of foreign money that may be subsidizing domestic political lobbying."

Doggle didn't react.

"And," Mann continued. "We've identified that the ANGER group accepted contributions from groups linked to terrorist activity."

"He's a little one-eyed, stuttering weasel," Doggle said. "But he's no terrorist. C'mon, Mr. Mann, in the midst of this national energy crisis and a tsunami striking our shores, doesn't the president have better things to do than spy on nerdy publicity seekers."

"The FBI is going to publicly announce the investigation, and we wanted you to be aware of it, knowing your recent partnering with the ANGER leader."

"Partnering?" Doggle said. "I've talked with him, but I've met with hundreds of interested parties on the energy bill."

"You may want to take a peek at these," Mann said. He turned the envelope he was holding upside down and several photographs spilled out. He handed the pictures to Doggle, who wheezed while leaning over his desk to accept them.

Doggle was silent for about a minute, examining the photographs one by one, often tilting them ninety degrees as if a different perspective would clarify the images. Finally, the Congressman tossed the photos back at Mann and snorted. Mann did not retrieve the pictures from the front of the desk.

"So, what is this supposed to prove?" Doggle said.

"As you noticed, everyone in the photos is identified. They show Mr. Winkle accepting money from lobbyists connected with the Chinese, Russian, Saudi, Venezuelan, and Iranian governments. We have videotape as well. Those who support his organization in the United States may believe they are doing the world a favor. But in reality, they are only playing in the hands of governments who want to see the power of the United States weakened. Without oil, coal, and natural gas, the U.S. will be only a toothless remnant of an economic power. Do you want to be associated with Mr. Winkle when he is exposed for what he is—a front for radical Islamic governments and our fellow fair-weather friendly commie superpowers who would like to see America, as Ronald Reagan might have said, on the *ash heap of history?*"

Doggle didn't flinch. "I have very little connection with Winkle's environmental group. I don't see how this affects me."

Mann slipped out another smaller six-by-nine-inch manila envelope from a vest pocket and tapped it on his fingers.

"What's that?" Doggle asked. It appeared to Mann that Doggle increased his interest as the corpulent congressman leaned forward in his chair. The chair's wheels squeaked like the sound of a door opening in a haunted house.

"In the course of the investigation, I'm told, the FBI also collected some seemingly irrelevant evidence that has nothing to do with Winkle or his connection with several members of Congress. When I became aware of what was uncovered, I knew right away that neither the bureau nor the Freeman administration wanted to reveal too much. It could become, let us say, embarrassing to several individuals."

"What's in the envelope?" Doggle asked point blank.

"Something that both of us would rather not see the light of day," Mann answered. "And I'm sure for the benefit of all, we can bury the hatchet and reach agreement on this energy bill."

Doggle stared at Mann with a poker face and Mann returned the glare, neither moving a facial muscle. Whatever was in the envelope seemed to give Doggle thought to pause. Or would he think it was a bluff? Doggle was in Congress for a long time, and he had a colorful history on and off the House floor—who knows whose bones an FBI probe might dig up?

Doggle heaved a wheezing sigh and said, "I didn't think President Freeman played these games, Mr. Mann."

"Not the president," Mann replied. "This is just between you and me congressman, old classmates who care about this great institution."

"And if I call your bluff?"

"If I open this sealed envelope here, congressman, we'll both know the contents. And you know all about these darn leaks in Washington."

After a few moments, the haunted-house-door-opening squeal howled again, this time like a tape of the sound in reverse as the fat man leaned back in his chair. "For the good of the country, I am willing to bend a bit … if the president does," Doggle said, his eyes not leaving Mann's.

"That's the spirit of compromise," Mann said, returning the envelope back into his vest, unopened. "The president wants to see all interested parties get what they most want."

"Twenty billion for the biofuel development project."

"How about ten?"

"Fifteen."

"With no demand for public hearings on the Atlantic Outer Continental Shelf gas-gathering system?"

"I can't promise that," Doggle said. "The cat's already out of the bag."

"Well, the president will look for your support to develop this most important resource."

"We need the energy," Doggle said, grinning. "We cannot depend on corn alone."

"Thank you, congressman."

When Mann left Doggle's inner office he smiled at a pretty brunette secretary with petite, rectangular-framed dark eyeglasses. He pulled the small, unopened manila envelope out of his pocket.

"Excuse me," he said, well out of Doggle's earshot. "Would you mind throwing this in the trash?"

"Sure," she said, taking the thin envelope and tossing it in a wastebasket adjacent to her desk.

Mann thanked her, engaged in a bit of small talk, and then left the Sam Rayburn Office Building to return to the White House. Mann wondered what went on in Doggle's mind. He didn't demand to see the contents of the envelope. How could he possibly know what was in it and if it was worth capitulating on the energy bill? What did he have to protect? His image? His reputation? His congressional seat? His unknown actions that may be less than legal? If you thought about it, it was scary. But whatever it was, it did not matter a hill of beans to Mann. He reached consensus with the major force in Congress that was holding up the legislation. And it was worth it. No, the president didn't play by these games. He was a lily-white Beaver Cleaver who played by the rules. But the president will never know. He will be relieved that Doggle decided to play ball. It will be just one of those mysteries of lawmaking. Mann smiled. He was glad to be on the side of Nathaniel Patrick Freeman, the most honest man he ever met. But the young president still had a few things to learn about power. And poker. Mann thought about the envelope and its mystery that seemed very clear to Congressman August Doggle. It will have to remain mysterious for now. Because what Mann deposited in the trash of Doggle's office was just an envelope. An empty envelope. There was nothing in it. And there never was.

CHAPTER 67

▼

"Three of us cannot fit on there," Danielle warned, frowning at the back of the pipeline pig. Perhaps her idea was pie in the sky.

"I'm not sure two of us can," Cowboy added, grunting, his arm in a makeshift sling that Danielle rigged up in a hurry with, of all things, her bra. Cowboy said his shoulder might be dislocated.

"You two can fit, and you will," Akmed said. He pointed toward an adjacent doorway. "There are pressurized masks with oxygen tanks available in the emergency compartment on that far wall. Get them quickly."

"Akmed," said Danielle.

"I am not going, Danielle," he said.

"We are not leaving you here."

"We can make it work somehow," said Cowboy.

"Impossible," Akmed said. "The pipeline seal must be closed from the inside. There is no way to pressurize the pig through the line without the seal. Someone must stay behind, and it must be me."

"I run this rig," Cowboy said. "I guess you can say I'm the captain. So what I say goes."

"If I could go with you, I would not survive."

"Who says?"

Akmed looked downward and expelled a sigh. "My friend, I knew of the plan to sabotage this platform. I was asked to participate. Though I decided against it, I knew I was not the only one on board."

"We can get you out of this," Cowboy said. "We'll vouch for you."

"If I am allowed to repatriate to Palestine, I will be killed along with my remaining relatives. If I get to America or England, I will be arrested and my relatives will be killed anyhow. If I stay here, you can escape, and my family in Palestine might remain safe. It is the only alternative."

"There has to be a better way, Akmed."

Akmed gently placed both of his palms on Cowboy's shoulders. "Many years ago, I faced a similar choice. I made a choice of death but Allah would not permit me to be a killer or be killed. He had other plans. I believe the Almighty One spared me for a larger purpose. That is, not to sacrifice my life to kill innocents, but, as the prophet Jesus said, *lay down my life for my friends.* Now I must make that choice."

Cowboy was speechless. Tears filled Danielle's eyes. Frigid seawater was now up to their calves and rising by the second.

They retrieved the oxygen masks and small connecting tanks and Akmed reviewed how they operated and what the two would experience inside the pipeline on the mechanical pig.

"Goodbye, my friends," Akmed said with the first relaxed smile he showed to anyone since perhaps his childhood. "And remember my brother," Akmed said to Cowboy.

"What Akmed?" Cowboy asked.

"It works. The hydrate withdrawal test *was* successful. You must not let anyone stop this project because of this accident—this sabotage. There are limitless supplies of energy under the sea for your people and my own. Remember to use it wisely."

Cowboy nodded, biting his lip.

"Now get going," Akmed said. "You don't have much time."

Cowboy and O'Day turned toward the pipeline opening and were face to face with a handgun—Sheldon's SIG-Sauer. Dr. Samatha Edison, eyes full of fire, held the firearm with two trembling hands. The gun waved in her nervous grip like a traffic light in a windstorm.

"I'm afraid you can't do that," Edison said.

"What the fuck are you doing?" said Cowboy, moving his injured arm and groaning in pain.

"We looked for you," Danielle said.

"Now you found me," Edison said, her voice quavering. Blood trickled down the side of her face from a wound on her left temple. Akmed stood paralyzed, his eyes focused on the gun.

"It's okay," Danielle said, pleading with her hands. "Akmed is innocent. It was Sheldon who sabotaged the project. He escaped in the bathysphere."

Edison laughed. "He's not going far."

"What are you talking about?" Danielle said. "We have to get out of here— you can come." Danielle turned her head towards the pipeline pig, ready to explain the escape plan. *How could three of them fit on the back of the pig?* She would figure out a way.

"You move and I'll put a hole in your forehead," Edison said, her perpetual lock of hair waving in front of her face like a horse's tail.

"Put the six-shooter down, Edison," Cowboy said. "We're all on the same side."

"And what side is that?" Edison said. "The side of eventual destruction of the earth?"

Cowboy stared at Edison like she was a drunken lush fallen off a barstool. The NOAA scientist altered the aim of the gun from person to person to show she could shoot any one of them. The dried rivulet of blood visible on the side of Edison's face looked like a route on an eerie roadmap.

"Did you whack your head or something?" Cowboy said. "You're talking crazy."

"Crazy? You are the crazy ones."

Danielle stepped forward and halted when the SIG-Sauer zeroed in on her nose. "Samatha," she said. "What's wrong? Sheldon was the one who caused the blowout."

"Sheldon? That idiot should be dead by now."

"I believe she injected a sample of hydrogen sulfide into the bathysphere's oxygen tanks, adulterating the air supply," Akmed said.

Danielle cried out in confusion. "Samatha!"

"A bitter end that was intended for all of you. But now you'll suffer a different fate." Edison spoke in sporadic ravings. "Sheldon didn't do anything other than be the boorish moron he was. You'll never learn, you fools. Try to violate the earth and you kill yourselves."

What? Danielle thought. *This brainy scientist has lost her mind.*

Cowboy stepped in front of Danielle, clutching his injured right arm, and Edison swung the gun toward his chest.

"You did it, didn't you?" Cowboy said.

"Did what?" Danielle asked.

"Sabotaged the project with Sheldon." He looked at Akmed and Danielle. "She never supported this idea and then she found her chance to scuttle it. Edison is the brainchild of the rupture of the hydrate formation. She knew just how to destabilize it. Sheldon didn't know his ass from a gas well in the ground. He just went along for the ride, probably bribed by somebody. But she did it. She caused the blowout."

"That's quite perceptive for an oakie from Muskogee," Edison said, a sinister smile on her face.

Danielle looked at Edison in disbelief. "Why?"

"Simple," Cowboy said. "She's an eco-terrorist. One of those Earth-firsters or something."

"You are the murderers!" Edison answered.

"Murderers? You caused a blowout that not only damaged this platform, but likely caused a tsunami that has probably hit the east coast of the United States and killed thousands of Americans."

"Don't show me your soft side, cowpoke. The coast has been evacuated because of the hurricane. The tsunami wave was a small one—it's only a warning. It will only sink a few docked yachts owned by some greedy tycoons. But it's the price we must pay to learn we cannot tamper with the earth or we all will die."

"From what, Chicken Little? A little carbon dioxide that comes out of your mouth with every breath? Here …" Cowboy puffed a forced breath toward Edison like he had a contagious disease and was trying to infect her.

"You are a fool," Edison said, shaking the gun in his face. "This project must fail or all of humanity is doomed. Increased use of fossil fuels leads the entire earth to devastation. Global warming will not kill thousands—it will kill billions of all species. It will destroy life as we know it, and I am not going to let that happen."

"You can't be serious," Danielle said. "You care about people."

"She cares about puppy dogs and the trees they piss on," Cowboy said sarcastically. "As for human beings, fuck 'em."

At that moment Akmed, who remained silent during the exchange, took a step away from the group and tumbled toward a nearby chair as if struck by lightning. Edison swept the gun in his direction, taking her eyes off of Cowboy. Akmed was lying like a strewn bag of laundry over the chair and the nervous NOAA scientist appeared that she would fire the weapon out of panic.

With her face turned to the side, her blood-soaked cheek was the perfect target for Cowboy's fist. With his uninjured left arm, he threw a roundhouse blow that met Edison's chin perfectly. The impact of the punch sent the slight-of-frame scientist reeling backward. As she lost her balance, hands windmilling wildly, the handgun discharged, with the volley headed in an unknown direction. As the earsplitting report echoed in the metal-walled room, Edison splashed to the water-covered floor like a KO'd boxer. It reminded Danielle of the old ice-tea commercials where a thirsty person fell backward into a cool, refreshing pool after taking a sip.

"I never liked her much," Cowboy said, brushing off the knuckles of his left hand.

Once Edison settled on the floor, her head nearly submerged in water, a gruesome underwater swell of cerise liquid bloomed around her black hair. The bullet found its mark. She shot herself in the head.

Danielle bent down to attend to Akmed, who remained slumped against the console chair.

"What's the matter with him?" Danielle said, grasping Akmed's head in her hands.

"He's okay," Cowboy said. "He should be around in a minute. Akmed has a medical condition he tries to keep secret—narcolepsy. Not good for his playboy image. He tends to fall asleep at the most inopportune times."

Akmed stirred in Danielle's arms, and then opened his eyes. She hugged him, hard.

"Just kidding," Akmed said, getting to his feet as lucid as before. "I was only providing a distraction for John Wayne to do his thing."

Cowboy laughed. "You devil, you."

Danielle nodded at Edison. "What about her?"

"Who cares?" Cowboy answered, pointing at the limp body nearly half encased in bloody water. "She's a mass murderer and she's dead," he said in cold frankness. "She wanted to go down with the ship, anyway. Besides, there's no more room on the bus."

The rig jerked again as if experiencing another tremor. Seawater flowed into the compressor room with more force.

"We have no time to waste," Akmed said. "You must go now!"

Cowboy and Akmed hugged and kissed one another's cheeks. They retrieved the oxygen tanks and masks, stepped onto the rear platform of the pipeline pig and Danielle grasped Akmed in a tight embrace.

"There's got to be another way," she sobbed.

"As your Jesus said, *I am the way*," the geophysicist said.

Tears dropped down her cheeks. "I'll never forget you." She kissed him, passionate and deep.

"I'll see you again," Akmed said softly, "in Paradise."

Cowboy reached out a hand and pulled Danielle up to the pipeline pig. They had donned their oxygen gear and additional clothing they scrounged up in the area to insulate themselves from the cold. The pipeline was heated to prevent freeze-ups, but the expected forty-degree temperatures inside the long tube would not be comfortable. Cowboy knew enough about the mechanics of the pipeline pig to instruct Akmed of what to do. After Akmed manipulated the controls to direct the prodigious mechanical pipeline-cleaner into the vacant tunnel, he closed the pressurized seal to the pipeline without looking at Danielle. He spoke in Arabic from the heart part of the declaration of independence of the state of Palestine:

"In the name of God, the Merciful, the Compassionate, 'O God, Master of the Kingdom, Thou givest the Kingdom to whom Thou wilt, and seizest the Kingdom from whom Thou wilt, Thou exaltest whom Thou wilt, and Thou abasest whom Thou wilt; in Thy hand is the good; Thou art powerful over everything …' Almighty God has spoken the truth."

Akmed rapped on the metal door with the butt of the SIG-Sauer he picked off the water-covered floor next to Edison's corpse. He pressurized the line with nitrogen and with a pull of a lever that engaged the compressor, he started the pig on its way. The pressurized gas would not propel the device all the way to shore—they would have to depend on the pig's battery power. But at least it would give them a head start. Cowboy had programmed a computer that would lift the huge line off the seafloor and to a shallower depth. Akmed knew that if the pipeline severed, it would fill with water and likely sink, killing Danielle and Cowboy by crushing them with the pressure of tons of seawater. He did not tell them that—they probably already knew. And they had enough to worry about, including the battery power of the pig, whether they had enough oxygen in their tanks to make it to the coast, and if they would die of hypothermia before personnel at the shoreline compressor station discovered them.

After he was sure the pig was shooting through the line with its two human passengers, Akmed sat and waited for the control chamber to be filled with ice-cold seawater, leaving him in a liquid sarcophagus that would bring him a slow and agonizing death. He gripped the SIG-Sauer that ended Edison's life in his powerful hands. He prayed for redemption.

Allah Akbar, Allah Akbar, Allah Akbar.

CHAPTER 68

▼

The only way Cowboy and Danielle could fit into the narrow space on the back of the pipeline pig was by entwining their arms and legs in a position that resembled something out of a Kama Sutra sexual guide. At least with the air mask and tank on their backs they did not have to get their faces close together, Danielle thought. She tried to inch away from him, but Cowboy's one-armed Herculean grip pulled her tighter to his body.

"I'm not playing grab ass," Cowboy said. "When that first blast of pressured nitrogen hits us, you are going to be blown off the back of this pig unless you hold on tighter."

She knew he was right, and this was no time for modesty. She was afraid. She tried not to think about being propelled through a four-foot-wide pipeline like a human spitball through a giant straw. She was claustrophobic in the shower and now they were going to be in a 100-mile-long hole curled up like college kids in a phone booth below the surface of the ocean that may very well end up being their tomb. She was already breathing heavily when she tasted the plastic odor of the air mask. It was nauseating and suffocating.

"Are you ready?" Cowboy asked.

She nodded her head to Cowboy and gripped him tighter. He wrapped one leg and his good arm around her torso and buttocks tighter and the other leg entwined around booster handles on the back of the pig.

"Just close your eyes and hold on," he said.

There was a knock of metal on metal, Akmed's signal that he was about to pressurize the line. Moments later, Danielle heard a terrible hiss, like the roar of a dinosaur in her ear and then a push. It did not feel like wind, it felt like a wall crashing in on her. Suddenly, the pig skidded along, almost effortlessly, though she felt incredible pressure against her body. They moved like a piece of aluminum siding ripped off a house in a hurricane and flung down a seaside street. It felt like falling. Perhaps this was what skydiving was like. Danielle briefly thought of the irony—afraid of heights, horrified of closed-in spaces, and the dread of being submerged in water. Here were all of her fears wrapped up into one, and she was in the middle of a terror enchilada. Soon, she could not think and she could not see, so she gripped the small crucifix and chain that encircled her neck as if it were a talisman. She closed her eyes in this potential hundred-mile tubular coffin. And she prayed. She prayed. She prayed Hail Marys and Our Fathers and every stanza from her Catechism book that could be pulled from her memory.

Hail Mary, full of grace … Our Father, who art in heaven … make me a shadow of your peace … Oh, God … Oh God! … Jesus Christ!

She hung onto Cowboy tighter, but there was no need. The pressure of the line pressed them against the back of the pig like the centrifugal force of a spinning carnival ride. The raucous sound of the pig's wire brushes scraping the sides of the line was deafening. The noise didn't resemble a pig squealing. It sounded like an army of hogs howling in agony as their throats were cut with rusty razor blades. She was losing consciousness. Fading away. Falling into a bottomless hole into Hell. Her last lucid thought was feeling a large bump, as if the device struck some unseen obstacle in its path, and then the realization that the jolt ripped her satellite phone from her belt and she had no idea where it fell.

"That two-faced b-b-bastard. That b-b-back-stabbing son-of-a-b-b-itch. That f-f-f-f-fat f-f-f-f-fuck!"

With those words, the rankled Herbert Winkle shouted as he watched CNN. He turned to Olga Stevick, who sat with him in Congressman Doggle's inner office watching a small television, waiting for the energy committee chairman to return from the floor of the House of Representatives. Stevick faced Winkle with a blank expression, silent, as if she had quietly passed on in her chair.

"You knew about this, d-d-didn't you?" he said, shaking a newspaper as if it were a dirty rag.

"I knew Doggle was close to a settlement with the Freeman administration. I did not know any details."

"B-Bullshit," the little man said, his left eye wandering and glassy. He fingered his greasy black hair. "Y-Y-You sold me down the river—you will probably be standing next to that trader at the bill signing with the p-p-president."

"For someone who knows how the art of compromise works, you seem to be disappointed that you don't get your way *all* the time, young man."

"D-D-Doggle is caving in to Freeman. He is going to endorse drilling off the coasts that most likely caused the tsunami and he is going to buy into this preposterous carbon sequestering plan—all for some price ceilings of newly discovered natural gas and his stupid ethanol f-f-funding."

"Price controls are important to us senior citizens," said Stevick. "It may keep many of us alive in the wintertime."

"And this new fossil-fuel drilling is a death sentence for your g-g-g-randchildren."

Winkle dropped his head into the newspaper and held it like a makeshift hat, shielding himself from imaginary rain. All of his efforts seemed to have been defeated. He was sure he could have dethroned the coal, oil, and gas industry for good. The fossil-fuel industry titans and their greed caused all the hurricanes, the tsunami, global warming, and famine. Science was now in his camp. He believed the public was finally ready to end the polluter's monopoly on energy. Now it seemed like his main ally turned into Benedict Arnold.

"That d-d-double-crossing asshole," he cried. "That bribe-taking, pig-swilling, sell-out b-blimp."

"Well, hello congressman," Stevick blurted.

Winkle's head surfaced from underneath the newspaper to see the rotund representative sliding behind his desk like a docking dirigible. *Did he hear the insults?*

"Sorry to keep you waiting," Doggle wheezed as if he just completed a triathlon. "I ran up here from the House floor."

Ran? Winkle thought. The only way this tank could run would be by rolling downhill.

"What is the meaning of this?" Winkle said pointing at the television, building bravado with every word. He shook the newspaper as if it were a club. "You caved! We had a chance to end the insidious fossil-fuel industry and you c-c-capitulated."

"Mr. Winkle, Mr. Winkle," Doggle said, collapsing in his leather chair that flattened with the sound of a truck engaging its air brakes. "Would you like half a loaf or none at all?"

"W-W-What did the president promise you—more of your corn-fuel money? A presidential visit for your next f-f-fundraiser—what?"

"Mr. Winkle, be satisfied that you are living in a free nation with a government where majority rules but the minority's rights are protected."

"What in the devil are you talking about?"

"I'm talking about you Mr. Winkle, hobnobbing with Russian spies, accepting contributions from Chinese communists, and sympathizing with activists in league with Islamic terrorists. Do you know this nation still shoots traitors when the mood arises?"

Winkle's breath was sucked out of his lungs. "S-S-Spies ... t-t-terrorists.... you're ins-s-sane."

"Tell it to the FBI."

"I have no foreign connections," the environmentalist said, suddenly losing his stutter. "I serve on an international environmental board with Russian and Chinese climatologists as well as many other representatives throughout the world. But I don't know what you're talking about—spies, terror—"

"You've been duped Winkle. They've been using you. Russia and China are doing whatever they can to reduce the economic power of the United States and they have found a friend in you. Don't you know that we can virtually eliminate carbon emissions in the United States but it won't mean a hill of beans to your global-warming paranoia? China will soon outpace the U.S. with carbon emissions—do you think you are going to change the Red Communist's policy with protest marches, press conferences, and cute little green bumper stickers? China wants to pass us up economically and they will use all the Middle East oil to do so. And Russia would like nothing more than to see the frozen tundra of Siberia turn into the fertile fields of Kansas and melt the Arctic ice so they can drill for more carbon-producing oil and gas and sell it to Europe. How stupid can you be? You might be able to change the mind of a clueless soccer mom in Columbus, Ohio, to get behind your leftist campaign to save the globe, but good luck with the Ruskis in Moscow and the Chi-Coms in Beijing. Get with the program Winkle. You got half a loaf. Take your winnings and go home."

Danielle's head was drowning in black. The collision of the pipeline pig with whatever-it-was twisted every joint she thought she had. But she didn't think she broke anything. But still, she could hardly move. She could hear Cowboy's moaning. "My arm, my arm," he repeated. But she did not see him. They were motionless now. Were they all the way to shore? Was this the end of the pipeline? Or was it just the end of the line for them? What did the pig hit? Perhaps a clump of frozen carbon dioxide hydrates in the line? She had no bearings; she had no sight. She dropped the satellite phone. Would it have even worked inside the line? She had no way of knowing. How would anyone know they are there? *Knock three times on the ceiling of the pipeline?* Then, despite the agonizing pain, she thought. *How can we get out of here?* There could be tons of seawater on top of this line. *How can we be rescued?* She didn't even know if she was upside down or right side up.

Her hand, folded up over her head, slid down the side of her face. The mask was still attached. It was okay. But she gasped for air. She must be sitting on the hose or something, or perhaps the tank broke. She could not breathe well. Maybe her chest was crushed. She was bitter cold. She slowly ran her hand down her body—it was soaked. With sweat? With seawater? With fluids inside the pipeline? Or was it her blood? As she ran her hand up and down, it bumped a wallet-sized object. What was this? She clasped her fingers around it and ran them across what felt like smooth metal. Then it registered. It was her cellphone. She plucked it from her shirt pocket and brought it up to her face. Flipping down the thin cover she reached for where the power button was located and pressed. A blue glimmer of light emitted from the device. She could not read the words or numbers on the phone. Her mask was fogged up with moisture from her breath. But there was light.

CHAPTER 69

▼

She can't be out there, Dan O'Day thought, standing outside in the midst of a series of bulbous gas scrubbers that looked like small space capsules in an alien parking lot. He stared out to the horizon that displayed the Atlantic Ocean. *She's an O'Day; she will find a way.*

His cellphone rang. At first he ignored it, but then he glanced at the device. He didn't recognize the number, but he answered anyway.

"Hello?" he said. Then angrily, "Hello?" The connection was lost. The storm played havoc on cellular systems. *A hang-up from a wrong number?*

A thought dawned on him.

"Who around here has a computer with Internet access?" he asked a compressor worker who was cleaning up some of the debris at the station.

The compressor station worker shrugged, and then remembered. "There's a wireless laptop in the foreman's field office I think," he said.

"Show me," O'Day said.

In a minute, they arrived at a one-room office trailer that had only space for a single chair. A laptop computer sat on a makeshift desk, its plastic dustcover keyboard caked with dirt. After locating the supervisor, O'Day spoke to him.

"Could you log on your computer for me? This is an emergency."

"We already have one buddy," the surprised foreman said. "We've just received an alert that says the offshore rig may have sunk, we have missing personnel, and contaminated hydrogen sulfide is running through the pipeline."

"I know—I've received my orders from corporate to look into it," O'Day lied. "Can I use your computer just for a minute?"

The pot-bellied, middle-aged supervisor looked uncertain for a moment, struck a few keys with two of his large fingers on the keyboard and in seconds he was attached to the Internet. He turned his chair over to O'Day.

"This should just take a minute," O'Day said. He punched in a few keys and was instantly connected to the global-positioning website that he paid $39.95 a month for—so far for nothing. He pulled out his wallet and entered the keycode for his daughter's satellite phone and checked the number. For security reasons, the actual number of the satellite phone alternated every hour. But with his master code he could check the current number used by the device. He located the number on the site and then he punched up the last number received on his cellphone and compared them. They didn't match.

"Son-of-a-bitch," O'Day said.

He struck more keys, some too quickly, forcing him to backspace several times. He entered another command trying to find where the satellite phone was located anyway. Just because Danielle didn't call him didn't mean he couldn't discover where the unit was. It should pinpoint the location within five meters, the company promised, but so far, the damn thing never worked. He didn't expect it to this time, either. But suddenly, coordinates jumped on the screen, but they meant little to O'Day. He clicked an option showing a wide-range map of the northern hemisphere. A red dot blinked where the satellite phone was last located—it did not show a current connection. It was offshore North America. He clicked another button that zoomed in the map. The screen came up slowly from top to bottom, like it was a NASA photograph coming in from the surface of Mars.

"C'mon, c'mon," O'Day complained.

Finally, the map narrowed the location to a spot approximately fifty miles off the North Carolina coast.

He selected another tab that joined the location with satellite photos that gave a recent overhead satellite picture with the locator device linked with it. He zoomed in closer. He saw nothing but the ocean. He selected maximum telephoto zoom. Again, nothing but a nebulous photo of water waves. It didn't make any sense. The location of the satellite receiver was nowhere near where the gas collection platform was supposedly located. Unless she was on the helicopter and it crashed into the sea.

Then his cellphone rang again.

Danielle randomly pressed buttons—she couldn't remember where the numerical keys were, but instead pressed a button that brought up her address book. She had no idea who she was calling and she couldn't speak with the oxygen mask on, but she pressed buttons anyway. Maybe she could reach the office and they could track her down. Somehow. She tried a couple of times. Then the blue haze of the phone disappeared. The battery must be dead. Had her brilliant brainstorm escape plan put the two of them into a Houdini-like inextricable trap?

It must be Maureen again, nagging me, O'Day thought, annoyed. He was going to shut if off when he glanced at the number. The same number—*a fucking wrong number twice?*

"Who the hell?" he wondered aloud. Again, he went to shut the button off and he read the final four numerals. He didn't recognize them. Or did he? Wait, yes, he did. The exchange was from Manhattan. It was Danielle's phone. It had to be. He never called her, but he had seen the number on the caller ID at home when she phoned her mother. But how can she be calling from her cell? Cellphones don't work out on the ocean. Someone must have stolen it. Or they found it and were trying to return it. Wait a minute—she could be already safe on shore.

He answered. He was impatient. Irritated. Fucking angry. "Hello? Hello?" He barked in the receiver several more times, but nothing but silence answered him.

It was Danielle's phone, but there is no way she could call, unless she was already on or near shore. There was no other way to get off that offshore platform than by helicopter. But he thought the last helicopter perhaps crashed into the sea. If she was on it, then how could she call him? There were no boats, they couldn't paddle a lifeboat 100 fucking miles in a hurricane. There was no way to get to land. He glanced down at the plant blueprint design hanging on the wall of the workstation. Numerous lines and symbols showed miles of interlocking pipes, valves, and regulators. On the schematic however, was something that he didn't notice the first time he looked at it though it stood out as naked as a jaybird. Two blue lines running from the plant off the coast and a blinking pulse on the end of one of them.

"What's this," he asked the foreman, pointing at the pulsing light.

"Someone from the offshore platform shot a pig through the empty pipeline for some reason—probably part of whatever malfunctions happened out there."

The synapses in O'Day's brain fired.

"How big are these lines—what diameter?" O'Day asked.

"Forty-eight inch—biggest pipeline pig in the world."

"Four feet. Of course, holy shit, of course." He smiled, forcing looks of curiosity from his onlookers. "She's an O'Day. She's in the fucking pipeline! How can you open the line up and get the pig out?"

The foreman shook his head.

"We can't," he said. "The storm surge has damaged some of our compressor controls—we'd have to do it manually and it would take hours."

"Got a welding torch around?" O'Day barked.

"I imagine," said the compressor worker.

"Get me one."

He turned to the foreman who looked at him as if he were mad. "Can you show me where the pig is?"

"Well, we could ballpark it."

"Do it and get me as precise as you can," he said pointing at the schematic.

The operator suddenly looked less than cooperative.

"Look, we don't have any orders from corporate that we know of. I can't take responsibility—"

O'Day stood and cut him off, dwarfing the foreman by his ursine size and whispered, "Just get me there."

CHAPTER 70

$$\blacktriangledown$$

The air was laced with the petroleum smell of motor oil. Miss Prissy sounded as if she were a panting dog after chasing a rabbit on a sweltering day. Cowboy could not see her through his mask; a cloud of condensed moisture lined the inside plastic lens. But he knew Danielle was hyperventilating. Anyway, it was pitch dark and silent as a tomb with the exception of the two of them breathing.

Curiously, his broken arm did not hurt any longer. He must be losing consciousness. His oxygen tank was depleted. He pulled off his mask to somehow catch his breath. He had nothing to lose. Besides its sickly odor, the air was sticky and seemingly void of life-giving oxygen. As his head swam with turbid thoughts, he saw multi-colored sparks that spun in his vision like a kaleidoscope like the sights he saw after being whacked in the head by the four-foot wrench. His head was swimming. He was drowning in thin air. He coughed up a metallic viscous fluid that he assumed must have been blood, but in the darkness he could not tell. He had no idea where he was. He was not sure if he was awake.

The American Energy lawyer continued to suck breath like a miniature bellows trying to ignite coals from a moribund fire. Cowboy reached toward the sound and felt hard plastic. It was Danielle's mask. She must be out of O_2 as well. He could not suck enough air into his lungs, but it was more than the void he experienced in the mask. With his good arm he pulled the mask from his companion's face. Her head and hair, soaked with sweat in the black sauna, fell down and was limp. Cowboy barely harbored the strength to reach and feel for a pulse. He felt the side of her long, slender neck and at least felt warmth. His own head fell backwards and the brightly colored sparkles of light faded away into blackness.

*   *   *   *

The welder's helmet strapped on Dan O'Day's head resembled that of a hockey goalie's mask. He donned a pair of insulated fireproof gloves, and then ignited the acetylene torch. He straddled the huge four-foot diameter pipeline between his legs as if he was riding a giant earthworm. The large pipeline surfaced from the ground just before the wall of the compressor station.

"This line doesn't have gas in it I hope," O'Day said.

"Nah," the foreman said. "This is the output carbon dioxide line flowing out to sea, but it's been shut off. The input gas line is on the other side of the station."

"Let's hope or I'm going to be the first welder in space."

O'Day snapped down the metal and glass protective shield over his face and flared the blue-flamed torch against the metal line. It was just like old times. Immediately a fireworks display of sparks set off in all directions. He had not welded a piece of pipeline in seven years, but the torch in his hands felt like an old leather baseball mitt, comfortable and warm, formed for his hand only over many years through pressure and sweat. Though the metal tube was not tremendously thick, whatever alloy it was made of was as tough as titanium, he thought. It was slow going. But after five minutes, O'Day sliced a six-inch narrow slit through the top of the pipe.

It was either the blinding light or the air that revived Cowboy. He wasn't sure which, but it felt like a slap of a hand or a cold mixed drink in the face, which in his habit of hitting on women in bars he had experienced a few times in his life. The scintillating flashes of color he imagined suddenly halted and a loud metal-on-metal clang echoed through the four-four-wide tube. It sounded as if it were only yards away.

"Hello?" a voice echoed through the hollow line. He saw a spot of light moving through the darkness like a laser beam. Could he be dreaming?

"I think I see something!" another voice barked with a hollow, sewer-like resonance.

Cowboy pushed himself toward the light and once he assured himself it was no dream, he turned back to the silent body of the American Energy lawyer.

"Hey counselor!" he grunted. "This is our stop."

With his powerful arms, Daniel O'Day lifted the nearly unconscious Danielle from the pipeline pig and pushed her through the hole in the top of the pipeline.

The oxygen-filled air revived her a little bit and her eyes opened to a squint, and then shut from the pain of the blinding daylight.

"Daddy," she said, softly. "I'm so sorry, Daddy."

Her father crawled out of the line and cradled her in his arms. "You have nothing to be sorry for. You are my little *girl* and there is nothing to be afraid of now."

Danielle collapsed in exhaustion, but her father knew she would be okay. After all, she was an O'Day. He swayed her back and forth like a baby and sang the Irish ballad: *"Oh, Dannie girl, oh Dannie girl, I love you so."*

When Cowboy was pulled out of the pipe, groggy, but conscious, O'Day looked at him suspiciously. His daughter's shirt was soaked through, clearly outlining her breasts, and Cowboy's injured right arm was supported by a woman's bra used as a sling.

"It's not what you think," Cowboy said.

President Freeman signed—without public fanfare—the emergency energy bill that passed both houses of Congress faster than "shit through a goose," as chief-of-staff Mann quipped. The sudden agreement with congressional leaders did not come without strings. The independently elected president pledged to leaders of both parties that he would not run for a second term, returning the presidential arena back to the two fighting factions. By doing this, he hoped to avoid a witch-hunt in Congress that would attempt to skewer him like a cube of meat. The energy bill included both carrots and sticks to encourage more domestic energy production and punish wasteful uses of fuel. Addressing the public during a major evening speech from the Oval Office, the president not only took full responsibility for the failure of the hydrate-extraction experiment that not only cost billions in taxpayer dollars to develop, but also for the resulting tsunami, though it was caused intentionally by saboteurs. It killed dozens of people along the Carolina and Virginia coasts and resulted in billions of dollars of property damage. But, Freeman vowed the search for clean, affordable, *domestic* energy would continue.

"America will not cower from this challenge," Freeman said, staring right at the camera that broadcast his words to millions. "We will seek those responsible for attacking our shores, but we will not risk the lives of our soldiers or innocents of other nations for energy alone. This nation endured a civil war, slavery, world wars, changes to our constitution, recessions, depressions, and seemingly impossible tasks such as landing a man on the moon. We will overcome this challenge as well. But it will not come without sacrifice by each and every American. But hope prevails. There may be limits to traditional energy sources on this globe of ours, but there is no limit to our innovation, persistence, or our quest to let the citizens of our nation and all nations secure life, liberty, and the pursuit of happiness."

After the teleprompter ended and the networks returned to regular programming, the president sat in his chair and wondered whether the nation had learned its lesson. He smirked. Probably not.

978-0-595-42924-0
0-595-42924-6

Love
Edelstein

Printed in the United States
77387LV00003B/44

9 780595 429240